Praise for BRENDA NOVAK's
EVERY WAKING MOMENT

"Strongly defined characters, sizzling sexual tension
and a tautly constructed plot steeped in danger
blend brilliantly in Novak's exceptionally intense,
powerfully emotional novel."
—*Booklist*

"*Every Waking Moment* is the kind of romantic suspense
that has no easy place to stop for minor things
like eating or sleeping. A Perfect 10."
—*Romance Reviews Today*

"Brenda Novak's gift lies in grabbing the reader
by the throat and not letting go until the very end....
Fast-paced scenes filled with sparkling dialogue,
romantic tension and a series of pulse-racing plot twists
bring the story to a heart-stopping climax.
An exciting, compelling, entertaining read."
—*Midwest Book Reviews*

"*Every Waking Moment* is an absolute must-read."
—*Writers Unlimited*

"A page-turner. A darn good read."
—*All About Romance*

"*Every Waking Moment* will keep you turning the pages,
hoping for the best, fearing the worst and appreciating
the world of suspense and intrigue only Novak
can create from scenarios that are far too possible."
—*Books*

"The story's stron
starts on the first pag

BRENDA NOVAK

DEAD
SILENCE

MIRA®

Recycling programs
for this product may
not exist in your area.

ISBN-13: 978-0-7783-2885-8

DEAD SILENCE

For questions and comments about the quality of this book please contact us
at Customer_eCare@Harlequin.ca.

www.MIRABooks.com

Printed in U.S.A.

To Donna Hayes,
Publisher and CEO of Harlequin Enterprises—
a savvy, classy woman. Most readers never know the
people who work so hard behind the scenes to
make it possible for an author to share her stories with
thousands, sometimes millions, of readers, but writers
know them and appreciate them. Thank you, Donna,
for navigating the tricky waters of publishing so well.
It's great to have someone I trust at the helm!
(Thanks, too, for supporting so many charitable causes,
including my annual online auction to benefit
diabetes research at www.brendanovak.com.)

Dear Reader,

Welcome to Stillwater—a small fictional town in the backwoods of Mississippi, where everyone knows everyone else *and* their business and it's very hard to keep the kind of deep, dark secret that has been haunting the Montgomery family for eighteen years. I'm excited about this series. If you've read my DUNDEE, IDAHO series for the Harlequin Superromance line, you probably know how much I love connected books. My characters become friends I'm sad to part with when "the end" arrives. I feel that way about Grace from this story. I admire her strength and sympathize with her struggles. Her past would not be an easy thing to live with, nor would the ripples caused by what happened that long-ago night, the night that started everything, the night she'll never forget….

Please feel free to write to me with questions or comments. You can reach me via my Web site at www.brendanovak.com, where you can also sign up for my periodic contests. (Details are posted on the site.) You can also check out excerpts and reviews for this and other books, see what's coming up next, or help me reach my fund-raising goal for diabetes research (my youngest son has Type I). I hold an online charity auction at my Web site every year, where I auction off great items donated by many famous authors, as well as others. Check
it out. Maybe you'd like to donate something—or just shop. If you don't have Internet service you can write to me at P.O. Box 3781, Citrus Heights, CA 95611.

To your health and happiness…

Brenda Novak

"The happiest women,
like the happiest nations, have no history."
—George Eliot (Mary Ann Evans,
English novelist, 1819–1880)

1

Grace Montgomery pulled to the side of the narrow country road and stared at the rambling farmhouse in which she'd grown up. Even in the heavy, blanketlike darkness of a Mississippi summer night, with only half a moon grinning eerily overhead, she could see that her older brother kept the place in good repair.

But that was all sleight of hand, wasn't it? Things weren't really what they seemed. They never had been. That was the problem—why she'd promised herself she wouldn't come back here.

The yellow light gleaming in an upstairs bedroom winked out. Clay was going to bed, probably at the same time as he did every night. Grace couldn't understand how he could live alone out here. How he could eat, sleep and work the farm—only forty paces away from where they'd hidden their stepfather's body.

The warning chime signaling that she'd left her keys in the ignition sounded as she got out of her small BMW. She hadn't planned to venture onto the property. But now that she was here, she had to see for herself that even after so many years there was nothing to give them away.

Her cotton skirt swayed gently against her calves

as she walked down the long drive. There was no wind, no sound except the cicadas and frogs, and the crunch of her sandals on gravel. If she'd forgotten anything, it was the quiet in this part of the state and how brightly the stars could shine away from the city.

She pictured herself as a young girl, sleeping on the front lawn with her younger sister, Molly, and her older stepsister, Madeline. Those were special times, when they'd talked and laughed and gazed up at the black velvet sky to find all those twinkling stars staring right back at them like a silent promise of good things to come. They'd all been so innocent then. When Madeline was around, Grace had had nothing to fear. But Madeline couldn't stick by Grace's side every minute. She hadn't even realized she should. She still didn't know what it was like for Grace back then. She'd been at a friend's house the night everything went wrong.

Despite the humidity, Grace shivered as she came upon the barn. Set off to the right, it lurked among the weeping willows and poplars. She hated everything associated with the old building. It was there she'd cleaned out the stall of the horse her stepfather wouldn't let anyone but him ride. It was there she'd gathered the eggs and fought with the mean rooster who used to fly at her in an attempt to gouge out her eyes. It was there, in the front corner of the building, that the reverend had kept a small office where he retired to write his Sunday sermons—and to delve into that locked file drawer.

The smell of moist earth and magnolias brought it all back too vividly, causing her to break out in a cold sweat. Curving her fingernails into her palms to remind herself that she was no longer a powerless girl, she immediately steered her thoughts away from the reverend's office. She'd promised herself she'd forget.

But she certainly hadn't forgotten yet. Despite her best efforts, she couldn't help wondering if that stifling room was still untouched. Except for what the reverend had kept in his file drawer, the office had been left intact, as if he might someday reappear and want to use it. Her mother had insisted they'd be foolish to change anything. She'd drilled it into all of them, except Madeline of course, that they must continue to refer to the reverend in the present tense. Folks in town were already suspicious enough.

Stillwater's residents had long memories, but eighteen years had passed since the reverend's sudden disappearance. Surely after so much time Clay could dismantle that damn office....

A deep voice came suddenly out of the dark. "Get the hell off my property or I'll shoot."

Grace whirled to see a man at least six foot four inches tall, so solidly built he could have been made of stone, standing only a few feet away. It was her brother, and he had a rifle trained on her.

For the briefest of moments, Grace wished he'd shoot.

But then she laughed. Clay was as vigilant as ever. Not that she was really surprised. He'd always been The Guardian.

"What? Ya'll don't know your own sister anymore?" she said and stepped out of the building's shadow.

"Grace?" The barrel of the hunting rifle dove toward the ground and he twitched as though tempted to gather her in a hug. Grace felt a similar response, but made no move toward him. Their relationship was too...complicated.

"God, Grace. It's been thirteen years since you left.
I barely recognize you. You could've gotten yourself
shot," he added gruffly.

She said nothing about that brief cowardly impulse:
One bullet could end it all.

"Really?" she murmured. "I would've recognized
you anywhere." Maybe it was because she thought of
him so often. Besides, he hadn't changed much. He
still had the same thick black hair—even darker than
Grace's—that swirled up off his forehead. The light,
enigmatic eyes that looked so much like her own. That
same determined set to his prominent jaw. He'd put on
a few more pounds of muscle mass, maybe, which
made her feel small at five-five and a hundred and
twenty pounds. But his bulkier size was the only difference.

"I expected you to be asleep," she said.

"Saw your car pull up out front."

"Wouldn't want to let just anyone go creeping
around out here."

If he heard the taunt in her voice, he didn't respond
to it. Except to glance furtively toward the copse of
trees that served as a marker for their stepfather's
grave.

After a stilted silence, he said, "Living in Jackson
must agree with you. You look good."

She'd been doing quite well in the city. Until
George E. Dunagan, Attorney-at-Law, had asked her
to marry him. When, for the third time, she couldn't
say yes, even though they both knew she wanted to,
he'd finally broken off the relationship. He'd told her
he didn't want to hear from her until she'd seen a therapist and resolved the issues of her childhood.

She'd tried visiting a therapist—but counseling

hadn't helped. There were too many realities she didn't want to examine. Others she *wanted* to share but couldn't, not with a therapist or anyone else, including George. Although George had recently relented and started calling her again, Grace's problems still stood between them.

She hoped that wouldn't be true for much longer. Either she'd overcome the past or the past would overcome her. She couldn't know how it would all end. She could only promise herself that she wouldn't return to her life in Jackson until she'd come to terms with what had happened in Stillwater.

"I keep busy," she said.

"Mom tells me you graduated first in your class at Georgetown."

Six years ago… She gave him an indifferent smile. He sounded impressed. But what she achieved never satisfied her for long. "Amazing what you can do when you apply yourself, huh?"

"How'd you get into a school like that?"

She'd left town two days after graduating from Stillwater High, worked as a waitress at a greasy spoon in Jackson in order to scrape by, and spent every available minute—for two years—studying for the entrance exams. When she wound up with an almost perfect score, no one seemed to care too much about her high school GPA. She managed to get into the University of Iowa, and after that she'd been accepted at Georgetown.

But she didn't see any point in discussing the details with Clay. She didn't look back on her college days, when she'd slept only three or four hours a night, with any pride or nostalgia. While everyone else juggled school *and* a normal social life, she'd kept to herself and tolerated nothing less than academic excellence.

She'd been trying to make up for the past, trying to prove that she was more than everyone thought. But after graduating from law school and working as an assistant district attorney for the past five years, she'd finally realized that running away wasn't the solution. She *still* couldn't move on with her personal life.

"I got lucky," she said simply.

He glanced at the house. "Wanna come in?"

Hearing the hope in those words, she studied the deep porch where they used to sit on the steps and listen to their mother read scripture. The reverend had demanded they study the Bible for an hour each day. But it hadn't been a bad experience. Holding a glass of lemonade, Grace would feel the oppressive heat of a summer's day cool slightly as evening approached. She'd hear the lilt of her mother's voice as the boards beneath the old rocking chair creaked and the lightning bugs danced near the porch light. She'd always enjoyed it—until the reverend came home.

"No, I—I'd better be going." She started edging away. Seeing Clay, knowing he was still on guard, was enough. She couldn't face any more memories tonight.

"How long will you be in town?"

She paused when he spoke. "I don't know."

He scowled, and she thought he looked rather harsh for such a handsome man. Evidently, carrying the family's dark secret was taking its toll on him, too. "What brings you back after all this time?" he asked.

She narrowed her eyes in challenge. "Sometimes I feel like doing the right thing and telling everyone what happened here."

"How do you know it's the right thing?" he asked softly.

"Because I've spent the past five years championing the truth and making people take responsibility for their actions."

"Are you sure you always get the right guy, Grace? And that he gets the appropriate punishment?"

"We have to trust the system, Clay. Without it, our whole society falls apart."

"Who deserves to pay for what happened here?"

The man who was buried in the ground. But Clay already knew that, so she didn't respond.

"Why haven't you come forward before?" he asked.

"For the same reason you're still guarding this place with that gun," she admitted.

He studied her for several seconds. "Sounds like you have a tough decision to make."

"I guess I do."

No response.

"Aren't you going to try and talk me out of it?" she asked with a bitter laugh.

"Sorry," he said. "You have to make your own choice."

She hated his answer and nearly told him so. She wanted a fight, something tangible to rail against, someone to blame. Leave it to Clay to sidestep her so easily. But he changed the subject before she could say anything.

"Did you quit your job?" he asked.

"No, I'm on vacation." She hadn't missed a single day of work in five years. The state owed her two months, and she'd taken a leave of absence beyond that.

"You picked an interesting place to spend your vacation."

"You're here, aren't you?"

"*I* have good reason."

She'd expected him to resent her for leaving, like their mother did, but she sensed that he was glad she'd escaped. He wanted her to stay away, to go and live her life and forget about him, Stillwater, everything.

His generosity made her feel even worse—for wanting the same thing. "You could leave if you really wanted to," she pointed out, although she knew that in his mind it wasn't really true.

His mouth was a straight, resolute slash in his face. "I've made my decision."

"You're a stubborn son of a bitch," she said. "You'll probably live your whole life out here."

"Where're you staying?" he asked instead of responding.

"I rented Evonne's place."

"Then you already know about her."

Grace steeled herself against the ache in her chest. "Molly called me when she died."

"Molly was here for the funeral."

"Molly comes here for a lot of things," she said, bristling even though there was no censure in his voice. She wanted to act the way Molly did, to come and go as she pleased, to behave as if she was just like anyone else. But she couldn't cope with all the contradictions. "Anyway, I was right in the middle of a very important trial." Which was true, but Grace hadn't made the slightest attempt to get away. Three months ago, she'd been too entrenched in the belief that she'd *never* come back. For anything. Except maybe her own mother's funeral—and even that was questionable.

"I know Evonne meant a great deal to you," he said. "She was a good woman."

A childless widow with sable-colored skin and eyes that saw the best in almost everyone, Evonne Walker had been sixty-five when Grace left Stillwater. Regardless of the weather, she used to sit beneath the awning in her front yard on Main Street at the corner of Apple Blossom, selling handmade soaps and lotions and, depending on the season, produce from her garden, eggs from her chickens, bottled pickles, peaches and tomatoes, sweet potato pies and brownies.

Evonne had been an oddity in Stillwater for three reasons. There'd never been any love lost between her and the reverend, she'd always minded her own business, and she'd been kind to Grace.

"She mailed me all her recipes, you know," Grace said. The package that had arrived from an attorney's office about a week after the funeral was what had finally convinced Grace to come back. That, and George's insistence that she deal with whatever it was that was causing her reservations about their marriage. Although she and George were speaking again, he'd given her a three-month ultimatum. He said he didn't want to spend the rest of his life waiting for something he was beginning to think would never happen.

Clay shifted the gun to his other arm as though he felt awkward still holding it. "Folks around here think those recipes went with her to the grave."

"No." They'd been a parting gift—the only package Grace had ever received from Evonne.

"She probably chose you because you helped her so much when you were a teenager," he said.

Grace thought it was because Evonne had an inkling of what had gone on at the farm, knew without ever being told.

Grief mingled with the guilt, regret and confusion

Grace already felt, and the lump that swelled in her throat made it difficult to speak. "Nothing's easy, is it, Clay?"

"Nothing's easy," he agreed.

She took a step down the drive. "It's late. I'd better go."

"Wait." His warm hand curled around her wrist for a moment. Then he let go as if he feared she might take exception to his touch. "I'm sorry, Grace. You know that, don't you?"

She couldn't stand the tortured expression on his face. She preferred to imagine him as indifferent, didn't want to know he was suffering as much as she was. She couldn't bear that, too.

"I know," she said softly and slipped away.

You have to make your own choice....

Clay's words ran through Grace's mind like a litany—all night and all morning. Her brother had implied that he wouldn't blame her if she came forward. He hadn't pointed out the very serious consequences, nor did he mention the people who'd be hurt. He'd simply shoved the decision right back in her lap.

Somehow she both loved and hated him for that.

God, what she wouldn't give for one clearly defined emotion....

The doorbell rang. Shoving the box she was unpacking to the right, she climbed to her feet and crossed the hardwood floor. Evonne's sisters and cousins had claimed most of the furniture in the house; they planned to have a yard sale with what remained. But Grace had contacted Rex Peters, the town's only real estate broker, and rented the house just in time to save the last of the dishes, kitchen utensils, cleaning supplies, an odd table here and there, gardening rakes and hoe and a few pictures. Now she was expecting George to deliver her bed, dressers, sofa, chairs and dinette set from Jackson. She was staying in Stillwater for three months—she had only that long to "make peace with her family," as George put it—but she needed furniture all the same. It made no sense to rent when it would have to come from Jackson, anyway.

For one second, she hoped George would be in a hurry to get back home. Since their sort of reconciliation, relations between them were awkward at best, and although she should've been eager to see a friendly face, she felt far less anticipation than she should have. She couldn't deal with the pressure of knowing he wanted something from her she couldn't yet give. And she was afraid he might want to make love. She struggled in that area more than any other.

The doorbell sounded again.

Apparently, he *was* pressed for time….

"Coming." She swung the door wide, but it wasn't George who stood on her step. It was a darling little boy with gray eyes, a patch of freckles across his nose, and tufts of blond hair sticking out from beneath a baseball cap.

"Hello," she said in surprise.

He wrinkled his nose as he gazed up at her. "Hi."

She waited, but he didn't say anything else.

"Can I help you?"

"Want me to mow your lawn? For five dollars?" he asked.

Grace raised her eyebrows. "Are you old enough to handle a lawn mower all on your own?"

His expression told her he didn't appreciate her

doubting his ability. "I used to do it for Evonne," he said indignantly.

For years, whenever Grace came by on her bicycle, Evonne would offer her some small job. Grace doubted Evonne ever really needed the help. She'd managed on her own for a long time. She only provided the opportunity as an excuse to send home some of the peaches or pickles Grace loved, and maybe a few dollars.

Lord knew Grace's family had needed the money, especially after Irene insisted Clay go away to college.

"I'm saving up," he added.

Grace couldn't resist a smile. "For what?"

He hesitated. "It's a secret."

"Oh." She eyed his muddy sneakers, his blue jeans, which were worn through at the knees and his over-size T-shirt. He definitely wasn't clean, but he looked as though he might have started out that way this morning. She couldn't decide whether he was well-cared-for or not. "How old are you?" she asked.

"Eight."

Even younger than she'd thought. From his build, she would've guessed nine. Poking her head outside, she glanced up and down the street, but she didn't see anyone who might be with him. "Are you a neighbor?"

He nodded.

"I see. Well, since a lawn mower wasn't one of the items left behind by Evonne's family, I think you've got yourself a job."

Instead of beaming at her, as she'd assumed he would, he turned and scrutinized the yard, thoughtfully scratching under his cap as though he was at least twenty years old. "You want me to do it today?"

"Probably not. Seems pretty short to me."

He scowled, obviously less than pleased with the loss of an immediate opportunity. "I could pull weeds," he suggested.

"For five dollars?"

"Not if you want me to do the garden in back."

She didn't blame him. The garden sprawled over a quarter of an acre and was entirely overrun. "Okay, how 'bout you do the front and back planter areas?"

"Will you throw in a cookie with that five bucks?"

She wanted to laugh but squelched the impulse. She suspected he'd be offended if he knew she wasn't taking him as seriously as he expected. "You drive a hard bargain, my friend."

"It's only a cookie."

"But I'm just moving in. I don't have any cookies."

He frowned, considering. "Can you get one by to-morrow?"

"You're willing to work on credit?"

"Sure." He smiled for the first time, revealing the fact that he was missing two front teeth. "A cookie to-morrow's better than none at all, right? Maybe you'll even give me two, since I had to wait."

Clearly, he was a bright boy. "What's your name?" she asked with a grin for the devilish glint in his eyes.

"Teddy."

"I'm Grace, Teddy. And it sounds like we have a deal."

"Thanks!" He dashed over to the flower bed and began pulling weeds just as a moving van rambled down the street. George, driving the rental truck.

Her on-again, off-again boyfriend smiled and waved when he saw her, then pulled into the drive.

"This is quite a house," he said as he got out.

She motioned him up the walkway. "Come see. It's

old, but I love the high ceilings and heavy-paned windows, the wallpaper, the floors. It's so…*her,* you know? I close my eyes and I can practically smell the spices she used. It's almost like she's still here."

"Who's 'she'?" he asked.

"Evonne."

"The woman who died recently? The one who used to sell things in her front yard?"

Grace nodded and held the door for him.

"How'd you manage to get her house?"

"I told you on the phone when I gave you the address, remember?"

"I'm sorry. I was preoccupied with the Wrigley case. It's going sideways on me."

She closed the door behind him. "The intruder rape?"

"Yeah."

"That *is* a problem," she said. But she found it difficult to really empathize. She'd seen the evidence stacked against his client, knew in her bones that the thirty-year-old bricklayer was dangerous and violent. She certainly didn't want to see this guy walk away from what he'd done just so George could win the case.

"Yeah, it is. But tell me again how you got this house. You seem happy with it."

"It was just a matter of timing, really. Evonne's family wanted to sell. But real estate isn't moving very fast around here, so I convinced them to collect three months' rent before putting it on the market."

"You're not going to get too comfortable here, are you?" he asked.

"In *Stillwater?*" she replied. He was the one who'd pressed her to visit, to finally resolve the situation between her and her family. Now he wasn't pleased that she'd taken his advice?

"Oh, yeah." He wiped the bead of sweat rolling down from his dark hair, which was beginning to thin on top. "Guess not, huh? You hate this town."

It really wasn't that clear-cut. But he'd been raised by two affluent, doting parents and had a younger sister who adored him. He didn't understand how complex her background was, how literal the skeletons in her closet. As a result, he preferred to dismiss her reservations about marriage. *Can't you just...get over it?* he'd asked before their last breakup.

She wished she could.

"I have no problem with the countryside, the slow pace of life, the architecture," she said as he looked around. It was the memories that plagued her. And, today, the heat. But she had to contend with the heat in Jackson, too.

"You're right. There's something classic and dignified about this place," he said.

"Let's go into the kitchen. I'll get you a cold drink."

He jerked his head toward the front. "Who's the boy weeding outside?"

Teddy had rocked back on his knees and silently appraised George as he walked by, but Grace could see through the window that he was back at work.

"One of the neighbor kids."

"He's a handsome boy. Good thing he's not twenty years older. I'd worry that he might steal you away."

Grace hesitated, easily recognizing the subtle plea for reassurance. She cared about George. Even if he didn't always understand her needs, he'd been a loyal friend. Once her heart was whole, she planned to marry him and start a family.

"You're not going to lose me," she said.

He caught her hand and leaned in to kiss her forehead. "I'm glad to hear that. When you come home, we'll forget about everything and move on."

We'll forget... He often tried to encourage her with such talk, but he had no scars to worry about. He simply didn't want to hear anything that wasn't a "yes."

"Of course we will," she said, because she needed him to maintain his faith in her.

He studied her as though he wasn't quite sure whether or not to believe that. Then he kissed her.

Grace slid her arms around his neck and enjoyed the kiss—until he deepened it. Then she felt that old stubborn resistance rise inside her like bile. Pulling away, she smiled to cover her less-than-enthusiastic response. "Let's get you something to drink, okay?"

"Sounds good." He followed her, stepping around the few boxes she'd brought to Stillwater in her car. "What're you going to do with yourself here, day after day?" he asked.

"I've been thinking about that."

"So have I. Why don't I bring your computer, so you can act as a paralegal for me?"

She cocked an eyebrow at him. "You'd jeopardize your clients by allowing a prosecutor access to your files?"

"My gosh, Grace, would you relax? You're off for three months. You won't be handling any of these cases."

It would still be a huge breach of ethics. Grace wasn't interested. "Thanks, but no thanks," she said. "I left my computer behind for a reason. I want a clean break from anything to do with my job." She was determined to finally face her demons, not anesthetize herself with more of the same routine.

"Then what?"

In the kitchen they were surrounded by tall, painted cabinets and elaborate crown molding. "I'm going to use the recipes Evonne sent me."

His expression turned condescending. "Make homemade soaps and lotions and stuff like that?"

"Exactly." Removing a pitcher of raspberry iced tea from the refrigerator, she poured him a glass.

"Now I'm not worried at all," he joked.

Grace handed him his drink. "Why not?"

"I can't see my talented little prosecutor sitting outside, peddling homemade foodstuffs. At least not for very long."

Grace tucked the wisps of hair that had fallen from her ponytail behind her ears. Maybe it wouldn't be as mentally challenging as the work she was used to, but it wouldn't be as hectic, either. An assistant district attorney was always cleaning up other people's messes, trying to put things right—or as right as they could be after a violent crime. Now, she yearned to forget the burglary, rape and murder cases she'd prosecuted and create something simple and pure. "It'll pass the time while I'm here," she said instead of arguing.

"And make you desperate to get back to a real job."

"Possibly."

"I give it a week."

Grace thought she might last a little longer than that. Maybe she wasn't too excited about what lurked at the farm. But—she glanced around the well-loved kitchen—here in Evonne's house, she felt at home for the first time since she could remember.

2

Grace's cell phone rang early the following morning. Expecting it to be someone from the office, she bolted awake and scrambled to answer before the caller could be transferred to voice mail.

A second later, she remembered helping George lug her bed up the stairs to what had been Evonne's bedroom.

She wasn't even in Jackson, she realized. She was in Stillwater. And she was staying here for some time.

"No one's going to steal me away, George," she muttered, and pushed the Talk button, thinking he might want to let her know he'd made it home safely last night. Fortunately, he'd been eager to get back to the Wrigley case and hadn't pressed her to sleep with him.

"Hello?"

"You've got to call Mom. And Madeline."

It was her younger sister, Molly, who worked for a clothes designer in New York City. As a teenager, Molly had been almost as eager to get out of Stillwater as Grace. She'd spent her first year after high school helping their mother move from the farm and get settled in town. But after that she'd obtained a grant from the federal government that allowed her to attend the

Fashion Institute of Design and Merchandising in Los Angeles. Except for a few visits to Jackson each year to see Grace, and to Stillwater to see Irene, Clay and Madeline, she'd been gone ever since.

Grace rubbed a hand over her face in an attempt to revive herself. "Why?"

"They know you're in Stillwater."

"Clay told them already?"

"From what I heard, you stopped by the farm night before last. How long did you think he'd wait?"

"Until I was ready, I guess."

"Did you ask him to keep your presence a secret?"

"No. I knew he'd tell Mom anyway."

"There you go."

Stifling a yawn, Grace kicked off the sheet that served as her only covering. Six-thirty in the morning, and it was already hot and sticky. The open windows and the fan whirring softly in the corner seemed to make little difference. But there wasn't any more Grace could do, except maybe sit in a tub of ice cubes. Evonne's house had no air-conditioning. "Okay, I—I'll call them later this morning."

"Did you know Mom's seeing someone?" Molly asked.

The sleepiness Grace had been fighting suddenly evaporated. "After all these years? You're kidding."

"No."

"When I talked to her a few weeks ago, she didn't mention anyone."

"The relationship—if that's really what it is—is pretty new. When I called Clay on Saturday, he said she's been gone a lot, and that she's been acting very secretive. So we're guessing she's involved with someone."

"Do you think he's from around here?"

"If so, I can't imagine who it would be. You know how poorly the people of Stillwater have always treated her."

"It's not as bad as it used to be, is it?"

"Of course not. But there are still plenty who'll never accept her."

"Not while they suspect what they do," Grace added.

Molly ignored the comment. "Anyway, if she's found someone special, I say it's about time. Considering what she's been through, she deserves a good man."

"What if he isn't good?"

"The odds have to work for us at some point, don't they? Surely she couldn't get three bad ones in a row."

Nothing was certain. Even if Irene *was* seeing someone special—a good man—did he deserve to get mixed up with their family? Not that he'd even know the worst of it. That was part of the problem Grace faced with George—her inability to be completely honest with him. "I don't see how she can do any worse than she did with our father and the reverend."

"Our father had his moments."

"Before he ran off."

"My point exactly. It was more like one big mistake, not two. Mom wouldn't have married the reverend if she hadn't been so desperate. She was only trying to keep all of us together."

"I know." Grace didn't blame Irene for buying into the dream the reverend had represented. He'd seemed like a solid family man, someone who'd stand by her, as well as her children and his own daughter, instead of shirking responsibility the way their real father had.

No one would've believed that Barker, a well-liked hardworking preacher, could possess such a dark side.

"So why didn't you tell me?" Molly asked. The tone of her voice indicated she'd shifted to a new topic.

"Tell you what?" Miserably hot, Grace pulled off the T-shirt she'd slept in and sat directly in front of the fan in her panties. The sweat moistening her bare skin made the air feel cooler.

"That you were finally returning to Stillwater."

Grace had thought about it. She knew Molly would've joined her, had she asked. Molly was the pleaser in the family; she tried to take care of everyone. But Grace refused to lean on her the way their mother did. "It came up at the last minute."

"Somehow I find that hard to believe."

"It's true."

"You had to make a lot of arrangements."

"Which came together quickly."

"If you say so." Obviously, Molly didn't want to argue further. "How does it feel to be back?"

Dropping onto the bed, Grace stared up at the ceiling, searching for an answer to that question. She was definitely apprehensive about being here. But for now, in this moment, she seemed to belong in Evonne's space. And not having to hurry off somewhere or finish something felt good.

"It's okay," she said.

"How long are you planning to stay?"

"I've got the house for three months. But I'm not sure I'll last the whole time."

"Please tell me you were going to call Mom."

"I was. I just—I've been busy."

"A phone call only takes a minute."

"Molly, don't start."

"I won't, because I'm in too much of a rush. I'll be late for work if I don't get a move on."

"I'll let you go, then."

"Call me if you need anything."

"I will." Grace knew her sister was about to hang up, but she had one more question. "Mol?"

"Yeah?"

"How do you do it?"

"Do what?"

"Come back here, visit Clay in that…that house, have lunch with Madeline, when you know—"

"I don't think about it," her sister interrupted.

How could she *not* think about it? The man who used to be their stepfather was dead. Ever since Grace had helped drag his body down the porch steps, where Clay loaded it into a wheelbarrow, she'd spent almost every night fearing she'd wake up to find the reverend staring in her bedroom window.

"I know Madeline's still hoping her father will drive back into town and surprise her someday," Molly went on. "But you and I know the reverend's gone, Grace. Gone for good. And the world's a better place for it."

"Amen to that," she murmured. "Except it's not so simple."

"It can be if you'll let it."

Did she really mean that? If so, how? "What if someone finally figures out what happened? These days, cold cases are solved all the time. Someone could discover the car in the quarry. A storm could unearth something too macabre to imagine. A particularly credible witness could set the conflicting stories straight."

"Calm down. It's been eighteen *years*. We're fine."

"The people of Stillwater will never forget, Molly. They thought that bastard could walk on water. They didn't know him the way we did."

"They can't even prove he's dead. You, of all people, should understand how the legal system works."

She, of all people... Somehow Molly wasn't making Grace feel any better. The fact that they were still conspiring to hide what had happened so long ago troubled Grace because it suggested that maybe she was still who she used to be and not who she'd become. "You'd better get to work."

"We'll talk later."

"Fine." Grace hung up, then walked to the window to gaze down on Evonne's backyard. She could tell that Evonne's family didn't care as much about the garden as Evonne had. It didn't look as though anyone had tended it since her death.

Grace was going to change that—

Suddenly, she realized that a black SUV had come to a complete stop in the side street just beyond the fence.

"Oops," she muttered and jumped out of sight. Had the driver seen her? It was possible. She'd hung a sheet over the bare window, but she'd tied it back in the middle of the night, hoping for more air.

Embarrassed, she bit her lip as she wondered what to do about it. But there wasn't anything she *could* do.

Whoever it was couldn't have seen a great deal from that distance, anyway...she hoped.

Putting on a spaghetti-strap T-shirt, some shorts and a pair of Keds, she headed downstairs. She'd call her mother and Madeline in an hour. First, she wanted to start on Evonne's garden.

* * *

Kennedy Archer cursed at the coffee he'd spilled in his lap when he saw the topless woman at the window. Evonne's house wasn't on the market yet, so he hadn't expected to see anyone inside. Least of all a woman as stunning as the dark-haired beauty who'd just flashed him. Especially at six-thirty in the morning. Judging by the way she'd darted out of sight the moment she realized he was there, she hadn't meant to put on a show. But a body like that was quite a sight for a man who'd been celibate since the death of his wife two years earlier.

"Daddy? You okay?"

Kennedy pressed his cell phone tighter to his ear. As timing would have it, he'd answered his son's call seconds before noticing movement at the window— and cried out when the coffee scalded him.

"I'm fine, Teddy," he said, still trying to hold the hot liquid puddling in the crotch of his pants away from his more sensitive parts. "What's up?"

His son lowered his voice. "I don't want to stay with Grandma today."

Kennedy was well aware of that. Heath, his ten-year-old, seemed to handle Camille Archer quite well. Heath rarely complained. But he was calm, patient, deliberate—a bit of an intellectual. Camille always called him her "good boy."

Teddy, on the other hand, had a completely different personality. Active, headstrong and already opinionated at eight years of age, he challenged his grandmother at every turn. Or that was how Camille interpreted it. They plowed into one power struggle after another. Yet Kennedy knew that with the right touch Teddy wasn't a difficult child at all. When

Raelynn was alive, she'd been very close to their youngest son.

"Where else would you like to go?" he asked.

"Home."

"You can't go home. There's no one to watch you there."

"What about Lindy?"

Lindy was a sixteen-year-old neighbor. At least Kennedy thought of her as a neighbor. His house sat on quite a bit of land, so there wasn't anyone in the immediate vicinity. He liked Lindy, but the last time she babysat, she'd invited her boyfriend over and they'd watched R-rated horror movies with the boys.

Kennedy no longer trusted her judgment. "Not Lindy. But you could go to Mrs. Weaver's."

"No, I hate it there!"

Kennedy wished Raelynn's parents hadn't followed her brother to Florida ten years ago. Teddy got along better with Grandma Horton than Grandma Archer. But, of course, he only saw his other grandparents once or twice a year. "Teddy, we've been through this before. Considering our options, my mother's is the best place for you. Anyway, it's not all torture. She took you to the zoo in Jackson last week, remember?"

"That was fun," he admitted. "But…now I'm bored. Can't you come and get me?"

"Sorry, buddy. I've got to work today. You know that."

"Then take me with you," he breathed into the phone. "I like playing in your office at the bank."

Kennedy maneuvered his Explorer to the side of the road. The street was still empty, but he needed to reach the napkins in his glove compartment and do what he could to keep the coffee from spilling elsewhere in the car. "I can't. Not today. I'm meeting my campaign director and several key supporters for breakfast. Then I've got to speak at the Rotary Club. After that, I have a shareholders' meeting."

"Why do you have to run for mayor?"

Kennedy wondered if now might be a good time to tell Teddy about Grandpa Archer. It would be easier to discuss the subject when Kennedy didn't have to see his son's face, when he himself could be more objective about the doctor's findings. But he couldn't expect Teddy to deal with that kind of news on his own. Not after losing his mother.

"Your grandpa's retiring, which will leave the seat vacant for the first time in thirty years. It's something I've been planning to do since I was little."

"When's the campaign over?" Teddy asked.

"November. Then, win or lose, life should get easier."

Teddy groaned. "*November?* I'll be back in school by then."

"I know. This has been a tough year." But certainly no more difficult than the one before.

Yanking his mind away from those first few months without Raelynn, Kennedy went through his schedule and decided he could skip meeting Buzz and the guys at the pizza parlor later this afternoon. He liked getting together with his friends occasionally. They'd known each other since grade school. But Teddy's needs came first. "Why don't I pick you up at four o'clock and take you and Heath out for ice cream?" He supposed they could even stop by the pizza parlor afterward to say hello to the gang.

"Can we go at six instead?"

Kennedy stopped swiping at the coffee in his lap. "Six? That's when I usually pick you up."

"I know, but Grandma said she'd take us swimming at four."

"So you have something fun planned."

"Not until four!"

"Come on, Teddy."

There was a lengthy pause. "Can we go camping this weekend?"

"Maybe."

"Say yes, *please?*"

"I'll say yes *if* you can manage not to argue with Grandma today."

A dramatic sigh met this response. "*O*-kay."

"What's Heath doing?"

"Watching TV. Until we go swimming, that's all there *is* to do. Grandma's afraid we might get a speck of dirt on her carpet."

"I thought you were having fun with that mowing service you started."

"Uh-oh, Grandma's comin'," he said and hung up.

Kennedy knew Camille would consider Teddy's plea to escape her place a personal betrayal. She tried to please him and his brother. But it was difficult for her to be around kids five days a week after not having any for so long. And yet she needed Teddy and Heath with her. Looking after the boys helped keep her mind off his father's diagnosis. She often tried to convince Kennedy that they loved every minute they spent with her.

Uh-oh, Grandma's comin'....

Evidently, Teddy was learning how to avoid a confrontation with her.

Chuckling, Kennedy slipped his phone into the extra cup-holder on the console. His youngest son was a handful, all right—but in a boisterous, exuberant way. If Camille had been younger and if she wasn't so stressed, she'd be able to see that.

"He'll survive another day," Kennedy told himself. Camille's domineering personality might not blend well with Teddy's, but she loved both boys as much as she loved him. No one, not even Teddy, questioned that.

He glanced at the clock on the dash. He had to get going. He had a lot to do today. And thanks to his sudden glimpse of that woman in the window, he wouldn't be able to start any of it until he went home to change.

"You weren't going to let me know you're in town?"

Still on her knees, Grace shifted around to see her mother standing in Evonne's backyard. Irene came to visit Grace in Jackson about once a year, but this was the first time since Grace had graduated from high school that they were both in Stillwater.

Clearing her throat, she rose stiffly to her feet. She'd meant to garden for only a couple of hours, but the morning had gotten away from her. It was after noon. Somehow, restoring Evonne's garden had turned into her mission for the day. Even with her clothes sticking to her, and the knowledge that she'd be sore tomorrow, it felt good to dig and pull weeds and work the earth, to save one plant after another from the neglect of the past few weeks.

Because of the muddy gloves on her hands, Grace wiped the sweat from her forehead with one arm. "I'm sorry," she said, attempting a smile. "I meant to, Mom. I just…got busy."

Irene motioned toward the garden. "I guess these weeds couldn't wait?"

Obviously her mother was hurt. Drawing a deep breath, Grace crossed the lawn to give her a hug. Grace was excited to see Irene, even though she'd dreaded this moment. She admired her mother, missed her, but Irene stirred too many other emotions, as well. "They bother me," she admitted. "I'm sure Evonne wouldn't like it. And—" she stepped back and removed her floppy hat to check the gray sky overhead "—I thought I'd get as far as I could before the rain starts."

Irene didn't appear convinced that Grace's concern over the weather had stopped her from calling. But Grace doubted her mother would push the issue. Over the years, they'd established a pattern for dealing with the strain between them, which was better ignored than confronted.

"You're looking good," Grace said, and meant it.

"I'm too fat," Irene responded, but if she had any weight to lose it wasn't more than ten or fifteen pounds. And the fact that she dressed up for even the smallest errand provided sufficient proof of her vanity.

"No, you're just right."

Grace's smile grew more genuine when she saw her mother brighten at the compliment. Although Irene was only five-two, they had the same oval-shaped face and blue eyes. Grace generally pulled her dark hair into a messy knot at the back of her head and wore little makeup. Her mother went heavy on the mascara and deep-red lipstick, and backcombed her hair into a style vaguely reminiscent of Loretta Lynn.

"Molly told me you're seeing someone," Grace said, eager to discover whether her sister was right.

Irene waved a dismissive hand. "Not really. She and that guy she brought for Christmas are dating again, though."

"Bo's just a friend, and you know it. But you're try-ing to change the subject, and that gives me the im-pression you're hiding something."

"Who would I be seeing? No one around here has ever liked me," she said with a self-deprecating chuckle.

Whether or not that was the case now, it'd been true in the past. When Irene married the Reverend Barker and moved with her three children from neighboring Booneville twenty-two years ago, Grace had been only nine years old. But nine was old enough to understand that the whispers she frequently heard about her mother weren't particularly flattering.

Look at her, walkin' 'round with her nose in the air. I swear I've never seen a more uppity woman.... As if we don't have a dozen ladies right here in Stillwater who would've made our good reverend twice the wife.... Why, Irene's gotta be ten, fifteen years younga than he is. She's afta his money, that's what she's afta.

The reverend had only a modest living and the farm. But that was still more than Irene and her children had possessed in Booneville. And it was enough to make the people of Stillwater resent them. They'd been out-siders, treated as if her mother had taken something she had no right to.

Of course it hadn't helped that the reverend made subtle yet demeaning comments about his new wife at every opportunity—even from the pulpit. Or that the blush of excitement her mother had experienced in the beginning faded fast as Irene came to know her new husband better.

Grace had always marveled at how loyal this town had been to Barker, that such an evil man could con-vince so many he was a saint.

A calloused hand closed over her arm, and a low, gruff voice grated in her ear, "Don't make a sound." When she whimpered, the man she called Daddy squeezed tighter, using the pressure to warn her of the consequences should she disobey. Madeline, his own daughter, slept in the bed directly across from her. But Grace knew he'd get his revenge if she woke her stepsister—

"Grace, what's wrong?" her mother asked.

The memory shattered. Folding her arms tightly across her body to ward off the chill left in its wake, Grace forced a trembling smile. "Nothing."

"You're sure?"

"Positive," she said, but the peace and tranquility she'd enjoyed earlier eluded her now. It felt as if she'd stepped out of the sun into a cold dark cellar. The images and sensations she worked so hard to avoid seemed to bang around inside her head. "I—it's too hot out here. We should sit on the porch," she said and started for the house.

"After thirteen years...I can't believe you're back," her mother said as she followed.

Grace spoke before she could catch herself. "I can't believe you never left."

"I couldn't leave," Irene said indignantly. "Do you think I'd abandon Clay?"

"Like I did?"

Her mother looked stricken. "No, I—I didn't mean that."

Grace pressed three fingers to her forehead as she sank onto the porch swing. Of course. No one who knew the truth ever blamed her. They pitied her, didn't know what to say or how to make things better. But they didn't *blame* her. She was the one who blamed herself. "I'm sorry." She willed her pulse to slow, her calm to return. "Coming here is difficult for me."

Her mother sat next to her and took her hand. She didn't say anything, but held on while they rocked back and forth.

Oddly enough, the tension eased. Grace wished her mother had been capable of reaching out to her eighteen years ago….

"Evonne's place is nice, isn't it?" Irene said at last.

"I like it here," Grace told her.

"Will you be staying long?"

"Three months. Maybe."

"Three months! That's good." Letting go, her mother stood. "I love you, Grace. I didn't say it enough, and I…I let you down. But I do love you."

Grace didn't know how to respond. So she asked the question she'd wanted to ask Irene for a long time. "Does ignoring something ugly mean it doesn't exist, Mom?"

Her mother studied her for several minutes, her eyes clouding with her own pain. "Does acknowledging it make it go away?" she countered. "I did what I had to do. Someday I hope you'll forgive me for that." With a final wave, she set off across the porch, her heels clacking on the wooden boards until she reached the lawn. "I've got an appointment. Call me later if…if you'd like to see me again."

"I'll call," Grace said and watched her go.

The cool, dim interior of the Hill Country Pizza & Pasta Parlor finally brought Grace a welcome reprieve from the heat. She'd just showered, but it was the hottest part of the day and she already felt sticky again. The air had grown muggier and muggier all afternoon, but it had yet to rain. She guessed the rain would fall tonight as a constant drizzle.

"Here's your pizza."

The teenage girl who'd taken her order hovered at the table with a small pie. As Grace moved her salad to the side, the door opened and a small group of men walked in.

"Thank you," she said to the waitress and immediately averted her face. She didn't want to make eye contact with anyone, didn't want to be noticed or drawn into conversation. She'd only come to have an early supper and to escape the heat.

But it wasn't three minutes later that she heard the same men talking about her.

"I swear it's her, Tim."

"Grinding Gracie? Nah…"

"It is! Rex Peters told me she was coming back to town."

"What for?" someone else asked. "I thought she'd become an assistant district attorney somewhere. There was an article about her in the paper."

Grace couldn't decipher the response. She told herself to block them out and finish her food. But a moment later, someone gave a low whistle and said something about how good she looked, and she couldn't help glancing over.

One of the men stood at the front counter. He had his back to her as he ordered, but the other four were the jocks she'd admired so much in high school. Seeing them made her skin crawl. She no longer wanted to be here, didn't want to acknowledge them. She wasn't the person she used to be.

"Maybe we don't recognize her with her clothes on," Joe Vincelli said. The meaningful snicker that went with those words brought his name back to Grace right away. He was the reverend's beloved nephew. He'd also coined the humiliating nickname that had been written on her locker and echoed after her in the halls.

"Shut up, she'll hear you," someone growled. Was it Buzz Harte? She couldn't be sure. He seemed to have changed the most; he'd certainly lost a lot of hair.

More murmuring and a few muffled guffaws made Grace's ears burn. Heart pounding, she stared down at her plate. Fourteen or fifteen years ago, she'd had sex with at least three of these men in fumbling back-seat trysts or behind a building. Obviously, they remembered those encounters with far more relish than she did. She didn't know how she could've allowed anyone to use her so terribly, especially the boys who'd attended high school with her.

Except that she'd been searching for something she couldn't find....

Feeling faint, she wiped off the sweat beading on her upper lip, and wondered if she could slip out of the restaurant without having to pass right by them.

Then Joe's voice carried to her again, louder than the others, and it was as if no time had passed at all. "She was one hell of an easy lay, wasn't she? All you had to do was crook your finger, and she'd spread her legs. I did her once behind the bleachers with my parents sitting about ten feet away."

Grace's chest constricted as they laughed, which made it difficult to breathe. With Joe, it had been even more complicated than wanting so desperately to be liked. She'd felt she owed him some type of compensation for the loss of his uncle.

"She once asked me if she could be my girlfriend

for a few weeks," Tim said. His voice was much lower than Joe's, but she heard enough words to be able to string them together. "I told her yes before I screwed her, then broke up with her right after." His subsequent laugh was a bark of disbelief. "It's amazing how anyone that stupid could get into Georgetown."

Someone—Buzz?—must've smacked him because he groaned.

"*Stupid?* Come on. She's definitely not stupid. She was—" his voice dropped, but she managed to cull the meaning "—screwed-up…something weird going on in that house…."

"There wasn't anything weird going on until they killed my uncle," Joe said defensively.

"You don't know what happened to your uncle," Tim said, a little more clearly. Joe started to argue, but Tim raised a hand. "And, trust me, they were weird from the beginning."

"Because of her bitch of a mother," Joe grumbled.

After that, there were several whispered remarks. But Grace wasn't listening; she was struggling to hang on to her composure.

Unfortunately, her stomach wasn't cooperating. It churned and ached as her mind painted pictures of what she'd done with these men when they were boys.

She'd tried to make up for those mistakes ever since. But it wasn't enough, was it? It was never enough.

"Go say hi to her, Joe," Tim said. "Maybe you can do her right here. If you make her squeal, maybe she'll tell you what happened to your uncle."

Joe's response was a muted snarl as the man who'd been ordering now joined the others at the table. "What're you guys talking about?" he asked, his words resonating clearly.

Grace hadn't seen this guy's face, but she didn't need to. It was Kennedy Archer—the most handsome, the most athletic, the most admired of them all. She knew him instantly but couldn't stop herself from looking up to confirm it.

He hadn't gotten fat. Nor had he gone bald, like some of his friends. He was still tall and broad-shouldered, with dark-blond hair and dimples on either side of his poster-boy smile. And, according to the campaign signs all over town, he was running for mayor, hoping to take the seat his father had occupied for so long.

Their eyes met. Surprise lit his face as recognition dawned, and he quit yanking on the tie he'd been trying to loosen.

Grace turned immediately away. In the restaurant business, four o'clock was the slowest part of the day. What were the chances that Kennedy Archer and his bunch would gather at the pizza joint while she was here, just like they used to when she worked behind the counter at sixteen?

She remembered watching every move they made, trying to anticipate their needs, to be funny, cool—and had to bite her lip to contain her roiling emotions. She hadn't expected to confront them all at once, hadn't prepared herself for the feelings that doing so might evoke. It seemed as though they'd shoved her back into the skin of the needy child she used to be.

How could she let that happen? Why hadn't she seen it coming?

She'd been too focused on what mattered to her as an adult, of course. Clay and Irene—and her stepsister Madeline, whom she hadn't called yet. High school was like another life to her, a dark time when she'd despised herself far more than anyone else could.

Suddenly, she realized she couldn't stay where she was any longer. Bile rose from her stomach, burning the back of her throat....

Standing with as much dignity as she could muster, she hurried to the back of the restaurant and into the bathroom.

Once the door closed behind her, blocking out the curious stares that had followed her from the table, she launched herself into a toilet stall and fell to her knees, just in time to lose what little she'd eaten of her dinner.

3

She wasn't coming back. The other guys had finally forgotten "Grinding Gracie" and gone on to talk about the election, the price local farmers were getting for cotton, a father/son fishing trip they were planning to take together in August. But Kennedy found himself glancing over at the table where Grace Montgomery had been sitting. Her food was still there. She'd eaten a little salad, but her pizza was untouched and growing colder by the minute.

Was she okay? He rocked back in his chair to check the darkened hallway that led to the restrooms, but he didn't see her. How long could it take to go to the bathroom?

"Kennedy, what's wrong with you, man?" Joe said, nudging him. "You too good for the rest of us now that you're going to be mayor?"

"I've always been too good for you bastards," he teased as he lowered his chair. But after a few half-hearted remarks about the fishing trip, he let the conversation slip away from him again. He was waiting for Grace to come out. The guys had been groaning and whistling at her while she walked to the bathroom, making stupid comments that said they had more testosterone than brains. He wanted to say something to Grace that would smooth it all over, help her feel welcome. If he could.

Another ten minutes passed. Their own pizza came. They devoured it, and still she didn't appear.

He checked the hall once again. Nothing.

"Why are you so preoccupied?" Buzz asked.

"I'm not," he said, but he'd been thinking about the topless woman he'd seen in the window earlier. Now he knew who it was. Grace. She had to be staying at Evonne's place. There couldn't be two women with a body like that.

But why was she renting a house when she had a mother, a brother and a stepsister in town who each had plenty of extra room? What *was* it with that family?

They polished off another pitcher of beer—no sign of Grace. "Where is she?" he asked Buzz.

"Who?" Tim responded, overhearing.

"Never mind," Kennedy grumbled.

"Looks like Grinding Gracie's left her pizza for us," Ronnie said. "You guys think I should take a piece? Wouldn't that be funny, to have her come out and see her pizza half gone?"

"Do it," Joe urged.

Ronnie's chair raked the carpet as he stood, but Kennedy caught him by the arm. "Sit down."

"Come on, Kennedy, it's just a joke."

"Forget it. You know she had a rough childhood. Give her a break, okay?"

Joe arched an eyebrow at him. "I never knew you had a thing for Grinding Gracie. The way I remember it, you wouldn't touch her with a ten-foot pole." He lifted his nose. "You were an Archer."

"I was with Raelynn," he said evenly.

"Yeah, he had a girlfriend," Buzz added.

"So did I," Joe replied with a careless laugh. "Grinding Gracie didn't interfere with that. It wasn't as if I'd ever *like* her or anything."

Kennedy had known these guys since grade school, but sometimes they got on his nerves. Especially Joe, who in situations like this seemed to bring out the worst in everyone. If not for what Joe had done for him when they were only twelve years old, Kennedy doubted they'd even be friends. "I don't want to hear it."

At the irritation in Kennedy's voice, they stared at him for several seconds. A few muttered about the pressure he was under. But after a while, the tension eased and they started talking about the Jaguars and what kind of football season they could expect.

Kennedy listened until he couldn't stand wondering about Grace anymore. Then, with a silent curse, he got up and went to the woman's restroom. "Grace?" he said, knocking on the door. "You okay in there?"

No reply. Just the sound of the fan whirring inside.

"Grace? If you don't answer, I'll have to come in."

Still nothing.

He began to enter—and caught a brief glimpse of her staggering to her feet. But then she hit the other side of the door and held it closed with the weight of her body.

"I—I'm…fine," she said. But her words were broken as though she had to gulp for the air to speak.

Judging by the unusually pale face and saucerlike eyes he'd seen in the mirror, he knew she couldn't be fine. She was sick. He could smell it.

"Do you need a ride home?" he asked.

There was no response, but she was leaning against the door, and he didn't want to force it open.

"I could give you a lift right now."

"No, you…you go on back to your friends. They're pretty funny…I—I wouldn't want you to miss anything."

Shit. She'd heard them, just as he feared. He tried to open the door again, but it wouldn't budge. "The guys—they can be idiots sometimes, you know? I often wonder if they'll ever grow up. Forget about them, okay? They don't mean half the things that come out of their mouths."

The sound of fabric brushing against the wood led him to believe she'd just slid to the floor.

"Grace?"

"Leave me alone." Her voice was more strident now, but it came from much lower, confirming his suspicion that she was on the floor. "I—I'm not one of your many admirers, so…do us both a favor and go."

Go. With a sigh, Kennedy told himself to do just that. But he couldn't; the words he'd heard his friends say, and how deeply he suspected they'd hurt her, wouldn't let him. He paced the short hall several times. Then he realized that Joe and the others were still waiting to see what would happen, and decided to take Grace out of the spotlight by returning to the table.

"You get anything good?" Joe asked and everyone laughed.

"He'd be smilin' if that was the case," Tim said.

Kennedy scowled. "You guys can be real assholes, you know that?"

Hunching over the sink, Grace dabbed a wet paper towel to her forehead. She needed to gather the strength to walk out of the pizza parlor. But she was hoping Kennedy and his friends would leave first. She'd face them all later, when she was better prepared.

Breathe deeply. In and out. In and out. She'd be okay. She'd survived a lot worse than this. It was just the surprise, the throwback to old times that bothered her.

Forget them. You don't need them. You never did....

The voice of a little boy heading into the opposite restroom rose in the hallway, and she decided to make her move. The approach of the dinner hour meant there were probably a lot more people in the restaurant. Even if Kennedy Archer and his friends were still around, maybe she could slip by without being noticed. Even if they saw her, she didn't care. The initial shock was over. What more could they do?

She splashed some water on her face and patted it dry, then marched into the dining area. Beer mugs, paper plates and silver pizza pans littered the table where Kennedy and his friends had eaten, but the seats were empty.

Allowing herself a small sigh of relief, Grace ignored the food that had grown cold at her own table and went swiftly outside. She dug through her purse for her keys while she walked, telling herself she'd be back at Evonne's in a matter of minutes. But the moment she glanced up, she saw that Kennedy Archer wasn't gone, after all. He was leaning against the front bumper of a Ford Explorer that was parked next to her Beemer.

It looked as if he was waiting for someone. She hoped it wasn't her.

For a few seconds, her footsteps faltered. She'd have to walk around him to get in. But she wasn't about to let the sight of him stop her. She wouldn't let him or his friends hurt her ever again, she thought, and picked up speed.

As she stepped off the curb, he shoved away from the Explorer as if to intercept her, but she circumvented him easily enough.

"Excuse me," she murmured and unlocked her car. She might have been talking to a stranger.

Throwing her purse into the passenger seat, she slid inside, welcoming the feel and smell of the familiar leather. But when she pulled on her door, she realized it wouldn't close because he was holding it.

She looked into his face, and let every ounce of the derision she felt for Stillwater's spoiled, selfish, insensitive men show in her eyes. "Is there something I can do for you?"

The look registered. He stepped back as though she'd slapped him, but didn't release her door.

"I just wanted to say—"

"Don't bother."

"But—"

"I know you, remember? I'm sure you and your friends can recall a great many things about me, and I don't blame you for not being impressed. But I also remember a great many things about you and am equally unimpressed. So save your feeble attempts to be a nice guy for someone who can't see the shriveled heart behind that phony smile."

With that, she glanced pointedly at the hand holding her door, and he finally let go.

Kennedy watched Grace pull out of the lot. Obviously, she wasn't the "I'll do anything to make you like me," girl she'd been in high school. He wanted to believe she'd confused him with Joe, or maybe Tim, but he knew she hadn't.

As he climbed into the driver's seat of his own vehicle, he remembered Joe bragging to the varsity football team that he could get Grace to have sex with him anytime, anywhere. To prove it, he'd convinced her to meet him in the locker room after the game the following Friday.

Kennedy hadn't stayed for the show, but he'd listened as avidly as everyone else to the gossip that had circulated afterward. He'd even laughed when Joe explained how he'd promised to take her to the prom only to stand her up.

"*I* never laid a hand on her," Kennedy said aloud in an effort to ease his troubled conscience. But his conscience wouldn't relent. Maybe he hadn't been directly involved—but he hadn't done much to stop the others from calling her names, had he? He'd been there, standing next to the guys who'd nudged her or tripped her. He'd chosen to ignore it when they slipped a pincher bug into her food at lunch. He'd only intervened when Raelynn was there.

Raelynn… God, he missed his wife. He'd never known anyone so sweet, so perfect. She used to plead with him to make his friends stop mocking Grace, to persuade them to leave her alone. For Raelynn's sake, he'd stepped in now and then. But his own mother often spoke of Grace's family as if they had no right to breathe the same air as decent people, and he'd taken his lead from her.

His regret tasted bitter as he shut his car door and started his engine. There'd been times he'd felt sorry for Grace, but mostly he'd tried to pretend she didn't exist. The way she'd stare at him with so much longing in her eyes made him uncomfortable. He hadn't been mature enough to realize that he had a responsibility to help her. Or maybe he simply hadn't cared enough to bother. No one had cared. Except her family. When Molly reached high school and walked into the girls' bathroom one day to find her sister with Tim, she went home and told their older brother. Clay came to school the next day and broke Tim's nose.

Clay's involvement finally scared off the guys who were using Grace sexually. But the damage had already been done. The name-calling and other cruelty continued.

His cell phone rang. Kennedy glanced down at it, surprised to see his mother's home number listed on his caller ID. Camille was supposed to be at the community pool with the boys. What were they doing home already?

He punched the Talk button. "Hello?"

"Have you heard?" she asked.

"Heard what?"

"Grace Montgomery's back in town."

No kidding. He pictured the woman who'd just accused him of having a shriveled heart and a phony smile. She'd been attractive in high school. It wasn't her looks that had marked her as an outcast, only her neediness. But now she was even prettier. Eyebrows that had been too thick were now slender and arched; teeth that had been slightly crooked were perfectly straight. She still had the same olive-colored skin, ice-blue eyes and dark, thick hair. The contrast was striking, but it was her high cheekbones and stubborn chin—both of which had been too severe for a young girl—that really set her apart. Beyond her stunning figure, of course. She'd developed before all the other girls, which certainly hadn't helped her situation growing up.

"Kennedy?" his mother prompted when he didn't answer right away.

"I know she's back," he said.

"Who told you?"

"I just ran into her at the pizza parlor."

"Someone said she's driving a BMW. Is that true?"

He knew his mother would feel better if he told her Grace's car was one of the smaller, less expensive models, but he couldn't bring himself to do it—for that reason. "It's true."

"How do you think she got it?"

Did it matter? Why shouldn't Grace have something nice? "I have no idea," he said.

"I can't imagine. District attorneys don't make that much. Especially assistant district attorneys. Maybe she married for money, like her mother, and now she's back because her husband's already gone missing."

"You're being ridiculous, Mom," Kennedy said with a heavy dose of annoyance. "The reverend wasn't exactly a millionaire. If Irene Montgomery married him for money, she sure didn't get a lot."

"She got the farm, didn't she? Clay *still* lives there."

Kennedy could see they were heading for an argument and changed the subject. "Why aren't you at the pool?"

"They closed at five for cleaning."

"So the boys got to swim for only an hour?"

"That's long enough, isn't it?"

He could imagine Teddy's disappointment after having waited all day. "I'm on my way. I'll see you in a minute."

"Will you be staying for supper?"

"No, I want to get home." He'd been doing well lately, adjusting to the loss of Raelynn. He'd been thinking about other things, worried about his father and swept up in the campaign. But tonight he felt his wife's absence like a gaping hole in his chest.

"I've got steaks and barbecue beans and corn," his mother said. He knew she enjoyed taking care of him, enjoyed feeling needed and important. And he appreciated everything she did. For an only child, that kind of intense focus often came with the territory. Sometimes it was too much. But with his father ill, he needed to give her extra support, which made it difficult to keep her at a healthier distance.

"Thanks, but there're plenty of groceries at home."

She gave a snort of displeasure. "Why would you go anywhere else when I've got dinner ready?"

"How's Dad?" he asked instead of answering.

"Fine. He's going to beat this. He knows it and I know it."

Kennedy wished *he* knew it. Maybe if Raelynn hadn't died, he'd have more faith. But the luck he'd experienced early in his life didn't seem to be holding.

After dialing and hanging up—twice—Grace gripped her cell phone with more resolve. She had to contact Madeline. She'd been in town for two and a half days. She'd seen Clay and Irene, even several of the jocks from high school. She couldn't procrastinate about calling her stepsister any longer. In some ways, she didn't want to put it off. She loved Madeline. It was just that she felt too much like a hypocrite pretending to be a good sister, a good friend, when she knew what she knew.

"Hello?"

"Maddy?"

"Yes?"

Wearing a fresh pair of shorts and a tank top, Grace lay in the hammock that hung from two oak trees on the left side of the property, nursing a glass of iced tea. She planned to spend a few hours in the kitchen later, but she couldn't remember the last time she'd paused to notice a sunset, let alone watch it.

After reveling in the quiet spectacle for the past five minutes, she thought she could understand why some people said that joy was in the simple things.

"It's Grace."

"Grace! Why haven't you called me?"

"I've been busy getting settled. But don't worry, I'm staying for several weeks, at least."

"*Weeks?* Are you kidding?"

"No."

"That's wonderful! I drove by Evonne's earlier hoping to catch you, but you weren't home."

Grace refused to think of the pizza parlor debacle. "I was picking up a few groceries." She took a sip of her iced tea, remembering her mad dash into the Piggly Wiggly, where she'd quickly gathered a few essentials before she could run into anyone else. "How're things at the paper?"

Madeline had worked as the editor of the *Stillwater Independent* since graduating with a journalism degree from Mississippi State University. She'd actually bought the paper last year when the original owners retired, with ten thousand dollars down and monthly payments that would stretch out over five years. So now she owned it *and* edited it—and struggled to pay her bills. Grace had often wondered where her stepsister might've ended up if her father hadn't disappeared. *The New York Times? The Washington Post?*

When they were growing up, Madeline had talked a lot about working for such a prestigious paper. As it was, she seemed hesitant to leave Stillwater for any length of time. Grace suspected she was afraid her father would come back while she was gone. Or that someone else she loved might disappear from her life if she didn't keep careful watch. Ironically, Madeline was closer to Irene and Clay, even to Molly in some ways, than Grace was.

The past had affected them all very differently. Grace hated leaving herself vulnerable, so she tried to wall people out. Madeline was afraid she'd lose the people she loved, so she tried to wall them in.

"The paper's doing well," she said. "Our circulation's been growing, especially since I started the section called 'Singles.'"

"Is that some type of classifieds?"

"A once-a-week showcase on two singles, one female, one male."

"Interesting."

"It is. It helps people get to know each other. What are you doing tonight?"

Grace thought of the note she'd found stuck in her door and couldn't resist a smile. *Do you have my cookies? Teddy.*

"I'd like to do some baking."

"Seriously?"

Her smile widened. "Seriously."

"Sounds like fun to me. Could you use some help?"

Grace's heart beat heavily for a moment before she managed an answer. "Sure."

"I was planning to watch a video with Kirk, but I see him all the time. I'd rather be with you."

"Are you two getting serious?"

"Not at all."

"You're as bad as I am. You've been seeing him for three years, Maddy."

This observation met with an audible sigh. "I know. The relationship never progresses. The friendship's too good to go our separate ways. But we're not in love enough to marry."

"Well, Molly and Clay are doing no better," Grace said.

"Clay could get married. Lord knows, plenty of women want him. He just doesn't seem interested in anything that lasts more than a single night. He was actually voted 'Most Eligible Bachelor' *and* 'Least Likely to Marry' in the poll I did for *Singles* a few months ago."

Grace could understand why Clay might hesitate to make a commitment. How could he move someone into that house and still hide the secret? What if his wife wanted to relocate at some point? Half the town would tear the farm apart searching for Lee Barker.

"And Molly's only twenty-nine," Madeline was saying. "That's not too unusual."

"Twenty-nine is definitely old enough to be married," Grace said.

"True."

Grace didn't want to examine her own situation, which was probably coming next, so she changed the subject. "What about bringing Kirk with you tonight?"

"That's a thought," Madeline replied, not questioning the shift in topics. "He just called to say something happened at the tavern last night that he wants to tell me about." She lowered her voice, infusing it with meaning. "I think it concerns Dad."

Grace had been pushing off on the ground with one foot. Now she stilled the hammock. "In what way?"

"I don't know. He was at work and didn't get to explain before he had to go. But it sounds promising."

Not this again. Poor Madeline. "Maddy, you have to let it go, okay? It's not good for you to obsess over..." She'd been about to say "the reverend" but forced herself to say "Daddy."

The reverend himself had told his stepchildren to call him Dad, and had gotten very angry when they didn't, especially if other people were around when they slipped up. Once he was no longer part of their lives, their mother had insisted they continue the practice for the same reason they couldn't pack up the office in the barn.

"Until my dad met your mother, it was just me and him," Madeline said. "He was all I had."

Her mother had committed suicide three years before the reverend married Irene. Grace had always wondered exactly what had caused her severe unhappiness and guessed she'd come to know the real man behind her husband's pious mask. But no one ever talked about her. Even Madeline pretended Eliza Barker had never existed. Grace assumed Madeline hadn't forgiven her yet.

"I know how much he meant to you, but—"

"I need some closure, Grace. If he's dead I'll have to accept that, right? Then I'll know he's not coming back. Like my birth mother. That's something, isn't it?"

"Does Kirk believe he's dead?" Grace asked.

"Of course. But unlike most other people around here, he's not blaming Irene."

"That's good," Grace said with a fake laugh. "I'd hate to have anyone like that influencing you."

"She's part of the reason I can't quit searching for answers," Madeline replied. "I'm determined to finally prove to this town that she's as innocent as you or I. They've been so unfair to her—and to you and Molly and Clay."

After the reverend disappeared, Grace's family was all Madeline had. Grace supposed she could've moved in with her cousins, but she'd never been particularly close to them. Not only that, her stubborn loyalty to Irene separated her from Joe's family almost immediately.

Grace pressed the cool glass to her cheek and closed her eyes. "I appreciate that, Maddy."

Her stepsister grew silent, then said, "We'll be over in an hour, okay?"

"Maddy?" Lowering her drink, Grace opened her eyes.

"What?"

"Where does Kennedy Archer live?"

"In the old Baumgarter place."

The Baumgarter place was a fabulous Georgian that sat back from the road a couple miles south of town. Grace remembered it well. Besides the fact that it was a landmark in Stillwater, Lacy Baumgarter had been one of the most popular girls in school and had held many lavish parties at that house.

Not that Grace had ever been invited….

"It's a beautiful home," she said, trying to keep her voice neutral.

"You should see how Raelynn fixed it up. After the Baumgarters moved away, the Greens bought it. They wound up getting a divorce, and Ann kept the house but couldn't afford to maintain it so it fell into disrepair. Finally, she sold it to Kennedy and Raelynn, who restored it."

"Wonderful." Grace pictured the SUV she'd spotted on Apple Blossom this morning and felt a moment's relief. On the way home from the pizza parlor she'd realized that Kennedy's Explorer was black and had begun to think the driver of that vehicle might've been him. But if he lived in the Baumgarter place, chances were fairly good he wouldn't be on Apple Blossom at six-thirty in the morning.

"Why do you ask?" Madeline wanted to know.

"I thought maybe he lived in town."

"Nope. You heard he's running for mayor, didn't you?"

"I've seen the signs." They were everywhere, but it looked as though Councilwoman Nibley was running against him and launching a pretty aggressive campaign of her own.

"I've endorsed him at the paper. Will you be around to vote?"

Grace set the hammock moving again. "I want to support you and your paper, Maddy, but I probably wouldn't vote for Kennedy even if I was here for the election."

"You don't like him?"

Grace didn't hesitate. "No."

"Really? Why not? He's nice. And I feel sorry for him."

"He comes from the most powerful family in Stillwater, he's handsome, fit and rich. What's to pity, Maddy?" Grace asked dryly.

"He took Raelynn's death really hard. I've never seen a man cry like that at a funeral."

Grace remembered her mother's mentioning the car accident that had claimed Raelynn's life. "I feel bad about his wife," she admitted.

"They'd been together since their sophomore year."

Grace had gone to high school with them, so she

was unlikely to forget that. "I know. But she was one of the kindest people I've ever known. He didn't deserve her."

A stunned silence met this response. "Do you have something *specific* against Kennedy Archer?"

Besides the fact that, unlike so many of his friends, he hadn't found her worthy of notice? Grace couldn't decide which was worse—being taunted and used or not being good enough to get that much attention. Somehow the contempt Kennedy had shown her in high school stung more than Joe's or Pete's cruelty. He'd never actively abused her. But she'd always known that if he'd broken rank with the others, they would've liked her, too. Kennedy was the leader. He formed his own opinions and judgments, and for the most part the others followed him. It was Kennedy she'd not so secretly admired. Yet Raelynn, the one girl who shouldn't have been nice to her, had been kindest of all. And Kennedy, the one boy who could've changed everything, hadn't bothered to acknowledge that she was alive.

"Nothing specific," she said. "See you when you get here."

"How's your mowing service going?" Kennedy asked Teddy as he backed out of his parents' drive. Kennedy had told Camille he wasn't staying for dinner, but his father had seemed particularly interested in seeing him tonight, and his mother had everything on the table when he'd arrived. He'd decided to stay for his father's sake, and they'd eaten together. Then he and Otis had talked politics for a while. It was nearly eight o'clock by the time he'd collected his boys and, taking the leftovers Camille wanted to send home with him, gone outside to the Explorer.

"He got into trouble today and had to sit in the corner," Heath volunteered. Kennedy's oldest son was now big enough for the passenger seat, but Kennedy made him sit in back, where it was safer. Raelynn had been on her way to have her hair cut when she veered into the center of the road to avoid a car that had suddenly turned in front of her—and hit a semi coming from the other direction. Nothing could've saved her from an impact like that. But Kennedy wasn't taking any chances with his children.

"Shut up, Heath," Teddy said. "You don't have to tell Dad *everything*."

Kennedy glanced at his youngest son in the rearview mirror. It was getting dark out, but he could still see Teddy's scowl. "What happened?"

"Nothing."

"What'd you do?" Kennedy persisted.

Heath pointed at his window as they drove past Evonne's. "He went to that house."

Kennedy guessed Grace had parked her Beemer in the detached garage because it was no longer sitting out front, as it had been when he passed by earlier. Kirk Vantassel's truck was there now, and all the lights were on inside the house, which meant Grace was probably entertaining her stepsister. Madeline had been seeing Kirk for a long time. "Why'd that upset Grandma?"

"He's supposed to stay away from Main Street. It's too busy."

"I went through the alley and the back gate," Teddy argued.

"That doesn't matter, stupid," Heath replied. "Evonne's dead. Someone else lives there now."

"Hey," Kennedy warned, but Teddy was already responding.

"*You're* stupid! I *know* someone else lives there. I met her. She gave me an extra dollar for pulling weeds and said I could mow the lawn in a few days."

"You have to mind Grandma," Heath said. "He can't go there anymore, right, Dad?"

Kennedy turned left at the stop sign and, another block down the road, Evonne's house disappeared from his mirrors. He knew Grace didn't like him and was tempted to tell Teddy to stay away because of that. But he remembered all too well how isolated she'd been as a girl and was determined not to support that again. "I don't see why it would be any different than working for Evonne."

Teddy made a face at his brother. "See?"

"Grandma won't like it," Heath said.

"So? Grace is giving me cookies tomorrow," Teddy insisted. "Now I'm not gonna bring you one."

Heath stuck out his tongue in return. "You wouldn't anyway."

"Maybe I would," Teddy said.

Kennedy thought there was actually a pretty good chance of it. Teddy might be headstrong, but he was also generous. "I'll tell Grandma it's fine for you to help Grace every once in a while."

"Grandma's going to be m-a-d," Heath said. "I don't think she likes Grace."

"Grandma doesn't even know her," Teddy said.

"Yes, she does," Heath replied. "I heard her on the phone. She said that Grace is a tramp and her mother killed some reverend dude."

The frustration Kennedy sometimes felt toward his mother reasserted itself. "Grace Montgomery graduated first in her class at Georgetown, which is a very tough law school. And she's become an excellent assistant district attorney. There was an article in the paper not long ago saying she's never lost a case."

"What does that mean?" Heath asked.

"It means she's earned some respect, okay? And your grandmother doesn't know that *anyone* killed the reverend."

"You'd have to be an idiot to believe anything else," Heath said.

Kennedy twisted in his seat to give his oldest son a pointed stare, and Heath immediately backed off. "That's what Grandma said," he added sheepishly.

Rubbing the five-o'clock shadow on his jaw, Kennedy returned his focus to the road. "Sometimes Grandma says a little too much," he said, although almost everyone in town suspected the same thing. He'd even wondered on occasion. "The Reverend Barker went missing years ago. No one knows what happened to him."

"Does that mean I can go to Grace's tomorrow, Dad?" Teddy said.

Kennedy remembered the resentment shining in Grace's eyes when she'd looked up at him in the parking lot of the pizza parlor. "Does she realize you're my son?"

"I don't know."

"Has she said anything about me?"

"No."

"Okay, you can mow the lawn, but don't go inside the house."

"Why not?"

"That's the rule. Either obey it or stay completely away."

"What about my cookies?"

"She can give them to you at the door, okay?"

There was a moment of silence, but Teddy sounded somewhat mollified when he answered. "Okay. I left her a note. I bet she'll have them for me tomorrow."

"Will you bring me one, too?" Kennedy asked.

"Cookies have carbs, Dad," Teddy replied.

Kennedy chuckled. "Do you even know what carbs are?"

"No, but Grandma does. She hates them."

"That's because she's watching her weight."

"Mom used to make the best cookies," Heath said.

Kennedy heard the melancholy in his son's voice and felt the familiar weight of his loss. Heath and Teddy missed their mother terribly. Kennedy missed Raelynn, too. He missed her fingers curling through his hair, her laugh, her presence in their home. He also missed not having to deal with his overbearing mother on a daily basis.

"I'll get you *both* one," Teddy said softly.

Again, Kennedy remembered the look Grace had given him. "Just don't mention that one of them is for me," he added with a rueful laugh.

4

"So...tell her," Madeline prompted, nudging Kirk Vantassel's foot with her own.

They were sitting around the coffee table in the living room, relaxing after the impromptu dinner Grace had served—chicken and pasta with a green salad and sourdough rolls. Kirk had brought over some Vicki Nibley for Mayor signs, and Madeline had made a big deal about what traitors they were not to support the candidate endorsed by her paper. Kirk admitted he didn't have strong political views. He said he was just trying to help his father get a date with Vicki, who'd been a widow for nearly five years. His reasoning made Grace laugh. But now that Madeline was changing the subject, she felt a measure of unease trickle through her veins. Grace knew from their earlier conversation that her stepsister was leading them straight to the topic she least wanted to discuss.

"Tell her what?" he asked, sprawled out on one end of Grace's plush, olive-colored sofa.

An illegitimate baby, Kirk had been raised by his grandmother in the small brick house next to the library on First Street, until his father was old enough to take him. Because he was eight years older than Grace, she hadn't had much contact with him when she lived in Stillwater. But she'd always liked him. He was the strong silent type, immovable in his loyalties and affections. And he wasn't bad-looking. He had a crooked nose—something he'd acquired playing football—and fine brown hair that lacked body. A pair of intense brown eyes easily redeemed his appearance, however. And he had great hands. Large and masculine, with plenty of nicks and gouges from his work as a roofing contractor, they were very different from George's long, narrow fingers and perfectly manicured nails.

"Tell her what you heard at the tavern last night. I didn't bring you over here just so you could wolf down two plates of pasta," Madeline teased, pulling her long auburn hair over one shoulder.

Picking up her wineglass from the table, Grace stood and crossed the room to stare out the front window. Barker would never be forgotten, she thought bitterly. Even after eighteen years, it seemed that every conversation, at least with anyone remotely connected to Stillwater, included him—if not directly, then in some kind of subtext.

"I ran into Matt Howton," Kirk said.

Grace sipped her wine. "*Matt?* I don't recall him."

"He's John Howton's oldest. Tall, skinny guy, about twenty-three. Works for Jed Fowler down at the auto shop."

At the mention of Jed Fowler, tension knotted the muscles in Grace's back and shoulders. "What did Matt have to say?"

Kirk leaned forward, resting his elbows on his thighs and letting his hands dangle between his knees. "We were just kicking back, having a few beers and shooting some pool, you know? And then he asked me how

Madeline's doing, which led to the fact that you're in town, which led to what he thought about your stepfather."

"And?" Grace asked, bracing herself.

"He suspects Jed Fowler might've had something to do with what happened," Madeline inserted, as if she couldn't wait for Kirk to get to the point.

Grace wasn't surprised by this declaration. Matt wasn't the first to suggest the taciturn repairman had been involved in the reverend's disappearance. But the excitement in Madeline's voice indicated there was more. "Did he say why?"

"First, you know Lorna Martin, who lives behind Jed's shop, says that on the night our father disappeared, she heard Jed's truck pull in around midnight, right?"

Grace nodded.

"The light went on in the shop and stayed on until 3:00 a.m.," Madeline continued. "She insists it's the only time she's ever seen him there so late."

"She reported that to the police," Grace said.

"*Now* tell her what Matt said," Madeline urged Kirk.

"Matt claims Jed has a file drawer he always keeps locked," Kirk said.

Grace's stomach began to hurt. She'd had enough of locked file drawers. From her experience, nothing good was ever inside. "So?" She scowled as she turned to face them. "Maybe he's got something valuable in there."

Kirk's eyebrows notched up, as if it surprised him that she wasn't more excited about the news. "Maybe he does, and maybe he doesn't, but according to Matt, he acts very strange about it. Matt was doing some stuff in the office two days ago and happened to find the drawer unlocked for a change. Curiosity got the better of him, so he opened it. Jed walked in at that moment and got so angry he nearly fired him."

"I've never seen Jed angry," Grace said. "I've never seen him express *any* emotion."

"Exactly," Kirk agreed smugly. "Obviously, there's something in that drawer he doesn't want anyone to see."

Jed had long been a dangerous variable. "What could it be?" Grace asked.

"Maybe it's evidence," Madeline replied.

"If he's guilty of murdering our…father, why would he hang on to something that could possibly incriminate him?" She'd used her prosecutor's matter-of-fact tone, but she knew of at least one very plausible reason he might've done exactly that—if he were the culprit. And Madeline launched right into it.

"Who can say for sure? But it happens. I've seen enough forensic shows to know that much." She drained her glass. "Heck, you've probably dealt with a few criminals who've kept trophies, haven't you?"

"One." Not that she wanted to be reminded of it. She was silent for a few seconds. "I thought you'd decided it was Mike Metzger?" she said at last.

A week before he went missing, the reverend had caught nineteen-year-old Mike smoking pot in the bathroom of the church and turned him in to the authorities. Mike hadn't been too happy about it. He'd made a few threats before the reverend disappeared and afterward admitted he was glad Barker was gone. But his mother swore he was home in bed on the night in question, and the circumstantial evidence pointing his way wasn't strong enough for police to press charges. Mike was now in prison for manufacturing crystal meth in his basement, but Madeline had sworn for years that he was to blame for her father's disappearance.

A furrow developed between Madeline's large hazel eyes. "I've never wanted to believe it could be Jed," she muttered. "I've always liked him. But there's no denying he's a bit…different."

Grace couldn't argue with that. "It's easier to imagine Mike doing something horrid."

"Right. But I think I might've been too closed-minded. We already know that Jed was at the farm that night, working on the tractor."

"He was in the barn. That doesn't necessarily make him guilty of murder. Mike lived less than a mile away. That's certainly a walkable distance."

Rising, Madeline poured herself and Kirk some more wine. At least five-eight, she was tall, slender and regal. Only the light dusting of freckles on her nose detracted from the sophistication of her appearance. "Jed had a better opportunity."

Kirk scooted forward a little. "Picture this. The reverend comes home from the church, sees the light on in the barn and walks down to see how the tractor's coming along. He and Jed argue, get into a scuffle—"

"Argue over *what?*" Grace asked. "At least Mike had a motive. Why would Jed want to hurt our dad?" The word *dad* tasted so bitter on her tongue she almost couldn't say it.

"They could've had a disagreement over anything," Kirk said.

"But our father never even came home that night." Grace consciously steadied her hand so she could take another sip of wine before repeating what she'd said hundreds of times before. "If his car had pulled up, I would've heard him."

"Maybe you were preoccupied," Kirk said.

"No. He—he expected our chores to be done. We always watched for him, didn't we, Madeline?"

"Usually," she said with a nod.

Grace drew a deep breath. She'd watched for him more carefully than the others. "He never drove up on the night of August third," she stated calmly.

"What else can you remember?" Kirk asked.

Far more than she wanted to. She remembered how hard it'd been to wipe the sticky blood from her hands. The sound of the shovel scraping through the mud. The smell of rain and damp leaves. She remembered sitting in a tub of hot water, shivering, her teeth clacking together while her mother scrubbed her clean as if she was a baby. And she remembered the pink color of the bathwater when she got out.

She fought to blank her mind. "Nothing special," she said. "That night was no different than any other."

"Except that Jed never came to the door to get paid for his work. Don't you think that's strange?" Madeline asked.

It was strange. Grace didn't know what he'd seen that night. Or whether he'd ever divulge it. At times, she believed he'd fixed the tractor and gone home without noticing anything amiss, just as he'd told the police. At other times she was certain he knew much more than he was saying. "Maybe he saw that Dad wasn't home yet and decided not to bother us."

"Or he was too busy hiding the body and hightailing it out of there," Kirk volunteered.

Grace shook her head. "Jed's not the type. You still

haven't given me a motive. Why would he want to harm the town's most popular spiritual leader?"

"He didn't consider him a spiritual leader," Kirk responded. "He quit going to church several months before the reverend disappeared. Don't you remember? One day he got up, walked out and never returned."

"He's not the only person to ever quit church."

"He's the only one I know who walked out in the middle of a sermon delivered by your father."

"Maybe he didn't like the way Dad preached." Grace hadn't liked it, either—not once she realized that what came out of his mouth had no correlation to what was in his heart.

"I went to Jed's repair shop with Daddy once in a while," Madeline said.

"Was there a problem between them?" Grace knew there wasn't, so she risked another sip of wine.

"I sensed *something* unfriendly going on. When Daddy invited him back to church, Jed said he'd already heard more than enough from a man *like him*." She ran a finger around the rim of her glass. "That shows some animosity, doesn't it?"

"But the police couldn't find any evidence to indicate that Jed did anything wrong," Grace said, finally facing them.

"They never really looked. They pumped him for information, trying to get him to point his finger at Mom—that's it."

"And now you think *he's* the one guilty of murder?" She realized after she'd spoken that she'd emphasized the wrong word. Fortunately, no one seemed to notice.

"Daddy didn't drive off into the sunset, Grace. He wouldn't leave me hanging. He wouldn't leave Mom, you, Clay, Molly, the farm, his congregation. Not after what my real mother did," she added softly. "He hated her for taking the easy way out."

Grace bit her tongue. Madeline must've seen some of the cracks in her father's marriage to the woman from Booneville, sensed the growing strain between him and his stepchildren. But it seemed that she'd chosen to ignore certain incidents and remember the past differently. If not for her loyal support and insistence that Irene was a good wife and mother, Grace thought the investigation might've gone on for years. They might even have gone to trial without a body. "But *Jed,* Maddy? He has no history of violence."

"He's not telling the truth about that night," she insisted.

Did Madeline really want the truth? Grace longed to tell her to forget her father. To let what had happened go—because she'd only suffer more if she ever found the answers she craved. She stood to lose her mother, her sisters, her brother… Hadn't she lost enough?

"You weren't even there." Madeline had been spending the night with a girlfriend, completely unaware that anything unusual was happening at home. But then, she'd been unaware of a lot of things. The reverend made sure of that.

"Jed said something strange to me once when I was at the shop to pick up my Jeep," Kirk said. "At the time, I blew it off. But after talking to Matt…"

Grace stared at her own reflection in the window again. "What was it?"

"I was asking him about that night. At first, he wouldn't say much, just gave all the same old lines. But when I asked him what *he* believes happened to Lee Barker, he said he thinks Madeline's father got exactly what he deserved."

A shiver ran from Grace's head to her feet.

"What he *deserved?*" Madeline repeated. "See, Grace? My dad was a preacher, for heaven's sake. A good man. What could he *deserve?*"

Grace closed her eyes, yearning for the innocence Madeline took for granted. "It means Jed didn't like him, that's all."

"No, it's more than that," Madeline said. "And I'm going to prove it."

The rain came in a constant downpour that night. For the first time since Grace had moved into Evonne's house, she felt out of place as she sat alone on the leather couch in the living room, watching the water cascade down the back windows. Her conversation with Madeline and Kirk bothered her, but no more than the storm. She kept picturing the gullies formed by the runoff, the water moving the topsoil at the farm, dumping it into the irrigation ditches and washing it far away from the trees behind the barn. They hadn't had time to dig much of a hole....

But no one had found Barker's grave in eighteen years.

She poured herself some more wine. What if Madeline managed to convince the police that Jed had killed her father? Would he defend himself by revealing all he knew? What would that be? And how would she face Madeline again if her stepsister ever learned the truth?

She sipped her chardonnay, remembering her encounter with Clay a week ago. She'd told him she was here to decide whether or not to come forward. But that was a lie. Her hands were tied, and they both knew it. Or she would've told the truth years ago.

So why was she here? To find some way to justify her continued silence, she decided. To live with what had happened. That was all.

Trying to shake off the foreboding that seemed to hang around her like cobwebs, she set her glass aside and used her cell phone, which lay on the seat next to her, to call Clay.

"Hello?"

She took a small measure of comfort in her brother's deep, steady voice. "I hate nights like this," she said without a greeting. "Don't they make you want to sit out on the porch with your gun—see what might turn up?"

There was a significant pause. "Nothing's going to turn up, Grace. Not while I'm here."

She rubbed the goose bumps from her arms. "But the rain…"

"It's just rain."

"It's not just rain. Combined with the heat and the smells creeping in from outside… It brings it all back so vividly. Like it was yesterday."

"It wasn't yesterday," he said. "It was a long, long time ago. Everyone's moved on."

"That's bullshit, Clay." She pulled a lap blanket over herself, even though her skin felt clammy. "*You* haven't moved on. You're still guarding that damn farm. *I* haven't moved on. I'm right back where I started. Even Madeline hasn't moved on. She's continuously searching for her father, for answers. Now she's convinced it was Jed."

"There are others who think the same thing," he said.

"Well, she's out to *prove* it."

He didn't hesitate. "She won't be able to."

"She can try, and trying might make the difference. I've seen it before. One person who won't let go of an old case, driving an investigation until—"

"Without a body, suspicions and accusations are as pointless today as they were eighteen years ago," he interrupted. "The police won't reopen the case without new evidence. You've dealt with criminal law long enough to know that."

Grace rubbed her forehead. She'd also dealt with criminal law long enough to see the exceptions. "This is why I stayed away. I didn't want to be terrified every time it stormed. I didn't want to hear Madeline's anguish over her father and continue lying to her."

The tension-filled silence made Grace believe Clay struggled with the same things. But then he said, "It's okay, Grace. It's over. I won't let anything more happen."

Someone knocked at her front door. Surprised, she glanced at the clock over the fireplace. It was nearly midnight.

"Someone's here," she said.

"This late?"

"Maybe Madeline forgot something." She got up and checked the peephole at the door. "I have to go."

"Who is it?"

"Joe Vincelli."

"Vincelli! What's he doing at your place?"

"I have no idea. But if I don't call you back in the next five minutes, get over here, okay?"

"Let me talk to him."

She didn't want to drag her brother into this. It was important she fight her own battles. Besides, he'd done enough for her in the past. "Let me see what I can do first," she said and hung up.

As she opened the door, a gust of moist wind ruffled her hair, and the soft thud of the rain grew louder. "Can I help you?"

Joe grinned as his eyes roved over her. "Noticed your lights on, so I thought I'd stop by."

"Why?" she said without returning his smile. "Are you lost?"

Chuckling, he rubbed the cleft in his chin. Now that he was older, the heavy shadow of beard covering his jaw, combined with his close-set eyes and crooked eyeteeth made him appear almost wolfish. "Come on, we could have a drink. For old time's sake. I saw you at the restaurant earlier but we didn't have a chance to catch up."

"Maybe that was because you were too busy bragging to all your friends that you 'did me' when we were sixteen."

At least he looked ashamed as he scratched his neck. "Yeah, well…I didn't mean anything by it."

Grace's hand tightened on the doorknob. "Go home," she said. "I don't want anything to do with you."

"There's no need to be unfriendly." He leaned against one of the porch columns and lit a cigarette. "Why can't we have a little fun?" he said, letting the smoke curl out of his mouth.

"Together?"

He winked at her. "Wouldn't be the first time."

"We have only one problem."

"What's that?"

"I wouldn't let you touch me again if you were the last man alive."

His smile faded as he shoved off from the post and jutted his chin toward her. "I guess you've changed, huh?"

"I guess I have," she said.

He gave her another sly grin. "I bet not that much."

"Probably more than you're capable of understanding." She looked him up and down and made it plain that she wasn't impressed with what she saw. "You, on the other hand, haven't grown up at all."

His stare hardened, and he took another drag on his cigarette. "Think you're too good for me now that you're some hotshot *assistant* district attorney from Jackson? Is that it, *Grinding Gracie?*"

The smoke from his cigarette drifted toward her, burning her nostrils. "The name's *Grace*," she replied. "And I've always been too good for you, Joe. I just didn't know it."

"Kiss my ass." He tossed the butt away and began to stalk off, then pivoted to face her. "You asked for what you got back then." He pointed at her. "You were nothing but a cheap slut."

"Don't ever approach me again," she said and closed the door.

"Bitch!" he yelled, throwing a rock at the house.

Grace drew the bolt, then leaned against the wall nearby, hugging herself. *Go away....*

"Maybe I'll take a backhoe to that farm you used to live on, see what *I* can come up with," he yelled. "Uncle Lee had to go somewhere, didn't he, Grace? People don't vaporize into thin air. Everyone in this town knows where he went, even if you and your family won't admit it."

She didn't respond. She knew a lot of people considered Joe a hero for risking his own life to save Kennedy from drowning in the Yocona River when they were kids. But she saw very few positive qualities in him.

"Which one of you actually did the deed?" he went on. "What'd it feel like, huh?"

Grace covered her face.

"Even if it wasn't you, you could still go to jail. But being a lawyer, you gotta know that."

God, it would be so easy to discover the truth—if anyone really knew where to look.

"You're gonna be sorry you treated me this way," he shouted.

A moment later, the engine of his truck roared to life. When she peered through the window, she saw him back up and spin out on her lawn before disappearing down the street.

You're gonna be sorry... echoed in her ears.

He won't do anything, she told herself. Clay wouldn't let him.

But Joe wasn't their only worry. All that business about Jed's locked file drawer frightened her.

Her phone rang.

"You okay?" Clay asked as soon as she answered.

She wasn't sure. She wanted to pack up and head back to Jackson, to hide beneath the law-and-order persona she'd created and the pile of work she did each day. But something told her it was already too late. "He...he's never liked me," she said.

"Why'd he come by?"

"Just to remind me of that, I guess."

"You're not going to let him get under your skin, are you, Grace?" Clay asked.

She'd certainly let Joe and his friends unsettle her in high school. But she wasn't in high school anymore. She was stronger now. The past thirteen years had to stand for at least that much.

"As far as I'm concerned, Joe Vincelli can go to hell," she said.

"Good girl."

* * *

Grace called her mother first thing the following morning. She might've waited too long to make the initial contact, but she wasn't going to hurt Irene a second time. She'd come to Stillwater to salvage her relationship with her mother, not destroy it. "Would you like to come over for breakfast?" she asked, propping herself up in bed against her pillows.

As Irene started to speak, Grace heard a man's voice in the background.

"Is someone there?" she asked.

"Of course not," her mother replied quickly. "It's only eight o'clock."

Grace frowned. Could it have been the television? Or… "If you'd rather do this some other day, Mom—"

"I don't want to put it off. You'll be leaving too soon as it is. Just…just give me an hour or so to get ready."

And get rid of whoever had probably spent the night.

"Okay…"

"See you soon."

When her mother hung up, Grace dialed Madeline's number. "I think whoever Mom's seeing might be over there right now," she said when her sister answered.

"Did she say she had company?"

"No, but I definitely heard someone."

"It's weird how she's acting."

"I don't get why having a boyfriend is such a big secret. Does she think it might upset one of us? We're all in our thirties, for crying out loud. Except Molly. But even she's twenty-nine."

"Maybe she's seeing someone she's afraid we won't approve of."

"Who could that be?" Grace kicked her sheet to the bottom of the bed.

"I have no idea."

Irene was still an attractive woman. If not for that night eighteen years ago, and all its consequences, Grace suspected her mother would've remarried years ago. Especially once she no longer had four children at home. "I guess she'll tell us when she's ready."

"I suppose," Madeline agreed.

Grace got up and walked to the window. This morning she was wearing a spaghetti-strap T-shirt with her panties, but after yesterday, she was careful to stand to one side as she looked down at the garden.

The weeds were gone, the rows carefully tended. Grace found the sight of everything she'd done gratifying, even though her muscles were so sore she could barely move. "I wonder if Mom has to work today."

"You didn't ask?"

"I was thrown by the deep voice in the background."

Madeline laughed. "I'm sure she'll be going to work. Mrs. Little depends on her to run the boutique pretty much every day—except Sunday and Monday, when they're closed."

"Could it be Mr. Little?"

"Mr. *Little?*" Madeline repeated.

"Maybe Mom's having an affair with a married man."

"God, I hope not. For lots of reasons, but mainly because folks around here would crucify her."

"They've never allowed her to keep a low profile."

"She'd better be particularly careful right now."

"Why?" Grace asked.

"Because you're back. Their interest is piqued."

Besides dealing with Evonne's family and the real estate agent on the house, and visiting the pizza parlor and grocery store, Grace had kept to herself. How could she be the cause of heightened attention? "What difference does that make?"

"You've been gone so long folks are curious. So many people have asked me about you, I was thinking of doing another piece in the paper."

"You're joking."

"I'm not."

"Don't waste your time," Grace said. "Why would anyone around here want to read about me again?"

"You're attractive yet aloof. That combination drives people crazy. Anyway, I think they should hear about everything you've accomplished in the past thirteen years."

Forever the advocate. What would the family have done without Madeline? "You've already made sure of that. Mother sent me the article you wrote last year."

"I didn't write it because you're my sister. It's not every day that someone from Stillwater graduates first in her class at Georgetown, then goes on to become an assistant D.A. who never loses a case."

"So? I've only been working for five years. I'm sure I'll lose in the future. Anyway, you know what the good citizens of Stillwater think of me, Madeline."

"Which is why I like to let people know how badly they've misjudged you."

Grace doubted Madeline's articles would change anyone's views. They'd always remember how she'd behaved when she was a teenager, when she was trying to save herself and destroy herself at the same time. "No article."

"We'll see how hard up I get for news this week,"

Madeline said as if it was all decided. "What're you doing tonight?"

"Nothing." For once, Grace didn't have a pile of cases to clutter her desk or her mind. She knew she'd get an occasional call from the office to ask about something she'd worked on in the past, but all her cases had been reassigned.

"Should I come by after work?"

"When time do you get off?"

"Around five. Unless there's a late-breaking story. But late-breaking around here is a cow getting out of its pasture at closing time." She laughed. "I think I can handle that without staying too late."

"Should I make dinner?"

"You cooked last night. Why don't I bring pizza?"

Grace thought of the little boy who'd left her that endearing note and knew he'd probably come by to pick up his cookies. She wanted to be able to send home something extra, just in case his folks were as poor as her mother had once been. "No, I'll make lasagna."

"I love lasagna."

"Should I drive by Mom's duplex?" Grace asked, returning to her curious conversation with Irene. "See if there's a car parked out front?"

"Mom wouldn't be that obvious."

"How do you know?"

"Because I've already tried it," she said. "Several times. There's never any car."

Grace moved away from the window and started peeling off her clothes in preparation for a shower. "You're an investigative reporter. Can't you find out who this guy is?"

"I suppose I could, but…to be honest, I'm torn between respecting her privacy and appeasing my own curiosity. And I'm also a little afraid of what I might find."

"Sometimes ignorance is bliss," Grace agreed, and wished Madeline could apply that to her father.

"True. Anyway, we'll talk more about it this evening."

"See you later."

"Grace?"

"What?"

"Any chance you'd be willing to go over to the auto shop with me late tonight and poke around?"

Grace froze as she was sliding off her panties. "*Late* tonight? Why am I getting the impression you mean after Jed's closed up?"

"Because I do."

Her chest began to burn as she stepped out of her panties and kicked them aside. "You want to break in?"

"I just want to see what's in the file drawer."

"In the middle of the night?"

"When else would I be able to get inside? If he's innocent, it won't matter that I took a peek."

"Except that breaking and entering is illegal! If we get caught doing something like that, we could go to jail. And I'd lose my job. Then you'd really have a story for your paper."

"We won't get caught," Madeline said. "You know the police in this town sit at the coffee shop all night. Besides, I have a police scanner in the car. I can make sure they're off doing their thing before we ever go in."

"Maddy—"

"Just think about it, okay? I don't want to do it alone."

Grace turned off the fan because she suddenly couldn't stand the constant motion. "What about Kirk?"

"He would've helped me last night, but I hadn't made up my mind yet. And now it's too late. There was a message on his answering machine. Della's suffered a stroke. She's never been much of a mother to him, but she's in the hospital in Minnesota and he's flying up there this morning to be with her."

The lintel of the bathroom door offered Grace the support she needed. "So it'd just be you and me?"

"We can do it. I *have* to see what's in that drawer. Before he moves it."

Grace nibbled nervously at her lip. "But he knows Matt was snooping around. He's probably moved it already."

"It's only been two days, and he has a lock on it. There's a chance he hasn't."

"I don't see what we have to gain, Maddy."

"Are you kidding?" Madeline asked, incredulous. "We could learn the truth! Don't you want to discover what happened to Dad? Aren't you *dying* to know?"

Grace wished to heaven she *didn't* know. "Of course, but—"

"Maybe this will finally provide us with some answers."

"And maybe it won't."

"Not finding anything gives us information, too."

"Such as?"

"You know what Lorna Martin said. The night Dad disappeared is the only time she remembers seeing Jed at his shop so late. What does that tell you?"

"That Lorna's a nosy neighbor?" she said, stalling for a moment to think.

"That he did something out of the ordinary."

Grace imagined searching through Jed's shop and grimaced in distaste. She didn't want to invade his privacy. Besides, he was odd. She wasn't sure what he'd do if he happened to catch them. "Madeline—"

"Please, Grace? Will you do it? For me? I *need* to see what's in that drawer, if only to reassure myself that there's no connection."

Tears had entered her stepsister's voice. Grace pressed her knuckles to her lips, trying to decide what to do. "If—if we go there and we don't find anything, will you give up on Jed?" she asked.

There was a long pause. "If I can."

That was hardly a promise. Grace still wanted to say no. But she had to show some support. Otherwise, Madeline might start wondering about the real reason for her reluctance. "Okay, I can't promise anything. But I'll consider it," she said and hung up.

Tossing the phone on the bathroom counter, she raked her fingers through her hair. Damn Matt Howton. Why'd he have to open his big mouth?

Breaking and entering was a crime. But Grace wasn't afraid of getting caught as much as she feared having Madeline suspect the truth.

5

After her conversation with Madeline, Grace couldn't shake a sense of apprehension. When her mother arrived, she went through the motions of making breakfast, but she felt as though the floor beneath her might give way, plunging her into a hole so deep she'd never get out.

Coming back to Stillwater would change her life. She'd known that all along, intuitively. It frightened her. And yet she couldn't bring herself to leave again. Not yet. For the past thirteen years she'd been pretending she was someone other than she was. But she refused to live like that anymore. She wanted to be able to forgive herself, to move on emotionally.

She just wasn't sure how to do that, or if it was even possible. And she definitely wasn't convinced that breaking into Jed's automotive shop would help anyone.

"Why are you so quiet this morning?" her mother asked, pouring syrup on the pancakes Grace had put in front of her.

Grace carried a pitcher of orange juice to the table. Irene had been pretty quiet herself. She'd shown up late and more than a little flustered, still insisting that she'd spent the morning alone.

"Just thinking," Grace said.

"About what?"

Returning to the counter, Grace added some bacon to her own plate before sitting down across from Irene. "Madeline."

"She does a really nice job with the paper."

Grace could tell from her mother's deflecting comment that she didn't want to talk about anything too deep. She'd always preferred to ignore the potentially upsetting.

Grace wished she could go on pretending that the veneer her mother valued so much was real. But she couldn't. That was why she worked tirelessly to protect the vulnerable and bring those who victimized others to justice. Why she'd ultimately had to come back to Stillwater. "She thinks she knows who killed her father," she said.

Irene made a face. "That Mike Metzger is a devil, isn't he?"

Mike wasn't a good man. But he hadn't killed Lee Barker, and Irene knew it.

"She's written some nice articles about you," Irene said. "She's very proud."

Grace knew Madeline had heard the rumors about her and the boys at school, but she'd resolutely ignored them. Or maybe she'd just refused to believe them, as she refused to believe the suspicion and accusations surrounding the Montgomerys.

"She's always stood by us," Grace said.

Her mother took a sip of juice. "I didn't give birth to that girl, but she's every bit one of my own. And I know she feels the same way."

Grace gaped at Irene. She knew she shouldn't say it. But she couldn't help herself. It drove her crazy that

Irene seemed to take no responsibility for the past. "Provided she never finds out, right?"

A pained expression appeared on Irene's face. "She won't."

More denial.

"She could."

No answer.

"I think we should move the body," Grace blurted.

Irene blinked in surprise. Even Grace couldn't believe what had come out of her mouth. Going to such great lengths to continue the cover-up might only make things worse. And yet…what else could she do? Let the people she loved suffer for something that wasn't their fault to begin with?

Her mother blanched. "Grace, please. I don't want to talk about…any of that."

Grace lowered her voice. Now that she'd actually stated the thought she'd squelched so many times before, she grew very convinced that they needed to act on it. "Mom, I realize this is difficult. I'm not trying to upset you. I just…I'm telling you we have to move the body."

"Stop it," Irene whispered harshly, glancing around as though someone might be in the house with them, listening. "We'll do nothing of the sort."

"Last night Joe Vincelli came over, threatening to take a backhoe to the farm."

"Why would he do that? After eighteen years?"

"Because he feels we're hiding something."

"But Lee went missing so long ago. His family won't speak to me when we pass on the street, of course. But Joe's never caused us any trouble. Why would he start now?"

Grace rubbed the condensation from her glass.

"Because he's not thirteen anymore. And because he's a vengeful son of a bitch."

Irene smoothed several nonexistent wrinkles on her skirt. "The police searched the farm, and they didn't find anything. Joe won't, either."

"But he's not the only threat. Madeline's just as determined to look for answers. If she prints possible leads in the paper again, it'll never end. Folks around town are already dredging up all the old tales about who saw what when. Maybe in some other place, a bigger place, the scandal would've been forgotten by now. But not here, especially with Joe's family in town, believing we got away with murder. And not with Madeline running the newspaper and keeping her father's disappearance constantly in the public eye."

"It's only natural she'd want to know."

Grace grabbed her mother's arm. "Mom, the sharks in this town have been circling for years, biding their time, waiting. Something could give us away. We need to get rid of the reverend's remains while we still have the chance. Bury them deep in the woods."

Her mother raised her juice but her hand was shaking too badly to manage another drink. Returning the glass to the table, she covered her mouth. "No. I—I can't face it."

"We *have* to make some changes," Grace insisted. "Clay can't live on that farm forever. He deserves some freedom, to marry, to move on. If we get rid of the remains, there'll be nothing to tie us to the reverend's disappearance. But if anyone ever finds that body where it is…"

"Heaven help us," Irene finished with a whimper.

"Exactly."

Her mother began to wring her hands. "But it's been so long. That—that night…" She stared at her plate, obviously replaying scenes in her mind that she'd rather not see. Eventually she shook her head. "No, we should sit tight. If we change…the place, we could make a mistake, miss something, leave evidence—and then Lee will win in the end. He'll destroy me, us, even Madeline."

Irene was getting too worked up.

Suddenly, Grace saw how fragile her mother had become, and let go of her arm. Taking a deep breath, she pushed the food around on her plate as it grew cold. Irene no longer had the strength or the presence of mind she'd once possessed; they couldn't rely on her for the kind of decisions she'd made, with Clay's help, in the past. Maybe Clay had figured that out first. Maybe that was why he shielded her so well.

"I'm sorry," Grace said. "Don't—don't worry about it, okay? I was wrong. We're fine."

Irene's eyes darted around the kitchen. "You really think so?"

"I know so." Grace patted her forearm. "I let Joe spook me and I…overreacted, that's all."

"You're sure?"

Grace assumed a calm she didn't feel. "Positive."

Her mother nodded. "Good. I'm glad to hear it. I—Everything's going so well for us now. Finally. It—it wouldn't be fair if—"

"I know." Grace motioned to her mother's plate. "Are you finished?"

"Yes."

"Let me take this."

Standing, she carried the dishes to the sink, wondering what she was going to do now that her mother couldn't cope with the past. "Do you like your job at Amelia's Dress Boutique?" she asked, to provide a refuge in the conversation.

"I get a twenty percent discount there," Irene said, eagerly following her lead.

"You have good taste. You always look so nice." Grace smiled encouragingly. "Here, I'll walk you to the car. I don't want to make you late," she said. And for the first time since her return, she realized how important it was that she'd come home. Not only did she need her family, her family needed her.

Teddy Archer stood on the doorstep of Evonne's house, and wondered whether or not he should knock. His father had dropped him off at his grandmother's place a while ago, but he'd known it was far too early to visit anyone. He'd forced himself to wait as long as he could—and hoped it was long enough. But now that he'd reached the porch, he could see a couple of Vicki Nibley For Mayor signs leaning against the house and guessed his new friend was "in the enemy camp," as his grandmother put it.

Grandma hated anyone who liked Mrs. Nibley. She called Mrs. Nibley a "bleeding heart liberal" and said she and her friends would ruin the town. But Grace didn't seem so bad to Teddy. She'd given him that extra dollar when he pulled weeds for her, hadn't she? It was probably still okay if he collected his cookies.

Making his decision, he knocked and straightened the bill of his ball cap while waiting for Grace to come to the door.

Once she appeared, he immediately felt better

because she seemed genuinely happy to see him. "Hello," she said.

Shoving his hands in his pockets, he jerked his head toward the deep ruts he'd noticed in the lawn just before he'd seen the campaign signs. "Someone gave you a lawn job last night."

She followed the direction of his gaze. "I know."

"You do? Who was it?"

She frowned. "A man named Joe."

Teddy recognized that name. "Vincelli?"

"That's him. You know him?"

"Yeah, he's funny."

"Maybe some people think so. But I'm not too impressed."

Not everyone liked Joe. Teddy had once heard a friend of his grandmother's say she felt sorry for Joe's parents, that their son was a "no account" boy. He wasn't sure what that meant exactly. But he knew it wasn't good. And he knew there were some things he wasn't supposed to repeat, so he didn't mention it. Instead, he pointed toward the signs. "You're voting for Mrs. Nibley?"

"I am."

"How come?" he asked, squinting up at her.

"I'm not a big fan of Kennedy Archer."

"Oh." She didn't like his father, either? He wasn't sure what to make of that.

"What about you?" she asked. "If you were old enough to vote, who would you choose?"

"Not Vicki Nibley," he admitted.

"So you're an Archer man?"

He nodded.

"Do you know him?"

He nodded again. He thought he should probably tell her that Kennedy was his dad, but he was afraid she'd hate him, too, if he did. "He's nice," he said, hoping to win her over.

"If you say so." She was still smiling, but something in her voice told Teddy he hadn't convinced her. "Are you ready for your cookies?"

They'd finally arrived at the cookies. He grinned. "Yeah."

"Great. I baked a big batch for you last night. Should I get the phone so we can call your mother? Let's ask if you can come in and have a few cookies with a glass of milk."

Teddy tilted his head to look past her and into the house. He could smell the yummy aroma he remembered so clearly from his mother's kitchen; he wanted to go in and pretend his house would smell like that again someday.

But his father had told him he couldn't go in her house. Staring at the porch floor, he scuffed one sneaker against the other. "Um…my mom's not home."

"Who's watching you, then?"

"My grandmother," he said. "She already knows I'm here."

"You're sure."

He nodded, but she still seemed hesitant.

"In that case, why don't we spread a blanket under the trees and eat out on the back lawn?"

Even if she didn't like his father, she seemed really nice. And eating on the back lawn was probably okay. It was still outside, wasn't it? "That'd be good," he said in relief. "And when we're done, maybe I could work for you again today. If you need me."

The smile that beamed down on him felt like sunshine.

"I was about to unlock the toolshed and visit the root cellar, which is always an adventure."

"Why is it an adventure?" he asked.

"Have you ever been there before?"

"Once, with Evonne. I helped her bring up some beets."

"Don't you think it's spooky, with all those spider-webs?"

"I'm not afraid of spiders." He stood taller so she'd believe him, even though the root cellar *was* a little scary. "But why do you want to go into the cellar?"

"To count what's left of the bottled peaches and to-matoes. I'm going to reopen Evonne's Homestyle Fix-in's."

"Her stand?" Excitement buzzed through him like a horde of bees. When he'd started spending his days at his grandmother's last summer, Evonne had let him come over a lot. Somehow being at her place made him feel happy inside. "I can count really good."

"I'll bet you can," she said with a laugh. "In any case, I'm glad to have your company." She held the door a little wider. "Would you like to help me carry everything outside? After our snack, we'll get busy."

Teddy hesitated for only a second. He wouldn't be inside long, so it wasn't as if he was *really* disobeying his father. Besides, his dad would expect him to help. Helping was always the right thing to do. Even Grandma said that.

"Okay." He followed her inside and, a moment later, the familiarity of the house seemed to enfold him in a warm embrace.

Kennedy stood in his office at the bank and stud-ied the large painting of Raymond Milton that hung on his wall. As a child, Kennedy's father, Otis Archer, had lived in the neighboring town of Iuka in a home with a dirt floor. He'd had a widowed mother and ten siblings. He hadn't graduated from high school because he'd had to run the cotton farm on which his family lived—and he'd had to work at the gas station in town when he wasn't on the farm. With no money for college, the prospects for improving his situation were few. Yet he'd managed to convince Raymond Milton, who'd made a fortune in trucking when Iuka was the most important shipping point on the Mobile and Ohio Railroads, that he had the capacity to make it big. Milton lent him a little seed money and, when he was only twenty-five, Otis had started Stillwater Trust Bank and Loan.

By thirty, Otis had made his first million and won the heart of Milton's youngest daughter, Camille, who'd married him shortly after. At forty, Kennedy's father had become mayor of Stillwater and, when Grandpa Milton died the year Kennedy was born, Otis inherited another million.

Otis Archer had gone from being a poor, uneducated boy to the most important man in Stillwater. He'd built quite a legacy.

His secretary buzzed, but Kennedy didn't respond. After the call he'd just had from the police chief, he knew it would be Joe. Besides the fact that he didn't want to talk to his friend, he had an off-site meeting and needed to leave so he wouldn't be late. But something about his grandfather's portrait held him fast. Although the town wasn't as sophisticated as a lot of other places, Kennedy loved Stillwater. He thought he'd make a good mayor. He'd certainly been groomed for the job, was comfortable with the path that lay ahead. But he wasn't ready to see his father's memorial picture hang-

ing next to his grandfather's. It was too soon after Raelynn's death to say goodbye to another member of his
family.

"I told her your car was still in the lot."

Kennedy turned as Joe Vincelli barged into his office. "What a surprise to see you."

Joe didn't pick up on the sarcasm in his voice.
"Why didn't you answer when Lilly buzzed?"

"I was preoccupied."

Joe's eyebrows shot up; apparently he considered
that a pretty lame excuse. But then, no one else knew
about the cancer slowly destroying Otis's body. Neither Kennedy nor his parents wanted word to get out.
The bank's stock would plummet once investors realized that the chairman of the board probably wouldn't
live through Christmas. And Kennedy wasn't sure he
could take the pity he'd receive.

He wasn't sure how they'd keep his father's con-
dition a secret, when Otis started chemotherapy
next month. But for the good of the bank and its
employees—and for the sake of preserving the privacy
he and his mother both prized—he knew they'd try.

"What's up?" he asked as though he hadn't already
heard.

"I want McCormick to reopen my uncle's case."

Kennedy looked at his friend, wondering why, after
so many years of letting the case grow cold, Joe was
so keen on another investigation. Sure, Barker was a
member of his family. But Joe had been thirteen when
the reverend went missing. And he'd never pressed
particularly hard for a resolution before. "Chief
McCormick called me a few minutes ago to say you'd
been in," he admitted.

"He told me he couldn't reopen the case without a

reason," Joe said, slouching into a seat. "But I know if you'll put a little pressure on him, he'll do it."

"What good would it do to reopen the case?" Kennedy asked.

"Maybe we'd find something this time."

"And maybe we wouldn't."

"Come on, Kennedy. We all know Clay or Irene killed my uncle. It's time to prove it. And think what a great running platform it would make for you. Vicki Nibley wouldn't have a prayer if you were responsible for figuring out what went on at the farm that night."

Kennedy moved back to his desk and sat on the corner. When they were twelve and Joe's father had taken them camping, Kennedy had slipped on a slick rock and fallen into the Yocona River. It was barely dawn. Joe's father was still sleeping, and there was no time to get him. It was Joe who'd jumped in to save Kennedy from the brutal current that had swept him under the ledge of a second massive rock. He'd nearly forfeited his own life in the process.

Kennedy owed Joe a lot, but this wasn't right. "I'm not worried about the mayoral seat," he said. "If I lose, I have enough work here at the bank to keep me busy."

"What are you talking about? You've dreamed of filling your father's shoes for years."

"It won't destroy my life if I don't take public office."

"Don't you want to know what happened to my uncle?"

Kennedy was curious. Everyone was. Grace's sudden return had started tongues wagging all over again. Some people said they saw the reverend's car pull into his own drive that night so long ago; others said they saw him heading out of town the opposite way. According to Kennedy's conversation with McCormick a few minutes earlier, one woman had even come forward to say she'd seen the reverend in a mall in Jackson only a few months ago. Most people, however, pointed fingers at Irene or Clay. Some claimed Grace had killed him, although she was just a young teenager at the time. Only Madeline, who was gone the night everything happened, was free from accusation.

Kennedy had a few suspicions of his own—but, like everyone else, he had no proof. And he felt the gossip was getting out of hand. He was more intrigued by the kind of person Grace had become than what'd happened to the reverend. There was something tragic about her, something fragile and vulnerable despite the tough exterior she tried to show the world. The contrast between her beauty and the darkness of her past fascinated him.

He'd lain awake last night marveling at what she'd been able to accomplish after leaving Stillwater with only a high school diploma—and remembering what he'd seen in the window.

"Of course I'd like to know," he said. "But not badly enough to make the Montgomerys miserable unless we have more to go on."

Joe stretched out his long legs. "Then do it for me."

Kennedy had feared this was coming. Although Joe had never before held the incident at the Yocona River over his head—which was one thing Kennedy had always admired about him—Kennedy couldn't help feeling obligated to Joe in ways he wasn't obligated to anyone else.

But the thought of what it would do to Grace still made him pause. "I can't. I don't have that authority."

Joe grimaced. "We both know your father owns this town. Lately he's been turning everything over to you. Talk to McCormick. Make him do something."

Joe had his better moments. He was a funny drunk and would do almost anything for his friends. But he had a mean streak the others didn't possess and a less-than-impressive track record. He'd been divorced from the same woman twice and, if not for his parents, probably wouldn't have a job. His folks owned Stillwater Road & Gravel just north of town. They let Joe pretend to manage it for them, but he spent most of his time hanging out, having lunch with the gang, chasing women or bugging Kennedy to lend him more money.

"Why?" Kennedy asked.

"Because a crime's been committed!"

"We don't know that." Kennedy suspected Grace had already paid a heavy price for that night, whether whatever had happened was her fault or not. And even though he had to admit that Joe might be right about her family, he felt strangely reluctant to pursue it.

"Why not make sure?" Joe pressed. "Fix it so I can take a backhoe to the farm and dig around. If there's a body there, I'll find it."

"The police searched the farm. They found nothing to warrant the use of a backhoe."

"Come on! That was before old man Jenkins retired, and you know as well as I do that Jenkins couldn't find his own ass without a guide. We had the equivalent of Barney Fife running the investigation."

"Regardless, McCormick would need another warrant, which wouldn't be easy to obtain. Not when the police have already been given one shot. This may come as news to you, but judges don't take invading people's privacy lightly," Kennedy said. "And Clay's like a junk-yard dog. You know that. He isn't going to give his permission."

"Judge Reynolds would listen to you."

Kennedy recalled how Joe had acted at the pizza parlor. "This is not about obtaining justice for your uncle, is it?"

"No," he said with a scowl.

"Seems to me you're more concerned with hurting Grace than anything else."

"You mean *Grinding Gracie?*" Joe chuckled as though she wasn't worthy of so much attention. "That's bullshit. Why would I want to hurt her?"

"I don't know. But if that's what you're after—" Kennedy toyed with the glass paperweight that had been a gift from his staff at Christmas "—what you did in high school was enough."

"Screw you," Joe said, jumping to his feet. "I didn't do anything to Grace in high school!"

The telephone rang. Kennedy raised a hand to indicate he'd be a minute and took the call, hoping the interruption would ease the tension in the room. But Joe simply cursed and started for the door.

"Some friend you are," he muttered. Kennedy waited for him to add, "You wouldn't even be here if it wasn't for me." But he didn't. He disappeared down the hall.

Kennedy wanted to go after him. He wanted to tell him to forget the past and get on with his life—and let Grace do the same. But Camille was on the other end of the line, saying, "Hello? Kennedy? Are you there?"

Dropping his head in one hand, he massaged his temples. He could sense from the edge in his mother's voice that something was wrong. "I'm here," he said. "What is it?"

"You need to talk to your son."

He immediately knew she didn't mean Heath. "What's Teddy done this time?"

"He went over to Grace Montgomery's just before noon."

"We already talked about this. I gave my permission for him to mow her lawn."

"But I told him to be back an hour ago."

Kennedy checked his watch. "Maybe he lost track of the time."

"That's no excuse. How can I let him leave the house if he can't obey a simple rule like 'be back by two'?"

His mother had a point. Teddy needed to be trustworthy. "Right," Kennedy said. "I'll talk to him tonight, okay? See what's going on."

"No, you should go over there right now. It's been *three* hours, Kennedy. I don't like it. Grace is not a nice person."

"I don't think she's half as bad as you imagine. She's an assistant district attorney, Mom. And from what I hear, she's a damn good one."

"I don't care if she is. You know she wasn't exactly an exemplary citizen when she lived here before. Are you willing to risk something happening to Teddy?"

She'd hit him in his most vulnerable spot. After losing Raelynn, he wasn't about to take anything for granted. "Of course not." He swallowed a sigh. "I'll go there right now." Even if it made him late for his meeting.

"You do that. And tell Teddy to get home."

Kennedy sidestepped making a commitment. "I'll call you back."

* * *

No one answered the door at Grace's, so Kennedy peered in the windows. It looked as though she'd made herself at home. The living room had a circular rug with an overstuffed couch and chair, a magazine table, a coffee table and an old-fashioned secretary in the corner. He could see a mahogany table and chairs through an opening that led into the dining room, and leather sofas in the family room beyond that. The furniture seemed to be a mix of old and new—nothing terribly fancy—and yet she'd created a combination that suggested she had good taste.

"Anyone home?" he called, and knocked again.

There was no response, although her BMW was in the garage. He'd checked before coming to the door.

Feeling his first shiver of alarm, he circled the house, hoping he could get in through the back. But as soon as he opened the gate, he heard a woman's voice—and stopped.

Was it Grace?

Standing behind the poplar trees, which shielded him from view, he peered through the branches.

It was her, all right. And Teddy was with her. But she wasn't doing anything diabolical to him. They were sitting at a patio table, reading a book.

"Why do you think he'd go into such a dark cave?" she asked as they studied one of the illustrations.

"He's curious, I guess," Teddy said.

"You'd never go into a dark cave alone, would you?"

"No. I want him to do it, though. Don't you?"

She laughed. "Spoken like a true boy. You already have a love of danger."

"Do you think he's going to get hurt?"

"Or lost," she said. "Let's see." She turned the page and started reading again. She was wearing a T-shirt and a pair of shorts, but no shoes, and her shapely legs were crossed at the ankle beneath her chair.

Kennedy could hardly believe what he was seeing.

"He *is* getting into trouble," Teddy breathed in obvious concern as the boy in the book slipped down a slope and fell through a hole into complete blackness. "Someone will come and help him, won't they?"

"Maybe," she said. "But you can't expect others to save you. You have to save yourself. Always remember that."

"Why won't other people help you?"

She hesitated for a second. "Sometimes they can't hear your cries."

Kennedy got the funny feeling that she wasn't talking about the story and experienced another twinge of guilt for all she'd suffered in high school. But he could tell that Teddy wasn't in any danger. On the contrary, his son was getting a dose of the comfort and closeness he'd craved so badly since losing his mother.

Not wanting to interrupt, Kennedy backed out, closed the gate with a tiny click, and slipped away.

When he was in his car, he phoned his mother. "Teddy's fine," he said. "Nothing to worry about."

"Is he coming home?"

He turned onto Main Street. "Not yet."

"Why not?"

"He's busy."

"Is he still with *her?*"

Kennedy didn't want to describe the tender scene he'd just witnessed. He was profoundly grateful that Grace could be so kind to Teddy, even though she didn't like *him.* "He's sweeping out her garage," he lied, because he thought his practical mother would accept that answer more readily.

But he'd underestimated her dislike of Grace.

"What's she planning to do, work him all day, then pay him a buck or two? Are you going to let her take advantage of him that way?"

"She's not taking advantage of him," he snapped. "I've got it handled."

A surprised silence followed this outburst, and he struggled to restrain his emotions. Maybe there were things about his mother that grated on him, but her intentions were loving. And she was dealing with a lot right now—too much. He'd often thought of getting another babysitter for the boys, but he knew none of them would be any happier. His children wanted what they'd had before, when their mother was alive; Camille would take his defection as a sign that he believed she wasn't doing an adequate job.

"I've already looked into it," he said, softening his voice. "Everything's fine. He'll get home when he gets home."

"You should've told him to come right away, like I asked you to."

"Because you want to read to him?"

"What?"

"Never mind," he said and hung up.

6

Country-western music poured out the open door of the pool hall adjacent to Jed's Dependable Auto Repair. Grace, standing flat against the outside wall, knew that if she leaned forward just a little, she'd probably see half the men who lived in Stillwater throwing darts, playing pool or drinking beer. But approaching the back of the automotive shop from the direction of the pool hall was still their best option. Located on Main Street several blocks from Evonne's, Jed's shop wasn't far from the busiest intersection in town. They couldn't go in through the front. And Walt Eastman's Tire Center on the other side had a big dog in the yard.

Dressed in a black T-shirt and jogging shorts, with her long hair tucked up inside a baseball cap, she pressed herself more tightly to the outer wall of the building.

"Tell me Jed doesn't have a dog, too," she whispered to Madeline, who was similarly dressed, except that she carried a backpack.

Her stepsister shook her head. "No. Walt's the only one with a dog. And the juicy steak I brought will keep that boy busy."

"Great. So all we have to worry about is getting caught and going to jail?"

Madeline brandished the chain cutters she'd removed from her backpack. "No one's going to jail. You heard the police scanner. It's coffee and doughnuts. Again."

"You're talking about the scanner back in the car, right?"

"I don't want to carry it around, do you?"

Grace preferred to travel light, in case she needed to run like hell. "No."

"That's what I thought."

"So what's the plan now that we've come this far?"

Madeline finished zipping up her pack and stood. "Kirk scouted it out for us before he left. He said there's a double gate at the back of the yard secured by a chain and padlock. We simply cut the chain with these, slip inside and take a look around. How hard can that be?"

Grace propped her hands on her hips. "Kirk told you how to break in to someone's business?"

"Once he realized he couldn't come along."

"Why not wait for him?" If only Grace could stall for enough time to talk Clay into moving the reverend's remains *before* Madeline drew any more attention.

"And let whatever's in that file drawer disappear?"

"It could be gone already."

"We have a better chance now than later." Madeline slung the backpack over her shoulder again. "Besides, there's no telling when Kirk might get back. His mother could be in the hospital for days, even weeks."

When Grace didn't appear convinced, Madeline's eyebrows drew together in an expression of impatience. "We're not going to steal anything, so quit worrying. This is no big deal."

It *was* a big deal. It was such a big deal that Grace's heart was beating faster than a hummingbird's wings. And it didn't help that she could see Kennedy Archer's SUV in the lot and knew he was inside the pool hall with all his friends. If she and Madeline got caught, they'd have plenty of witnesses to their humiliation.

But Grace hadn't known that Kennedy and Friends would be at the pool hall when she'd let Madeline persuade her to join this crazy scheme. She hadn't even considered the fact that Let The Good Times Roll was so close, or that on Thursdays the owner featured margaritas for a dollar. She'd thought exclusively of her stepsister. When Grace initially refused to accompany her, Madeline had started off alone, which made Grace give in and go after her. She couldn't sit at home while her sister broke into the automotive shop. Because she already had the answers Madeline wanted so badly, Grace felt responsible for the risks her stepsister was taking.

"I'm an assistant district attorney," she whispered, breathing deeply and resting her head against the gritty surface of the brick wall. "I can't believe I'm breaking the law. I prosecute scum like us."

"You can't prosecute anyone the cops don't catch, right?" Madeline looked carefully around the corner to see down the alley. "And we know the cops are exactly where I said they'd be. Nothing ever happens in Stillwater. They're not expecting trouble."

Grace wished it wasn't so damn hot. She was feeling light-headed. "Okay, let's get this over with. You want me to go first?" If she couldn't talk her stepsister out of this misadventure, she had a strong desire to be finished with it as soon as possible, which provoked a certain recklessness. She wanted to rush forward, cut the chain, do the search and get out.

"No, I'm the one who got us into this. I'll go first." Madeline darted off, circling around the parking lot.

Grace hesitated, listening to the buzz of conversation drifting out of the pool hall along with the music, then quickly followed. By the time she caught up, the dog next door was busy devouring the steak Madeline had tossed it and ignoring them completely.

That was a positive omen. But step two of their plan didn't go quite so smoothly. Cutting a chain wasn't nearly as easy as it looked on TV. They both had to grab hold of the cutters and squeeze with all their might before the chain finally fell to the ground. Then it thudded in the dirt with a quiet jingle—but to Grace that jingle sounded as loud as crashing cymbals.

"See?" Madeline said as though the noise didn't bother her in the least. "The hard part's already over."

Grace glanced behind them. No one came out of the tavern—and no lights flashed on in the houses that backed onto the alley.

Maybe Madeline was right. Maybe she was overreacting. They were only going to slip in, check a file drawer or two and slip out. Stillwater was a sleepy town; a quick peek at Jed's cabinets couldn't be *that* dangerous.

"Let's go." Her stepsister stepped through the gate, but Grace yanked her back.

"Not without gloves, Maddy. Where are they?"

"Anyone in town could've touched this gate."

"I don't care. We wear them starting now."

"Okay. You're the D.A."

"Don't remind me."

Setting her backpack on the ground, Madeline

reached into a front compartment and handed Grace a pair of yellow rubber gloves.

Grace blinked in astonishment. "You're kidding, right? You want me to debut as a criminal looking like I'm about to wash someone's dishes?"

"I brought what I had."

"I have a really bad feeling about this. If nothing else, it's unauthorized entry of property."

"You mean trespassing?"

"And forcible entry/vandalism," she added, eyeing the cut lock, but she allowed Madeline to tug her into the yard.

When they arrived at the building, Grace wanted to immediately duck inside its dark confines. But, like the gate, it was locked. Which didn't come as any big surprise. "How do you plan to get in?" she asked.

Madeline removed her gloves and shoved them at Grace. "Hold these," she said, and fished a nail file from her "crime kit."

"You know how to pick a lock?" Grace whispered. "Who taught you that?"

"Who do you think?"

"Kirk again? Should I be worried about you dating him?"

Madeline chuckled as she worked. "When he was a kid and he got into trouble, his dad would lock his bike in the shed. Kirk figured out how to pick the lock so he could get it out after his father went to work."

"Your bare hands are touching that knob," Grace pointed out. Talking helped calm her nerves, made their actions seem more natural somehow. But knowing her sister was leaving fingerprints everywhere didn't help Grace's peace of mind.

"I'll wipe it off before we leave."

"Maddy, I'm sure Jed had nothing to do with what happened eighteen years ago," Grace said. "Can't we just go home?"

Madeline was too busy with the lock to listen. "Shh…"

"What if someone comes by later, notices that the shop's unprotected and steals everything? It'll be our fault."

"Who'd steal a bunch of car repair tools?"

"You'd be surprised. I've met folks who'll steal anything."

"Not in Stillwater. People here rarely even lock their houses. But we'll make the gate look the same as we found it, just in case."

"That's some consolation," Grace said sarcastically.

"Quit worrying."

The lock-picking was taking *forever.* Grace hovered in the shadows of the corrugated metal building and glanced nervously toward the pool hall. "We'll probably find a bag of pot or something. That'll be the big secret. And what do we care if Jed smokes weed? It doesn't affect our lives in the least."

"We could find something a lot more relevant than weed."

"*If* we ever get in."

With a curse, Madeline yanked her file from the lock.

The tension in Grace's body edged up yet another notch. "What is it?"

"I can't—"

Two men ambled out of the pool hall. At the sound of their voices, Grace pulled her stepsister down to the ground, out of sight. The chain link fence surrounding the property certainly didn't give them much cover.

"Who is it?" she breathed when the two men stood talking in the parking lot.

"Marcus and Roger Vincelli," Madeline whispered.

"*Joe's* dad?"

"And his brother."

"Oh, God," Grace said. "Is Joe with them?"

"I don't think so."

Finally, the men climbed into their respective vehicles and drove off. When nothing but music broke the silence, Grace and Madeline got to their feet.

"Hurry," Grace prompted, more than a little spooked.

"I can't trip the lock," Madeline complained, frustration lining her forehead. "I can't find the tumbler. It's different than the ones Kirk had me practice on last night."

"So we can go home?" Grace asked hopefully.

"No. We'll have to use the crowbar."

"The *what?*"

Madeline was already removing a crowbar from her pack.

"Madeline, we can't—"

Before Grace could even get the words out, Madeline had inserted the iron bar into the doorjamb. A moment later, a terrible scraping and wrenching blasted the air, then a *pop* sounded as the door broke open and swung wide. The dog next door barked, then apparently returned to his steak bone.

Grace stared wild-eyed around them. She was positive someone would come this time. But several seconds passed, and she heard nothing to indicate they'd drawn any attention.

"I hope you're not going to turn on the lights," Grace said, thrusting her stepsister's gloves at her as they hurried inside.

"Of course not. Here." Madeline put a long heavy object in Grace's hands. A moment later, when Grace found the switch, she realized it was a flashlight.

"You've thought of everything, I see."

"You take that side, I'll take this one."

The shop was a rectangular room with a cement floor, a reception counter in front and a bathroom in the far corner. It smelled of motor oil and featured a scarred wooden desk and racks and racks of auto parts—definitely not the kind of place in which Grace felt very comfortable. But now that they'd broken the door, she decided it was better to commit herself to the task at hand. Maybe if Madeline saw that they weren't going to find any evidence here, she'd give up trying to prove that Jed had caused the death of her father.

"So far it looks like an auto repair shop," she said.

Madeline swept her flashlight around the room. "There're some filing cabinets along that wall."

"There're some on that wall, too," Grace said, pointing at them.

"I'll take the ones behind the desk. You take the ones in the corner."

With a shrug, Grace moved to the three tall filing cabinets near the bathroom. The drawers of the first were labeled—work orders, parts orders, paid bills and catalogs.

The constant whine of the toilet running in the bathroom got on her nerves as, behind her, Madeline opened and closed file drawers with wild abandon. The beam of her stepsister's flashlight bounced as she moved—until she found a drawer that was locked.

"Here it is," she breathed.

Grace turned expectantly. "You want me to help you get it open?"

"No, I've got it. You might as well search the rest of the filing cabinets and the desk, just to be sure."

Madeline took another small tool from her backpack, along with the crowbar, and Grace turned back to her own searching. She didn't want to watch what Madeline was about to do. The list of their crimes was already scrolling through her head.

When she heard a large bang, Grace knew Madeline had managed to jimmy the drawer open and cringed at the thought of Jed finding it like that in the morning.

"Try not to mess things up too badly," she cautioned. "I feel terrible about this."

"I had to break the lock," Madeline said. Her voice was too filled with anticipation to allow for much remorse. "That's not a tremendous amount of damage— for a break-in. He'll hardly know we were here."

"Right. He'll probably think he busted his own locks. Happens all the time."

Madeline didn't answer. She was too intent on going through the drawer.

"Anything?" Grace asked.

"Not yet," she murmured.

All Grace could hear of the music at the pool hall was the percussion thumping rhythmically through the walls. Jed had been in business a long time and, as she moved to the second file cabinet, she began to believe he'd kept every slip of paper he'd ever come across.

"Talk about a packrat," she grumbled. "Some of these work orders are more than ten years old." The next drawer went back even farther than that.

Madeline said nothing.

"Maybe someone should tell Jed the IRS can't audit you for tax returns older than seven years."

"You tell him," Madeline murmured. She had a folder in her hand and was looking through it carefully.

Grace was still halfheartedly rifling through her own files. "I'm not going to tell him anything."

"Mmm…" Madeline said.

"Maybe you should write an article on record-keeping for the paper," Grace suggested. "You could use Jed as an example."

"Good idea."

Madeline wasn't listening. Giving up on the nervous chatter, Grace closed the bottom drawer of the middle filing cabinet and moved on to the third and last cabinet, which was pretty old and beat up. Dust an inch thick rested on top, along with baskets of ancient work orders yet to be filed and even a cracked coffee mug. In here, the records were fifteen, sixteen, seventeen years old.

"Jeez," Grace said and almost shut the top drawer before even delving inside. What was the point? Madeline had already found the mysterious locked drawer and was busily combing through it.

But then she noticed something that made goose bumps stand out on her arms. The dates on the folders were growing closer and closer to that fateful night eighteen years ago. She wondered if Jed had kept the work order from when he'd fixed the tractor, and what it might say.

Her scalp began to tingle as she quickly thumbed through the August invoices. She didn't find one dated that particular night, but she found one for the following day.

Taking off her gloves so she could grip the thin paper, she pulled it from the file. It was made out to her mother, which seemed a little odd. The reverend had always handled everything anyone could loosely interpret as "man's work."

Holding it in one hand, she thumbed through the next drawer and the next. All previous invoices showed the reverend's name. Had the sudden switch occurred because Jed already knew, the very next morning, that the reverend wasn't coming back? If so, he was the only one. It had taken two days for the community to launch a search. A full-grown man had never gone missing from Stillwater before. The reverend's car had disappeared, as well, so at first everyone had assumed he'd taken off somewhere and would soon be back.

Grace checked on Madeline again. When she found her examining items and letters in a cigar box, she returned her attention to the invoice. Other than her mother's name, Jed had meticulously recorded the parts he'd ordered and installed in the tractor, his time and the amount due. But unlike all the other invoices she'd seen in the drawer so far, this one wasn't marked *paid*.

Hadn't he collected? Grace couldn't remember. Of course, she knew he'd never come to the house *that* night. But what about later?

"There's nothing here," Madeline said, dejection dripping from her words. "Just some old love letters from a woman named Marilyn, a two-dollar bill that has *I love you* written on it, and pictures of three kids I don't recognize."

"I'm not coming up with anything, either." Grace put the invoice back and was about to close the drawer when her eye caught something black and shiny stuffed below the hanging file folders. Curious to see what it could be and why it was there, she shifted so Madeline couldn't see what she was doing. Moving some files, she pulled out a pocket Bible—and nearly dropped it again.

It was the one the Reverend Barker had carried everywhere like a small day-planner.

The one she thought they'd buried with him.

Kennedy was hoping to finish Joe Vincelli off quickly by sinking the eight ball on his next turn, after which he planned to call it a night. He liked hanging out at the pool hall on Thursdays. Since Raelynn's death, it was the only social outing he participated in with any regularity. Fortunately, his kids really liked Kari Monson, the middle-aged single woman who lived next door to his parents. Kari worked days but often helped Kennedy if he needed babysitting in the evening. He knew she'd already have the boys in bed. But it was getting late, and he had a big day tomorrow. He needed to head home.

On the other side of the table, Joe bent over the smooth green felt, running his cue stick lightly through his thumb and finger as he considered the various shots open to him. Three striped balls remained on the table to Kennedy's one solid, so Kennedy was trying to be patient. But he was beginning to wonder if Joe would ever take his turn. "Come on. I want to go home *sometime* tonight."

"Give me a second," Joe barked and moved to the end of the table to check the angle of yet another shot. Although Joe's earlier visit to Kennedy's office hadn't gone particularly well, they hadn't mentioned it since arriving at the pool hall. They hadn't talked about Grace at all. But Kennedy could feel the added tension between them. Joe *really* wanted to win this game.

"I'll give you an extra shot if you need it," Kennedy said. "Just go."

"You won't give me anything." Joe straightened and raised one eyebrow to ensure he'd made his point. "I don't need you to make concessions."

Kennedy waved off the waitress, who was coming around to ask if he wanted another drink. "Enough with the competitive bullshit, okay? You've circled the table three times. It's only fifty bucks. Let's go."

Finished with his game at the next table, Buzz carried his beer over so he could watch. "Who's winning?"

Kennedy didn't respond, and neither did Joe, but that was answer enough. If Joe had been winning, he would've made some wisecrack.

"That's your best angle right there," Buzz said, trying to encourage the continuation of the game. But Buzz was better friends with Kennedy than he was with Joe, so it didn't surprise Kennedy when Joe discounted the advice and stooped to take an entirely different shot.

Joe's shadow stretched over the table, then the cue ball clacked against its target and sent the striped thirteen racing for the corner pocket.

At the last second, it banked off the side and veered off in the wrong direction.

Kennedy knew he was in a perfect position to end the game. Before he could do that, however, Ronnie Oates, who'd just left for home three minutes earlier, came rushing back into the pool hall.

"I think someone's breaking into the auto shop next door!" he said. In his excitement he sounded as though he'd been running much farther than the distance from the parking lot to the building.

"Who'd want to rob old Jed?" Joe muttered. "Hell, if someone's that desperate for a wrench, he can have one of mine."

"All I know is that I saw the beam of a flashlight inside," Ronnie said. "Let's go take a look."

Kennedy gazed longingly at the eight ball. One more shot…just one, and the game would be over. But Joe and the others were already pouring out the back. Even if he sank it, there'd be no one to witness the victory. Then, when Joe came back, he'd say they had to play again.

"There *is* a flashlight or something over there," he heard someone else shout.

He laid his cue stick across the table. He supposed he might as well go see what was happening. Probably just a bunch of kids out to cause trouble, but it was Thursday, not Friday, which was a bit odd. And Jed's Dependable Auto Repair made an unlikely target.

"Call the police," he yelled over to Pug, the bartender.

Kennedy waited long enough to see the man pick up the phone and dial. Then he strode into the parking lot.

Shouts rose outside as Grace stared at the Bible she'd just discovered and, for a second, her knees threatened to give out on her. They were going to be caught—exactly what she'd feared.

A thump indicated that Madeline had dropped her flashlight. Scooping it up again, she turned it off. "Someone's coming," she whispered. "Let's get out of here."

The dog they'd been so careful to feed at the tire shop next door began to bark at the noise.

Grace didn't know what to do. Should she leave the Bible in the file drawer? Or try to take it with her?

Panic made it difficult to think. Turning off her own

flashlight, she shoved the Bible back inside the drawer. Then she realized that the break-in might raise enough questions that someone else would search for the reason they'd been interested in the place at all. If the Bible surfaced, embossed with the reverend's name and containing his margin notes, whoever found it would go straight to Jed. Then he'd be forced to tell where he got it and how. And he could only have gotten it the night the reverend died. Grace remembered how the Bible had fallen out of her stepfather's jacket as they dragged his body down the porch steps. She'd tried stuffing it back in, but…had it fallen out a second time, farther away, on the dark wet ground?

She didn't know. It could have. She'd been out of her mind that night; they'd all been out of their minds.

"Grace!" Madeline cried, already at the door.

Grace squeezed her forehead with one hand. *Think! Oh, God. What do I do?*

There was no time to do anything. The shouting and footsteps were growing louder. She could even recognize a few of the voices.

Slamming the drawer, she turned to follow her stepsister. But just as she reached Madeline, she realized she *couldn't* leave the Bible behind. It could destroy her whole family.

"We have to split up," she said. "You go that way, and I'll—" she searched frantically for another option "—I'll sneak out the bathroom window."

"But what if—"

"Go," she said and gave her stepsister a little shove.

Madeline touched her arm to let Grace know she'd heard and ducked outside.

Run, Grace thought, as though they could communicate telepathically. *Run*. But she couldn't move very fast herself. She felt her way through the dark, back to the filing cabinet, where she retrieved the Bible and slipped it into the waistband of her shorts.

The men were at the door. She had to reach the bathroom. Unless she wanted to try hiding under the desk, it was her only chance of escape.

Her hands instinctively groped for her flashlight. She hated the dark. But she didn't know where she'd put the damn thing after shutting it off.

Then she heard someone yell, "I see him! Over there!" and the footsteps raced off in another direction.

Madeline! Grace wasn't sure whether or not her stepsister would be able to get away. But that suddenly became a secondary concern. She had to take the reverend's Bible and destroy it while she had the chance.

Finally she found the bathroom and eyed the small window above the toilet. She could see a slice of moon gleaming far above and longed to climb out, as she'd told Madeline she would. That window faced away from the dog and the noise. But it was too high. Even if she could get through, she was afraid she'd fall to the ground and break her neck.

Going out the front was her only option, although she was afraid the police were on their way and might spot her as they drove up.

Skirting the reception desk, she peered through the door, which stood slightly ajar from Madeline's rapid departure.

She could hear no sirens. Just the melee going on down the alley, and the dog next door, barking wildly.

She had at most a few seconds in which to disappear before everyone came back to see what had been damaged or stolen....

The leather cover of the Bible felt like a hot brand on the skin of her back—the reverend's brand. She wanted to toss it away and pretend she'd never seen it. But she couldn't. She had to burn it so no one would ever find it again.

Begging for a miracle, she darted outside and hurried around the building.

She managed to clear the yard with little sound. When she entered the alley, she began to feel more hopeful.

She was out. But what now?

She needed to climb Lorna Martin's fence. If she could cut through the neighborhood while everyone's attention was elsewhere, she still had a chance of escape.

Kennedy couldn't believe his eyes. He'd been leaning against the back of his SUV, waiting to see if the others caught the burglar who'd broken in next door, when a second guy emerged from the shadows of the auto shop. Dressed all in black, the dark figure hurried across the alley and scaled Lorna Martin's fence.

It was a kid, just as he'd suspected. Had to be. The person's frame wasn't big enough to be a man. And no man he knew climbed a fence like that....

Kennedy glanced around as though expecting someone else to go after him. But the guys who'd left the pool hall were already much farther down the alley. There was nothing to do but go after the little thief himself.

"Hey, hold on there!" he called.

The boy ran even faster, but now that he'd committed himself, Kennedy was dedicated to catching him. He jumped the fence, too, and nearly ran into Lorna

Martin's husband, who came barreling out of the house wearing a bathrobe.

"Kennedy?" Les said, stopping abruptly. "What's going on? What are you doing here?"

Kennedy swerved around him. "Some young kid just came through here," he called back as he ran. "Did you see him?"

"No, but judging from all the ruckus, he's down there." Les pointed in the direction of the others.

"There's two of 'em," Kennedy said and continued to sprint to the front.

Les yelled something after him, but Kennedy didn't stop. He wasn't about to let some stupid kid get away with breaking into one of Stillwater's businesses. Whoever this was, he needed to be taught a lesson before he did anything worse.

When he reached the street, Kennedy saw a small, dark shape dart around the corner four houses down and knew the culprit was probably heading for the woods. If Kennedy didn't catch up to him soon, he might never find him. Not alone. And not in the dark.

He pounded along the sidewalk, but when he got to the corner, he could no longer see any movement. The streetlights illuminated nothing more than a row of dark houses and shiny black asphalt.

He stopped, taking a deep breath as it began to rain. Where had the boy gone? They'd both be soaked in a matter of minutes, which didn't sound particularly appealing.

Not that Kennedy was ready to give up. Gazing at the railroad tracks that passed through the meadowlike land, he realized the boy must've cut over already. If not, Kennedy would've seen him.

Obviously, the troublemaker didn't know this area

very well. How was he planning to cross the creek? Maybe he could hide in the woods, but unless he planned to swim in the dark, he wouldn't get very far. The creak formed an arc that hemmed him in on three sides.

Jogging through the meadow, Kennedy cleared the railroad tracks and entered the woods. But he couldn't see much. The dense foliage blocked out most of the moonlight. He knew the boy could be headed in any direction. Or maybe he wasn't moving at all. Maybe Kennedy was wrong. Maybe he knew the area as well as Kennedy did and was simply lying low, hoping Kennedy would eventually give up.

Kennedy stood still, listening. An owl hooted, but he heard nothing more.

Walking deeper into the trees, he went toward the creek, his movements as stealthy as possible, pausing often to listen. Two could play the waiting game. But he spent at least ten minutes in the woods and heard nothing, saw nothing move.

He began to wonder if he should go back and summon a group with flashlights to help him search the area. He was about to act on that thought when he heard a startled cry.

The boy was close. Much closer than he'd expected. And it sounded as if he'd hurt himself.

It was over. Kennedy had him now.

Creeping forward, he strained to see in the dank, thick darkness. What had happened? He couldn't imagine—until a shaft of moonlight filtered through the trees, giving him a glimpse of what lay ahead. Evidently, the boy had gotten himself tangled up in the blackberry bushes that covered the low areas near the water.

He was probably pretty scratched up. But Kennedy wore a pair of long pants and wasn't worried about such minor injuries. Launching himself into the thicket, he grabbed the kid by the back of the shirt and hauled him out of the briars without bothering to make sure his exit was gentle. Then he sat him hard on the ground.

"What the hell do you think you're—" Kennedy started, but the boy rolled over and tried to regain his feet so he could run, which forced Kennedy to tackle him.

"What's the matter with you?" Kennedy cried when they hit the ground. But a split second later, he realized that the body under his was far too soft to belong to a boy.

Knocking off the baseball cap that shadowed the burglar's face, he stared in astonishment.

It was a woman, all right. But not just any woman. It was Grace Montgomery.

7

Grace couldn't breathe. She couldn't think straight, either. Only one thought crystallized in her mind—and if a thought could be sound it would've been a blaring horn: *escape!* She tried to shove Kennedy off or wriggle out from beneath him, but she was shaking from the adrenaline rushing through her body—and he was too strong.

"Let me go!"

"Stop fighting!"

She couldn't. She was desperate. If he caught her with the reverend's Bible, she stood to lose much more than her job.

"Calm down," he said. "I—I didn't mean to hurt you—" He pinned her left hand down over her head. "I expected—" he grabbed her other hand as she clawed the ground in hopes of finding a root or something she could use to pull herself out from under him "—you to be a teenage boy."

Before she could respond, Grace heard another voice. Joe Vincelli was coming through the woods toward them. "Kennedy? Where are you, man?"

Grace froze, wishing the spongy ground would simply give way and swallow her whole.

Kennedy lifted his head but didn't respond. It was

difficult to make out his expression. Everything was a series of dark, wet shadows.

After a long second, she felt his attention shift back to her. "What are you doing?" he whispered gruffly. "Why'd you break into Jed's auto shop?"

She refused to answer him, refused to so much as manufacture a lie. What difference would any response of hers make? He'd always thought she was trash. In his mind, this would only prove that he'd been right all along.

"It's okay." His tone was gentler now. "Just tell me what's going on. I have no idea what it could be, but I'm hoping you have a good reason for this."

He spoke as if addressing a frightened child. But that gentleness was too obvious a falsehood for someone who knew him and his friends the way Grace did. They told so many lies with their lips and hands and bodies....

She struggled to control her fear as she glared defiantly up at him.

"Grace?" he prompted.

The rain began to fall harder. The water already absorbed by the ground soaked through her clothes as she blinked to keep the drops out of her eyes. In her peripheral vision, she could see the beam of Joe's flashlight darting among the trees.

"Hello?" Joe shouted, drawing closer. "Kennedy, where are you? I can see someone's been through here."

Obviously, Joe wasn't having much difficulty following them. They'd left a trail of smashed plants— and he had a light.

Grace squeezed her eyes shut, expecting that light to find her at any second. But it never did. The next thing she knew, Kennedy jumped up, hauled her to her feet and pushed her into the trees behind him. "Get out of here," he said.

Kennedy couldn't believe what he'd just done. He'd let a burglar go—and he was running for mayor of this town.

He told himself it was because an arrest would cost Grace her job, and he couldn't stand to see that happen without knowing the whole story. But deep down, he knew his motivation was much simpler. He'd felt the tremors going through her body, sensed her terror even though she wouldn't explain or ask him for help, and he'd wanted to protect her. He'd remembered her sitting next to his son saying, "You can't expect others to save you. You have to save yourself."

For a split second, he'd been tempted to use his body to shelter hers from the rain while he cradled her safely against him. She seemed so aloof and yet so damn fragile. *I've got you, pretty baby. I'll save you.*

But that was craziness. She saw him as her enemy, not some kind of savior.

Joe emerged from the trees. "There you are. Why didn't you answer me?"

Kennedy stepped back—and his foot landed on something square and soft yet solid. A book? It wasn't a plant or a rock. And he doubted it had just dropped from the sky. Chances were that Grace had lost it when he tackled her.

He blocked Joe's view of it in case whatever it was might give her away. "Someone else darted out of the auto shop, so I came after him. Nearly had him a minute ago, too."

Joe pointed his light at the blackberry bushes that

sloped down to the water. Because they were more resilient than most plants, it wasn't quite as apparent that someone had been through them, but Kennedy could see Joe was wondering. "Maybe it's not too late," he said, edging toward them. "Come on."

Kennedy recovered the object on the ground and shoved it up under his T-shirt, into the waistband of his jeans. Then he caught hold of Joe's arm. "I've been in there already."

Joe kept scanning the area with his light. "Still, whoever it is couldn't have gotten far. The creek's right there."

The wet object pressed against Kennedy's stomach did feel like a book. But why Grace would steal a book from Jed, he couldn't imagine. "He's gone. And it's raining. Let's head home."

"We're already wet."

"I'm telling you, he must've doubled back. I don't think he's in here anymore."

"Did you get a good look at him, at least?"

"Whoever it was wasn't very big. I'm guessing it was a teenager."

Joe pivoted in a circle. "I'll give you a hundred to one it wasn't a teenager."

The protective instinct that had surprised Kennedy a few moments earlier rose inside him again. He didn't understand why Grace affected him so deeply now that they were adults. He knew he wanted her to forgive him so he could forgive himself for how he'd treated her in the past. But he also wanted her to *like* him, which didn't make sense.

Maybe it was the challenge, he decided. He'd always made friends easily, had never met with much resistance.

Or maybe he wanted to make a difference in someone else's life, the way Raelynn had made a difference in his. Grace needed him. He felt compelled to be there for her this time, to do what he could to compensate for everything she'd suffered before.

"Why do you say that?" Kennedy asked and started out of the woods as though the argument was settled.

"I think it was Kirk Vantassel," Joe answered, falling in step beside him.

Kirk was taller than Kennedy or Joe, and Kennedy had just said that the culprit was small. But he didn't point that out. "Why Kirk?"

"Because it was Madeline Barker who broke in. We chased her down in the alley."

The rain had soaked through Kennedy's shirt, plastering the cotton fabric against him. He used his arm to subtly shift the book to his side, where he could better hide it. "Madeline's a model citizen. Why would she break into Jed's shop?"

"She's convinced he killed her father. Told us she was searching for evidence."

That made sense to Kennedy. Madeline was always coming up with possible scenarios to explain her father's disappearance. She'd printed several in the paper. Maybe she'd uncovered a new lead.

Kennedy could easily imagine how eager she'd be to pursue it. She loved the Montgomerys, had been defending them for years. He could even see her recruiting Grace to help her tonight. Was the book some type of evidence, then?

"Did Madeline *tell* you Kirk was with her?" he asked, squinting up at the rain.

"She claims she was alone. But when Les told me

you followed someone else through his yard, I knew she had help."

Kennedy kept his eyes trained on the circle of Joe's flashlight moving over the ground directly in front of them. He was tempted to look behind but wouldn't let himself. Surely Grace would give him enough time to get rid of Joe before trying to head home. "Did you and the others turn her in?"

"No. She promised to pay for the damage she caused, so we let her go. She's already been through a lot."

They reached the edge of the meadow, where moonlight made it easier to see, especially in contrast to the darker woods.

"Losing her father was tough on her," Kennedy agreed and, since the weather provided the perfect excuse to hurry, he started to jog. He wanted to get Joe out of the area as soon as possible, and he wanted to see what he'd found. The book pressed to his side seemed to have the soft leather cover and thickness of a Bible. But it couldn't be, could it? As far as he knew, Grace wasn't particularly religious. Neither was her family. A few years after the reverend went missing, the Montgomerys quit church altogether, giving the townspeople something else they could point to as proof that they were lost souls. And Kennedy highly doubted she'd take a Bible from Jed's shop. Even if Jed had one there, why would anyone steal it?

"Having your uncle go missing was probably hard on the Montgomerys, too," he said, to keep the conversation going.

"That's bullshit," Joe said, catching up to him. "If you ask me, Madeline needs to look a little closer to home if she wants answers. It's like I said at your office—you should pressure McCormick to reopen the case. This wouldn't have happened if the police were making any progress."

Kennedy flung his wet hair out of his face. "You think we'd be doing Madeline any favors by going after her family—again?"

"The truth is the truth," he responded between breaths as they ran. "She deserves the truth, no matter what it is."

Kennedy knew Joe wasn't pushing the issue for Madeline's sake and almost volunteered that Grace had been with Madeline at Jed's, helping her search for evidence. He was tired of Joe's unrelenting prejudice. But he thought it was better not to mention Grace in connection with the break-in. McCormick might've let Madeline go. Everyone liked Madeline. Grace, on the other hand, wasn't nearly as popular in Stillwater as her stepsister. Kennedy suspected they'd lock her up for the same infraction.

"Do Irene, Clay and Grace deserve to suffer through another investigation?" he asked, because Joe had slowed and he didn't want to lose his attention.

Joe was busy shining his light on the woods behind them. But at this question, he pivoted and started walking again. "Hell, yeah, if they're as guilty as I think they are. Justice needs to be done."

"Justice. And what if they're not guilty? Where's the justice in disrupting their lives?"

He shrugged. "Them's the breaks, you know? It could happen to any of us."

They crossed the railroad tracks. "Pretty easy for you to say," Kennedy muttered. "Since nothing like that ever has."

Joe pulled Kennedy to a stop. "Wait a second. I'm

on the victim's side. *Something* happened to my uncle," he argued. "I think it's damn time the police figured out what, don't you?"

Jerking his arm free from Joe's grasp, Kennedy sheltered his face with his other hand. "What's really driving you on this, Joe? That's the part I'm missing."

"The truth, like I said. It should be important to you, too." Rain dripped from the ends of Joe's hair, which curved in toward his face. "Are you going to help me or not?"

Kennedy remembered Grace's unequivocal rejection in the parking lot of the pizza parlor. He knew of only one thing that might make Joe vindictive enough to force an issue that could hurt Grace so badly. "You want to get with her again, don't you. You want to get with her and she won't give you the time of day."

Joe snapped off his flashlight, but Kennedy could still see that he was scowling. "Hell, no. What would I want with Grinding Gracie?"

Kennedy pictured the intelligence in Grace's blue eyes. Those eyes were older than her years, as if they'd seen far too much, but they were also mysterious, compelling and deep enough to drown in. He thought he could suggest exactly what Joe might want. "She's a beautiful woman, something special."

"Special?" Joe scoffed. "I've slept with her before. Everyone has. Except you maybe, and that was only 'cause of Raelynn."

Kennedy ignored his comment. "But it's not the same, is it? We were just kids. She didn't know who she was then, had no identity. She was a lost girl letting you use her body because she didn't really own it yet. Now she's attractive, successful and completely indifferent to you, me, to all of us."

Joe rubbed his jaw and gave the trees one final sweep with his light. "She's still the same to me," he said and stalked away. But Joe was lying. Kennedy doubted there was a man in town, at least a single man, who wouldn't give just about anything to make love with Grace as an adult.

Even he wanted that.

Clay stopped pacing his kitchen to stare at Grace, his mouth a grim line. "That can't be."

"It's true." She hugged the thick towel he'd given her closer to her body. The night was balmy, even at nearly three in the morning. But she was chilled. After her long trek home in the rain, she hadn't bothered to change or dry off. She'd grabbed her car keys and driven straight to the farm.

"But we buried that Bible with him," Clay said as if the strength of his conviction could make it true.

"It must've fallen out. It did once. On the porch steps."

"We would've seen it."

"How can you say that?" Grace asked. "It was so dark. Can you remember *everything* that happened? Were you thinking that clearly?"

Grace sometimes wondered if any of them had been thinking at all. Especially Clay. Hiding the body and driving the reverend's car into the quarry had been his idea, a decision they'd had to live with for eighteen years.

But what better option did they have? They couldn't have gone to the police. Grace knew that now as well as she'd known it then. No one in Stillwater would've believed them; no one would've listened. They would've demanded retribution for the loss of their beloved preacher.

"We were so careful," he said.

"Evidently we weren't careful enough."

"But Jed's never said a word about the Bible." Clay's hand rasped over his whiskers as he rubbed his jaw. "Not to me. Not to Mom. Not to the police. Why?"

"I have no idea."

He sat on the edge of the table beside her. "Where do you think it is now?"

"Kennedy Archer or Joe Vincelli must've picked it up. That's all I can figure."

Surprisingly, Clay's face filled with hope. "Maybe they didn't see it. Maybe we should go back and search some more—"

She shook her head. "No, I know where I lost it."

It must have happened while she was wrestling with Kennedy. She'd had the Bible right before that. But she didn't want to talk about her little scuffle. No one needed to know Kennedy had caught her—or let her go. She'd dropped the Bible trying to get away. That was the pertinent information.

Still, as much as she told herself it didn't matter, that she had more pressing concerns, she couldn't avoid the question that had nagged at her ever since: *why had he helped her?*

"Once the coast was clear I scoured the area," she said. "It's gone."

Clay stood and began to pace again. "Joe Vincelli will take it to the police for sure."

"I know."

"So will Kennedy Archer."

Grace didn't immediately respond. She wasn't sure what Kennedy would do. She still couldn't believe he'd let her go and wondered if he already regretted it.

"He'd have to," she said at last. "He can't get involved in anything like this."

"I'd better call Mom," Clay said. "Prepare her, just in case—"

A knock sounded at the door. Was it Joe? Kennedy? The police?

Grace's nerves drew taut. It seemed as though she'd always watched the threshold of that door with trepidation. When she was young, she'd feared the moment the reverend returned home each day. Now she feared those who wanted to know where he'd gone.

"Go upstairs," Clay murmured. "I'll handle this."

Grace had parked her car in the gravel lot behind the house, so it couldn't be seen from the street. She was tempted to slip out the back and drive off into the night while she had the chance. But then she heard Madeline's voice through the door.

"Clay can you hear me? Clay, open up!"

Clay didn't move right away. Instead, he glanced at Grace. "Do you think she knows about the Bible?"

"If she does, it won't be long until all hell breaks loose. She'll go straight to Jed and demand he tell her where he got it."

"And, from his perspective, I can't think of one reason in the world why he shouldn't tell her."

Grace dropped her head in her hand. "Of course he'll tell her. He'll have to. Everyone will be ready to lynch him."

"Clay?" Madeline called, banging some more. "Hurry, damn it! I need you. I can't find Grace."

Clay squeezed Grace's arm, then crossed the living room to unlock the door.

Madeline rushed in as he opened it. "Oh, God, Clay, I really did it this time. I talked Grace into—"

She stopped the second she saw Grace sitting at the table and hurried into the kitchen to embrace her. "There you are! I'm so sorry! Are you okay?"

"I'm fine." Grace met Clay's eyes over their step-sister's shoulder. Obviously, Madeline hadn't heard about the Bible, or her greeting would've been far different. If Joe had found it, he'd have gone directly to the police, eager to let everyone know he'd been right all along. Which meant Kennedy Archer had it.

Joe. Kennedy. Clay. Madeline. Irene. Grace hated the complexity of her relationships here in Stillwater. But... She thought of George and realized they were complex everywhere. The man who claimed he wanted to marry her hadn't even called in the past couple of days, although she needed his reassurance more than ever.

"I'm so glad you're safe," Madeline said. "I'm sorry I got you into that!"

"It's okay," Grace assured her. "Tell me what happened to you."

"They caught me in the alley." Madeline lifted her chin. "But I put up a good fight."

From the bruise on her stepsister's cheek, that certainly appeared to be true.

Suddenly Madeline seemed to notice the deep scratches on Grace's bare legs, her hands, her face. "God, look at you," she said, motioning toward a particularly deep gouge. "You're even more banged up than I am."

"I hid in the blackberry bushes down by the creek," Grace told her.

"They didn't find you, did they?"

Grace remembered the solid feel of Kennedy's muscular body as he landed on top of her, the power in his arms as he forced her hands over her head, and felt a very strange response in the pit of her stomach. *I didn't mean to hurt you....*

He and his kind always meant to hurt. That didn't explain why he'd let her go, but...obviously he wasn't really himself tonight. "No, they didn't find me."

"Good. They know *someone* was with me, but I wouldn't tell them who. I don't think they're interested in pursuing the issue anymore. They know why I was there. They know I didn't take anything and that I'll pay for the damage."

"That's good," Grace said, but it was difficult to smile and act relieved when she knew that Kennedy would come forward eventually. Her possession of that Bible revealed far too much.

And she could easily guess what Madeline would think of her when he went public with what he had.

Kennedy sat in his kitchen. The book he'd carried home from the woods was indeed a Bible. But not just any Bible. It had belonged to the Reverend Barker. His name was embossed on the front. His handwriting was all over the inside of it. Kennedy could even remember seeing him take it out of his pocket.

Frowning, he turned the thin pages. The notes in the margins unsettled him because they revealed in very subtle ways a man obsessed with his own power, not God's. Kennedy had been young when the reverend went missing, but the words he'd been studying for the past hour painted a picture of a man far different from the image he'd always maintained—far different from the pious man most people believed Barker to be.

There was a full page where Barker had written about Grace. He'd noted certain things she said, things she did, how she looked. Some fairly explicit poetry a few pages afterward seemed connected to her, as well. Unless Kennedy was assuming more than was really on the page....

He tried to steer his thoughts in a different direction. Maybe Barker was simply overjoyed to have a new daughter.

But if so, where were his notes on Molly? Why would he single Grace out the way he'd done?

Kennedy couldn't come up with a good reason. No matter how he interpreted what he read, he got the same feeling. The reverend was obsessed with Grace.

That sent chills down Kennedy's spine. He closed the Bible and shoved it away from him, but couldn't take his eyes off the embossed name. Eighteen years ago, she'd been just a girl, the same age as Kennedy.

Standing, he went to the window to peer out at the long drive that led to the highway. He had to be wrong. The reverend was a man of God. It was Kennedy who'd been having sexual fantasies about Grace. Not when they were younger, of course. But now. He couldn't forget the sight of her naked in that damn window.

Rubbing a finger over his lips, he turned back to see the reverend's Bible lying on his table. He felt like he imagined King David must've felt after seeing Bathsheba. If he had David's power, if he knew Grace would come willingly, wouldn't he send for her? Right now? Tonight?

Probably. But, he reminded himself, it was Bathsheba who'd brought about David's downfall....

With a sigh, he jammed a hand through his hair and walked quietly to the small music room just off the entry. Maybe he was half-crazy with missing Raelynn.

Maybe Grace evoked in him a very basic, almost primitive urge to possess her, an urge that was stronger than he'd ever experienced before. But the fact remained that the reverend had gone missing under mysterious circumstances. That Grace and her family had long been suspected of having something to do with it. And that Kennedy had just found this Bible, which had been the reverend's constant companion, on Grace's person.

He had to hand it over to the police, didn't he? He had to let them do their work.

And yet he already knew how things would go. Once word of this got out, almost everyone in town would turn on Grace and her family, and Joe would lead the pack. At best, the Montgomerys would suffer through another lengthy investigation. At worst…

The plush carpet gave silently beneath his feet as he crossed the room. He didn't want to think about the worst. Especially because there *was* something out of the ordinary between the reverend and the Montgomerys. Something dark, even sinister. He could feel it. But he hated to venture a guess as to what it was—and doubted Grace would ever tell him.

Circumventing the baby grand piano, he sat in one of two leather wing-back chairs. He'd felt the tremors going through her body when he'd caught her tonight. Yet she hadn't expected or asked for any kindness from him. She'd lain beneath him, her heart beating as fast as a captured rabbit's, her body shaking while she waited for Joe as if he carried the executioner's ax.

Kennedy picked up the telephone on the table next to him. He'd driven past Grace's house on his way home to find everything dark. Because he'd realized by then that the book he'd found was the reverend's

Bible, he hadn't gone to the door. He'd wanted some time to think about all this before he spoke to her. But now that he'd had the chance to look at it...

Lifting the receiver, he dialed information.

"City, please," a woman said.

"Stillwater. It's a new listing, for Grace Montgomery."

There was a momentary pause, then, "I'm sorry, I don't show anything for a Grace Montgomery in Stillwater. Would you like to try somewhere else?"

"No, thanks," he said and hung up. Grace obviously hadn't ordered telephone service, which made sense. From what he'd heard she was only in town for a few months. If she had a cell, she wouldn't need a regular telephone. But he didn't know how to get hold of that number.

He checked the grandfather clock out in the entry hall. It was probably just as well that he couldn't call her, he decided.

Retrieving the Bible, he hid it in his sock drawer until he could decide what to do with it. Suddenly he was more interested in what had gone on in the months leading up to the reverend's disappearance than he was in the actual night.

Because he suspected that what had happened then would explain all the rest.

When Grace returned home, she found a note shoved into the doorjamb.

Immediately apprehensive, she turned to study the bushes, the road behind her, the deep shadows by the garage and the far end of the porch, wondering if whoever had left it was still around. After everything that had occurred, she was expecting a fast reprisal. The past couple of hours felt very much like being tied to a railroad track and hearing a train whistle in the distance. The crossing barrier was lowering; the lights were flashing. She knew a locomotive was moving down the track. She just didn't know when it was going to hit her.

But no one seemed to be lurking near the house.

Taking the folded note with her, she went inside, locked the door and sat in the dark living room, listening to the clock tick. She wasn't sure she wanted to know who the note was from, let alone read what was written inside. But ignoring the crossing guard and the flashing lights wouldn't stop that locomotive....

Resigned, she crossed the room to turn on the light and slowly unfolded the paper.

Where are you, pretty lady? I think maybe we got off on the wrong foot the other night. I'm not a bad guy—definitely willing to forgive and forget, if you are. High school was then, this is now. Give me a call.

Joe had signed his name—and jotted down his number.

With a grimace, she stared at his bold yet sloppy writing. He didn't get it. He thought it might take a little more effort than it used to, but he could still have her if he wanted.

Shaking her head, she walked around the room, lighting all the candles. Then she used one narrow taper to burn his note in the sink.

So much for Joe. He'd *never* hear from her.

After rinsing the ashes away, she called George. She needed to remind herself that she had another life besides the one she was living right now in Stillwater, that she had the hope of something better—a husband, a family.

But George didn't answer.

She looked at her watch. It was almost five in the morning. Which meant he was probably sleeping. She'd expected that. But she craved the sound of his voice. And he'd always picked up when she needed him at odd hours.

She tried again. "Hello, this is George E. Dunagan. I'm unable to come to the phone right now—"

Hanging up, she stood at the doors that opened onto the back porch, watching the trees sway in the wind and feeling very much alone in the creaky old house. George was probably sleeping more deeply than usual, she decided. He hadn't called her the past couple of days because he'd been busy. It was probably that intruder rape case he was working on, the one he'd said was going sideways when he'd brought her furniture over a week ago. She knew how crazy a defense attorney's job could be. All that shifting and slanting and hiding of the truth took considerable effort.

Chastising herself for being sardonic—including him with so many of the defense attorneys she knew—she promised herself she'd call him in a few hours, when he reached his office. Then she went upstairs.

The rain had stopped. She was glad of the storm; it would lower the temperature and the humidity for a day or two. But she didn't like the low, keening whistle of the wind. The sound brought back those years when she'd huddled, frightened, beneath her blankets. Too afraid to move. Trying not to breathe. It had been a blustery night just like this one when she'd first heard that ominous creak in the hall and seen the looming shadow of her stepfather in her bedroom doorway....

"He's dead. Dead and gone," she whispered. She'd helped bury him. They'd all helped. But, sure enough, when she closed her eyes, he had his nose pressed to the glass of her living room window.

He was back. And he was trying to get inside the house.

8

The next morning, Kennedy sat at the kitchen table and watched his youngest son dig in to a bowl of Honeycomb cereal. He'd wanted to talk to Teddy about Grace before the incident at the pool hall. But it'd seemed a little hypocritical to tell his son he had to spend less time with the woman whose cookies they were all so greedily devouring. She'd also sent home a pan of lasagna and some garlic bread, which his mother had grudgingly passed along. They'd eaten it for dinner. He had to admit it'd felt good to have a homemade meal with his boys that he hadn't cooked, one without his mother's presence and the constant worry that gnawed at him every time he looked at his father.

"You're downing that cereal pretty fast," he said, folding the newspaper he'd been reading and putting it next to his coffee cup. "Where's the fire?"

"What fire?" Teddy asked, his mouth full.

"It's a figure of speech. I'm asking why you're in such a hurry."

His youngest son paused briefly to glance up at him. "We need to go, don't we? You have lots to do."

"Somehow that's never motivated you to get ready so fast before."

Teddy kept his eyes on his food and continued to shovel cereal into his mouth.

"Last week you hated going to Grandma's. Suddenly I get no complaints," Kennedy went on.

Teddy's spoon hovered a few inches from his mouth. "It's not so bad anymore."

"The question is why."

No answer.

"You like Grace's cookies that much?"

"I like Grace," Teddy said. "It's fun at her place."

Heath finished drinking the milk left over from his cereal and banged his bowl onto the table. "He was gone *all* day yesterday," he volunteered. "Grandma was *so* mad she said she was going to box his ears."

"Tattletale!" Teddy cried.

"Whoa." Kennedy reached across the table and squeezed Teddy's arm, because he was the easiest one to reach, before the brief exchange could erupt into a full-blown argument. "Settle down. Grandma already asked me to talk to you about the amount of time you're spending over there."

"Grandma doesn't like Grace just because she's voting for Vicki Nibley," Teddy complained.

With a scowl, Kennedy let go of him. "Is she *really* voting for Mrs. Nibley?"

"She has some Nibley signs at her house," Heath said. "Grandma spotted them yesterday and said, 'It figures.'"

Come to think of it, Kennedy had seen them, too. He'd told himself at the time that it didn't matter to him, but it bothered him more than he cared to admit. "What do you do when you go over there?" he asked, wondering if his son would mention the reading.

"Just...work," he replied with a shrug.

"What kind of work?"

"We cook. We count the jars in the cellar. We—"

"How do you cook if you're staying outside?" Kennedy interrupted, arching a knowing eyebrow at him.

Teddy's face turned red. "I wasn't inside very long, Dad. And…and we *had* to cook," he added beseechingly. "If we didn't, we wouldn't be ready for today."

"Something special is happening today?"

"We're going to open the shop."

"What shop?"

"Evonne's Homestyle Fixin's."

Kennedy blinked several times. "You're kidding me."

"No." Excitement sparkled in his youngest son's wide gray eyes. "We have twenty-two jars of peaches, eighteen jars of tomatoes—"

"Does Grace need the money?" Kennedy asked.

"She told me I could charge whatever I want. And she's gonna split it with me."

"So probably not."

"I think she misses Evonne. Like me." He assumed a more grown-up air. "She wants to take a page out of Evonne's book."

"Which means…"

His shoulders rounded again. "I don't know. That's just what she said."

"It means—" Kennedy started.

"I remember," Teddy interrupted. "It's living the simple life…or something like that."

Kennedy laughed.

"She's probably going to take a lot of naps," Heath piped up. "Right, Dad?"

"Living the simple life is definitely about slowing

down for a bit," he replied. "Considering what she normally does, I'm sure that's a good idea."

"What does she normally do?" Heath asked.

"She's an assistant district attorney, remember?"

"No." Teddy shoved his bowl away. "What's that?"

"A lawyer."

"What's a lawyer?"

"Someone who knows the laws we live by in this country."

Teddy licked the milk mustache from his lip. "Yeah, that's it. She said she's taking a vacation from the laws."

"From practicing law," Kennedy corrected, but Teddy took no notice.

"She's *really* nice."

Kennedy folded his arms. "I'm still waiting to hear why you disobeyed me."

"She needed my help."

"Having a good excuse doesn't make it okay," Kennedy pointed out.

Teddy's eyebrows gathered above the bridge of his small nose. "We leave the back door open to catch the breeze," he said as though that somehow improved the situation. "And sometimes we sit out on the porch and drink fresh-squeezed lemonade."

"You do?" Heath said, his tone jealous. "I like lemonade. Can I come, too?"

"Maybe," Teddy said, but it was easy to tell he'd rather have Grace all to himself.

Kennedy wondered how he should respond to his son's disobedience. Grace's personal life worried him. He hadn't forgotten the ominous Bible in his sock drawer. He'd barely slept because of it. And yet he'd already seen how Grace interacted with Teddy. He felt quite certain she'd never hurt him. "You disobeyed me, so you have to be punished."

"How?" Teddy asked.

"You'll have to do some extra work around here this weekend."

Teddy didn't even bat an eye. "Okay. But I can still go over to Grace's today, right?"

Kennedy's jaw dropped. He didn't care about the extra work? "I don't know about that."

"Please?" he begged. "She *needs* me."

"If I let you go there again, you can't stay so long. It upsets Grandma. Just visit for a couple of hours and head back."

"But Grace and I have a lot to do!"

Kennedy assumed the role of a stern parent. "Do you want to be grounded in addition to the extra work?"

"No." Teddy stared glumly up at him, making it difficult for Kennedy to be angry. "But it's stupid if I have to stay at Grandma's all day. No matter what I do, she says, 'Stop that! You're making me nervous.'"

"If you want to help Grace open the shop, you're going to have to compromise."

"But—"

"Teddy…" Kennedy warned.

Finally, his son seemed to get the point. "O-kay," he said with a pained sigh.

"And do me one other favor."

Teddy's expression grew leery. "What's that?"

Kennedy grinned. "Bring home more of those cookies."

Teddy's eyes lit up as though he'd just been given

a gift. "I will if you'll let her go camping with us this weekend."

"What?" Kennedy said.

"She loves the outdoors. She told me so herself. That's why she likes to be in the garden."

"I don't think so, Teddy. I'm guessing she wouldn't want to go even if I invited her."

"Sure she would, Dad! I bet if you let her go camping with us, she'd even vote for you. She just needs to get to know you, right?"

Feigning disinterest, Kennedy picked up the newspaper next to his empty plate. "Maybe another time, buddy."

But Teddy wasn't taking no for an answer. "*Please,* Dad? I know you'd like her if you'd give her a chance. I know she'd like you, too. Then you wouldn't have to worry about me when I'm over there."

Kennedy had no idea how to respond. Teddy seemed on the verge of tears.

"We're planning to do the stand all next week," his son added hopefully.

"I'll think about it," Kennedy said, putting off the inevitable disappointment his real response would engender. But he regretted softening that much when Teddy's smile stretched wider than he'd seen in months.

"Thanks, Dad. You're the best!"

Kennedy started to say he hadn't agreed—then clamped his mouth shut again. He didn't have to say no. The moment he invited her, Grace would do that for him.

"No problem," he said. "Just don't be disappointed if she can't come, okay? She might have other plans."

"She doesn't have other plans," he replied confidently. "She hardly knows anyone here. And she really likes me."

It wasn't her affinity for Teddy he was worried about. It was her lack of affinity for *him*.

As soon as she stepped out of the shower, Grace tried George's office number. She'd tried calling him twice already, but Heather, his secretary, said he hadn't come in yet. He usually hit the office at eight, so it seemed odd that his secretary didn't know where he was at ten o'clock, but Grace assumed he must've had a court date he'd forgotten to mention.

"George E. Dunagan's office."

"Hi, Heather. It's Grace again. Is George in yet?"

There was a slight hesitation. "Um, I'm not sure. I've been on the phone."

Being on the phone meant she couldn't see him when he walked in? "Could you check, please?"

"Ah, sure."

"Thanks," Grace said, perplexed by the strain in his secretary's voice.

There was a long pause but finally George came on the line.

"Grace?"

She sighed in relief. "George. There you are. I was beginning to think you'd been abducted by aliens or something." She laughed, but he didn't join in.

"What's up?" he said.

She straightened, trying to figure out what had changed. "Nothing, really. I just wanted to check in with you. We haven't talked for a few days."

"I've been busy." He didn't elaborate. "How's Stillwater?" he asked after a moment of awkward silence.

"Okay, I guess."

He covered the phone and spoke to someone else.

"Madeline talked me into breaking into an auto repair shop last night," she said because she knew he wasn't listening.

"That's nice," he said when he came back on the line.

Grace moved over to her dresser, where she'd put a picture of them having dinner for her birthday. "George, what's going on? You're acting so distant."

"Listen, Grace, I've got another call, and it's one I have to take. Can we talk later?"

A sick feeling settled in the pit of her stomach. George had never treated her so coolly. Why wasn't he pressing her to come home early? Why wasn't he asking if he could drive out and spend the weekend with her? He'd always done that sort of thing in the past. "Is there something I should know about?" she asked.

"I can't explain right now. I've got a lot going on."

She couldn't imagine how he could be any busier than usual. And he'd always had time for her before. But she let him go. "Sure," she said. "You're okay, aren't you?"

"I'm fine," he replied and hurried off the phone.

He was fine. He'd said so himself. So why was every nerve screaming that something was wrong? George had always been so steady, so resolute. He couldn't have changed his mind about wanting a relationship with her, could he? Not when she needed him most....

Grace was still staring at the phone when Teddy knocked. She'd been expecting him, but after talking to George, she wasn't sure she wanted company—

until she opened the door and Teddy promptly presented her with a dandelion.

"I picked it for you," he said proudly.

She smiled. "Thank you. It's beautiful." Somehow his sweet gesture made her feel better. Nothing was really wrong between her and George. Eventually, they'd marry as they'd planned all along and have a boy just like Teddy.

In any case, she had enough to worry about without stressing over George. The reverend's Bible was floating around somewhere.

"You all ready to open the shop?" she asked.

"Yeah!"

She was almost as excited as he was. Selling Evonne's handmade soaps, lotions and preserves was one way to feel close to her again. "Do you have your grandma's permission to be here?"

He glanced at the Nibley for Mayor signs on her porch, the ones she'd been meaning to put in her yard, then scuffed one toe against the other. "Yeah."

She sensed he had something else to say, but he didn't come out with it. Every time she asked about his family, he clammed up. She guessed his home life was so bad he didn't want to discuss it. "Teddy?"

He looked up at her. "What?"

"I want to meet your parents."

"This weekend?" he said hopefully.

"Today."

"Okay." He nodded. "But my mom's gone and my dad's at work. So can it wait till after we set up the stand?"

She didn't see why not. "Of course," she said, and a warm feeling lingered in her heart as she waved the boy inside. How such a random pair of lost souls had managed to find each other, she didn't know. But it seemed fitting that they'd met at Evonne's. "Come on, we'll start bringing out the peaches."

"Do you think we'll make lots of money today?" Teddy asked, setting his lawn chair as close to Grace's as he could.

Grace studied the fruits and vegetables and other things they'd laid out for sale. At the last minute, Teddy had asked if they could bake a big batch of chocolate chip cookies. Grace wouldn't have done it, except he'd said he'd mow the lawn in exchange for any that were left over at the end of the day, and she wanted him to have them. She suspected there'd be quite a few extras. Folks had to be missing Evonne's peaches and tomatoes they'd grown up eating. But Grace wasn't sure that something *she'd* made would appeal to the people of this town. Especially considering one of the theories that had circulated—that she or her mother had poisoned the reverend.

"Maybe a few bucks," she said with a shrug.

"Who do you think our first customer will be?"

"I don't know," she replied, but it didn't take long to find out. Almost as soon as the words were out of Grace's mouth, a white sedan pulled to the curb and Mrs. Reese, one of her former high school teachers, got out.

Grace's hands tightened on the arms of her chair. This woman had once thrown a ruler at her for being unable to answer a question in class. In high school, Grace hadn't done much homework. She'd been too busy working at the pizza parlor and helping with the farm—and worrying, always worrying, about the shallow grave in the backyard. During those years, it had been a struggle just to sleep through the night.

"I heard you were back," the white-haired Mrs. Reese said when Grace greeted her.

"Yes, for a few months."

"I see." Her eyes scanned the items on display. "I must say I'm glad to hear you've turned your life around. Making assistant D.A. and all that. Came as a bit of a surprise, to be honest with you." She focused on the Vicki Nibley For Mayor sign Grace had finally placed in the yard. "But I can't say as I like your politics."

"Then I can't say as I like yours, either," Grace responded.

Mrs. Reese's mouth opened and shut twice, but nothing came out. Turning to Teddy, she frowned. "Your grandma know you're over here?" she asked.

Teddy wouldn't look at her. His chin bumped his chest as he nodded vigorously.

"I can't imagine she likes it."

Grace cleared her throat. "Did you stop for a reason, Mrs. Reese?"

The older woman glared at her, then waved at the jars of peaches. "Those Evonne's?"

"They are. We brought them out of the cellar just yesterday."

"I'll take three jars."

Grace let Teddy collect the money. Determined to remain polite, she nodded as Mrs. Reese glanced her way before returning to her car.

"What was that all about?" Grace asked Teddy as the older woman disappeared around the corner.

"I guess she doesn't like Mrs. Nibley," he said sheepishly.

Grace studied him more closely. Something was going on here, and she figured she'd waited long enough to find out what. "Mrs. Reese acted as though she knows your grandma pretty well."

A pained expression appeared on his face. "*Everyone* knows my grandma."

"Who is she?" she asked, but before he could answer, a 1950s truck stopped at the curb and her heart leapt into her throat. It was Jed Fowler. She knew because he'd been driving that truck ever since she could remember.

He emerged looking ruddier than ever. He'd obviously lost some weight, but he still had a barrel chest and wore the same style coveralls she remembered from when he'd come out to fix the tractor all those years ago. A tattered red ball cap advertising his auto shop covered his head, so she couldn't tell if he'd lost any more of his hair.

Wondering what the police had told him about last night—if he knew it was Madeline who'd broken into his shop—she stood up as he walked over. "Hello, Jed," she said nervously. "How are you?"

When their eyes met, she got the impression he could see right through her. Had Kennedy told him she'd been with Madeline? That she was the one who'd taken the reverend's Bible?

She wiped her clammy hands on her cotton skirt and took a deep breath. "Something I can get for you today?"

"You make those cookies?" he asked, pointing to one of five platefuls at the far end.

"I did."

He picked up a bar of soap, smelled the lavender, then grimaced and put it back. "I'll have a jar of pickles."

"That it for you?" she asked.

Teddy hovered eagerly at her elbow. "I'll take the money."

Jed's eyes rested on the boy. He seemed as surprised as Mrs. Reese to see Teddy, but handed him a twenty while motioning toward the cookies. "Give me a plate of those, too."

He was buying her cookies. That made Grace feel even worse about last night.

She helped Teddy calculate the change, which he dropped into the old man's callused palm. Jed started to walk away—but Grace called him back. "Mr. Fowler?"

He turned.

Folding her arms across her chest, Grace forced herself to go on. "I—I heard about what happened last night. I'm sorry, truly I am."

She swallowed hard, wondering how he might respond. But he didn't say anything. Which wasn't all that unusual. His gaze wandered to Teddy again. Then he nodded.

Grace's heart was still pounding as she watched him climb into his truck. She hated the thought that she'd been an accomplice to breaking open his door and invading his privacy.

"What happened last night?" Teddy asked.

She didn't answer. She wasn't about to tell him. She had her own questions. "Why is everyone so surprised that you're with me?" she asked.

"I don't know," he said. But he was staring at his shoes again.

"Who's your grandmother, Teddy?"

The sun nearly blinded them as midafternoon approached. He lifted a hand to shade his eyes. "Can I tell you later? When you meet my dad and he asks you to go camping with us?"

"Camping?"

"Yeah. I asked him if you could go and he said yes!"

"Teddy—" Grace shook her head, trying to stay focused on the bigger question. "Tell me about your family."

"I don't want to."

"Why not?"

"Because we just got the stand going. And if you don't like what I say, you'll want me to go home."

"That's silly. I don't care who your family is."

"You don't?" He seemed relieved.

"Of course not." She tugged on the bill of his ball cap, and he grinned.

"That's good," he said. "Because it won't be *my* fault if my dad beats Vicki Nibley, right?"

His *dad?* Grace's knees went weak. "What'd you say?"

Obviously confused by her response, he glanced between her and the Vicki Nibley sign closest to them. "I won't be mad at you if Mrs. Nibley wins," he told her.

She brought a hand to her chest. "You're not telling me you're Kennedy Archer's son!"

He nodded, but only halfheartedly as if he was afraid to admit it.

"You can't be," she said.

He bit his lip. "Why not?"

"Because you don't look anything like him."

"I don't?"

"No!" she said stubbornly. But now that she knew, she could see *some* resemblance. Teddy had his father's square jaw, wide mouth and confident, All-American smile. He also had the Archer bone structure, which would probably make him a very handsome man some day.

"Everyone says I look like my mom," he said.

That was true, too. In certain ways. How had she missed it?

Grace hadn't expected Kennedy Archer's son to be running around on his own at eight years old—that was how! She hadn't expected Kennedy Archer's son to be allowed to get dirty or rip out his knees or mow other people's lawns. But most of all, she hadn't expected to *like* anyone so closely related to Kennedy Archer.

"Why isn't someone watching you?" she asked. She was trying to curb her disappointment, to hide it— but that wasn't easy.

"I told you, my grandma watches me."

"She can't. She lives out of town, down by the—"

"She moved," he broke in. "A long time ago."

"Where?"

"Around the block."

"What?"

"Grandpa wanted to be closer to the bank," he explained.

Around the block. Closer to the bank. Of course. It all made sense. Teddy had lost his mother, so someone had to watch him during the day. Why not Grandma Archer?

Which meant...

Grace pressed her fingers to her temples. That

had been Kennedy in the black SUV the morning she'd been caught unawares. He'd probably been dropping his boys off at his mother's house and gotten quite an eyeful.

"Oh, boy," she muttered, dropping into her seat.

After several long seconds, Teddy tentatively tapped her on the shoulder. "Grace?"

"What?"

"Are you mad at me?"

"No, of course not," she said, but she didn't know what she was going to do. She couldn't hang out with Kennedy's son. Kennedy might've let her go last night, but she was pretty sure none of this was over yet.

"What's wrong, then?" he asked.

She rubbed a hand over her face. "Um…I just need some time to think, okay, Teddy? Why don't you…" Her mind grasped for something that might make him happy and buy her some time. "Why don't you take all the cookies home with you? And…and we'll talk later, okay?"

"You don't like me anymore," he accused.

As she looked into his troubled face, her heart threatened to break. "Teddy, that's not it at all. You see, your father and I…we've never been friends."

"He thinks *you're* nice."

"No, he doesn't. We…I can't believe he'd even allow you to be here. He doesn't know about it, does he?"

"He knows," Teddy insisted. "He said to thank you for the lasagna. And he asked me to bring him some more cookies. He *loves* your cookies."

She'd made dinner for Kennedy and his sons last night. She'd thought she was sending food to a poverty-stricken family with a darling little boy who needed her. She hadn't realized she was wasting her time and effort on the likes of Kennedy Archer, who could buy his children the best of everything.

"He even said you could go camping with us," Teddy added, as if that might help.

Camping again. Grace couldn't imagine that Kennedy had plans to invite her anywhere. "Teddy, you have a family who loves you and takes good care of you. You don't need me."

Tears filled his eyes. "I'm never coming back here!" he cried and ran away.

Numb, Grace sat staring at the food spread out on the table before her, and thought about the books she'd planned to check out at the library. Teddy had never heard of Lemony Snicket. She'd wanted to read him the whole "Series of Unfortunate Events."

But she was running into too many unfortunate events of her own.

His mother was calling—again. Sometimes Kennedy wished he could go through a whole day without being interrupted by her. She always had some complaint or suggestion. If Rodney Granger had surplus peaches on his trees, she called to see if he and the boys wanted to go pick a few pounds. She called to let him know she'd be renting a carpet-cleaning machine and to ask if he'd like to borrow it. She called to tell him she'd won him another vote whenever she convinced a Vicki Nibley supporter to switch sides. For the most part, it was pretty thoughtful stuff. It was just…constant. Sometimes she made him feel claustrophobic. But there wasn't much he could do, since she was watching his boys every day. He certainly didn't want to leave them with anyone else. Maybe his mother wasn't the most soft-spoken person in the world, but she was very responsible. And she was family. If Raelynn's death and his father's cancer had taught him anything, it was to value those relationships.

Stifling a sigh, he pushed the Talk button on his phone because he knew she'd only call back if he didn't. If she reached his voice mail twice in a row, she called his secretary and started tracking him down that way. "Hello?"

"Kennedy?"

"What?"

"We have a problem."

"What's wrong now?"

"Teddy's upset."

"Why? Did he get in trouble for coming home late again?"

"No. He came home early. But he went straight to the tree house and won't come out. Something happened while he was over at that woman's house."

Grace. Besides Irene, Grace was the only one his mother called "that woman." "Do you know what it could be?"

"He won't say."

The disapproval in her tone screamed, "I told you he shouldn't have been allowed over there!"

"Put him on the phone."

Kennedy waited several minutes. He was beginning to believe his mother wasn't able to coax Teddy into talking to him when his son finally picked up. "Hello?"

"Hey, buddy. What's going on?"

"I'm not in trouble," he grumbled sullenly. "I came home on time."

"I know," Kennedy said. "I'm just calling to see what happened at Grace's today."

"Nothing happened."

"When I drove past her place at lunch, the stand

was up, but you two weren't around. Didn't you open the shop?"

"We opened it for a little while, but—" his voice cracked "—she doesn't want me over there. She doesn't like me anymore."

Kennedy remembered them reading together at the patio table. "What makes you think that?"

"She told me to take all the cookies and go home."

"Maybe she was tired and wanted to have a nap."

"She wasn't tired."

Kennedy switched the phone to his other ear. "How do you know?"

"Because I told her you were my dad."

He sat up straighter. "She hadn't figured that out?"

Silence.

"Teddy?"

"I couldn't tell her, Dad. She wants Vicki Nibley to be the next mayor."

"So why'd you tell her today?"

"I wanted to wait till you could ask her to go camping. But Mrs. Reese came to buy some peaches and said Grandma wouldn't like me being there."

It was easy for Kennedy to picture the old battle-ax doing that. Grace had been in her English class, too. She'd sat in the back corner, where Joe's girlfriend threw spit-wads at her and Mrs. Reese wondered aloud why Clay's little sister couldn't keep up with the rest of the class. "I'm sure that went over big."

Teddy sniffed. "I don't think she likes Mrs. Reese."

"Probably not." Kennedy could certainly understand. Mrs. Reese was a busybody who took too many liberties in dispensing advice. "Don't worry. Everything will be okay."

There was a momentary lull in the conversation, but when Teddy spoke again, Kennedy heard a surge of hope in his voice. "Dad?"

"What?"

"Do you think you could go over to Grace's and show her that you're a nice guy?" he asked plaintively.

"Are you serious?"

"Yeah! She said you've never been friends. But you could say you're sorry."

"Teddy—"

"You made *me* say I'm sorry to Parker McNally, even though he hit me first."

"You bloodied his nose."

"He started it—but you said sometimes being big enough to say you're sorry is more important than who started it."

"This is different."

"How? You want to be friends with Grace, don't you?"

Kennedy had walked right into that one. "Of course I do. It's just…I don't know, bud."

"Come on, Dad. We were going to open the stand every day next week. And camping won't be any fun without her."

Kennedy rested his head in one hand. "Teddy—"

"*Please,* Dad? She's my *best* friend."

Kennedy's heart felt as if it had jumped into his throat. He couldn't speak. Teddy used to say his mother was his best friend.

"Daddy? Are you there?"

"I'm here."

"Will you do it? For me? *Please?*"

Kennedy took a deep breath, then let the air seep

slowly between his lips. "Sure," he said at last. "I'll go over there."

"Be really nice, okay? And when you ask her to go camping, tell her we're going to make s'mores. She'll like that."

Kennedy wasn't convinced Grace would even let him speak to her. "My going over there might not make any difference."

"It will," his son said, happy again, and disconnected.

Kennedy hung up the phone. He was sorry about what'd happened in high school. Terribly sorry. He felt he should apologize to Grace. But he was pretty sure she wouldn't want to hear it.

9

When she came to the door, Grace was wearing a white cotton blouse that contrasted nicely with her olive skin, a long red, orange and pink skirt with a bracelet around one narrow ankle and no shoes. Kennedy caught a glimpse of the shiny pink polish that covered her toenails, thought how delicate and feminine her feet looked, and wanted to continue to stare at the ground rather than face the scratches on her cheek from last night and the wary expression in her eyes. But he owed her an apology and, although it had taken Teddy to motivate him to deliver it, he was glad to finally be here.

"Hi." He'd already loosened his tie. Shoving his hands in the pockets of his suit pants, he stepped back so she wouldn't feel threatened by him in any way.

She hovered by the door as if she might need to lock him out at a moment's notice, so he doubted his attempt to convince her that she was safe had much effect.

"Hello," she said, her voice far more uncertain than welcoming.

Kennedy attempted a charming grin and jerked his head toward the stand she'd erected in the front yard. "Looks like you've been busy. Got any more peaches?"

Her eyes focused briefly on the stand. "You're here to buy peaches?" she asked skeptically.

"Not really," he admitted.

She raked one hand through the layers of her hair, which fell loose around her shoulders. "You've come about last night."

The tone of her voice seemed to add "at last." But he still didn't know what to think about the Bible he'd found. Or what to do with it. "No."

She raised her eyebrows.

"It's Teddy. He called me a few minutes ago."

Her chest lifted as though she'd just drawn a deep breath. "I'm sorry. I didn't mean to hurt him. I would never purposely take my feelings about you and your friends out on a child."

He winced. She hated him enough that not doing so required conscious effort?

Of course she did. But realizing it didn't make an apology any easier.

"I wouldn't have let him in if I'd known," she added, clearly trying to reassure him that it was an innocent mistake. "Anyway, he'll get over the disappointment. He and I barely know each other. In the future, just…just tell him whatever you think—that I'm not a good influence. And maybe for a week or two, I'll hold off reopening Evonne's stand. That way I won't be so visible to him."

Stepping closer, he put a hand on the door. To his surprise, she didn't try to close it.

"Grace, I'm sorry."

She inched backward in an obvious attempt to put more space between them. "For what? Teddy was no trouble."

"I'm not talking about Teddy. He had my permission to come over here. I figured he would've told you by now that he's my son. Or someone else would. Anyway, I'm sorry for what I did—and didn't do—in high school."

"I don't want to talk about high school," she said. "What happened then, happened. You can celebrate the letters you received in football and basketball and baseball. You can line up your prom pictures and your report cards and smile proudly. But I…I was stupid and desperate and…" She let her words dwindle away. "I just want to forget those years."

"Does that mean you won't forgive me?" he asked.

Several lines creased her forehead as she stared past him. "Will you give back what you took last night?" she asked, focusing on him again.

What did he say now? If she was involved in the reverend's death and he returned that Bible to her, he'd be aiding in the cover-up. If he took it to the police, he could be consigning her to who knew what kind of hell. Yet he couldn't keep it. He didn't want anything to do with it. If anyone ever found it, he'd have to explain where it came from.

Could he trust her? He couldn't say, not without knowing her better. "Will you go camping with me and the boys this weekend?" he asked instead of responding.

Her eyes widened. *"What?"*

"Teddy's really counting on it." Kennedy wanted her to go, too. But he doubted she'd believe him even if he admitted it.

"No, of course not," she said. "I mean…unless…" She stopped, lowered her voice. "Are you offering me a trade?"

"For the Bible?" He hated to use it as leverage. He

generally didn't have to bribe women. But he needed to understand Grace better in order to decide how to handle what he knew.

"Will you give it to me if I go with you this weekend?"

He could always bring it along and give it back to her there, where they had plenty of privacy—if, ultimately, that was the decision he made. But he couldn't promise anything. "That'll depend."

"On what?"

"On how things go."

Her lip curled in disgust. "God, you're even more like Joe than I thought."

"I'm nothing like Joe!" he snapped.

"Oh, yeah? Well, I can already tell you how things will 'go.' I won't sleep with you, Kennedy. Not for *anything.*"

"I wasn't implying—" He stretched his neck as the full impact of her words sank in. "Wow, you really know how to hurt a guy's ego, you know that? Sleeping with me would be that distasteful to you?"

"I won't leave myself vulnerable to you. I don't care if you're going to be the next president of the United States. Those days are over."

"I wasn't trying to—" He paused. "I'm not asking for anything physical. It's just a camping trip, okay? It'll last three days and two nights. The boys will be there. You'll have your own tent."

Her expression softened slightly. "So this really is for Teddy?"

"More or less."

"You won't touch me?"

He let his gaze linger on her face. "Not if you don't want me to."

"And you'll give me the Bible?"

He'd consider it—for the price of an explanation. But he didn't add that. "Maybe."

Maybe was better than nothing. It could be her only chance to recover it. When she answered, he knew she recognized that. "Okay. I'll go."

"Good." He walked away but turned back when he reached his SUV. "I'll pick you up at eight o'clock tomorrow morning."

"Should I bring some food or—"

"I'll take care of everything," he said and left.

Grace watched through the window as Kennedy Archer pulled out of her drive. A camping trip. He wanted her to go into the woods with him and his boys. But she wasn't completely convinced it was wise to accompany him anywhere. She didn't like the strange emotions he evoked—the simmering attraction of old, the searing disappointment and embarrassment for her actions in high school, the burning resentment, anger, even humiliation she still felt. But she was fairly confident he wouldn't touch her if he said he wouldn't. And she had to get hold of that Bible.

Besides, she felt terrible about how she'd treated Teddy. He was too young to understand the complexity of her feelings toward his father and had taken her reaction to the news that he was an Archer as a personal rejection.

Her cell phone rang. Turning away from the window, she rushed to answer, hoping it was George. He hadn't called her since they'd spoken this morning.

"Any word on what went missing last night?" Clay asked.

Grace reeled in her disappointment. "Kennedy Archer has it."

"He told you so?"

"Basically."

There was a long silence. "Has he taken it to the police?"

"Not yet. I think he might give it back to me."

"You're kidding."

"No."

Grace heard Clay turn down the TV, which had been blaring in the background. "Why would he do that?"

"I'm not sure. I'll be able to tell you more on Monday."

"What's happening this weekend?"

"I'm going camping with him."

This information met with another prolonged silence, then her brother repeated, "You're going camping with Kennedy Archer."

"Crazy, I know."

"What about George?"

Grace lowered the blind against the sweltering heat. "Mom tell you about him?"

"Molly did, too. They said you were hoping to marry him. You think I don't know anything about your life?"

George had been acting so strange lately, she wasn't sure they were still together.

"I think we've broken up," she said.

"You're not sure?"

"No. Anyway, camping with Kennedy isn't a date."

"What would you call it?"

"An…outing with the kids."

"I can't imagine Kennedy Archer taking you camping with his boys unless he's interested in you."

"His youngest has been hanging out over here. It's Teddy who wants me to go."

Clay gave a disbelieving chuckle. "Yeah, right. Call me as soon as you get back. I can't wait to hear you eat your words."

"Just don't tell anyone where I'm going," she said. "We don't need to connect my name with Kennedy's and start a big fuss. It'll be easier to get that Bible back if he can continue on as he's always been."

"What are you going to say to Madeline, and Mom?"

"I'll tell them I have to go to Jackson to see George."

"Then that's my story, too. I'll talk to you later."

"Wait."

"What is it?"

"If Kennedy gives me the Bible and agrees to keep his mouth shut, don't you think we should move the—" she cleared her throat "—item we talked about?"

"No."

"But that way, even if it gets discovered, there'd be no evidentiary link to us." She realized what she was saying and quickly amended it. "If we're careful not to leave a link, that is."

"We can't be careful enough. It's not possible. We don't want to start digging around."

"We'll say you're making a few improvements to the farm. No big deal."

"Just get hold of the Bible, okay?"

Just get hold of the Bible? "You're sure about—"

"I'm positive."

She swallowed a sigh. "Okay."

A dial tone sounded in her ear. Frowning at the

handset, she considered calling George again but changed her mind. She refused to panic. There could be a thousand different reasons he hadn't returned her call.

But, deep down, she didn't believe any of them—except the one she feared most. He was giving up on her.

Fortunately, when Kennedy arrived at his mother's house, Teddy didn't press him for details about his visit to Grace's. As soon as he walked in, Teddy mumbled, "Did you do it?" and Kennedy nodded. Then Camille turned from peeling potatoes at the sink and started talking about how she'd known from the beginning that Grace wouldn't be nice to Teddy for very long. At that point, Kennedy and Teddy exchanged a knowing look and clammed up.

Although Kennedy refused to stay for dinner, it took him almost an hour to get his kids out of the house. First his mother needed help setting up a new printer. Then his father wanted to show him a biography on Jack Nicholson. By the time Kennedy drove away, the boys were starving and, despite his mother's tacit disapproval, they'd left a hot meal. But Kennedy wanted to get ready for the camping trip.

As they turned onto Main Street, he announced that Grace had agreed to go with them.

The news immediately silenced both boys' complaints about hunger pangs.

"Really?" Teddy said with eager anticipation.

"She said she'd go." Kennedy grinned, feeling more boyish than he had in a long while.

"No way! How'd you talk her into it, Dad?"

He'd used a small bribe, but he didn't give himself

away. He had a good reason for wanting to get to know Grace. He needed to decide if he still stood with his mother and everyone else where she was concerned. Or if he stood alone.

"So when are we leaving?" Heath asked.

Kennedy pulled into Rudy's Big Burger. He wasn't planning to cook tonight. They had too much to do. "First thing in the morning."

"Yippee!" Teddy cried.

Kennedy looked at his oldest son. "What about you, Heath? You glad she's coming?"

Heath hesitated, "Grandma won't like it…."

Kennedy parked the SUV. "Do we have to tell Grandma about everything we do?"

"No."

"Great. Then I say we keep this to ourselves."

"Okay," he said, that easily convinced, and climbed out.

Kennedy started to follow the boys toward the entrance, but Buzz pulled into the parking lot before he could reach the restaurant door.

His best friend rolled down his window. "Hey!"

Kennedy checked to make sure Teddy and Heath got safely into Rudy's, then walked over to say hello. As he drew nearer, he could see that Joe was in the truck with Buzz and felt his enthusiasm dim. Kennedy didn't like Joe nearly as much as he used to. Maybe that was because Joe seemed more egocentric by the day.

"You guys going to grab a burger?" Kennedy asked.

"No. Just saw your Explorer turn in and thought we'd say hello."

"Come in and sit down with us."

"We can't. Sarah's invited Joe to dinner." Buzz winked. "She's got her niece Melinda coming over."

"More matchmaking?" Kennedy wasn't sure how he'd been lucky enough to escape Sarah's eye as a partner for her recently divorced niece, but he was grateful. Melinda was too young. And he was tired of everyone in town wanting to set him up with some-one.

"She thinks I'm quite a catch." Joe stretched his arm across the back of the seat.

"Buzz is too loyal to tell her the truth, huh?" Kennedy and Joe always teased each other, but today Kennedy was at least partially serious.

Joe flipped him off, but Kennedy merely laughed.

"You and the kids can join us for dinner, too," Buzz said. "You know Sarah. She'll have enough to feed an army."

"Daddy!"

Kennedy turned as Teddy came out of the restau-rant. After making sure there were no cars, Kennedy waved him over, then put his hands on his son's shoul-ders and returned to the conversation. "Thanks for the invitation, but I think we'll eat here."

"Hey, Buzz, guess what?" Teddy said excitedly.

"What's that, kid?"

"We're going camping tomorrow."

Cursing silently, Kennedy tightened his grip on Teddy's shoulders, hoping to relay the message to shut up.

"You are?" Joe's enthusiasm indicated his interest was immediately piqued. "Where?"

"Pickwick Lake," Kennedy said, knowing Joe typ-ically liked to go farther.

"Why Pickwick?" he asked. "You always camp there."

Kennedy shrugged. "This is sort of a last-minute trip."

"If you're willing to go to Arkabutla instead, I'll go with you."

Joe loved to hunt and fish more than anyone Kennedy knew. And since all the other guys were married, he was forever searching for ways to entertain himself. But Kennedy had no intention of inviting Joe. After the pizza parlor incident, he could only imagine how happy Grace would be if Joe tagged along. "Maybe next time."

Buzz glanced at his watch. "We'd better get going. Sarah will be mad if we're late."

Kennedy thumped the door panel. "Have fun tonight. Tell Sarah and the kids I said hello."

"Will do."

"Don't break Melinda's heart, okay, Joe?" he added.

"Me?" Joe's smile hitched up on one side. "Come on, I'm too nice a guy for that."

Kennedy laughed as they drove off, but sighed in relief once they were gone. The last thing he needed was for Joe to find out that he and Grace were spending the weekend together and start running his big mouth.

Waiting for Kennedy and his boys, Grace twirled her rings around and around her fingers. Madeline had called wanting to come by last night, but Grace had complained of a headache and said she was going to bed. She didn't want to see her stepsister and pretend she didn't find anything at Jed's when she couldn't say with certainty whether or not that Bible would reappear and reveal her for the liar she was. She didn't want to talk to her mother, either. Feeling the way she did, she couldn't pretend she wasn't worried about the future, and knew she'd only upset Irene. With all that, and the whole town speculating as to why Madeline had broken into Jed's shop, Grace was actually glad she'd be out of town for the next few days.

Even if it was with Kennedy Archer.

She rubbed her forehead, wondering what the two of them would talk about. Back in high school, she'd stared longingly after him as he'd walked down the halls, or watched from the corner of the room as he'd slung an arm around Raelynn's shoulders, wishing, dreaming, that it could be her. But he'd barely acknowledged her existence. And since she'd returned to town, he'd caught her throwing up in the bathroom of the pizza parlor and fleeing the scene of a crime. Not impressive—and not much on which to build a friendship.

Teddy would be there, though. That boy had captured her heart. Maybe it was how sweet he was and how bright for someone so young. She'd never met a more loving child. As far as Grace was concerned, Kennedy didn't deserve Teddy any more than he'd deserved Raelynn. But life was never fair. She'd learned that long ago.

Hearing a car in the drive, she grabbed the cookies she'd baked and the small bag in which she'd packed a few toiletries, two pairs of shorts, some T-shirts, tennis shoes, suntan oil and a bathing suit. She'd told everyone in her family except Clay that she was going to Jackson for the weekend to see George—even though he hadn't returned her call—so she needed to slip away before someone spotted her getting into Kennedy's Explorer.

With that in mind, she opened the front door before Kennedy could knock.

"Hi," he said, disarming her with a smile so genuine she almost forgot she didn't like him.

"Wow," she muttered. "No wonder I was such an idiot."

He blinked in surprise. "What did you say?"

"Never mind." She let him take her bag while she locked the door, but he didn't walk off right away. He frowned at the flip-flops on her feet.

"You brought some proper shoes, didn't you?"

She nodded and moved toward the SUV, then stopped. "This is crazy," she said. "I shouldn't be going."

"Why?"

"I don't understand the point of it."

"Most people go camping to get away, have a good time."

She could relate to that; she definitely wanted to get away. But... "I know. It's just that we—"

"Will be fine," he finished. "You're not really going to disappoint them, are you?" He motioned to the car, where Teddy was hanging halfway out the window, waving at her. Another boy sat beside him, leaning up on his knees to get a better look at her.

She sighed. "I guess not."

"Good." Skirting her, he went to the back of the Explorer, where he loaded her bags. Then he brought the cookies around front.

"Hi, Grace!" Teddy said as she climbed in.

She smiled broadly at him. "Hi, Teddy."

"This is Heath." Kennedy indicated his other son as he slid behind the wheel. "He's ten."

"Another handsome boy," she said, and was rewarded with a shy smile.

They were all handsome, Grace realized. Especially Kennedy. If the boys grew up to resemble their father, they'd probably break more hearts than they could count.

With a sudden frown, she turned to stare out her window.

Kennedy must have sensed her change in mood because he squeezed her elbow. "Relax, okay?"

When she glanced over at him, the smile he gave her was impossible to resist.

Smiling in return, she buckled her seat belt and he handed her a coffee cup that had been in one of his cup holders. "It's hot. Be careful."

"Thanks."

"There's cream and sugar in that bag by your feet."

"We got doughnuts, too," Teddy announced, brandishing a large white bag.

"Sounds good," she said.

"We all guessed which kind would be your favorite," Teddy explained.

She could tell he thought he'd won. "So what made it into the bag?"

"For you? One of each," Kennedy said. "A chocolate doughnut with sprinkles, an apple fritter and a maple bar."

Teddy leaned forward. "Which is your favorite?"

"Who chose the sprinkles?" She expected Teddy or his brother to pipe up. She couldn't imagine Kennedy picking sprinkles, but he was the one who grinned at her.

"I did."

She arched her eyebrows. "Oh. You like sprinkles?"

"No, I was picking for you. That's your favorite, right?"

Clearing her throat, she turned her face away. "Actually, that's the only kind I *don't* like."

"Liar," he muttered and she couldn't help laughing.

"You'd better be careful lying to Dad," Teddy said. "Or it'll be torture time."

"What's torture time?" she asked.

"That's where he holds you down and tickles you till you beg for mercy," Heath said.

"Or he rubs his whiskers on your neck until you say 'uncle,'" Teddy added.

"I'd never say uncle," she said. "Not to your father."

Kennedy turned right on Mulberry Street and headed toward the Tennessee state line. To the boys, Grace knew he seemed as calm as ever, but she could see the devilish glint in his eye. "Then I suggest you never lie to me," he said softly. "Otherwise, I might have to prove you wrong."

"He can make you say it," Teddy agreed, nodding with absolute conviction.

Grace studied Kennedy for several long seconds. "No, he can't. He'll never get the best of me."

"You can't stop him," Heath insisted. "He's too strong."

"The trick is not to fight. The trick is to play dead," she said simply.

Kennedy looked over at her. "Play dead?"

She settled back in her seat. "What fun is torturing someone who doesn't care?"

"Is it that easy not to care?"

"It can become a habit," she said.

"You have to let your guard down sometime, Grace."

The boys had lost the gist of the conversation but were still watching them curiously. "Why?" she asked.

"Protecting yourself that well means you risk missing out on something spectacular."

"Oh, well." She folded her arms. "At least I'll survive."

Some kind of emotion entered his eyes, but she had no idea what it signified. "That's no way to live."

She tossed him an empty smile. "Some people just do what they have to."

Grace reminded Kennedy of a cactus. She could be prickly, of course. But in his mind, the comparison had more to do with the arid emotional environment she'd experienced in the past, the way she seemed to store what she absolutely needed inside her, and how she tried so hard to take very little from those around her. He wasn't sure he'd ever met anyone who demanded less from others or worked harder to maintain a tough exterior.

"What would happen if you agreed to pretend we just met?" he asked as they took the turnoff that would lead them, in only fifteen more minutes, to the lake.

She'd been dozing, but when he spoke, she sat up. He could almost hear her defenses snapping back into place. "What do you mean?"

"I'm asking what terrible thing you think might happen."

"I don't know," she said.

"*I* don't think anything terrible would happen."

"Because nothing terrible ever happens to you," she pointed out. "You seem to have been born under a lucky sign."

He lowered his voice, even though the boys were so busy with their Game Boys he knew they weren't listening. "I've already agreed not to press you for anything physical. What else do you have to worry about? That you might enjoy yourself? That you might actually let someone get to know you?"

"You already know me."

He thought of the rumors that had always circulated about her and her family, the Bible she'd dropped in the woods, her guarded manner. "No, I don't."

"That's funny," she said. "Because I know you."

"Not really. We never—"

She cut him off. "I remember the presentation you gave in fifth grade on the bottle-nosed dolphin. You made a mosaic out of broken glass. You threw it away after you got your A, but I stole it out of the trash and took it home." She laughed softly at herself. "To me, it was the most beautiful thing in the world. I hung it on the wall of my room for four years."

She pulled on her seat belt, obviously lost in thought. "And I remember when you broke your arm playing basketball in seventh grade. I knew you must really be hurt when you started to cry." Her voice trailed off as though it had affected her deeply. "I watched your mother pick you up from school in her new Cadillac that day."

"That injury was Joe's fault," he said, feeling uncomfortable because he couldn't remember anything about her except the nasty things his friends used to say. "He fouled me hard when I drove to the basket."

She didn't respond to his comment. She was too busy recalling incident after incident. "I can still picture you riding in your father's convertible T-Bird when you were nominated for royalty in high school," she said. "I knew you'd win." She laughed again. "And so did you."

He wished she'd stop….

"Then there was the time you shaved your head, along with the rest of the football team. Not your best look, for sure, but you pulled it off better than most. And the winning touchdown pass against Cambridge Heights our senior year that put us in the play-offs. And your speech on graduation night—"

"That's enough," he said softly. Even he remembered graduation night. She'd come up and offered him a tentative smile as though she wanted to wish him well—and he'd turned away from her as if she hadn't been standing there.

She didn't say anything else, and they rode in silence until they reached the campground. When he'd paid the fees and backed into the space he'd reserved, the boys piled out, talking excitedly about the s'mores they had planned for later. But Kennedy caught Grace's hand before she could open her door. He felt guilty for treating her so carelessly when they were kids, wanted to say something that would somehow erase what he'd done. But he couldn't find the right words.

Turning her hand over, he traced one of the lines on her palm. "I guess you know me better than I thought," he said simply and got out.

10

Grace didn't know what to make of Kennedy. They hiked, they fished, they skipped rocks in the lake. He threw Teddy and Heath in the water. Then he threw her in, too. But he insisted on giving her a piggyback ride to camp so her wet tennis shoes wouldn't get caked with mud. And he set up her tent and gave her the best pad and sleeping bag they owned. When Teddy and Heath picked her some wildflowers, he even found an old can and filled it with water so they could set them on the wooden picnic table near the campfire.

"Teddy told me you like the outdoors," he said as she was sitting on a log nearby, doing a crossword puzzle with Heath and Teddy.

"I do." She smiled, enjoying the smell of the fish he was grilling for dinner. Surprisingly, she couldn't remember a time when she'd felt so relaxed, so far removed from Stillwater and everything that had happened there. It was the Kennedy Archer charm, and for once, she was basking in his light.

"What's four down?" Heath asked, drawing her attention back to the holiday-themed crossword puzzle. "A babbling what?"

"It's some form of water," she said, hoping to help him figure it out.

"A stream?"

"The answer has five letters."

Concentration etched a frown on Teddy's face. "Lake only has four…."

"River has five," Heath said.

"But the last letter is a *k,*" Grace reminded him.

"I know!" Heath cried. "Brook!"

She gave his shoulder a pat. "Good job."

"Now let's do six across," Teddy said. "A bedtime what?"

"Story?" Heath answered, then immediately corrected himself. "No, it can only be four letters, and there's an *i* in the middle."

"Kiss?" Kennedy said.

Grace glanced up to find him looking at her. When their eyes met, the fluttery sensation in her stomach reminded her entirely too much of the hero worship she'd experienced when she was younger—so she immediately bent over the puzzle again.

"Hey, you're right, Dad," Teddy said. "I think it *is* kiss."

"What's the next one?" Kennedy asked.

"Nine down," Heath said. "What you say on Valentine's Day. Will you be what?"

"My Valentine!" Teddy shouted.

"That's two words, dummy," Heath said.

"It was a good guess," Grace said to soften Heath's criticism. "But in this case, I think it might be 'mine.'"

Once again, Grace felt Kennedy's gaze on her but refused to acknowledge him.

"Do *you* have a Valentine?" Teddy asked as she watched him write the letters.

She scooted over because Heath was trying to

squeeze between her and a knot on the log. "You mean a boyfriend?"

"Yeah."

She thought of George's neglect. "No, not really."

"Not really?" Heath repeated.

"We've broken up," she explained.

Teddy leaned forward to see around the fall of her hair. "But you like him?"

"Sure, I like him."

"Are you going to *marry* him?" he said, his meaningful smile making Grace laugh.

"Maybe someday."

"Why not now?" Heath wanted to know.

Grace wished Kennedy would stop his boys from asking her such personal questions—but she doubted he would. Although he appeared to be focused on cooking dinner, she suspected he was listening as intently as they were. "I—"

"Don't want to get married?" Teddy inserted.

"It's not that. I just…I'm not ready, I guess."

"Oh." Teddy seemed to consider her answer. "When will you be ready? Next week?"

She laughed again. "Maybe when I move back to Jackson in a few months."

"I don't think you should ever move away." If Teddy had made this comment, Grace might not have been surprised. But hearing it from Heath, who didn't show his emotions to the same extent, took her aback.

"Why not?" she asked.

"Because then you won't be able to go camping with us anymore."

"I see. Well—" she grinned at Kennedy "—I'm sure there'll be another nice lady to take my place."

"My mom's the only one who's come with us before," Heath said.

The mention of Raelynn cast a sudden pall over the group, confirming to Grace how vital the wife and mother of this family had been to all of them. She put one arm around Heath and the other around Teddy. "I'll bet she's gazing down on you from heaven," she said.

Teddy searched the sky as if he hoped to see her. "You think so? Right now?"

"Probably. She was so good she must be an angel. I believe God allows angels to look after the ones they love."

Teddy blinked quickly, obviously fighting tears, and Grace decided to give the Archer men a moment of privacy. "I'm going to take a walk," she said. "You two help your dad, okay?"

"Okay," Heath said, but no one seemed particularly eager to focus on anything besides her. She could feel all three pairs of eyes staring after her as she slipped away.

Grace loved the cool lap of the water against her ankles, the sand squishing between her toes. But Teddy's questions about her boyfriend, and the strange way she felt whenever Kennedy looked at her, had her thinking of George. What was going on with the man she planned to marry? He knew she wanted to talk to him. Surely he'd had a moment to contact her since she'd called yesterday morning—late last night, if no other time. For the past two years, they'd been close enough to call each other regardless of the hour.

Taking her cell from the pocket of her shorts, she checked once again to make sure she had service.

Her signal was as strong as ever. Her battery was fine, too.

So much for that excuse, she thought, and punched George's number. His recorder answered almost before the phone could ring. "Hello. This is George E. Dunagan. I'm unable to come to the phone right now, but if you leave a message I'll get back to you shortly."

She waited for the beep. "George, why haven't you called me? I'd really like to hear from you, so give me a ring when you get a minute, okay?" she said and hung up.

It was Saturday evening. She and George generally went out with friends, to a movie or to dinner. Where was he tonight?

"Grace?" Kennedy came through the trees behind her. "Dinner's ready."

She nodded but continued to admire the reflection of the sunset on the glistening water. "Beautiful, isn't it?" she said.

When he didn't respond, she glanced back at him. "I've never seen anything like it," he replied, but he never took his eyes off her.

Kennedy watched Grace from across the fire, marveling at how comfortable she seemed to be with his boys. He wasn't sure what he'd expected, but it certainly wasn't the laughing, patient, doting woman he and his children had enjoyed for most of the day. When she was around Teddy and Heath, all trace of the hostility he'd witnessed at the pizza parlor disappeared. So did the distrust that entered her eyes the moment the boys wandered off and left her temporarily alone with him.

For the past fifteen minutes, the four of them had been roasting marshmallows, and she'd been smiling the entire time. Teddy and Heath kept accidentally setting their marshmallows on fire, but that didn't stop them from stuffing their mouths full or proudly offering the charred results to Grace.

For Grace's part, she accepted whatever Teddy or Heath gave her and pretended to like it.

"That was a good one, wasn't it?" Teddy said as she licked her fingers after eating another of his blackened gifts.

"Excellent," she said. When her eyes briefly locked with Kennedy's, he sent her a wry grin and she responded with a little shrug that made him wonder how Joe or anyone else could think anything but the best of her. Maybe she had a prickly exterior, but her heart was soft. Probably too soft for her own good.

Kennedy rotated the marshmallows on his own stick, being careful to keep them out of the flames. If they turned out perfectly, maybe Grace would accept one from *him*....

"Isn't this fun?" Teddy had chocolate spread from ear to ear, but his smile was almost as wide.

Grace rocked back on her log perch, leaning on her palms and stretching out the smooth, bare legs Kennedy had insisted she smear with mosquito repellant. "It is."

"You like being with us, don't you?" Heath asked eagerly.

He suspected that her slight hesitation was imperceptible to the boys, but Kennedy noticed it right away. "Of course," she said.

Teddy stabbed another two marshmallows with the pointy end of his stick. "Does that mean you're *not* going to vote for Vicki Nibley?"

Again, Grace met Kennedy's eyes through the rising smoke. "Someone needs to vote for poor Mrs. Nibley, don't you agree?"

"Not you," Heath said. "What about our dad?"

"I think enough people like your father."

"A man can never have too many friends," Kennedy said, moving his marshmallows to a safer part of the fire.

She wiped away the moisture on her lip caused by the heat of the flames. "So you have to go after the lone holdout?" she challenged.

He grinned at her. "So you have to side with the underdog?"

She laughed as she shoved the hair out of her face. "The underdog needs me much more than you do."

He was beginning to wonder about that. He couldn't stop his gaze from trailing after her wherever she went, kept imagining how her skin would feel if she ever let him touch her.

He raised his marshmallows higher above the hungry fire. What he wanted required a slow, steady hand. In this—and other things—he knew he could only be as successful as he was patient.

"Dad, your marshmallows are going to fall off!" Heath said only a couple of minutes later.

He saw that they were a toasty golden-brown and were sagging dangerously low.

Kennedy held a hand under his stick so they wouldn't drop into the dirt. "Now they'll melt in your mouth," he said and circled the fire to give them to Grace.

When she realized they were for her, she waved him away. "No, thanks. You go ahead."

He frowned, hoping she'd reconsider. "Are you sure? I made them for you."

The surprise in her expression told him he'd communicated the fact that it mattered to him whether or not she accepted his small offering, and he wished he hadn't been so obvious. Embarrassed, he started to turn back, but she reached out and caught his hand.

"Actually, they look pretty good. I guess I have room for one more," she said.

And that was when he knew he was right about Grace Montgomery—and almost everyone else in Stillwater, especially his mother and Joe, were wrong.

When Grace's cell phone rang, it was nearly three in the morning, but she didn't mind. She'd been lying in her tent for at least four hours, trying to sleep. But every time she closed her eyes, she saw Kennedy. She heard his laugh when he'd tossed them all so easily in the water. Felt the strength in his arms when he carried her back to camp. Saw the boyish eagerness on his face when she'd accepted his marshmallows.

Which made her particularly glad to read George's name on her lit screen.

"Finally," she muttered and pressed the Talk button. "There you are," she said. "I was beginning to think you'd forgotten all about me."

"Sorry. I…I should've called earlier."

The eagerness she usually heard in his voice was gone, and his tone suggested there was more he wasn't saying. "But—"

"This isn't easy for me, Grace."

Her stomach tightened into a hard knot, but she lowered her voice so she wouldn't wake Kennedy or his boys. "What's wrong, George?"

"I've met someone else," he blurted.

Grace sucked air between her teeth as though someone had just punched her. Could it be true? George loved her. She knew that. He'd always loved her. Which meant something else was going on. His faith was dwindling. She needed to convince him she'd be ready to make a commitment soon.

"George, you—you're overreacting to having me gone, that's all. I'll be back in a little while. I can come see you for a few days next week if you want."

There was a stilted pause. She could feel him weakening, so the resolve in his next words shocked her. "I can't, Grace. I've waited for you long enough. You know how I feel about you, how I'll always feel. But even Petra—"

"You've been talking to your sister about me?"

"Why are you whispering?"

"I'm camping with friends."

"What friends?"

"For someone who's seeing another woman, you sound pretty possessive, George."

"It's just that you've never mentioned any friends in Stillwater."

"You don't know them."

"Of course I don't know them. Who are they?"

"Someone I went to high school with, okay? It's no big deal," she said, and wished that was true. Unfortunately, anything to do with Kennedy seemed like a very big deal indeed. "What did Petra say?" she asked.

"I know you don't believe it, but she likes you, Grace. She's just worried about me. Says our relationship is too one-sided."

"One-sided means she doesn't think I care about you. I plan on marrying you, having a family with you. That's not caring?"

"If you really wanted to marry me, you would've done it by now."

Grace hid inside her sleeping bag, trying not to smell Kennedy's cologne on the lining. "That's not necessarily true."

"Yes, it is. Let's be honest. You practically cringe when I touch you."

Her hot breath bounced back at her inside the bag, making her think of a tomb. She was completely shut off. Alone. "No, I don't!"

"Do you assume I hadn't noticed?"

Grace stared into the blackness. Sometimes she tried to feign the interest she didn't feel naturally. But she didn't *hate* making love with George. He was patient, gentle. "I don't *cringe*."

"You don't enjoy making love."

"Once in a while that's true," she admitted. "But not always."

"Not always?"

At times she felt as though she was almost normal. "Right."

He chuckled bitterly. "That's real passion."

Grace wondered whether he'd feel any better if she finally explained *why* she struggled so much with physical intimacy. But she feared it was already too late. And she wasn't sure it would be fair to expect George to understand and compensate—which, knowing him, he'd probably try to do. The past was her problem. He had the chance to get out of the relationship, to start seeing someone who wasn't damaged as she was, and she cared enough to want that for him. Why should he have to pay for what had happened to her?

The tightness in her throat made it difficult to find her voice. "So who is this other woman?"

"You really want to know?" he asked.

"Maybe it would help if I could picture you with someone who'll make you happy."

He cursed softly. "Don't say that, Grace. It only makes this harder for me."

"Who is it?" she repeated.

"You know my secretary, Heather?"

Her mind flashed back to the strangled sound of Heather's voice the last time she'd called. "You're seeing *Heather?*"

"No, her older sister came by the office, and…well, we sort of hit it off."

Something sharp seemed to be stabbing Grace in the chest, again and again. Tightening her grip on the phone, she tried to slow her breathing, to bear the pain. "Have you slept with her?" she whispered.

There was an awkward silence. "Yes."

The darkness pressed closer. Hot. Cloying. Terrifying. Just like that night when she was thirteen and she woke with the reverend's hand clamped tightly over her mouth….

I won't think about it! But she couldn't stop the tears burning behind her eyes.

"That's how I…that's when I realized what it felt like to be with a woman who really wanted me," he said.

Grace couldn't speak. She didn't know what to say. She could imagine how wonderful it must've been for George to feel desired—and couldn't even hold what he'd done against him. This was her fault, not his. She couldn't give him what he wanted. She'd locked her sexuality away long ago. Those early experiences with the reverend had left too many scars.

She squirmed out of the sleeping bag, gasping for air.

"Grace?" he said after several seconds.

Someone was stirring in the other tent. She was afraid of waking Heath and Teddy. "What?" she managed to respond, her voice barely audible.

"Are you okay?"

She burrowed deeper into the bag, hoping to smother all sound along with the pain. "Yes," she lied.

Silence. "I'm sorry," he said at last. "I know we talked about trying again once you got back, but…I'm afraid to miss this opportunity with Lisa because I can't believe anything will really change between us."

"Don't apologize." She swallowed hard. "I—I understand."

"I never meant to hurt you, Grace."

"I know." Her nose was running. Sniffling, she wiped her eyes. "Can we still be friends?"

"I don't think so." He spoke as though the words had been wrenched from him, but they drove through her like a pickax. "I'm afraid we'd fall right back into the same relationship," he said. "Whoever I'm seeing could never compare to you. Not if I don't make a clean break and put what we had behind me."

Grace couldn't imagine returning to Jackson without George there, waiting for her. They'd been together for three and a half years. Except for the fact that he wanted to make love far more often than she did, their relationship was comfortable. But he was right. Their love life wasn't spectacular, and probably never would be.

"You've been good to me," she admitted, trying to keep the tears from her voice.

"I love you," he said.

For a second, Grace felt the worst kind of panic. She wanted to fight for him, promise him anything that would make him change his mind. But he deserved someone who was madly in love with him, who would marry him without reservation and who would enjoy the physical aspect of the relationship far more than she did.

"I love you, too," she admitted.

"Grace?"

He said her name with such doubt she fought a second impulse to capitalize on it. "You're doing the right thing," she said briskly and hung up.

Kennedy had heard the phone ring, the whispering and then the zipper of Grace's tent. He knew she was going somewhere. He guessed it was to the bathroom. But if she'd taken the flashlight he'd given her for that purpose, she didn't turn it on. And when she walked away, it wasn't in the direction of the Port-a-Potties, which were several campsites to their left.

Was she sneaking off to search for the Bible he'd stuck in the glove compartment of his Explorer? He probably would've let her go, but he didn't think that was it. Something had happened during that phone call. He hadn't heard enough to follow the whole conversation, but he suspected Grace was upset.

He listened to her footsteps recede. She seemed to be heading down to the lake.

Being careful not to wake the children, he slipped out of his sleeping bag, pulled on a pair of jeans and hurried after her. He felt reluctant to invade her privacy, but he wanted to make sure she was okay.

Following at a distance, he hung back in the trees when she got to the beach. Once she passed into the moonlight, he realized she was dressed in a bathing suit and planned to go into the water.

At that point, he almost stopped her. The weather had cooled. She'd freeze when she got out….

But then he saw her dash a hand across her face and thought maybe she needed the solitude.

Without a moment's hesitation, she waded into the water and plunged below the surface as though seeking oblivion.

Kennedy held his own breath until she came up for air, but he didn't feel much better when she began to swim hell-bent for the middle of the lake.

Eventually, she turned toward shore and he started to relax. But she didn't get out as he expected. Before she reached shallow water, she flipped around and glided out even farther.

"Shit." Shoving his hands in his pockets to help combat the chill, he shifted anxiously on his feet. He didn't want her in that big lake alone. The dark of night made the water look more like ink, and most of the time he could barely see her. What if she went under and didn't reappear? How would he ever find her?

He yearned to go in after her, but her grief seemed so profound. He knew she wouldn't welcome the intrusion. Maybe someone else could help her, but he was the last person she'd want as a witness to her pain.

She'll get out soon, he told himself. But the minutes ticked by and she didn't show any signs of slowing down.

She had to be exhausted. Not to mention half-frozen.

He couldn't take it anymore. Striding down to the water's edge, he cupped his hands around his mouth. "Grace!"

At the sound of his voice, she stopped. He was

pretty sure she saw him standing there, waving for her to get out. But it didn't do any good. A moment later, she continued swimming in the opposite direction.

"What the hell?" He almost called out a second time, but if she wouldn't listen, there wasn't any point. Besides, he might wake the boys and the other campers.

Nearly ripping his faded jeans in his rush to get them off, he tossed them on the sand. He was wearing only a pair of boxer briefs, but he didn't care about modesty. He couldn't see Grace at all.

The cold jolt of the water stole his breath as he dashed into it. Ignoring the sharp sting, he dived under. She was coming in whether she wanted to or not.

His lungs burned as he forced himself to go as far as he could without air. Finally he surfaced and began swimming freestyle. After several minutes, he stopped to get his bearings and heard her splashing not far ahead of him. Obviously, she knew he was coming and didn't want him to catch up. But Kennedy wasn't convinced she could make it back without him. Not after swimming so long already.

With a silent curse, he concentrated on closing the gap between them. By the time he reached her, her movements were growing sluggish. She was tired—and hurting somehow. But fear for her safety made him angry.

"What the hell are you doing?" he shouted, grabbing hold of her ankle and dragging her toward him.

"G-go away!" she gurgled, flailing her arms in the water.

He wiped the droplets from his face. "You're going to drown us both!"

She struggled to keep her head up. "I d-didn't ask you t-to come out here."

There wasn't anything to be gained by arguing. They needed to get back before she was completely spent. Circling her waist with one arm, he began towing her to shore.

"Let go of me," she said, trying to tear herself away. "I d-don't need y-you."

"You need me more than you think," he responded. "Quit fighting."

"L-leave me alone, and—and go b-back to your k-kids."

Her teeth were chattering so badly he could hardly understand her. "I'm not leaving you anywhere."

She pried at his fingers. "K-Kennedy."

He squeezed tighter. He needed her to understand how determined he was, before she exhausted his strength, too. "Relax. You're along for the ride."

She went limp, and he suspected she was actually grateful for an excuse to give in.

Kennedy could touch bottom long before Grace could. Breathing heavily, he stood at the earliest opportunity and pulled her against his chest, wanting to make sure he hadn't drowned her in his efforts to save her. "Hey," he said, his voice gentle now that he knew she wasn't going to disappear in the lake. "What's wrong? What happened tonight?"

She didn't answer, and he couldn't tell whether it was lake water or tears that rolled down her cheeks. "Who was on the phone?" he asked.

"No one," she said, shaking violently. He hugged her close. They were cold, but they'd be far colder once they left the water.

Although she stiffened at the contact, he ignored that, too, because he wanted to comfort her.

Surprisingly, as soon as his bare stomach touched

hers, she wrapped her legs around his waist and grabbed on as a child would. She even buried her face in his neck.

"You're okay," he said, tightening his arms around her.

They didn't speak for several minutes, but she slowly stopped shaking. After a while, she lifted her head. "Why are we camping together, Kennedy?" she asked. "Why did you bring me here?"

He couldn't help letting his gaze drift to her lips. He'd brought her because of the reverend's Bible. He had a decision to make. But he was fascinated with her, too. "I don't know," he said. "You—you get to me somehow."

She shook her head. "No. I'm no good for you. For your own sake, keep your distance." She tried to swim away, but he caught her easily enough.

"I'll decide what's best for me, Grace."

Their stomachs touched again, and so did their bare legs and arms. "But you don't know what you're getting into."

Considering her possible past, he supposed she was right. But she already mattered more to him than any uneasiness he felt about that. "I'm a big boy," he told her. "I think I can handle it."

"You don't understand—"

"Shh…" He didn't want to hear any more. Silencing her the quickest way he knew how, he rubbed his lips lightly against hers. In Stillwater, he'd told her he wouldn't touch her, but he hadn't expected her to take a swim in the middle of the night. Now that he had her in his arms, he couldn't seem to let go. Especially after she closed her eyes and parted her lips, as if she wanted him to give her a real kiss.

Taking her bottom lip in his mouth, he slid his tongue very deliberately against hers. He longed to slip his hand under the elastic of her bikini while he was kissing her, to press a finger deep inside her at the same time. But he had to be careful or he'd ruin whatever was happening between them. The way Grace made him feel wasn't anything he wanted to lose. She was the first woman he'd desired since Raelynn.

Slowly, the tension in Grace's body eased, and she opened her mouth wider. Her response made every muscle in his body grow taut with hope and expectation. "I knew you'd taste as sweet as honey," he told her.

She frowned in confusion.

"What is it?" he murmured.

"You just kissed me as if…"

"What?"

"As if I mattered to you," she finished.

He winced at the thought that she'd find it so hard to believe. "You do matter to me," he said.

She tried to pull away, but he wouldn't let her. "Don't," he said.

She scowled. "This isn't good."

"Are you kidding? It's the best thing I've felt in a long time."

At the hoarse quality in his voice, her eyes locked with his. "I know what you want," she whispered.

He brought his forehead to hers. "All I want is to hear you say you like this, too."

"No."

"You won't say it? Or you don't like it?"

"I don't like it."

He studied her, measured the feel of her body against his. "You're lying. Fortunately I can always tell."

"You don't know anything."

"You don't have to be afraid of me, Grace. I won't hurt you."

"I'm not afraid of you. I'm afraid of me."

"Why?"

Her demeanor changed instantly. "If I give you what you want, will you leave me alone?"

He could think of scarcely anything except getting rid of the scraps of fabric between them. He was rock-hard and breathing heavily. But he could tell she was looking for any excuse to write him off, and he wasn't about to hand her one.

Ignoring her question, he said, "Let's get you warm and dry," and began carrying her to shore.

She tried to stop him. "No. Let's finish this. Put it behind us."

"Maybe someday. Not now."

She lifted his hand to her breast, and his fingers curled instinctively around the soft flesh. "See? There you go. That's what you're after. I'll give it to you. Right here."

There was something reckless, even dangerous about her. Kennedy wanted to make love, but he knew her offer wasn't as straightforward as it appeared.

"And then what?" he asked hesitantly.

"Then nothing. It's over. You go brag to your friends, tell everyone in town they were right about me. Do whatever you want. But you have to promise you'll never contact me again."

With a grimace, he pulled his hand away. "Sorry, not interested."

"Still too good for me?" she taunted.

He caught his breath as she wrapped her legs around him and thrust her pelvis convincingly against him. She was after something. But it definitely wasn't sex. She wanted to diffuse the tension between them and move on. The question was why. The past? The present? Fear of intimacy? Fear of reprisal?

"Too good?" he echoed, laughing mirthlessly. "What's wrong, Grace? Feeling threatened?"

She immediately released him and started to tread water. "Of course not. I'm just looking for any angle to get my stepfather's Bible back."

"It's not that simple."

"I don't know what you mean."

"I think you're afraid you might actually like me if you gave yourself half a chance."

"I've always liked you," she said. "Who hasn't?"

He knew how she'd felt about him years ago. Was it possible those feelings hadn't completely disappeared? "You have a strange way of showing it," he said.

"And you have children to worry about. I'm the last person you should spend your time with. Take what you want from me, return the Bible, and that'll be the end of it."

"Oh, now I understand," he said.

"What?"

"You're willing to give me a quickie here in the lake so you can prove to yourself that's all I was after, is that it? Then you can convince yourself I'm the bastard you always thought I was."

"If that's the case, you should be damn glad of it." She sounded slightly panicked. "You're the one who'd benefit."

He resumed pulling her to shore. "No, thanks."

"Listen to me."

"No. You feel bad about something, and you're trying to make yourself feel even worse. But I won't allow you to use me to do it."

"Why do you care how I feel? What I think?" When she couldn't wrench her wrist away, she splashed water at him.

He turned his face in the other direction, but he wasn't about to let her go. No way would he risk having her swim back into the middle of the lake.

"Come on, Kennedy, I'm *Grinding Gracie,* remember? What was it Joe said at the pizza parlor? For a smile, I'll spread my legs? Well, this time I'm not asking for even that much."

"Stop it," he snapped. "What happened in high school makes me sick." He kept pulling her along.

"You afraid I'll tell someone about the two of us? That it'll ruin your spotless reputation if other people find out you wanted to get down and dirty with me?"

"I'm not worried about that."

"So what's wrong? Why the hesitation?"

"Maybe I don't like your terms."

"You don't want to give me the Bible?"

"It has nothing to do with the Bible."

"Then what *terms?*" she repeated in disbelief. "I said no strings attached. For a guy like you, how does an offer get any better than that?"

He whirled to confront her. "For a guy like me? You don't even know me! We're not in high school anymore, Grace."

"You think I don't know that?"

"I think it's hard for you to forget." He flung the wet hair out of his eyes. "And I hate that I'm part of the reason."

"If you don't want me, go on about your business." She could finally touch bottom. Using her newfound traction, she wriggled out of his grasp, but he turned around so fast her eyes widened.

Instinctively, she stepped back as his gaze wandered hungrily over her face, her mouth, her mostly bare shoulders.

"I want you all right." He untied the fabric of her bikini top, which fell down to reveal what he'd seen in the window, and dreamed about ever since. Still, he didn't touch her there. Lifting her chin with one finger, he brushed his lips over hers once again. "But it's not *sex* I'm after," he murmured. "I want to make love to you, Grace. In case you haven't learned it yet, there's a difference."

She didn't move, didn't speak.

He raised his head. "Now, if you're not back in your tent in five minutes, I'm taking that damn Bible to the police. Understood?"

Without waiting for an answer, he let her go. Then he left the water and marched off toward camp because he knew that if he stayed another second he'd take anything she was willing to give him, even if it wasn't everything he wanted.

11

Grace sat on the shore and stared out at the lake, not quite sure what had happened a few minutes earlier. She'd left her tent in a torrent of pain and somehow wound up in the water with Kennedy Archer, experiencing the very desire she couldn't summon for George. How could her life be so perverse?

Closing her eyes, she remembered the warm thrust of his tongue, the pressure of his erection as she tightened her legs around him. The memory alone caused goose bumps to rise on her arms. If only she could feel that for George, maybe she'd have a shot at happiness....

But *Kennedy?*

"No," she muttered and buried her face in her hands. She was shivering uncontrollably, but she embraced the cold, hoping its razor-like edge would remind her that she could never trust him, never believe that he might really care about her. She was so different from Raelynn, whom he'd idolized. And she was painfully aware of what she'd done with most of his friends. If she couldn't forgive herself for those incidents, how could she expect him to forgive her? They shouldn't even be seen together. His family would hate her. And she couldn't be any more honest with him about the events of eighteen years ago than she could with

George. The truth, if it came out, could destroy him as well as her.

But it was his two sons who worried her most. What if they began to care about her?

Resting her forehead on her knees, she wrapped her arms tightly around her legs and tried to stop shaking long enough to figure out what to do. She was tempted to leave town immediately, head right back to the big city. But George needed her out of his life, and her family needed her in Stillwater.

"Grace, come back to camp," Kennedy said from somewhere behind her, and she realized he hadn't gone to bed as she'd assumed.

She shook her head in disbelief. He was so responsible. He'd definitely make a good mayor, she thought.

"I'm coming." She stood, brushed the sand from her legs and met up with him halfway to their campsite. She'd tied her bathing suit on again, but when he looked at her, she still felt exposed, raw, hungry.

It's not sex I'm after. I want to make love to you, Grace....

What would that be like? For once, she wanted to hold nothing back. With him, she sensed that would be possible.

But she'd never find out.

They walked in silence, without touching. Once she reached her tent, she murmured a good-night and started to go inside, but Kennedy caught her by the wrist.

"Grace?" His voice was a mere whisper.

She looked up to find him wearing an intense expression.

"Do you know what's inside the reverend's Bible?"

"Inside it?" she echoed in confusion.

"Did you ever have the chance to read what he wrote?"

"No. What did he write?"

"A lot of it was about you."

She didn't dare say anything.

"I read it, and it's made me wonder…"

Apprehension gnawed at her, and her pulse raced. "What?" she said hesitantly.

"Did…did the reverend ever—"

Her stomach tensed. "I don't want to talk about him," she said.

Taking both her hands, he held them reassuringly. "Did he…you know, touch you when you were a girl? Touch you in the wrong places and in the wrong way?"

The breath seemed to freeze in Grace's lungs, creating a crushing tightness. For a split second, she wanted to admit it. To divulge her pain and outrage at last. To cast off the heavy burden of her filthy secret, a secret she hadn't even been willing to share with a therapist.

But she couldn't get past the feeling that she was somehow to blame for what her stepfather had done. Like those encounters with Kennedy's friends in high school, the shame of it burned her almost as deeply as the betrayal. Besides, she couldn't give anyone an inkling that she and her family might've had such a powerful motive for murder. Especially Kennedy. He knew about the Bible. She was sure he'd turn on her at some point. All his friends and his family were against her. And when he did, the consequences of one weak moment could destroy her entire family.

"No." She told herself to look him in the eye, but she couldn't. She was afraid he'd see right through her, the way he had when they were in the water.

She tried to move away, but he hung on to her. "I think he did," he said stubbornly.

He was pressing her, searching for the truth. She had to be more convincing. "Are you crazy?" She forced a scoffing tone into her voice. "There are people in this town who'd condemn even you for saying such a thing. The reverend was above reproach— wasn't he?"

His expression didn't change as he stared down at her. "I don't know. You tell me."

He seemed so aware of every nuance. She needed more space. "He—of course. I mean, everyone knows what a g-good man he was. He—" The words seemed to congeal in her throat. She knew she should continue to praise her stepfather, but she couldn't do it. Not here. Not now. Not to Kennedy.

"*Was* he a good man?" Kennedy whispered.

She struggled to hold herself together, trying to catch her breath. Too much had happened tonight. Everything was running into a great kaleidoscope of emotion. Pain. Anger. Disappointment. Arousal. Hope. Kennedy seemed to provide the anchor she craved, but she knew that was an illusion. As soon as she grabbed on, she'd find out there was really nothing there. He was Mr. Stillwater and she was Grinding Gracie.

"Did he molest you, Grace?"

She wanted to cover her ears. "No. Stop it! I can't—I…just shut up, please!" Finally, she managed to wrench free and dart into the protective cover of her tent. There, blinking back tears, she held her breath to see what Kennedy would do next. She prayed he'd accept what she'd told him and believe it. But she knew she hadn't been nearly as persuasive as she should've been. Especially when she heard him pacing outside.

"God," she heard him say. "If he's not dead already, I'll kill him myself."

Kennedy lay awake long after Grace had stopped stirring. He supposed she'd finally fallen asleep. He hoped so; she needed the rest. But for him sleep was impossible. He couldn't shut down. In his mind, he kept seeing the moonlight on Grace's ashen face when he'd asked if the reverend had abused her—seeing the truth in her eyes—and kept wondering how far the bastard had taken the molestation. Had he raped her? If so, how old had she been? And had he done it once? Twice? More?

The thought of the reverend forcing a small, defenseless Grace to lie beneath him evoked a white-hot anger.

Pressing his thumb and finger into his closed eyes, Kennedy attempted to blot out the vision. It was making him nauseous. Nothing could stop him from feeling Grace's fear and helplessness as an innocent child, the guilt and self-loathing she seemed to feel as an adult. What he now believed explained so much, didn't it?

He understood why Grace had acted out in a sexual manner during high school. He'd heard that was common with people who'd been molested as children. He also understood why she'd been so desperate for attention. With such serious problems at home, her emotional needs weren't being met. Even though the reverend was gone by the time she reached high school, things certainly hadn't improved, at least not a great deal. Her mother didn't have much of an education and wasn't well liked. The best job she could get required her to work long hours for little pay. The Montgomerys were surrounded by suspicion, constantly the brunt of jokes or the subject of snide glances and unkind whispers, many of which ended with "white trash."

The beautiful woman he'd just held in the water was anything but trash. Recalling the jibes and taunts his friends had lobbed Grace's way and, worse, the adoration and hope he'd seen shining in her eyes whenever she looked at him, turned his guilt into a physical ache.

"Why?" he muttered. Why couldn't he have stepped outside his perfect world long enough to show her some compassion? To help turn the tide of disapproval and dislike?

Obviously, he was as bad as Joe and the others. He'd done nothing. And yet she'd survived. She'd graduated from high school. She'd pulled herself together and gone to college, even law school. She'd become an assistant D.A. and never lost a case.

Impressive. Her accomplishments, once she left Stillwater, were *more* than impressive. And yet the scars remained. He knew that.

The day Clay appeared at school and bloodied Tim's face came to mind. Clay was incredibly strong, and had been even in high school. As a junior, he could bench-press over three hundred pounds. A plaque still hung in the weight room with his name on it—the "Over 300 Club." Kennedy hadn't achieved that status until he was in college, and he'd never beat Clay's record.

Had Clay or Irene discovered what the reverend was doing to Grace and killed him in an act of rage? Or had they acted more methodically to ensure that he could never hurt her again? It was even possible that little Grace had finally done something about the abuse, and her family was covering for her.

Regardless, Kennedy was certain the story they'd long told wasn't true. Before finding that Bible and seeing everything the reverend had written about Grace, he'd been willing to give them the benefit of the doubt. Sometimes strange, inexplicable things happened. But he couldn't accept that anymore. He suspected the Montgomerys were as guilty as everybody claimed.

But, knowing what he did, could he blame them?

The sun beat down on Grace's tent. She rolled over, still sleepy but unable to tolerate the sweltering heat. It was fairly early in the morning—about eight-thirty, she guessed—but the boys and Kennedy were already up. She could hear them talking, smell the bacon frying.

"She knows you're a nice guy now, right, Dad?" Teddy asked.

"We'll talk about it later," Kennedy replied, his voice low.

"She likes you. I can tell."

Kennedy cleared his throat. "Teddy, that's enough."

"Okay. But you like her, too, don't you? She's pretty, huh, Dad?"

"She's pretty," he admitted.

Grace muffled a groan as she recalled the events of the previous night in brutal detail. She'd kissed Kennedy, offered to have sex with him. She should be embarrassed about that, except she knew she'd do it again if it would put what they were feeling behind them. She could sense trouble coming, trouble that seemed particularly ominous when she thought about the recognition on Kennedy's face as she lied so poorly at her tent door a few hours earlier.

Why hadn't she been stronger?

Rolling onto her side, she spotted the cell phone. It wasn't until that moment that she thought of George. She'd lost the man she was going to marry. Almost every facet of her life had changed last night.

"She's *really* pretty," Heath concurred.

"Grab those eggs and bring them to me," Kennedy said.

Throwing off the cover of her sleeping bag, she told herself she might as well face Kennedy and get it over with. Maybe they could simply forget their encounter at the lake. Pretend it had never happened and go their separate ways.

But she didn't really want to forget what she'd felt.

"I can never get it right," she muttered.

"I think she's waking up," Teddy said with an eagerness that made Grace smile despite everything.

"Stay here, Teddy," Kennedy admonished. "Give her a chance to get dressed."

"I was just going to say hello," he muttered.

After pulling on a tank top and a pair of shorts, Grace gathered her toiletries, and stepped out of the tent wearing flip-flops on her feet. She knew her hair probably looked a fright since she'd gone to bed with it wet, but Kennedy didn't seem to notice. He turned at the sound of her approach and something invisible passed between them. It wasn't the self-consciousness she'd expected to feel. It was more indefinable than that. She'd never experienced it before.

Fleetingly, she remembered clinging to him, rubbing against him in the lake. Thank goodness they'd been dressed or things might've ended much differently.

"Morning," he said, handing her a piece of bacon.

She mumbled a response, focusing on the salty taste of the meat so she wouldn't have to consider that he now knew more about her than almost anyone else in the world.

"Pancakes will be ready in a few minutes," he said.

"Smells great." She wished she could read the expression in his eyes. "Do I have time to grab a quick shower?"

"Sure."

"I'll walk you over," Heath said.

Grace took the boy's hand.

"I'll come, too," Teddy said and insisted on carrying her bag.

The sound of an engine caught Grace's attention as they started off. She glanced back, expecting it to be another camper coming or going. But that wasn't the case at all.

They had company.

"Oh, no," she said, immediately recognizing the driver.

"What's the matter?" Teddy asked.

As Joe Vincelli hopped out of his truck, Teddy stayed at her side, but Heath ran over to greet him.

"Hi, Joe! I didn't know you were coming."

Neither did Grace. "You invited him?" she muttered to Kennedy. The sight of Joe reminded her that Kennedy had always been an enemy. How long would it be before he told his friends about the Bible and what had happened last night?

"No," Kennedy said, but there was no chance for him to explain.

"Here you are," Joe said. "I knew I could find you."

"What's going on?" Kennedy asked.

Joe's gaze cut to her. "When you mentioned you were going camping, you didn't tell me you were bringing Gracie."

"That's Grace," he said. "And you didn't ask."

"Grace. Right." The smile that curved Joe's lips indicated he found Kennedy's correction amusing. "Well, no worries. I'm here to save the outing."

"*Save* the outing?" Grace repeated.

"Don't you know? Politicians are notoriously dull."

"And you're…?"

"Compared to Kennedy, I'm the life of the party. I don't have a reputation to protect." He winked at her. "You and I are alike in that way, eh?"

"We're not alike at all," she said.

Again, he gave her a smile that indicated her response meant something significant to him. "If you say so." Reaching into his truck, he pulled out a box of doughnuts. "Anyway, I've come bearing gifts."

"Do you have any with sprinkles?" Teddy asked eagerly.

Joe shook his head. "You kidding? Only pansies like sprinkles. I don't like sprinkles. Do you like sprinkles?" he said to Heath.

"I like sprinkles," Heath replied.

Teddy shifted Grace's bag to his other arm. "Grace likes them, too.

Joe's eyebrows shot up as he looked at her. "Wow, your takeover is nearly complete. Good thing I came."

"And that means what, exactly?" she asked.

He chuckled softly. "Nothing."

"Damn right," Kennedy said.

Ignoring him, Joe nudged Heath. "Maybe if you could persuade Grace to be nice to me, I'd drive back to town and get her some doughnuts with sprinkles."

She raised one hand. "Don't trouble yourself on my account," she said and headed for the showers, knowing that whatever had happened yesterday, today was bound to be much worse.

Kennedy watched Grace walk away with his two boys. When they were out of earshot, he turned to Joe. "Why are you here? You had to leave at five in the morning to show up so early."

"I told you I might join you," he said indifferently.

Kennedy stared at him. "No, you said you didn't want to go to Pickwick Lake."

Joe sauntered closer, eating a doughnut in only two bites. "It's not that bad here," he said, still chewing.

"What changed your mind?"

"Since when do I need a reason to visit my best friend?"

"You knew Grace was here, too. How?"

Joe hesitated, as if he might continue to deny the motivation behind his trip, then shrugged. "Buzz told me he saw you drive out of town with a woman in the car."

Kennedy forked the rest of the bacon onto a paper plate. "And you found that compelling enough to track us down?"

"You haven't dated anyone since Raelynn died. I was curious to see which woman you had with you." He widened his eyes. "Never dreamed it would be Grace."

Kennedy didn't believe that for a minute. Joe hadn't seemed at all surprised to see her. "So now you know."

Joe made a clicking sound and stood with his feet apart, arms folded. "Yeah, now I know. But I should've guessed right off the bat. Makes sense, doesn't it?"

Kennedy knew he shouldn't ask, but he was bothered enough by Joe's attitude that he couldn't stop himself. "What makes sense?"

"Why you don't want to press McCormick to solve my uncle's case."

"I've already stated my reasons."

"I guess you did," Joe said with a chuckle. "You just didn't add that you're more interested in getting a piece of ass than in seeing justice done."

Kennedy put the spatula he'd been using on the tree stump that held the rest of his cooking supplies. "We've known each other a long time, Joe," he said, lowering his voice. "I owe you more than any other man. But if you ever say anything like that to me again, I won't hesitate to break your jaw. And believe me, the fact that I'm running for mayor won't stop me."

It seemed to take Joe a moment to absorb the fact that Kennedy meant what he said. When he finally realized it, the mocking smile slid from his face. "You'd let a woman come between us, Kennedy? *Grinding Gracie?* She's that good?"

Kennedy recognized the mean streak that occasionally appeared in Joe. He'd seen that look before, whenever Joe started a fistfight at the pool hall or got into an argument with his ex-wife. But Teddy and Heath were already racing each other back to camp, so Kennedy retrieved his spatula and tried to make the situation seem as casual as possible. "I wouldn't know."

"But you want to find out."

"I wanted some company. That's all."

Heath rushed to touch the truck before Teddy could. "I win!" he called out.

"You cheated," Teddy complained.

"No, I didn't," Heath said.

"You had a head start."

Heath brought a hand to his chest as though he'd been falsely accused. "I said, 'one, two, three, go.'"

"I didn't hear you!"

"Fine, let's race back."

"Okay. One, two, three, go," Teddy hollered and dashed off before his brother could do the same.

When the kids were gone, Joe nudged Kennedy with his elbow. "Listen, I'm sorry. I'm dissatisfied. Tired of being divorced. Tired of my job. Tired of doing the same old things. I admit all that. I'm even willing to admit that Grace seems to have changed a lot. I can see why you might be attracted to her. But she's still the same person, Kennedy. You shouldn't let that pretty face fool you."

"Don't worry about me."

"You're not interested in her?"

Kennedy tried to say he wasn't. Only he couldn't bring himself to do it. Grace might be everything he should avoid. But right now, she was everything he wanted. "I think she has a boyfriend in Jackson."

Joe snagged a piece of bacon. "Yet you risked taking her up here with you."

"Risked?"

"You know how people can be once a rumor gets started."

"I took her camping. Big deal."

Joe stole another piece of bacon and seemed to smile more easily.

"What's that grin for?" Kennedy asked.

He nodded in the direction Teddy and Heath had gone. "You need a good mother for those boys. And, considering your career, it has to be someone with an impeccable reputation. You're not likely to forget that."

It was true. But Kennedy didn't want to hear about it. Especially from Joe. "I might take her out a couple of times once we get back," he said.

Joe stiffened. "Why?"

"Why not?"

"Your parents won't like it."

"I'm thirty-one years old, Joe. I'm not going to base every decision I make on what my parents will or won't like." Although, with the state of his father's health, Kennedy knew he should probably be more sensitive to it than he sounded at the moment.

"Other people won't like it, either," Joe said.

"Are you talking about you?" Kennedy asked.

"She killed my uncle."

Kennedy kept his eyes on the bacon he was frying because now, more than ever, he thought that might be true. "Where's the proof?"

"That's the problem."

"You're working yourself up over nothing. It's not like we'd ever get married," he said.

"That's comforting, anyway." Joe nodded as though he'd finally caught on. But Kennedy wasn't sure *what* his friend had grasped. The only thing Kennedy knew was that Grace already meant more to him than Joe did. He was willing to risk his friendship with the man who'd saved his life for the one woman in town who, if he fell in love with her, would be least likely to love him back.

Grace took her time in the shower. She was hoping Joe would be gone when she returned. But he wasn't. He was lounging on a log near the picnic table, eating breakfast.

His eyes followed her from the moment she came

into sight until she sat in one of the three camp chairs across from him. She could feel Kennedy's eyes on her, too, and wished she didn't have to be here, with either of them. She couldn't stand Joe, and Kennedy knew too much for comfort.

"Are you hungry, Grace?" Teddy asked.

She nodded and Kennedy gave his son a plate with two pancakes, bacon and an egg to carry over to her.

"Want some juice?" Heath stood ready at the pitcher.

She smiled. She was coming to like Kennedy's older son as much as Teddy. "You bet."

Joe helped him pour the juice, then took the cup before Heath could and walked over to give it to her himself. "Nothing tastes as good as pancakes and bacon when you're camping," he said.

"I think the s'mores we made last night tasted better," Teddy said.

Grace had to agree with Teddy. But Joe was so eager to remain the center of attention he ran right over Teddy's comment without responding. "I make a mean Dutch-oven cobbler, don't I, Kennedy?"

Kennedy seemed more reserved today. "Yeah," he concurred, sounding pretty neutral. Grace couldn't tell if he was pleased to have Joe with them or not. He had a politician's impeccable manners, but he certainly wasn't going to any great lengths to make his friend feel welcome.

"I can make it for you guys tonight," he said.

Grace's food suddenly lost its flavor. Joe was staying all day?

"Do you like peaches or blackberries, Grace?" Joe asked and, if she wasn't mistaken, he smiled at her dawning realization.

"I don't have a preference," she said. She wanted to suggest they head back but she knew how disappointed Heath and Teddy would be and couldn't make herself do it. She'd survive until tomorrow. The one advantage of having Joe here was that she wouldn't have to worry about doing anything stupid with Kennedy.

"*I* like blackberries!" Teddy announced.

Joe tossed his empty plate in the black garbage bag anchored to the table. "Blackberries it is, then. Anyone interested in riding into town with me so I can buy the ingredients?"

Heath volunteered, but Joe gave Grace's foot a little nudge. "What about you?"

"No, thanks."

"Grace is going swimming with me, right?" Teddy said.

"Right," she replied.

"Hooray! I'll go change." Kennedy's youngest hurried to the tent.

"Kennedy, what about you?" Joe cast a sidelong glance at Grace, giving the impression he didn't want to leave Kennedy alone with her.

"No, thanks," Kennedy said. "I'm going to clean up."

Joe obviously wasn't happy that Heath was the only one who'd agreed to go with him. But a moment later he shrugged. "Okay. Let's go."

After climbing into his truck, he rolled down the window. "We'll be back in an hour or so."

"Make sure Heath wears his seat belt," Kennedy said.

Joe waved his words away. "Relax. You tell me that every time I take him somewhere. It's the law, remember?"

"One you don't seem to mind breaking," Kennedy responded.

"Personal freedom vs. personal safety," Joe said, a reckless glint in his eye. "No one's going to tell *me* what to do."

Considering his attitude and Raelynn's accident, Grace thought it was little wonder Kennedy would be concerned, but she didn't say anything until after Joe and Heath had driven off. Then she motioned toward the plastic tub Kennedy had just filled with soapy water. "I'll do the dishes. It's my turn. You go swimming with Teddy."

"I've got this," he said. "It'll only take me a minute."

She was about to insist but, deciding against it, started toward her tent instead. It was probably best to avoid contact with Kennedy as much as possible.

"Grace?"

She turned. "What?"

"Who called you last night?"

She hesitated, but ultimately couldn't see any harm in telling him the truth. "George."

"The man you want to marry?"

"That's him."

"And..."

She gave a little shrug. "I guess you could say the wedding's off."

"And the relationship?"

"That's off, too." She tried to inject some indifference into her voice but could tell from his expression that she hadn't managed it very well.

He stood clutching the frying pan he was about to scrub, as though he didn't know what to do with it. "I'm sorry."

"Don't be. He's better off," she said and went to change.

12

Kennedy sat on the beach with Joe, watching Grace play with Teddy in the water. His son was pretending to be a dolphin and splashed loudly while Grace guided him around, laughing. Kennedy noticed a marked difference in her when she was with children. She acted so carefree.

A few minutes earlier, Heath had presented her with a pretty rock. She'd made such a big deal of how beautiful it was, he'd been searching for another one ever since.

Her enthusiastic response made Kennedy want to get up and search for a pretty rock himself.

"When you invited her up here, did she agree easily?" Joe asked, crossing his long legs in front of him. Because Joe had more than his fair share of leisure time, he was deeply tanned and had been eager to remove his shirt. He claimed he wanted to catch a few more rays, but Kennedy suspected he was hoping to impress Grace.

She didn't seem to notice.

"Easily enough." Kennedy was wearing a T-shirt with his swimming trunks, but considered taking it off so he could get in the water.

"You asked and she accepted, just like that?" He snapped his fingers.

"Teddy's been spending some time at her place lately." Kennedy shoved the warm sand around with his bare toes. "I think she came because of him."

"So you're telling me she's more interested in your boys than she is you?"

Kennedy glanced up in surprise. "Probably." He didn't want to analyze Grace with Joe, didn't like Joe's attitude toward her.

Joe took a pull on the soda he held casually in one hand. "Why would you think that?"

"Because of the past, I guess."

"What happened wasn't our fault."

"Maybe *some* things weren't."

"You're saying other things were?"

Kennedy knew Joe was baiting him, but he cared more about answering this question honestly than whether or not Joe liked what he had to say. "More or less."

Joe scowled. "You had a girlfriend. You never even messed with her."

"Maybe not, but I certainly wasn't nice. And you and the others—"

"Don't try to put me on a guilt trip," Joe interrupted, raising a hand and shaking his head. "She couldn't wait to get her pants down."

Kennedy didn't appreciate the vision Joe's words created in his mind. "I don't want to talk about it."

"I'm just saying I wasn't going to turn her away. She was beggin' for it."

Kennedy felt his muscles tighten, but he knew better than to reveal how much Joe's words bothered him. Joe was *trying* to get a reaction, hoping to learn how deep Kennedy's feelings ran. "I think she's more upset with the way she was treated after those incidents than with the incidents themselves," he said calmly.

Joe gave a disbelieving bark. "What'd she expect?"

Kennedy had to work to keep the disgust from his face. "I sincerely hope you don't need me to answer that."

Grace squealed as she let Teddy dunk her in the water, and Joe returned his attention to the lake. "Whatever you think, it looks like she's back for more of the same. Only she's being selective this time."

"What're you talking about?"

"You don't suppose the fact that you're a rich widower has anything to do with the way she's doting on your two motherless boys?"

Kennedy was beginning to wonder how he'd tolerated Joe for so long. "No, I don't."

Joe chuckled. "I never figured you for naïve, but there you go."

"She's here because she enjoys Heath and Teddy," he said. He knew she'd also come to recover the Bible, but he didn't mention that. What she felt for Heath and Teddy was sincere. Kennedy could tell. He wasn't sure why she'd taken to them so easily, but he guessed it was because his boys weren't old enough to be a threat to her. They loved her, and she loved them back. Simple. Uncomplicated. Nothing to fear. If Kennedy was willing to settle for a strictly platonic relationship, she'd probably be friendlier to him, too. But the physical part of his attraction to her was too strong to deny. Even if he told her he wouldn't touch her again, she'd be able to feel that he *would* touch her if she ever gave him the chance. And that instantly relegated him to the "threat" category.

"You said earlier that you might take her out when we get home," Joe said.

"So?"

One eyebrow slid up. "Would you do that openly?"

Kennedy wished his friend would leave. He preferred swimming in the lake with Grace, Heath and Teddy to sitting on the beach with Joe. But he didn't want to interact too much with Grace under Joe's watchful eye. If Joe saw anything that made him uneasy, Kennedy had no doubt he'd go straight to Otis and Camille. He might anyway. "Maybe."

Joe sat up taller. "Really?"

"She was only thirteen when your uncle went missing. Forgive me if I don't see her as a homicidal maniac." Kennedy suspected he should care more about the past than he did. But at this point, what was happening in the present was far more important to him.

"What about her reputation?"

"I told you, she's different now."

At the irritation in Kennedy's voice, Joe paused, but only briefly. "Kennedy, screw her brains out if you have to. But don't let it go any farther. You have too much to lose."

"Your respect for women is inspiring," Kennedy said dryly.

"Cindy wasn't like Raelynn, or maybe you'd understand."

Cindy was Joe's ex-wife, but she wasn't nearly as bad as he made her sound. As far as Kennedy could tell, she'd tried to make their marriage work. It was Joe who'd caused most of their problems. He'd gambled away their money and cheated on her, probably more than once.

"It's hot out here," Kennedy said, unwilling to argue. "Let's go in the water." Standing, he pulled his shirt over his head and dropped it on the sand.

Joe rose, too, and grabbed Kennedy by the elbow. "If you got serious with Grace, your parents'll leave their money to charity."

"I'm more worried about being disowned than disinherited."

"Still, no woman's worth that amount of money."

"From what I hear, you have your own problems to worry about," Kennedy said.

Joe assessed him coldly. "What are you getting at?"

"Buzz said you're racking up quite a few new gambling debts."

A touch of belligerence showed in Joe's manner. "I can take care of them."

"I bailed you out last time. But I won't do it again. If your father finds out what's going on, I won't be the only one disinherited, so I suggest you mind your own business."

"And keep my mouth shut around your parents."

"Exactly."

Shaking his head, Joe laughed as though the conversation had been nothing but a joke all along. "I can't believe it. I'm being blackmailed by Dudley Do-right."

"If that's how you choose to look at it."

"Kennedy, if you take her out, they're going to hear about it without my help."

"At least you won't be involved, stirring things up and making them worse."

Joe sobered. "You think I'd do that?"

Kennedy doubted Joe would hesitate if there was something to be gained from it. "Of course not," he lied. "I'm just making sure you're covering my back, that's all."

"I've always covered your back, brother," Joe said. "Haven't I proven that?"

Joe's was the hand that had gripped Kennedy when he was drowning…. "Sure you have," he said. "Let's go swimming."

"There you are. We got no worries. What our parents don't know won't hurt 'em, right?" he said and took off for the water.

Kennedy didn't answer. He was thinking of the reverend's Bible, still in the glove box of his SUV, and wishing he could agree.

That night Heath and Teddy insisted on having Grace lie down with them so they could tell spooky stories in the dark. But with all the exercise they'd had, it wasn't long before the tent grew quiet. She could hear the steadiness of their breathing as they slept, but she stayed a while longer, simply because it felt so good to be with them, curled up in their sleeping bags, one on either side.

And she wasn't eager to face Kennedy and Joe again.

She could hear the men talking out by the fire. She liked the sound of Kennedy's voice, but since Joe had arrived, Kennedy hadn't been the same man. His eyes rested on her often enough, but he didn't speak to her if he could avoid it. He stood aside when Joe offered to rub sunscreen on her back and didn't step up when she refused, said nothing when Joe insisted on carrying her water during their hike, and watched silently as Joe baited her hook when they went fishing. Joe brushed against her at every opportunity, too—with a hand, an arm, his chest.

His touch made her recoil.

"I wish Cindy would get a freakin' job," Joe said, his voice rising easily to her ears.

"What do you care if she's still living off the divorce settlement?"

"It bugs me," he said. "Anyway, she has too much time on her hands."

Grace tried to block out his voice. The scent of dirt and lake water on the two sleeping boys made her smile. They'd had so much fun.

"I heard she wants to open her own restaurant," Kennedy said.

"Can you believe it? She actually had the nerve to come to me for money, wants me to invest ten thousand dollars." Joe laughed incredulously.

"Don't you owe her at least that much?"

"Hell, no."

"That's not the way she tells it. She says you pawned her grandmother's ring and—"

"I don't care what she says. I don't owe her jack shit. I paid for groceries and rent while we were married. Does she owe me for that?"

Grace felt herself drifting away and forced her eyelids open. She shouldn't fall asleep on Kennedy's sleeping bag. Getting up, she attempted to cross quietly to her own tent, but the zipper gave her away.

"There you are," Joe said. "Come sit down with us for a few minutes."

Grace would've refused, but she needed a drink of water, anyway, and a final trip to the restroom.

"Kennedy thinks I should give my ex-wife ten thousand dollars," Joe said as she poured herself a cup of water from the jug on the table and took the chair on the other side of the fire. "What do you think about that?"

Cindy had been one of the more popular girls in school. She and Joe hadn't gotten together until after

Grace had left Stillwater, but Grace thought they'd probably made a good couple because they were both so shallow. "I have no idea what you're talking about."

"I don't owe her anything."

"If you say so."

The shadows caused by the flickering fire made it difficult to see much detail, but something in Kennedy's expression made Grace wonder what he was thinking. Today, she'd sensed a certain amount of conflict in him when he was around Joe and was a little surprised by it. They'd always seemed so close.

"You ever been married?" Joe asked.

She took a sip of water. "No."

"Do you ever plan on marrying?"

Wincing at the reminder of her breakup with George, Grace cradled her cup in her hand. "At this point, I'm not sure. There's certainly no rush."

She already missed the security and affection George had provided. But she was also experiencing a slight sense of relief. She'd dragged around so much guilt for being unable to give him what he wanted that she felt lighter now. Somehow free.

Kennedy stirred the fire. She met his gaze through the sparks, then glanced away. Whatever was going on between them wasn't diminishing from lack of interaction. It was growing stronger, more difficult to resist. Remembering the taste and texture of his kiss, she felt an unmistakable response.

"Would you like a cup of coffee?" Joe asked.

She cleared her throat. "No, thanks. I'm about ready to turn in."

"So soon? Come on. I drove all the way out here to have some fun. The least you can do is hang out with me for a few minutes. There're so many things I'm dying to ask you."

The foreboding that plagued her so often returned. "I can't imagine why you'd want to ask me anything."

"I'm not the only one. You hold the key to the big mystery, right?"

"Wrong. I don't know where the reverend is."

"That's what you call him now?"

She cursed her stupidity. She'd been away from Stillwater too long. "What do you want me to call him?"

"If I remember correctly, it was always Daddy before."

"He never legally adopted me. And I'm thirty-one years old."

"Still, you could've said 'my father.' *I don't know where my father is.*"

The chill of the evening seemed to soak right through Grace's sweatshirt. She hugged herself for warmth. "I thought you might take exception to it."

"I see. But you didn't care about that when you were a kid."

"It never even occurred to me."

"And now you're all grown up." He grinned at Kennedy. "We've noticed."

Kennedy gave him a dirty look, but Joe didn't seem to let it bother him. "So what are your theories on the disappearance of my uncle Lee?" he asked. "Surely you've got a few ideas."

"Enough about your uncle," Kennedy said sharply.

Joe cocked his head to one side. "The subject doesn't interest you?"

"I'm sick of hearing about it."

"Then you're the only person who is. Except maybe for Grace."

"Daddy?" Teddy called from the tent, his voice filled with sleep.

"What is it, bud?" Kennedy responded.

"Heath just kicked me."

"Push him over."

"I tried. He's too heavy."

Kennedy shot Joe what looked like a warning glance as he strode past him to take care of his son. But when he ducked inside the tent, Joe leaned forward and propped his elbows on his knees. "Why don't the two of us try to put the puzzle together?"

"How do you propose we do that?" Grace asked. "He disappeared without a trace."

"Without a trace," Joe repeated. "See, that's where you lose me. I believe there has to be some clue, someone who saw *something*."

Like Jed Fowler.... "Who?" she challenged, knowing if Joe had anything solid she would've heard about it already.

"Nora Young had a meeting with him at the church. She claims she was still in the parking lot talking to Rachelle Cook when he locked up and got in his car. Rachelle confirms it."

"So? Dede Hunt saw him heading out of town at about eight-thirty."

"She thought she saw a car that looked like his. That's different." The shadows made his sly smile appear rather sinister. "And Bonnie Ray Simpson, the closest neighbor, said she saw his car parked in the drive around nine or ten."

"Bonnie Ray's an alcoholic."

"That doesn't mean she didn't see his car."

Grace leaned back, careful to seem completely at ease. "He never came home. Only my mother returned."

"When was that?"

"About nine. She came from choir practice at Ruby Bradford's."

"She didn't see him?"

"You know she didn't. I told you, he didn't come home."

Joe rocked back. "God, doesn't it drive you nuts, Grace?"

She took another drink of her water, watching him steadily over the rim. "What?"

"Not knowing."

"I've finally come to terms with it," she lied. She'd managed to block out part of that night—the part that came right after the reverend locked Molly out and right before her mother came home. But there was so much more that haunted her....

"You sound pretty certain that this mystery can't be solved," Joe said, clicking his tongue. "Do you know something we don't?"

She remembered Clay getting home shortly after her mother—heard the shouts, the terrible thud of fist on bone. "You've asked me that before. Do you think the answer's going to change?"

"I can always hope."

"You can hope that the Easter Bunny's real, too, but that won't make it so."

He studied her for a moment. "Your mother had a black eye the day after my uncle disappeared. And Clay had a cut lip."

"Clay was getting a plate from the cupboard and accidentally clipped her with his elbow. When he bent over to see if she was okay, she lifted her head unexpectedly and caught him in the mouth." There were more injuries that Grace remembered. But fortunately, they could be hidden.

"You're sure."

"Are you insinuating that your beloved uncle, a man of the cloth, would ever strike a woman? Or beat up a younger man?"

Joe chuckled at her neat dodge and drained the whiskey in his cup. "Maybe he was provoked."

"He was far too patient and gentle for that."

The zipper of the tent alerted them to the fact that Kennedy was back.

"What do you think, Kennedy?" Joe asked, setting his mug on the ground.

Kennedy moved to the picnic table and started stowing all the stuff the boys had left out. "I think you've had too much to drink. Why don't we all turn in?"

"The conversation's just gettin' good." Joe rubbed the whiskers on his chin. "Tell me what *you* think happened to him, Grace. Honestly."

"That's enough," Kennedy said. "She doesn't want to talk about it."

"I'm asking *her,* not you," Joe responded.

Kennedy whipped around. "I don't care. Leave her alone."

Grace caught her breath at the sudden tension between them—and sensed an increased malevolence in Joe as he glanced back at her. "Looks like you're coming up in the world."

"What do you mean by that?" she asked.

"Nothing," he said.

Something had been set in motion the day she returned to Stillwater, like a rock rolling downhill, gathering speed. It would crush her if she didn't stop it. She had to act. "What do you want from me?" she asked softly.

"You know what I want. The truth. And I want Kennedy to hear you say it."

"Joe—" Kennedy began.

Grace lifted a hand to stop him. She refused to come between Kennedy and his old friend. She wanted to leave Stillwater knowing his life was as perfect as it had always been. "Don't, he doesn't bother me," she said and stalked to her tent, doubly convinced that they had to move the reverend's remains. They had to hide them deep in the woods and let Joe search the farm. It was a gutsy move, but if it worked, she stood to convince the whole town that her family had nothing to do with the reverend's disappearance. Then they might be able to live normal lives.

The cool night air ruffled Kennedy's hair as he crouched outside Grace's tent. "Grace."

He heard her stir, but she didn't respond.

"Grace," he whispered again and scratched the nylon fabric with his flashlight to gain her attention.

"What?" She sounded groggy, confused.

"Head down to the bathrooms."

"But…why?"

"Shhh," he admonished, and said nothing more. He didn't want to wake Joe, who was sleeping off the whiskey in his own two-man tent.

Grace emerged wearing flip-flops, a pair of pajama bottoms and a sweatshirt turned wrong side out. She walked several feet before snapping on her flashlight. Then, as he'd directed, she started down the path to the Port-a-Potties. When she was halfway there, Kennedy fell in step beside her.

As he approached, the snap of a twig brought her light up so she could see him, but he quickly covered her hand to keep the beam on the ground with his. "What are you—" she started.

He squeezed to communicate the need for silence, and she let her words fall away.

When they reached the bathrooms, he turned off both flashlights and led her around the small building. He wasn't sure how he'd expected her to react to his late-night summons, but the way her fingers curled through his the moment he took her hand surprised him. She felt fragile and cold, which only made him more certain of his decision.

"Where are you taking me?" she asked.

He pulled her into the woods. "Here," he said when he was fairly confident they could speak without being overheard.

"Why?"

He squinted to see her more clearly. The towering trees obscured most of the moonlight. "We need to talk."

Wariness entered her voice. "No, we don't."

"Tell me about the Bible, Grace," he said. "What were you doing at Jed's? Why did you have it?"

She shook her head. "Stay out of it, Kennedy."

The questions were making him crazy, but he was better off not knowing. With a sigh, he stretched the taut muscles in his neck. "You're right. Forget I asked." What was the point? He had the Bible in his pocket. He'd brought her out here to give it back.

"So what are you going to do with it?" she asked. "Have you decided?"

He could tell she was wary of his answer. "What would your next move be if I turned it over to you?"

"Is that a real possibility?"

The suspicion in her voice made him a little angry. "You think I'd hold you, kiss you, tell you I want to make love to you, then throw you to the wolves?"

She didn't answer, but his anger wilted as he realized that was exactly what his friends had done to her, again and again, in high school. She could probably no longer link sexual desire with loyalty or anything positive.

"Would you hide it somewhere?" he asked.

"I'd burn it," she said simply. "And I'd ask you to forget you ever saw it, to go on with your life as if nothing ever happened."

He hesitated. "And you?"

"What about me?"

"Am I supposed to forget you, too?"

"What other option do you have?"

He couldn't really answer that, but he was too used to getting what he wanted to believe he couldn't have it now. Only death seemed capable of cheating him. "You feel what I feel, Grace."

She didn't agree, but she didn't deny it, either.

"It's true, isn't it?" he prompted.

When she stared mutinously up at him, he decided to prove it. Setting their flashlights on the ground, he slipped his hands under her sweatshirt and spanned her waist, rubbing her soft skin with his thumbs. She clasped his forearms, but he wasn't sure if she meant to hold him where he was or push him away.

"Touching you, even as innocently as this, makes me drunk with desire," he whispered. "I want to feel you beneath me, pulling me inside you."

She closed her eyes and swayed toward him, and his heart began to pound as his mouth found the curve of her neck. Breathing in the scent of their campfire, which lingered in her hair, he kissed the indentation below her ear while sliding a hand up her shirt. She moaned as he cupped her breast, as if she'd surrender all resistance.

But then she shoved away and stepped out of reach, leaving them both shaken.

"What's wrong?" he asked.

"We can't do this."

"Why?"

"Because I'm afraid of what you make me feel."

"Feeling isn't bad, Grace."

She raked her fingers through her hair. "It is for me. I'm not capable of loving you, just a little and only for a while."

Just a little and only for a while? Was that what he was asking?

Maybe so. He wanted a meaningful relationship, something to fill the vacuum Raelynn's death had created. But even if he and Grace could overcome their own history, he could never offer her a long-term commitment. The thought of them together would be enough to put his father in the grave. And that was only one of the many ramifications.

Yet he couldn't give her up.

"I've had a good relationship in the past. I know what it can be like," he said.

"What does that mean to *us?*"

"It means maybe you should trust me. I'm not like Joe."

"You're demanding I be vulnerable."

"I'm willing to be vulnerable, too," he said, even though he knew he'd be vulnerable in a completely different way.

She shook her head. "We'd be heading straight for a brick wall."

"Risk it," he entreated. "Lower your guard this once. See where our friendship leads."

She seemed to waver. "No," she said at last.

"Why not?"

"Because our friendship can't lead anywhere, Kennedy. I envy what you had with Raelynn. But I'm not her." She lifted her chin. "I only need to know one thing."

"The Bible."

"Are you going to give it to me?"

Kennedy started to reach into his pocket. He wanted to prove his loyalty, convince her that he wasn't trying to use her. But if Grace and her family really did have a hand in Barker's disappearance, could he let something so pertinent to what had happened go up in smoke? As damaging as Grace's connection to this Bible might be right now, if some other piece of evidence surfaced later, the reverend's notes could prompt a jury to draw the same conclusions he had.

Using the hand that had been about to reveal the Bible, he rubbed his face instead. "I can't."

"So you're going to throw me to the wolves, after all?"

He grimaced. "No. I already destroyed it."

"When?"

"Last night after you went into your tent."

Her eyes glistened as she stared up at him. "Why?" she said.

"Because I was upset," he told her. "He was a fraud. I hate him as much as you do."

She must have heard the truth in that statement because some of the stiffness left her stance. "You were right," she whispered, reaching out to grab hold of the nearest tree as if she needed the support.

Kennedy's heart leaped into his throat. "About what?"

"About what he did to me," she said. Then she scooped up her flashlight and ran away.

Kennedy remained where he was, letting the silence gather around him as he tried to digest what she'd just admitted. He'd never encountered the extreme emotions he was experiencing with Grace. Raelynn had been happy, sweet, consistent. They'd fallen in love young and maintained a close relationship with very few problems.

Grace was right—she was nothing like Raelynn. She'd been through hell and might never get over it. So why did he want her so badly? When logic screamed, "No! Absolutely not!"

Because there was one place, way down deep, that didn't care about logic at all. That part of him seemed to chant, "Yes, yes, yes!"

And it was getting louder....

Grace couldn't walk quickly enough. Hurrying out of the woods, she rounded the Port-a-Potties and went down the narrow path to the campsite, hoping to reach her tent before Kennedy could come after her. The Bible was gone. As much as she would've liked to watch it burn, part of her felt gratified that Kennedy was the one who'd destroyed it.

But there was still something about him that frightened her, and it had nothing to do with the fact that he could so easily unravel her family's dark secret.

She smiled bitterly. Who would've thought a ray of hope—hope that she might actually have a chance of being loved by the only man she'd ever really wanted—

would be the most frightening thing she'd ever encounter?

She marveled at the warmth she'd felt when Kennedy's hand held hers. Maybe it was just that she craved
some sort of vindication for being snubbed in the past.
But his voice, his touch, affected her like no other
man's—

A dark shadow loomed in front of her. Jumping
back, she barely managed to stifle a scream.

"Hey, it's me."

Joe. He stood before her wearing tennis shoes with
no socks, a pair of Nike shorts and a windbreaker that
was open to reveal his bare chest. Obviously, he'd
dressed in a hurry, just as she had.

"What are you doing out here?" he asked.

Grace grappled for the self-possession she'd lost
while speaking to Kennedy in the woods. "Coming
back from the Port-a-Potty."

"Where's your flashlight?"

"Here." She waved it between them as an excuse to
take another step away from him. "With this moon, I
didn't need it."

Tugging it from her hand, he flipped the switch and
pointed the beam behind her. She turned to look, expecting to see Kennedy walking up the trail—and said
a silent prayer of thanks to find no one there.

"You're alone?" he said in surprise.

She wasn't going to volunteer anything to Joe.
"What'd you expect?" she replied. "It's the middle of
the night."

At this, he pointed the light directly in her face. "I
thought maybe you were giving Kennedy a blow job."

Squinting against the blinding brightness, she
jerked the flashlight away and pretended his crudeness

didn't bother her. Anything else would only encourage him. "Considering he's sleeping in his tent, that'd be quite a feat."

Joe's smile changed. "He's not there. I checked. But you already know that."

She gave a nonchalant shrug. "All I know is that if Teddy and Heath are around, Kennedy's not far away. Maybe he couldn't sleep and got up to take a walk." Circumventing him, she started off again. "You might check the lake."

Joe laughed softly. "You know, Kennedy might be interested in you for the moment, Grace. He hasn't been laid in two years. But it'll be over as soon as he gets what he wants, so don't expect it to last."

Grace didn't turn around. "I don't expect anything."

"Yeah, right," he called after her. "Just like your mother wasn't after my uncle's farm. Only the stakes are much higher with Kennedy, aren't they? I have to hand it to you, Gracie. At least you know a real prize from a poor preacher."

13

Kennedy stood in the woods, wrapping the Bible in the empty black garbage bag he'd just removed from the trash can outside the restrooms. Now that he'd decided to keep it, he needed to figure out a hiding place. He didn't want to risk putting it back in the Explorer and having Grace or one of his boys find it. He wasn't excited about the idea of taking the Bible home with him, anyway. What would he do with it? The more work he put into concealing it, the more questions he'd face if something ever went wrong.

The best thing would be to get rid of it right here. Why carry it around? If he buried the reverend's Bible, the chances of anyone stumbling upon it would be slim, especially in such a remote location. And, if necessary, he'd know where to find it.

Locating a large, sharp rock, he began to dig at the base of a tall pine. It was late, and he was tired, but he wanted to bury the Bible deeply enough that some raccoon or other animal wouldn't unearth it.

While he worked, a door clapped shut at the Port-a-Potties not far away. Then a child cried and was quickly silenced in a nearby tent. Over all, however, the woods remained peaceful and still, allowing him to concentrate—until he heard Joe call his name.

"Kennedy?"

"Shit," he muttered, and turned off his flashlight as he hurried to finish.

"You out here, man?"

The hole he'd dug so far would have to be deep enough. Placing the Bible inside, Kennedy quickly covered it. He'd barely tamped down the dirt when he heard rustling in the trees.

"Kennedy?"

Kicking aside the rock he'd used, Kennedy stomped a few final times on the Bible's grave, then grabbed his flashlight and stood as Joe emerged into the clearing.

"Right here," Kennedy said.

"What the hell are you doing in the woods?"

Kennedy led Joe away from the disturbed earth. "Just thinking."

"About what?"

"Raelynn," he replied and prayed she'd forgive him for the lie.

"You're still not over her, are you," Joe said, his words more of a statement than a question.

Kennedy wasn't sure he'd ever be over Raelynn. She was part of him. She always would be. But he doubted Joe understood that, or the way things were beginning to change for him. Now that the acute pain of his wife's death had diminished to this terrible emptiness, Kennedy was beginning to crave new companionship. Love. Sex. Laughter. Commitment. Everything he'd enjoyed with Raelynn. "She was incredible," he said and meant it.

Joe nodded. "I agree. It won't be easy to settle for someone else after living with her." He chuckled. "Someone like Grace can't even compare."

Kennedy thought most of the people in Stillwater were judging Grace by the wrong standard. They were counting the number of times she'd fallen down—not the number of times she'd gotten up. "Certain events shape us into who we are," he said.

Joe shot him a confused look. "So what's your point?"

Kennedy wasn't completely clear on his own emotions. But he could tell Grace was different from the other women he'd known. "Would you be surprised if a flower bloomed if it was planted in a perfect spot of ground, where it received just the right amount of water and light?"

"You're asking me about flowers?" Joe replied dryly.

"It's an analogy, okay?"

"No, I wouldn't be surprised," he said with a shrug that let Kennedy know he was only playing along.

"Would you be surprised if a rare, delicate flower bloomed in a very hostile place, with little sunlight and even less water?"

"I don't see what—"

"Just answer the question."

Joe hesitated as though he might balk but finally relented. "Of course I'd be surprised."

"You'd want to protect that flower, right? You'd see it as a bit of a miracle."

"You're saying Grace is a miracle, Kennedy? She's slept with almost every friend you have. What's to admire about that?"

Joe didn't get it. Kennedy should have expected that. He considered pointing out all the less than admirable things Joe had done in his lifetime but decided there was no use. Slapping his friend on the back in an attempt to minimize some of the hard feelings they both had, he led him toward camp. "Forget it."

"We grew up together," Joe replied. "I thought I knew you. But you're starting to worry me."

Kennedy had begun to realize that Joe didn't know him at all. Funny thing was, they were probably better off for it. Facing their differences would, in all likelihood, destroy their friendship. "Don't worry," he said. "Nothing's going to change."

"You're sure?" Joe sounded skeptical.

"I'm sure," Kennedy said. After all, Grace would be gone in a matter of weeks or months. Then he'd *have* to forget her.

Joe waited for Kennedy to fall asleep before creeping out of the tent. He could scarcely believe what he'd heard Kennedy say—all that bullshit about rare flowers blooming in hostile places and miracles. Joe certainly didn't see Grace as a rare flower. He couldn't deny that she was attractive, but she and her family had gotten away with murder—and they'd been laughing behind their hands ever since.

It was the greatest of ironies that Grace had become a district attorney, although it was no wonder that she'd never lost a case. She probably knew exactly what to look for in a homicide. From watching her mother, or possibly Clay.

And now she had the nerve to think she could move back to town and thumb her nose at everyone she once knew.

Joe wasn't about to let her do that. Grabbing the flashlight Kennedy had left on the picnic table, he strode off toward the restrooms. He had to figure out what Kennedy and Grace had been doing an hour or so earlier. Surely they'd been together. It was too much to believe they just happened to leave their tents and wander through the woods at the same time.

The obvious answer was that they'd been fooling

around. But Joe didn't think so. There was too much tension. They'd each seemed taut as a bowstring, which sure didn't lead Joe to believe they'd just had sex.

So what, then? Why had they met in the woods?

Veering off the path toward the place he'd found Kennedy earlier, Joe turned on the light and began searching for any kind of evidence that Kennedy and Grace had been there together. He wasn't sure what he was looking for—a condom wrapper? a blanket?—but Kennedy must've had some reason for being in the woods. Joe had gone camping with him dozens of times since Raelynn's death, and he'd never slipped off in the middle of the night before. Not many people plunged into the forest to "think" at three in the morning.

The scent of pine needles and wet vegetation rose to his nostrils as he poked through the woods. He spotted something shiny, which turned out to be a crushed beer can. There was a cigarette butt and a soggy paper towel. But it was all garbage he guessed had been left behind by someone else.

It was too dark, he decided. Planning to search again in the morning, he trudged back to the tent.

Birds twittering loudly in the trees overhead woke Joe just after daybreak. Heath and Teddy were already stirring in the next tent. They all emerged at the same time, but when Joe didn't stop at the picnic table, they chimed in to ask where he was going. Mumbling that he had to use the restroom, he slipped off into the woods for another quick search.

Even with the sunlight peeking through the trees, he couldn't see anything obviously out of place—

certainly nothing to indicate what Kennedy and Grace had been doing last night. The only sign of activity in the entire area was a slight mound at the base of a tree, and it didn't even seem all that recent. Still...

Stepping closer, he kicked at a loose clod—

"Are you going to pee in the woods, Uncle Joe? Like you did last year?"

Joe spun around to see that Kennedy and Teddy had followed him.

"Yeah," he said as indifferently as possible. "I hate Port-a-Potties, don't you?"

"They stink." Teddy wrinkled his nose, then looked up at his father. "Can I pee out here, too? Huh, Dad? Can I?"

Kennedy's gaze rested on Joe a split second too long, in Joe's opinion. "No."

"Why not?" Teddy asked.

"Because there's a bathroom only fifteen feet away."

"But it *smells*."

"You'll survive," Kennedy said and led his son through the trees.

Joe stared after them until they disappeared, then urinated on the nearest tree for the simple satisfaction of doing something an Archer wouldn't. He didn't give a damn if there was a restroom *two* feet away. He'd do whatever he pleased—and if Grace stumbled upon him, so much the better. He'd like to show her that he had quite a bit more to offer than when they were kids.

He stroked himself a few times, smiling as he grew large. She'd be impressed, all right.

Teddy's voice, coming from the direction of the Port-a-Potties, intruded and Joe forced himself to zip his pants. But the appetites he'd stirred left him craving more.

He'd have to visit his ex-wife. Cindy occasionally let him stay the night, if he paid off one of her bills or fixed her car or whatever. She wanted to cut him out of her life entirely, but she was too poor and too lonely to actually do it.

Women were so much more accommodating when they had a few needs.

Pretty soon Grace would remember what that was all about.

Grace was eager to say goodbye to Kennedy. She wanted to be alone, to try and make sense out of everything that had happened over the weekend. But when he set her bag on the doorstep and began to walk away, she felt a strange sense of loss.

"Thanks for coming," he said, his manner as formal as it had been all morning.

Since their encounter in the woods, he'd grown distant. Polite. She hated that. She preferred him when he was teasing her or smiling at her in that mysterious way he had, which always made her feel like someone else, someone without a sordid past.

But she was a fool to acknowledge his effect on her. She knew that, too.

"Kennedy?"

He'd already started toward his SUV, where Teddy and Heath were waving and calling out their goodbyes. Smiling, she waved back at them.

"What?" Kennedy said.

A muscle flexed in his jaw when he turned.

"You're angry with me," she said, taken aback by the sudden revelation.

"No," he told her. "I'm angry with myself for getting into a situation I knew I should avoid."

As her breath seeped slowly through her lips, she squared her shoulders. "Well, it's not too late to save yourself."

She knew it had to come to this, but she almost wished he'd argue with her. His was the only kiss that had ever made her want to fight the defensiveness that caused her to shut down whenever she was approached in a sexual way. His was the only touch that generated enough heat to…maybe…purge her of the hateful memories that crowded too close whenever a man wanted her.

A frown created lines between his eyebrows but he didn't say anything.

"Your boys are wonderful, Kennedy. You're lucky— despite what happened to Raelynn. Although…I'm sorry about that." She regretted thinking he hadn't deserved his wife. They were perfect for each other. "You'll find someone else. Someone just as good."

"Stop it," he growled.

Wondering if it hurt him to talk about Raelynn, she switched topics. "Thanks. For the trip and for… taking care of you-know-what."

He studied her. "Just do me one favor, okay?"

She bit her bottom lip. "What's that?"

Lowering his voice so that only she could hear, he said, "Forget the reverend and the past. Somehow cut it away."

She didn't want him feeling sorry for her, so she nodded as though she'd already done it. "Of course."

When the lines in his face didn't soften, she wondered what she could say to convince him, but a sound drew their attention to the end of the drive.

Irene had pulled in next to Kennedy's SUV.

Under different circumstances, her mother's sagging jaw would've been funny. But Grace didn't feel much like laughing today. Joe didn't have any reason, at least that Grace could think of, to share the fact that she and Kennedy had been together this past weekend. Her mother, however, wouldn't be able to resist connecting her daughter to such an important figure.

Given how her mother had been treated over the years, Grace couldn't blame her. But she preferred to let the camping trip fade into the past without further notice. She refused to use Kennedy to build her own credibility or social standing.

"Why, Kennedy Archer. How nice to see you," Irene said, using every bit of her Southern charm as she got out and sashayed up the walk.

Kennedy gave her his politician's smile—Grace was coming to know the difference now that she'd seen something more personal—and offered Irene his hand. "Hello, Mrs. Barker. How are you?"

"I'd be fine, if you'd call me Irene." She fluttered her eyelashes. "We've known each other long enough for that."

"Of course we have."

"How's the campaign coming?"

"Not so good." He jerked his head toward the Vicki Nibley sign in Grace's yard. "It seems I have a particularly stubborn holdout."

Irene blushed prettily. "I'll see if I can talk some sense into her. You know, my other daughter, Madeline, supports you down at the paper."

"I'm grateful," he said.

Irene basked in his attention for a little longer. Then

her eyes slid to Grace—and widened. "Oh, my! Is that soot on your face?"

"I need a shower," Grace said, rubbing at her cheek.

"We went camping," Teddy shouted enthusiastically.

Kennedy stepped back to swat at his jeans. "We're all a bit dirty."

Irene pressed a ring-laden hand to her chest. "Ya'll spent the night in the woods *together?*"

Grace ground her teeth as Kennedy answered.

"Two nights, actually. In separate tents."

"Isn't that nice." She arched her eyebrows meaningfully at Grace. "I'm surprised Grace didn't mention she had such plans for the weekend."

"It came up at the last minute," she mumbled.

"And prevented you from going to Jackson, I see."

Kennedy's eyes rested on Grace. "I hope the fact that you didn't make it to Jackson isn't the cause of any…problems."

The way he said "problems," she knew he was talking about George. "No. That would've happened anyway."

Before Irene could ask what they were talking about, Teddy jumped into the conversation. "Mrs. Barker! Mrs. Barker, guess what?"

Irene managed to summon a smile for him, even though she was definitely more interested in Kennedy. "What, dear?"

"I can hold my breath under water almost as long as Grace."

"That's wonderful. Sounds like you had fun."

"We had a blast!" He rested his chin briefly on his hands, which were clutching the windowsill. Then his head popped up again. "Hey, Dad! Can Grace go with us to watch the fireworks next week?"

Kennedy cleared his throat. "We'll see, Teddy."

Grace shook her head. She was determined to keep a safe distance from Kennedy in the future. "I'm sorry, Teddy," she said. "I already have other plans."

"What are you doing?" Irene's voice was just sharp enough to communicate her opinion—that nothing could be more important than a date with Kennedy.

Grace struggled to come up with something. There wasn't a lot to do in such a small town on the Fourth of July. Almost everyone headed over to the high school to spread blankets on the football field and watch the fireworks. "I'm…going to be with Madeline," she said lamely.

"I'm sure Maddy wouldn't mind getting together the night before or the night after," Irene said.

Grace looked to Kennedy for help. But he sided with Irene. "Think you could arrange it?" he asked, the sparkle in his eyes telling her he was enjoying this.

"One vote isn't worth that much of your time," Grace said pointedly.

He cocked his head at a challenging angle. "Every vote counts."

Grace sighed. "I'll call you," she said.

"Please, Grace?" Teddy hollered, unwilling to be put off.

"You could bring Madeline if you want," Heath added.

Grace tucked a clump of her tangled hair behind one ear. "I'll ask her, okay, boys?" she called back.

"I'm sure she'll say yes," Irene confided to Kennedy.

"Great. I'll count on it, then." The smile Kennedy turned on Grace's mother was markedly warmer. "I'm glad we had the chance to chat, Irene."

"So am I," she said, obviously flattered.

Grace rolled her eyes. "We'll talk later," she told Kennedy.

He chuckled as he walked away. But backing out of her drive, he stopped, got out and yanked the Vicki Nibley sign from the grass.

"Mind if I remove this?" he asked.

Grace didn't bother saying no. She suspected he'd take it anyway. "If it makes you feel better."

He carried it to the back of his SUV.

"*I'm* voting for you," Irene volunteered.

With a final wave and another round of goodbyes from Teddy and Heath, he left, and Irene bestowed a smug smile on Grace. "Why didn't you tell me Kennedy Archer's interested in you?"

Grace opened the front door. "Because he's not."

"Looks that way to me."

"We're just friends."

"He seems pretty excited about having you join him for the fireworks."

"Which I can't do."

Irene remained on the porch, leaning over the railing to gaze after Kennedy's SUV. "Why not?"

"He's gone, Mother. You can come inside now." Grace held the door, and Irene finally stepped through the opening.

"Why can't you go out with him?" her mother persisted. "You haven't married George yet."

Grace dropped her keys on the small secretary in the living room. "George broke up with me this weekend."

"I thought ya'll were already broken up."

"We were, sort of. But now we're broken up without hope of reconciliation."

Her mother's face brightened. "That's even better."

"Thanks for the consolation," Grace said, leading her into the living room.

"Kennedy Archer is perfect for you. I like George, but—"

"But what?" Grace interrupted. "You've only met him once."

"I could tell that he's too dowdy for you."

"Dowdy?"

"And stiff."

Loyalty made her defensive. "He's a good man, rock-solid."

"Maybe, but he's not nearly as charming as Kennedy."

"George can be charming. He was just busy the day we came by."

Her mother perched on the edge of the leather couch. "He's not very handsome, either," she murmured.

"Yeah, well…" Grace wanted to spout off the cliché that looks could be deceiving, but her conscience wouldn't allow it. She was beginning to believe Kennedy was a nice man, too. "What you don't seem to understand is that I can't be seen with Kennedy. It'll start the whole town talking."

"Let them talk!" her mother cried. "It's about time the people of Stillwater realized we're as good as everyone else. Now that you've caught Kennedy Archer's eye—"

"I haven't caught his eye," Grace said. "His little boy comes over to see me sometimes. I'm a…a family friend."

"He needs a wife." She nearly swooned. "Imagine it, Grace. What if you were to marry Kennedy Archer?"

Grace *couldn't* imagine it. She was too different from the kind of wife he needed. "I'm not his type."

"You never know," she said. "Did you have fun camping?"

Grace thought of Kennedy holding her in the water, his lips on her neck—and heat rose inside her. She'd had fun, all right. In some ways, she'd never felt more complete. But indulging her attraction to Kennedy would inevitably set her up for a disappointment.

"We had a nice time until Joe Vincelli showed up."

Clamping her hands tightly together, Irene lowered her voice. "Did Joe say anything about Lee?"

"Nothing," Grace lied. She saw no need to upset her mother. Irene couldn't do anything about Joe.

"Good. That's good." Standing, she picked up her purse.

"You're leaving?" Grace asked.

"I was on my way to Madeline's for dinner when I saw you and Kennedy out front. Why don't you come with me?"

"No, thanks. I didn't get much sleep last night. I want to soak in a tub, then go straight to bed."

"Okay." She breezed toward the door. "I can't wait to tell Maddy you're seeing Kennedy Archer," she said. "Maybe she'll print something about it in her Singles section."

"No!" Grace shouted, following her. "Mom, promise me you won't tell *anyone* that I went camping with Kennedy."

"Are you kidding? That's the best thing to happen to our family in years."

"I'm serious."

"I'll be discreet," she said.

Grace wanted more of a promise. But it wasn't as

if she planned on seeing Kennedy again. One camping trip couldn't be construed as much of anything.

"Discreet is fine," she said. But she was a little worried when her mother smiled eagerly and hurried off as though she couldn't wait to tell everyone she saw.

The phone rang as soon as Grace climbed out of her hot bath. Wrapping herself in a towel, she hurried to the nightstand in the bedroom.

"Hello?"

"What's going on?" It was her sister, Molly, calling from New York. "How're things in Stillwater?"

"I'm not sure," Grace said. "It certainly hasn't been anything like I expected."

"Madeline told me about Jed's shop. I can't believe you let her talk you into that. You could be in jail!"

"Don't remind me," Grace said with a groan.

"What were you *thinking?*"

"What would *you* do?" Grace countered. "She was going, with or without me. I couldn't let her do it alone."

Molly said nothing for a few seconds, then murmured, "Well, at least you weren't caught."

Grace considered telling her about the Bible and Kennedy Archer. She knew she and Molly could be closer, if only she could lower her defenses. But, in the end, she decided to keep her mouth shut about both subjects. Kennedy was something she couldn't explain. Their history was too complex. And she didn't want to draw Molly back into what had happened eighteen years ago. Her sister had been so young at the time, she'd merely huddled in the corner, crying. She was the least affected of the family. To this day, Grace wasn't sure if Molly completely understood what had caused the events of that night.

Besides, the Bible was no longer a threat to them. "Have you talked to Clay?" she asked.

"Not recently. How's he doing?"

"Fine."

"Mom's really excited you're back," she said.

"She is?"

"She called last night to tell me the two of you are getting along better than ever."

Evidently, it didn't take much to please their mother. She and Irene hadn't spent that much time together, but relations, at least on the surface, were smooth, so Irene was satisfied. "Go figure."

"She still says she's not seeing anyone."

"I haven't found any proof that she is."

"She was acting strange, even on the phone yesterday."

"How?"

"Preoccupied. Too happy."

"Whoever it is, they're going to great lengths to hide the relationship."

"And that has me a little worried."

If Grace wasn't already so worried about other things, she'd be more concerned. "Hopefully, it's nothing."

"Are you okay?" Molly asked.

"I'm fine."

"Really? Will you be able to stick it out for the whole three months?"

Going back wouldn't be much easier. Grace thought of the pictures she'd shown various juries over the years. Those images would be imbedded in her mind forever, along with other, more personal images. And it would be difficult to see George. "I'm staying for now."

"Are you sure you don't want me to come out there?"

"Do you have any vacation days?"

"No, but I could try to arrange something."

"Don't. Everything's fine."

"You're positive?"

Grace's call-waiting beeped, saving her from having to convince Molly. "I've got another call," she said. "Can I get back to you later?"

"Of course," she said and Grace switched over.

"Do you have it?" Clay asked.

"Have what?"

"What do you think?"

The Bible. Of course. Grace released an audible sigh. "No."

A long stretch of silence met her response. "What happened?"

"He destroyed it."

"You're sure?"

"Fairly sure. I didn't see him do it, but he told me he did."

"You believe him?"

"He has no reason to lie. What good would it do him to hang on to such evidence? He wouldn't want to get caught with it."

"Does he know where you found it?" Clay asked.

Hearing a door open and shut in the background, she imagined Clay locking up for the night. "He asked me, but he didn't press for an answer. I don't think he really wants to learn the details."

Another long silence. "Which means he's interested in you, like I said," Clay muttered at last.

Grace didn't deny it. Kennedy *was* interested. He'd admitted as much. But whether or not he'd ever openly pursue her with the intention of establishing a serious relationship was another matter. She wouldn't let him even if he tried. "I think it's a question of wanting what you can't have."

"You don't return the interest?"

She heard the skepticism in her brother's voice and quickly moved to squelch it. "No," she said, but the fact that she'd just spent her bath fantasizing about Kennedy made the lie sound far too obvious to her own ears.

"Because of George?" Clay asked.

"George has nothing to do with it," she said. "He's met someone else."

"Since when?"

"He dropped the bomb Saturday night."

Clay whistled. "Nice of him to take you by surprise."

"He deserves a chance at happiness. I'm glad he has it."

"You deserve a chance at happiness, too," her brother said.

"What about you?" she asked, but he didn't rise to the bait.

"You've had quite a weekend," he went on.

Grace turned on the fan that would help her endure the heat and slipped into bed. "You don't know the half of it."

"What does that mean?"

"Joe Vincelli joined us on Sunday."

"Really? Why?"

"Ostensibly he came as Kennedy's friend. But Kennedy didn't invite him. I think he wanted to be sure Kennedy and I didn't get too close. He feels threatened by the fact that Kennedy and I are becoming friends."

"Did his feelings toward you make any difference to Kennedy?"

"They didn't seem to."

"So we don't have to worry about him."

"Yes, we do. Joe's not going to forget. He suspects too much." She hesitated, then plunged on. "I know you don't agree with me on this, but I think we should move the...the problem."

"Don't bring it up again," Clay snapped.

"We can't just close our eyes and hope for the best!" she responded.

"Digging around would only cause more problems."

"Not if we could hide what we were doing."

"We have to sit tight and wait for this added scrutiny to blow over," Clay said. "That's all."

Grace wasn't so sure the added scrutiny would blow over. Her own experience with police investigations led her to believe they'd be much better off getting rid of whatever remained of Lee Barker—if they could manage it without getting caught.

"You worry about your garden and your vegetable stand and Madeline and Molly and whatever else concerns you, and forget about the past, okay?" Clay said. "Leave that to me."

Grace pulled the sheet up to her chin. Arguing with Clay wasn't going to do any good. He was immovable. He'd always been in charge, and that was why she sometimes couldn't help blaming him as much as she blamed herself for how things had gone eighteen years ago.

"Forget the past," she repeated disbelievingly. Kennedy had given her the same glib advice.

"Exactly."

"Impossible," she said. Joe wouldn't let her forget. She felt certain of that.

14

Irene studied Francine Eastman, who was standing in front of her at the deli inside the Piggly Wiggly, wondering how to strike up a conversation. Fran, as her friends called her, ran a bridge club for the social elite—so, of course, Irene had never been invited.

"The macaroni salad looks good today," she said.

Since there were only the two of them waiting for Polly Zufelt to finish whatever she was doing in back, Fran couldn't possibly mistake the fact that Irene was addressing her. But Fran still gave her a frown that said, "Are you talking to *me?*" "I guess," she replied indifferently.

Irene straightened the pretty silk scarf she'd tied over her linen dress. "You gettin' ready for bridge club?"

Fran assessed her coldly. "It's Reva's birthday. Polly's just boxing up her cake."

Reva, who was married to one of the more affluent farmers in the area, was Fran's best friend. She came into the dress shop occasionally, but Irene didn't like her any better than she did Fran. "So you're having a little party when you're finished playing cards?" she asked.

"That's right," Fran said. "I suppose you're going back to work?"

Irene stiffened at the other woman's condescending manner. She knew Fran's words weren't a simple observation—they were a reference to the vast difference between them. "Yes, but I'm not in any hurry. I can take as long as I like," she said, then cursed herself for sounding so defensive.

Fran gave a little shrug. "I'm happy for you."

Polly returned with Reva's cake. "How's that, Mrs. Eastman?"

"Fine, Polly. Thank you."

Fran accepted the cake, but before she could put it in her cart, Irene spoke again. "Did you know Grace is back?"

There was a slight pause. "I've heard, yes," Fran said as though she hardly considered it good news.

"She's still not married, if you can believe it."

"I can't imagine why not," Fran replied with a smug smile.

Irene knew she was referring to Grace's reputation. Irene had heard the rumors that had circulated about her daughter, suspected many of them were true. But she blamed herself, not Grace. She should've gotten away from Lee as soon as she'd begun having misgivings about her marriage. If she hadn't been so reluctant to leave Madeline behind, and so afraid her children would starve or be split up, she would have.

"Oh, well," she said. "There's hope yet. Now that she's dating Kennedy, who knows what might happen?"

At that, Fran stumbled and nearly dropped the cake. "Kennedy who?"

Irene helped steady her. "Why, you know Kennedy Archer. His mother is one of your very best friends."

Fran's eyes bugged out as though she'd just swallowed her dentures. "It's not true," she breathed.

"Of course it is. He took her away for the weekend."

"Who said?"

"He did. Ask him."

"I think I will," she snapped.

Irene laughed softly to herself as Fran nearly twisted an ankle in her hurry to get out of the store. "Have a nice day," she called after her.

No doubt Fran had *several* calls to make. Irene didn't care if she told the whole town. In fact, she hoped Fran would start with Kennedy's own mother. Stillwater's future mayor had taken Grace along with his boys, so his intentions seemed honorable, and there wasn't a damn thing anyone could do about it.

"What can I get for you?" Polly asked.

Smiling broadly, Irene stepped up to the counter. "I think I'll forget about calories today and go for the Reuben."

On Tuesday when Kennedy returned from lunch, his mother was waiting for him in his office.

"Is Dad okay?" he asked, surprised to see her. Since she'd been taking care of the boys, she usually just called if she had any concerns.

Twin spots of color rode high on her cheeks as she stood. "You have the nerve to ask me that?"

Kennedy slowed his step, trying to figure out what was going on. Setting his briefcase on a credenza, he came around the desk, but he didn't sink into his chair. For this, he felt quite sure he needed to remain on his feet. Using his knuckles to lean on the desk, he waiting for the full brunt of her anger to hit. "Where're the boys?"

"With Otis."

"Dad's home?"

"He didn't go in to work this morning. He isn't feeling well." As much as Camille loved Otis and wanted nothing more than to see him healthy, she sounded almost triumphant to be able to tell Kennedy what he least wanted to hear.

Her words made his stomach muscles tense. He'd been dealing with his father's illness mostly by pretending it didn't exist. But he knew he couldn't do that forever. Sooner or later, it would have a significant impact on all their lives. "Are you going to take him to the hospital?"

"No. We've called the doctor. They're arranging for him to start—" she lowered her voice "—*treatment* next week instead of the week after. Until then, he's supposed to rest. Fortunately, he hasn't heard what you've been up to, or he'd be a lot sicker."

"What have I been up to?" Kennedy asked.

She closed the door and advanced on him. "Why did you do it?"

"That question might be easier to answer if you told me what you're talking about," he said, but he knew his mother had found out about Grace. When he'd taken Grace camping, it hadn't seemed like a big deal—just a weekend out with a woman he'd known in high school. But he hadn't stopped thinking of her since—which made the time they'd spent together feel like the betrayal his mother thought it was.

"Quit playing games with me," she said. "I'm talking about that Montgomery woman."

Finally taking a seat, he began going through the stack of messages on his desk, as though he wasn't all that concerned. "What about her?"

"What do you think? You took her away for the weekend."

"I wanted to get to know her," he said with a shrug.

"And?"

"That's it."

"That's it," she repeated in obvious disbelief. Shaking her head, she withdrew a flyer from her purse and shoved it at him.

Vicki Nibley's name, emblazoned across the top in big block letters, stood out larger than the rest. Below that, Kennedy read, "A candidate who cares about law and order. A candidate who supports the rights of victims and their families." At the very bottom, he found a personal endorsement—by Elaine, Marcus and Roger Vincelli. "Join us in supporting the only candidate who will fight for truth and justice."

Kennedy stared at the signatures, shocked that Joe's parents and brother had defected so quickly. They hadn't even called him!

"This is…unexpected," he said, glancing up at her.

"What did you *think* would happen?" his mother asked. "There're rumors flying all over town about you and Grace. You know that woman's reputation. Why would you open yourself up to such criticism? Especially before the election?"

Shoving back his chair, Kennedy stood. "Give her a break," he said. "She's never been convicted of anything. She's an innocent woman who—"

"Who what?" Camille interrupted.

"Who was mistreated as a child. Have you ever stopped to think why she might have behaved the way she did?"

"I don't care about that. I only care about you!" Camille's voice cracked as it rose, and Kennedy suspected she was close to tears. He couldn't remember ever seeing his mother cry—except when she'd told him his father had cancer. He'd known then that the world was coming to an end, because no one was stronger than Camille Archer.

It bothered him to know he'd upset her so badly. She was already going through a lot. "It's okay, Mom. I…I'll do something about this," he said, even though, at the moment, he had no idea what that might be.

Her nostrils flared as she worked to gain control of her emotions. "You'd better," she said at last.

Kennedy understood how deeply his father's diagnosis upset her. She'd built her life around Otis, his hopes and dreams, this town. "It's just an election," he reminded her gently.

"Don't you believe it." Her tone rang with determination. "What's happening could adversely affect your father. And I won't tolerate that!"

Kennedy wasn't sure how to console her, but he knew he could only go so far to please his parents, the Vincellis or anyone else in Stillwater. "I have to live with myself," he said. "I have to do what I think is best."

"Then do what you think is best. Just stay away from her."

He thought of the tentative arrangements he'd made with Grace to go to the fireworks. She'd said she'd call him, but she hadn't. He was taking that as a yes. "I'm not sure I want to turn my back on her."

"She doesn't need you."

"Maybe not, but having a friend in this town can't hurt her."

"It could hurt *you.*"

He skimmed over his mother's response. "And the boys? You think they should stay away, too?"

"Of course!"

"They're crazy about her."

"They wouldn't even know her if it wasn't for you."

He pinched the bridge of his nose. "They won't be happy about losing contact with her."

"Of course they won't," Camille replied. "She plays with them as if she doesn't have a care in the world."

"And why not?" he said, dropping his hand. "She's off work right now."

"She should be more productive and less…visible."

Obviously, it was the less visible part that interested his mother.

"Teddy and Heath were at her place just this morning," she went on, "sitting out on the lawn selling soap and cookies and whatever else."

"So?"

"She lives on Main Street, for crying out loud. Who knows how many people saw them? To make matters worse, she now has a Kennedy Archer For Mayor sign in her yard."

"She does?" he asked, oddly pleased despite everything.

"One day it's Vicki Nibley. The next it's Kennedy Archer. Tell me that doesn't make it look as though you put a smile on her face last weekend."

"God, you sound like Joe," he said.

"It's the truth."

Kennedy was still fixated on the sign. "Where'd she get one of my signs?"

"How should I know? Maybe Teddy took it from the garage and dragged it over."

"Main Street's a good location," he said.

"But now that you've seen this—" she smacked the paper he'd thrown onto his desktop "—you must realize that associating with her in any way, even having your sign in her yard, is the kiss of death."

"You're talking as if Vicki Nibley's already won. The election isn't over yet."

"If anything could cause us to lose, it would be Grace Montgomery."

Kennedy rounded his desk. "Everything will be okay, Mom." He would've drawn her into a comforting embrace, except he knew she'd remain stiff and awkward. His mother had always been loving but not particularly nurturing. She struggled with intimacy and preferred to show her devotion through dispensing advice and sacrificing her time to help him in various ways. His parents were alike in that.

"What made you take her to the lake?" she asked, perching on the edge of a chair.

"A lot of things. Mostly, I was thinking about a poor little girl who didn't have the chance at life she should've had," he told her.

"What's that supposed to mean? She was damn lucky Lee took her and her family in, that he put a roof over their heads."

"That's not all a child needs, Mom."

"So what are you saying?"

Kennedy scratched his shoulder, searching for some way to gain a little understanding and support for Grace. To an extent, he sympathized with Joe's family because they felt so wronged. But he didn't believe they were the only ones who deserved consideration. What had happened to Grace was grossly unfair. "I think she was abused," he said.

Camille grimaced in disbelief. "Oh, brother. If that's the excuse she's giving you, I'll bet anything it's a lie. Don't you see? She's trying to manipulate you."

Kennedy thought back on those few moments when he'd asked Grace about the reverend, and knew that what his mother said couldn't be true. No one could manufacture the desolation he'd seen on her face. The way she'd finally admitted it also rang true. "She didn't tell me she was abused. Not at first. I guessed."

"How?" she asked, leaning forward expectantly.

"Something tipped me off."

Camille shook her head. "No. She's a gold digger, just like her mother."

"That's not true."

"Show me one person who ever saw a mark on her."

Kennedy lowered his voice. "There are other types of abuse, Mom."

"Lee Barker was a preacher! I hope you're not insinuating what I think you're insinuating. Because if you're wrong, if you accuse a man like Lee, the backlash will be severe."

"I'm not insinuating anything. I have proof."

His mother stared at him for several seconds, then softened. "What kind of proof?"

Kennedy remembered Joe standing so close to the spot where he'd buried the Bible. Seeing his friend there had spooked Kennedy, made him consider going back and moving it. But he hadn't had the chance. And he'd decided soon afterward that he was probably being paranoid. If Joe knew anything about the Bible, he would've stormed the police station; he wouldn't have kept the news to himself. "It doesn't matter," he said. "What's important is that you know things aren't as we've always believed."

Camille examined her manicure. "Then bring this proof out into the open, so *everyone* will know," she said when she looked up.

"I can't." He wasn't even sure others would interpret it the way he did. There was nothing truly explicit on those pages. It was a feeling he'd gotten, the missing piece that had explained Grace's behavior—and why the Montgomerys might want to be rid of Barker.

"Why not?" she demanded.

"Because it could hurt Grace as much as help her."

"Kennedy, tell me what you have."

"No."

"Tell me!"

He raked a hand through his hair. "Don't worry about it, Mom. It's not around here, anyway."

"Who has it?"

"No one has it."

"Then where is it?"

"I buried it, okay?"

"You *buried* it? Why, for God's sake?"

He blew out a sigh. "Because it could hurt me, too."

"You've done something you shouldn't have," she said, a tinge of panic entering her voice.

"Some people would see it like that."

"Kennedy, what's going on?"

"Mom, I can't—you're just going to have to trust me on this."

"*Trust* you?"

"Why not?" he replied, growing impatient. "How long do I have to prove myself? Have I ever let you down?"

She narrowed her eyes.

"In recent years?" he clarified.

She seemed to waver. "What do you suggest we do?"

"I think we befriend Grace."

"What?" she cried, coming out of her chair.

"If we back off, it'll seem like an admission that we were doing something wrong in associating with her. Instead, we do the opposite, tout her innocence."

"Your father will never agree to an association with the Montgomerys."

"He will if you do." Although his father hadn't expressed any fears, Kennedy knew he was frightened of what lay ahead. He was relying on Camille to handle anything unrelated to his health and his job.

"You're taking a big chance, Kennedy. You realize that, don't you?" his mother said. "Maybe they haven't found his body yet, but somebody killed Lee Barker. If you're wrong about her and something unexpected turns up—"

The color suddenly drained from her face. "That's not what you buried, is it?"

"Of course not."

"Well?" she responded. "What am I to think?"

"You're to trust me, remember? Anyway, I've already made the decision." He held her gaze as he sat on the edge of the desk. "Are you with me?"

Several seconds ticked by. Finally, she nodded. "You're my son," she said. "Of course I'm with you."

"It might get a little rough, but I think we can ride out the storm."

"The Vincellis won't win. After this—" she wadded up the flyer and threw it in the wastebasket "—I'm going to make damn sure of it."

"We can take them," Kennedy said, smiling at his mother's spunk. But he was feeling far from confident. Aligning himself with Grace would alienate more people than just the Vincellis.

Camille hesitated at the door. "I hope you're right. I don't want to be sorry about this decision," she said and left.

Grace was surprised to see Heath and Teddy at her door late that afternoon. Judging by the way their grandmother had whisked them off earlier, Grace had assumed they were in trouble. But they didn't seem upset. When she answered their knock, they greeted her as enthusiastically as ever.

"Hi, Grace!" Teddy said.

Heath smiled up at her. "What have you been doing since we left?"

She'd sat out in the yard, reading a book for two hours. Then she'd closed up the stand because no one seemed interested in purchasing anything today. Plenty of folks slowed to stare at her, but no one stopped. "Making caramel apples," she said.

"For the stand?"

"For the two of you."

"I love caramel apples!" Teddy cried.

"How many did you make?" Heath asked.

"A dozen."

"Maybe we could try selling a few, just to see how they do."

Grace was quickly learning that, of the two boys, Heath was the cool-headed businessman. Teddy was the passionate one who led with his heart. "I already took in the inventory," she said.

"We'll help you bring it out again," Heath volunteered.

Grace wasn't sure she wanted to sit outside anymore. Something had changed in the past couple of days, something she could sense but not quite define.

She'd expected a reaction because of her involvement with Kennedy, but this went beyond that. It was as if the contempt and hatred she'd experienced when she was younger had increased tenfold.

She preferred to spend the rest of the afternoon in her garden. "If I'm going to be out in the heat, I should probably be pulling weeds."

"We'll help you do that later," Teddy said.

"Let's open the stand," Heath begged. "Can we, please?"

Grace considered his hopeful face. If the boys were that excited about trying again, she wasn't going to allow the people of Stillwater to stop her from saying yes. "Okay," she said, and they started hauling everything out again.

"Do you think we'll have more buyers now than we did this morning?" Heath asked as he arranged baskets of tomatoes, carrots, zucchini and peas on the table.

"I hope so." Grace didn't really expect much, but they'd barely finished setting everything out when Madeline pulled up to the curb.

"Here's someone already," Heath said.

"Hi, there!" Madeline hopped out of her Jeep, giving Teddy and Heath a smile as she strode onto the lawn. "Looks like you've got plenty of help this afternoon."

Grace waved. "I do."

"Why haven't you been answering your phone?"

"When did you call?"

"I've tried several times."

"I'm sorry. I must've accidentally turned it to quiet mode." Now that George had moved on, she didn't check it as often. "Did you need something?"

"Mom told me you were seeing Kennedy, but I

didn't believe it until I heard the same thing from three other people. I had to come over to find out if it was true."

"I'm not seeing Kennedy," Grace said.

Madeline popped the gum she was chewing and nodded toward Heath, Teddy and the yard sign. "Right."

"We're just friends," she insisted, but Teddy piped up at that moment with, "Grace went camping with us last weekend!"

Madeline tossed her gum into the bushes and chose a brownie. "So much for heading to Jackson, huh?"

"I didn't tell you because I didn't want you to make a big deal of it," Grace said.

"It *is* a big deal," Madeline told her. "Kennedy Archer? Do you know how many women would love to trade places with you?"

Grace arched her eyebrows. "If you write about this in the paper, I'll never forgive you."

Madeline didn't respond. She was obviously too busy admiring the campaign sign Teddy had hammered into the lawn. "Nice," she replied, her voice thick with brownie. "Mind if I get a picture? You could stand right behind it, beside Teddy and Heath."

"Madeline—"

A second car pulled up, bringing Teddy and Heath to their feet. Grace was grateful for the diversion—until she saw that it was Joe's ex-wife. Cindy hadn't changed much since high school. She was still as short as ever, had the same almost chubby build and round face. Only her hair was different. She'd dyed it darker than Grace remembered, and had it cut like a boy's.

Cindy remained behind the wheel of her pickup truck as if she wasn't sure whether or not to get out.

Teddy and Heath ran over and knocked on the window, and that seemed to propel her to action.

"Hi, guys," she said, but her voice was cautious, and she looked around as if she was concerned with who might see her.

"What's up?" Madeline asked.

"Nothing." She approached the table, immediately bending over the merchandise.

Teddy followed her closely, almost stepping on her heels. "What would you like?"

Cindy's eyes flicked Grace's way. "Did you make all this stuff?"

"Using Evonne's recipes," she said so that her involvement wouldn't deprive the boys of the sale they were so eagerly anticipating.

"I miss Evonne," Cindy admitted.

Grace nodded. They had that one thing in common.

"The brownies are good," Madeline said, dusting her hands.

Cindy smiled at Teddy, who was waiting for her to make a decision. "I'll have a brownie, then."

"What about a caramel apple?" Heath offered. "They're new."

"I'll have one of those, too." Her gaze slid back to Grace. "How much do I owe you?"

"I'll take the money," Heath said and paused to figure it out. "Two-fifty. Is that right, Grace?"

"Perfect." Grace didn't care how much he charged. She planned to keep only enough money to replenish her cupboards and let the boys have the rest. She wasn't running the stand for profit. It was more of a tribute than anything else, a way to try and achieve the kind of calm Evonne had always possessed.

Cindy extracted the change from her purse. But when

she'd collected her brownie and caramel apple, she didn't leave. She sidled closer to Grace's end of the table.

"Grace, I—I know we've never been friends, but—"

Suspicious, Grace narrowed her eyes. "What is it?"

Cindy glanced at Heath and Teddy, who were now trying to sell Madeline a caramel apple, and lowered her voice. "Joe's family is…sometimes difficult to get along with."

Grace had no idea where she was going with this. "I'm sorry," she said.

"For the most part, I know how to handle them. But—" she cleared her throat "—they've been talking a lot lately."

Grace became even more anxious. "About what?"

"You," she replied, then jerked her head toward the boys, "and their father."

"What I do is my own business," Grace said.

"I know. I agree. I'm not trying to upset you. I just… Kennedy's a good man, you know? I'd hate it if the Vincellis managed to hurt him."

"Hurt him?" Grace echoed.

"Haven't you heard? They're siding with Vicki Nibley just because he's become…er…friends with you." Taking a tightly folded piece of paper from her pocket, she handed it to Grace. "I thought you should know, in case you really care about him," she added and hurried back to her car.

Grace opened what looked to be a flyer.

"What's that?" Madeline asked, paying attention again now that the boys had finished wrangling a couple of dollars out of her for a caramel apple.

Grace shoved the paper into the pocket of her dress. "Nothing important," she said, feeling numb.

"Did Cindy give it to you?"

She nodded.

"What is it?"

"Just a political flyer."

Madeline took another big bite of her apple. "She supports Kennedy, right?"

"I think so."

"He's going to win."

Grace watched the boys as they added up how much they'd make if everything sold. "I hope so," she replied. But the Vincellis had never turned against the Archers before.

Nothing was certain.

The Fixin's stand was still open. They didn't have any customers just now, but Kennedy saw Grace out front, along with his two boys, and slowed. He had to hand it to his mother. It was nearly five-thirty, and she hadn't come to collect Heath and Teddy. Once Camille made up her mind to support something, she followed through without hesitation. The Archers were making a statement, one that could hardly be missed with Teddy and Heath spending so much of the afternoon in Grace's company, right in her front yard for the whole town to see.

Trying to shake off a sense of misgiving for dragging his parents into a situation that might not be best for them, he parked in the driveway.

"Dad!" Teddy cried and came running. Heath trailed behind him, his manner, as usual, a little more sedate.

Kennedy hugged both children, then walked over to Grace, who was sitting under the awning of her Fixin's stand, watching him. When he drew close enough, he could see the small droplets of moisture on her top lip and cleavage from the humidity. But to him she'd never looked prettier. She had her hair pulled back, and was wearing a simple cotton dress with black sandals.

"How's business?" he asked.

She didn't bother answering. She was upset about something, he could tell.

"What's wrong?"

"Do you know what the Vincellis are doing?" she asked.

Evidently, word was spreading fast....

Kennedy shrugged as though he wasn't concerned. "Don't worry about it."

"What are the Vincellis doing?" Heath asked.

"They're voting for Vicki Nibley," Kennedy explained.

Teddy's jaw dropped. "*Joe's* voting for Mrs. Nibley?"

"Joe hasn't signed anything that I've seen," Kennedy told them. "But I'm not sure how he feels. I haven't been able to reach him."

Teddy's expression grew troubled. "The Vincellis are our friends."

Kennedy put his hands in his pockets. "They have a right to choose who to vote for."

"But why wouldn't they vote for you?" Heath asked.

"They think Mrs. Nibley will serve their purposes better, I guess."

"What does that mean?" Teddy stared up at him.

"That she'll do what they want her to."

"Oh."

Kennedy turned to Grace. "My mother's expecting

me and the boys for dinner. Can we help you carry this stuff inside before we go?"

She shook her head. "No, I've got it."

"You're sure?"

"I'm sure," she said.

He waved Teddy and Heath toward the SUV. "Hop in and buckle up. Your grandpa's not feeling very well today. I don't want to keep him waiting."

"He's sick a lot," Teddy observed.

Kennedy needed to tell his boys what was happening to Grandpa. Soon. But tonight wasn't the night. There were too many other things on his mind.

"Why don't you take these to your folks," Grace said and gave him a jar of peaches, a jar of pickles, tomato sauce and some carrots and fresh herbs from her garden.

He wanted to refuse because he knew his parents didn't like her. But she was so sweet to send it, he couldn't.

"Thanks." He waited until the boys had carried the food to the car before letting his gaze settle fully on Grace. "You're beautiful, you know that?" he said.

Her brow furrowed as she looked up at him. "You have to stay away from me, Kennedy."

"Who says?"

"I do."

He grinned, hoping to soften her. "What if I can't?"

She didn't return his smile, or his playful tone. "Are you trying to make me fall in love with you?" she asked, her expression serious, worried.

"Are you trying to make me do the same thing?" he asked, losing the smile.

"No! I'm trying to leave you just as I found you. You and those boys. I—" she cleared her throat and lowered her voice "—I don't begrudge you what you've had in the past, Kennedy. I *want* you to have everything you desire."

He admired the black fringe of her lashes, the clear blue of her eyes. "What if that's you?" he said softly. "What if I want you, Grace?"

"Stop it, please! I'll ruin everything for you."

He tried to catch her hand as she got up and started for the house, but she sidestepped him at just the right moment. Then her feet flew across the porch, the door slammed and she was gone.

15

"Jed called me on Sunday," Madeline said.

Ever since Kennedy had left a few hours earlier, Grace hadn't been able to think of anything except the flyer. But mention of the man whose shop they'd broken into caught her attention quickly enough.

"He knows it was you?" Staring up at the waning moon, which looked like it was sitting on the back fence, she adjusted the volume on her cell phone so she could hear her stepsister above the cicadas.

"Yeah."

"What did he say?"

Madeline's voice faltered slightly as she answered. "He said he's sorry for what I've been through, but that he didn't kill my father."

Grace had been lying in her hammock, enjoying the aroma of rosemary and anise rising from her garden. Now she sat up and let her bare feet dangle over the side. "Do you believe him?"

"I guess."

The dejection in her stepsister's voice made Grace feel guilty for her own relief. Somehow, Lee Barker had managed to be a decent father to Madeline.

"He seemed pretty sincere," Madeline added. "He wasn't even mad about what I did to his shop."

"I can't imagine he'd call you if he was the one who hurt…Dad," Grace said.

"I know. I just…I have questions where he's concerned."

So did Grace, but they weren't the same questions. Grace wanted to find out how Jed had gotten hold of the reverend's Bible—and why he'd hidden it for so long.

"I asked him about quitting church," she said.

"What did he say?"

"A man has to follow his heart."

Grace pulled the hair off her neck, hoping the slight breeze stirring the trees would cool her. "Coming from Jed, that's a mouthful. What do you think he meant by it?"

"I asked him to explain. He said he worshipped God in his own way and didn't need someone like my father to tell him how he should live."

"Sounds like you got more out of him than most people," Grace said.

"I could tell he felt bad for me, that he was trying to make things better."

"He must like you. Years ago, when folks questioned whether or not he might've been involved in Dad's disappearance, he didn't proclaim his innocence, remember? He just went quietly about his business."

"I wish I hadn't broken into his shop," Madeline confessed. "He's unusual, but…I think he's a good man."

"He bought some cookies from me the other day," Grace said.

"He did?"

"I got the impression he was trying to let me know

he accepts who I am." It touched Grace that Jed, of all people, had reached out to her.

"He doesn't know you were with me that night, does he?" Madeline asked.

"Tough to say. Who told him it was you in the first place?"

"Who knows? Word's been circulating the way it always does in Stillwater. You should see all the letters and e-mails that have poured in to the paper."

"What about Chief McCormick?"

"What about him? I'm sure he knows it was me, too. But he hasn't contacted me. Unless Jed decides to press charges, I think he'll just let it go."

In that case, if Jed realized the Bible was missing, he might suspect someone was with Madeline. Had she found it, she probably would've printed it in the paper. "I don't think he suspects me," she said.

"Good. I'm taking enough flak for both of us."

"What do the letters say?"

"Some are sympathetic. Others criticize me for taking matters into my own hands. The worst tell me to ask my family to take a lie detector test before I go busting into someone's business."

Grace caught her breath. Madeline had never mentioned a lie detector before. Was she beginning to wonder? To toy with the idea of asking a few questions when she had a machine to tell her whether or not those she loved were responding truthfully? It had to be a temptation, didn't it?

The mere suggestion terrified Grace, but she couldn't slough off Madeline's words without giving herself away. "Do you need us to do that?" she asked, the beating of her heart vibrating all the way out to her fingertips. "Take a lie detector test?"

"Of course not," Madeline said. "I trust you. You know that."

Grace covered her eyes with one hand. Did Madeline really believe in her family that much? Or was she afraid of what she might learn? "Those things are notoriously unreliable," she said. To her own ear, she sounded as if she had something to hide. No doubt that was probably the D.A. in her.

In any event, Madeline didn't seem to notice. "A false positive is all we need right now," she agreed.

"You're not going to print any of the letters you've received about the break-in, are you?" Grace asked, changing the subject as soon as she dared.

"No. I feel a little uncomfortable about that, but—"

"Why?"

"Because I'd print them if what happened to me had happened to someone else. That's what good reporting is all about, you know? Tackling tough cases like this one, helping to ferret out the truth, bringing the moral issues to light."

The wind had come up and set the wind chimes moving. The melodic tinkling was a beautiful yet lonely sound.

Grace stared across the lawn and garden, thinking that what had happened to them could've happened to almost any family. Could've...but didn't. "You own the paper. You get to decide. That's one of the perks."

"Omitting a story just because I'm involved in it doesn't say much for fair reporting. But Mom's taken enough abuse. I'm not going to resurrect old tensions by printing this garbage. There are enough accusations flying around already."

The darkness in Stillwater was more complete than

anywhere else she'd ever been. It seemed to press closer, a velvet shroud that sent a trickle of unease down Grace's spine. She considered going inside, but the air in the yard was cooler. "Have you talked to Clay about the letters?"

"Yeah. He agrees I should toss them. So does Molly."

Lightning bugs hovered near Grace's porch light, glowing as if they were under some magical spell. "Have you figured out who Mom's seeing?"

"Not yet. I drove by there late last night, even forgot my scruples long enough to approach the house and peek in the window. But the drapes were pulled and I couldn't see anything. What about you?"

Grace had been far too involved in her own life to watch her mother very closely. "No."

"She's sure excited about you and Kennedy."

Grace nearly said, "There is no *me and Kennedy,*" but she knew her sister wouldn't believe her. Not after hearing Teddy and Heath go on about the camping trip, and how Kennedy had thrown her in the water and carried her to camp and roasted her some marshmallows.

"Have you heard that the Vincellis are suddenly campaigning against Kennedy?" Grace asked. She'd been too upset to broach the subject when Madeline was over earlier, hadn't wanted to bring it up in front of Heath and Teddy. But now she wondered if her stepsister could help.

"I have."

"Is there anything you can do to minimize the damage?"

"Like what?"

Pushing off with one foot, Grace set the hammock

in motion as the wind began to whip the fine strands of hair that had fallen from her ponytail. "I don't know. You could publish some kind of rebuttal."

"I wish I could, but that'd only make things worse. Folks around here know my connection to you."

"He'd make a good mayor."

"Don't worry, nothing they do will change the outcome of the election. The Archers are far more powerful than the Vincellis."

Grace stopped swinging. "This isn't about liking one family over the other. It's about disliking *me*." She was afraid the opposition would document the sins of her past and broadcast them all around town, and she feared that *would* hurt Kennedy's chances of winning. If the Vincellis caused enough of an outcry, they could even endanger *her* job. Mississippi was nothing if not devoutly religious. "Where does Joe stand in all of this? Do you know?"

"I've heard he's trying to remain neutral. Joe's pretty self-serving. He probably doesn't want to make enemies on either side, just in case."

She hoped Kennedy would go about his business, the Vincellis would be mollified, and everything would return to normal. Grace had tried to call him earlier to tell him not to let the boys come over anymore, but he hadn't been home.

"I hate Joe," she said.

"He's asked me out a few times," Madeline told her.

"I hope you didn't go."

"No. He doesn't know how to treat a woman. Anyone who's seen how he behaved with Cindy can tell you that."

Grace's phone beeped, and she knew instinctively that it was the call she'd been waiting for. "Somebody else is trying to get hold of me," she said. "I'll talk to you tomorrow, okay?"

"Somebody?"

"Stop it."

Madeline responded with a laugh and then a yawn. "Okay, sleep tight."

Grace doubted she'd get any sleep at all. She was too angry at the Vincellis—and yet, to a degree, she could understand. How would she feel if a member of her family suddenly went missing, and she suspected Joe or one of his relatives was responsible?

Taking a deep breath, she switched to the other caller. "Hello?"

"Sorry I missed you earlier." Kennedy. The sound of his voice seemed to rush around her with the wind. "I was still at my parents' house."

"How's your dad? Better?"

There was a slight hesitation in his response. "A little."

"I hope it's nothing serious."

He cleared his throat. "No, but he needs some tests. Do you think you could watch the boys tomorrow so my mother can go to the doctor's with him? I'd watch them myself, but I have meetings all afternoon."

Grace got up and moved to the porch, hanging restlessly over the railing. "You want me to babysit Heath and Teddy?"

"Do I have any other boys?" he said with a chuckle.

"Are you crazy?" she replied. "You have to keep yourself and your children away from me."

"I'm glad you didn't leave *that* on my answering machine."

"I shouldn't *have* to point out the reality of the situation."

"What reality? Why do I have to stay away?"

"You know why!"

"I'm not going to let the Vincellis dictate who I see, Grace."

A clatter in the alley caused Grace's stomach muscles to tighten involuntarily—until she heard a brief catfight and the cat she'd noticed while gardening came streaking through her yard.

"Then…I'll leave," she said. "I'll go back to Jackson. Immediately."

The thought had gone through her mind a million times since she'd seen that flyer. She hated to return to Jackson before she was expected at work, to face George and his new girlfriend, especially when staying in Evonne's house felt right in so many ways. This old home was becoming hers. It had embraced her as Evonne would have. But if by staying she made life difficult for Kennedy or his kids, she'd rather go. Her family relationships were better than they'd been in years. Maybe that small amount of progress was enough. Maybe she could go on and forget.

"Don't move away," he said.

"Why shouldn't I?" she countered.

"Because you belong here, at least for the summer."

And at the end of the summer? Maybe by then it would be too late to escape unscathed. Maybe it'd be too late for them both. "I don't belong anywhere. Definitely *don't* bring the boys, because I'm leaving," she said and hung up.

He was too stubborn. She had to leave Stillwater, she realized. The sooner the better.

Hurrying into the house, she dragged her suitcases out of the spare bedroom and began to pack.

* * *

After Grace disconnected, Kennedy paced the carpet of the parlor. He didn't know many houses that had a parlor these days, but his house was older than most, and that was what his wife had called this room. Here sat her grand piano, her music stand, her nicest furniture. Since she died, no one ever really came in here. Only Kennedy and occasionally Heath and Teddy—when they wanted to feel close to her.

Tonight, however, Kennedy couldn't feel any type of connection with Raelynn. He was too anxious. Had Grace been serious about leaving town? Surely not. He'd heard, from a variety of sources, that she had a three-month lease on the house.

If she did move, where would she go? Back to Jackson? Back to the man she'd planned to marry?

Kennedy didn't like that idea. He disliked it enough that he was tempted to jump into his SUV and drive over to her place, do what he could to convince her to stay. But he couldn't leave the boys alone, and it was too late to get a babysitter.

After several more passes across the parlor, he finally picked up the phone. The only thing he could think of was to call his mother for help. He knew she wouldn't like it, but she was the one person who, regardless of what happened in the world, had always been there for him.

The following morning, Grace tucked the hair falling out of her ponytail behind her ears, put on some water for tea and resumed packing. She'd fallen asleep not long after starting last night, and woken up late. But she didn't have that much stuff. She could finish in one day and head out tonight.

She'd have to leave behind a key and hire movers to deal with the furniture, though. George's support now belonged to someone else.

She thought of Madeline and knew she should call her. She should call Irene and Clay, too. They'd be willing to help. But she didn't know what to say to them. They wouldn't be happy about her leaving.

With a sigh, she sat on the floor, crossed her legs and leaned back on her palms. She'd felt she was finally beginning to heal. And now this...

The kettle whistled. Standing, she walked around the boxes she'd brought from the garage. Evonne had always enjoyed chamomile tea. Although it was already far too hot for anything served without ice cubes, Grace saw this cup as a final toast to her old friend.

Before she could pour the hot water, however, a knock sounded at the door.

"Grace?"

Hearing Teddy's voice, she cursed under her breath. What was Kennedy thinking? She'd told him she couldn't babysit. He was crazy for asking her in the first place.

But she was eager to see the boys one more time, to have the chance to say goodbye.

Hurrying through the living room, she threw open the door—and her smile froze on her face. The boys weren't alone. Camille Archer stood on the porch with them.

"There you are!" Teddy threw his arms around her waist.

Grace wasn't sure how to respond to his enthusiasm. She rubbed his back but felt acutely self-conscious beneath the hawklike gaze of Kennedy's mother.

"Hello," she said to Teddy and Heath before meeting Camille's pointed stare. "What can I do for you?"

Camille didn't answer right away. She was too busy scrutinizing every detail of Grace's appearance. Grace might've said something about how rude it was to stare, but there were the boys to consider. She didn't want to end up in a yelling match with their grandmother.

In the awkward silence, Heath inched close enough to get his own hug. Grace patted his back but didn't squeeze him as tightly as she ordinarily would have. She wanted to downplay these gestures of affection as much as possible, because she could tell that Camille was taking careful note.

When Camille finally spoke, she didn't bother with a greeting. "I hear you're moving."

Grace glanced over her shoulder at the boxes strewn about. "Yes. I have to return to Jackson."

"No!" Teddy cried.

Heath's shoulders drooped. "So soon?"

"Why now?" Camille asked. "Why are you doing it so suddenly?"

Grace didn't blink. "Because I need to go."

"Is it because you run at the first sign of a fight?"

Grace scowled. "Living here has always been a fight," she said. "I wouldn't have come back if I was afraid of the people here. I'm leaving for other reasons."

"Which are… "

"Frankly, none of your business."

Camille obviously didn't like her answer. Pressing her lips into a tight, colorless line, she folded her arms.

Meanwhile, Grace checked the street to see who might be watching them, and noticed Camille's cream-colored Cadillac sitting right out front. "You might want to move your car," she said.

Camille tilted her head at a jaunty angle. "Something wrong with the way I parked?"

Grace raised her eyebrows. "It's a very distinctive vehicle and, unless your goal is to antagonize the Vincellis, I suggest—"

"I don't give a damn about the Vincellis," Camille interrupted, waving an imperious hand.

That explained it. The Archers and the Vincellis were squaring off, starting a feud. But Grace didn't want Camille's pride to put Kennedy at even more risk. "I think we'd better go inside."

Camille might have argued, but Grace didn't give her the chance. She turned and walked in so that Camille, if she still wanted to talk, had to follow.

Kennedy's mother took her sweet time, but eventually stepped across the threshold and allowed Grace to close the door.

"So why are you here?" Grace asked, hoping to get to the reason for Camille's visit as soon as possible. Kennedy's mother couldn't have come to ask her to leave; Grace was already doing that. "It won't take me more than a day to get out of town," she explained, just in case.

"I want to know if you're leaving because of my son."

"Of course not," Grace said. "They need me in Jackson."

"*Who* needs you?"

"A...friend. And they could always use me at work."

"I see. Well, that creates a small problem."

Creates a problem? Certainly not for the Archers. "What problem is that?" Grace asked.

"Now that Raelynn is gone, and Kennedy's so busy at the bank, we need help with Heath and Teddy this summer."

"*We* need you," Teddy echoed.

Grace didn't acknowledge his remark. She was too shocked by what she'd just heard. "You want me to help with the boys on a regular basis?"

"I can hire someone if you'd rather not," Camille said.

Kennedy's mother had never spoken two words to Grace before. If they happened to meet, Camille walked right by. "Then hire someone," she said. "I can't do it. Surely you know what the Vincellis will make of that."

"Of course I know."

"Is that why you're here? To show them you can do whatever you want?"

"I'm here because my son asked me to come."

"You don't really want to leave, do you?" Heath asked. He and Teddy were gazing earnestly up at her, hanging on every word.

"It's not that I *want* to go," she explained. "It's just that…I'm busy. That's all."

"But what about our Fixin's stand?" Heath asked.

"And the garden?" Teddy added.

Their distress brought a lump to Grace's throat, but she wasn't about to reveal that to Camille. Squaring her shoulders, she said, "I'm sorry. My situation has changed. But you'll still have your father and grandmother and—"

Camille made a noise that caused Grace to glance up. "If you leave, you'll give the Vincellis what they want."

"Exactly," she said, even though there was much

more to her leaving than Camille could guess. "And maybe they'll let things return to status quo."

"That won't help *you*."

When Grace said nothing, something flickered in Camille's eyes that Grace had never seen there before. It was almost as if she'd caught a glimpse of the woman behind the austere mask Kennedy's mother showed the world. "But you're not doing it for you, are you?" she said.

"I don't know what you're talking about."

"You're in love with my son."

"No," Grace said. "We're complete opposites. We have nothing in common. You of all people know that. Anyway, I'm leaving. Nothing else matters."

"I'll be honest," Camille said. "I wouldn't be happy to see the two of you together, but—"

"Grandma!" Teddy complained.

"But what?" Grace said.

"You've rented a home for the summer. You should feel free to finish out your lease without worrying about how it affects us."

"Don't listen to Grandma," Heath said. "We *want* you to stay."

Teddy grabbed Grace's hand. "Please? You said you'd be here all summer, remember?"

Grace kept her focus on Camille. "If I stay, will you tell your son to keep his distance?" she asked.

"I'll tell him," Camille replied. "But he'll do exactly as he pleases. You should know that by now."

"And the Vincellis?"

"I don't need you to do me any favors where they're concerned," Camille said. "I can take care of my own."

The steel in her voice almost made Grace sorry for the Vincellis. They'd certainly taken on a formidable opponent. "Fine," she said.

"So you'll stay?" Heath cried.

"I'll stay," Grace agreed.

"Hooray!" Teddy whooped and hugged her again, and Camille nodded toward him and his brother.

"Does that mean you'll watch the boys this afternoon?"

Grace put a hand on each child's head. "Of course."

"Then I'll pick them up in a few hours." Kennedy's mother turned toward the door. Grace opened it for her, but she turned back before stepping outside. "Thank you for what you sent home with Kennedy last night. It brought back fond memories of Evonne," she said. She'd spoken stiffly, as though it had taken some effort, but Grace couldn't help feeling gratified. It was the first time Camille had treated her like an equal.

Kennedy's mother called while he was in the middle of reading through the latest shareholders' report, and worrying about what would happen to the bank the moment news of his father's illness went public.

His secretary and two tellers were in the conference room with him, collating a mailer that included the report. But when he heard Camille's voice, he told his mother to hang on a minute and walked into his office.

"What did she say?" he asked. Part of him wanted to hear that Camille had convinced Grace to remain in Stillwater. The other part recognized that he and his family would be better off if she moved. Without her in town, the Vincellis might relax and begin to forget again. God forbid they should keep pressing for answers. If that Bible ever came to light, along with his part in hiding it…

"The boys are with her now. I'm off to take your father to the doctor."

"So she's staying."

"I think so. For the summer, anyway."

Relief surged through him, despite his concerns. "That's good," he said, and hoped it was. "She shouldn't let the Vincellis run her out of town."

"I don't think they were running her out of town."

"She was leaving because of the trouble they're causing."

"She was leaving to protect *you,*" Camille said.

Kennedy wasn't sure how to respond to that. He knew Grace was trying to manage her own life and not create problems for him or anyone else. But he suspected the motivation to flee wasn't entirely unselfish. She was also trying to safeguard her emotions. Whatever was going on between them frightened her. In some ways, it frightened him, too. No other woman in town could tempt him to help cover up a murder; that was for sure. "I wasn't very nice to her when we were younger," he admitted, feeling bad about that all over again.

"Nobody was," his mother said. "I didn't want you getting mixed up with her kind, and let you know it. I did what I thought was best at the time. And I won't apologize for it," she added defensively.

Kennedy chuckled at this response. He hadn't asked her to apologize. Obviously, she was wrestling with her own conscience. "You liked her, didn't you."

"I didn't say that."

"But you did. Like her, I mean."

"I'll admit she's probably a better person than I expected."

There was a grudging tone to Camille's voice, but coming from his mother, it was still a huge admission.

"She has a good heart," he said.

"She's also very attractive."

"Really?" He smiled to himself as he remembered Grace naked in the window. "I hadn't noticed."

"You've noticed, all right. That's what has me worried."

Kennedy's father said something in the background.

"What did Dad say?" Kennedy asked.

"That you're thinking with another part of your anatomy and not your brain."

Kennedy scowled. "I haven't slept with her, if that's what he's getting at."

Camille repeated what Kennedy had said, which elicited a bark of laughter. "Maybe not yet," Otis muttered, sounding much closer to the phone.

"I heard that," Kennedy said wryly.

His mother laughed. "Apparently, your father's a bit skeptical of your motives."

"Dad doesn't need to worry about my motives. He needs to worry about getting well."

Camille immediately sobered. "He knows that, Kennedy."

"Tell him it's okay with me," Otis said. "You might not like it, Camille, but I don't mind. If Grace Montgomery makes him happy, then I'm happy. He's been a good boy his whole life, and I'm proud. Very—" his voice faltered "—proud."

Kennedy's throat constricted. His father had always been a stern man, a disciplinarian. He didn't share his emotions. Even now, he'd used Camille as a conduit. But what he said made a profound impact.

"Did you hear him?" Camille asked softly.

"I did," Kennedy replied. "But I won't accept goodbye, Mom. You tell him that, okay? I want him to see my boys grow up."

"He will."

"Tell him I love him, too," Kennedy added.

"It's time to clean out the reverend's office," Grace said. Now that she'd decided to stay in Stillwater, she wanted to go ahead with her plans to put the past behind her.

Clay pursed his lips but didn't immediately respond, so she turned to look out his kitchen window. A rooster very similar to the one she remembered from her childhood strutted in the yard among the hens, pecking at the dark earth. The barn she hated lurked right behind, its door yawning open. She grimaced at the sight of it, and looked beyond, to the creek, which evoked far pleasanter memories. Each summer, Clay had inflated old tire tubes and they'd floated down to the pond.

Too bad all the days of her childhood couldn't have been as pleasant....

Clenching her jaw, she tried to find some small corner of her soul where she could stow the bitterness. But she was running out of room.

"I'm not sure we should change anything right now," Clay said. "People around here are agitated enough, Grace. You know that."

"But I can't wait any longer," she told him. "I have to be able to effect a change here, to feel like I'm finally in charge. Otherwise, it's as if he still has some hold over this house, the land, us." She had to vanquish him.

"What about Madeline?"

Madeline was the reason they couldn't burn everything that had belonged to Barker, as Grace wished. "You can call her after we're done, tell her you boxed up his stuff and put it in storage. If she wants it, she can take it."

"I don't think she'll be happy about us doing something like that without including her. For all her talk about murder, deep down she still hopes he's coming back."

"She knows the chances of that."

"Knowing it and facing it are two different things."

"I *need* to do this, Clay," she said simply.

Clay stared down at his large hands, dirty because he'd just come from clearing the irrigation ditches. "Grace, I wish I could let you do what you want. I can't tell you how much I regret…"

"What?" she prompted.

He didn't continue. But Grace understood. He felt responsible for what had happened that terrible night when he was supposed to have stayed to watch out for her. She'd tried on various occasions to tell him that she'd been living in hell long before that. That under the circumstances, any other sixteen-year-old kid probably would've run off with his friends, just as Clay had. Why not? Barker wasn't at home, not at first. Clay hadn't even known what was at stake.

But the consequences of her brother's actions were so great, she couldn't convince him.

Maybe that was because, to a certain extent, she blamed him almost as much as he blamed himself. If only he *had* remained with her and Molly that night, as Irene had asked him to, maybe the reverend wouldn't have been in that mood *and* had the opportunity to take things so far.

Tasting bile at the back of her throat, Grace grabbed her purse. She did pretty well as long as she remained at Evonne's, or in town. But being at the farm was too difficult.

She turned to go but hesitated when she saw her brother's head hanging down. She wanted to comfort him. Why should they both suffer? His age at the time, his innocence, had to count for something, didn't it?

Forcing herself to drop her purse, she reached deep, beyond her own pain, and knelt in front of him. "That wasn't the first time, Clay," she admitted when their eyes met. "What Barker did…" She struggled for breath because, even now, if felt as though her stepfather had his hand on her throat. "It got worse with each encounter. He—he would've killed me eventually. I honestly believe that. He couldn't have kept what he was doing hidden for much longer. It was too…s-sick."

The sympathy and regret in her brother's face expanded the ache in her chest. She wanted to let Clay's love wash over her, heal her. Intellectually, she knew she wasn't to blame for what Barker had done. But her emotions contradicted what her brain told her. She felt she must have done *something* to cause what had happened to her. After all, the reverend had never hurt Molly or Madeline.

"Why?" Clay's voice was barely audible. "Why would anyone want to hurt you? You were always so sweet, so beautiful. You were only a child, for God's sake!"

"He hated me…." She struggled to drag the words out of the dark place inside her where the memories remained. "I think it was because he desired me, because he knew it made him the lowest of God's creatures to crave what he did." Sweat ran between her breasts and down her back, but she swallowed hard and forced herself to endure her body's reaction. For Clay's sake, she needed to talk about the abuse she'd suffered. "He blamed me for his…perversions."

"Why didn't you tell anyone?" Clay asked. "Mom would've helped you. *I* would've helped you."

This was the question she dreaded most, because there was no easy answer. Clay, Irene and Molly didn't understand what it was like to feel so powerless, so utterly defeated. "I couldn't," she said. "He…he threatened t-to use the knife the way he used so many other objects, to c-carve me up from the inside out."

"God, Grace."

A tear slipped down Clay's cheek. Grace steeled herself against the sight of it. She was feeling far too vulnerable, couldn't bear any more pain. But the torment in his expression meant she had to keep trying. Clay was big, strong, confident. He could fight almost any kind of foe with little fear of losing. He'd fought for her in the past. His problem was that he couldn't beat this.

Reaching up, she touched his cheek—and saw his jaw tense and his shoulders shake as he tried to contain his emotion.

"It's okay," she whispered. "It's okay."

He searched her face, and she managed to give him a watery smile. After eighteen years, she wanted to achieve forgiveness for them both. She knew it might take more time to forgive herself, but she could forgive Clay, couldn't she?

He must've recognized the difference in her because his arms went around her, gathering her to him as if she was still a little girl. "I'd give anything to go back," he said, and she finally felt the barrier she'd built between them crack and begin to give way.

She rested her head on his broad shoulders, soaking in the security he offered. He loved her. He'd tried. "I know."

When he released her, he scrubbed his jaw, wincing as if the fact that he'd broken down somehow embarrassed him.

"Let's go pack up that damn office," he said gruffly.

She stood and stared at him. "But you said... What about Madeline?"

"We'll make it up to her somehow." He started for the back door. "What you feel has to take precedence at some point, doesn't it? And I, for one, think you've waited long enough."

16

The office was stifling, with hot, static air that smelled of mildew. Cobwebs hung from the corners, and a leak in the roof had ruined some of the ceiling tiles as well as part of one wall. The damage reminded Grace of Barker's evil—slowly advancing from some unseen source, rotting everything in its path.

While Grace stood in the doorway, summoning the nerve to cross the threshold, Clay went over to lift the blind on the room's only window. Then he used an old rag to wipe the dirty panes.

When he finished, sunlight filtered into the dark place where Lee Barker had written his sermons and tortured his stepdaughter.

"Are you okay?" Clay asked.

She nodded.

He moved closer, obviously concerned. "Are you sure? You're pale as a ghost."

"*I'm* not the ghost," she said softly.

"Do you think he's watching now?"

"I hope so." She wanted Lee Barker to see that *she* was the one still living and breathing, that *she* could change her environment. She had the power now.

"I think he's burning in hell," Clay said.

Finally entering the room, she went to the file

drawer the reverend had kept under lock and key. She had no idea what he'd done with all the Polaroids he'd taken of her, but she knew he'd hidden some of them here. He used to whisper about them at night, when everyone else was sleeping. He'd told her that if she didn't let him touch her, he'd show them to her mother. The fear of seeing the disappointment in her mother's eyes—the same disappointment she felt for somehow bringing this on herself—kept her as pliant as modeling clay. She didn't want to be blamed for breaking up what was supposed to be an ideal match, for taking the food from their table, for causing Madeline to be ripped away from them. By the time the reverend became bold enough to invade her room, in addition to the occasional forced visits to his office, she was so ashamed and mortified by the thought of someone seeing those pictures that he no longer had to threaten her. She would've done almost anything to avoid the humiliation. *You don't want your momma to know what we do together, do you? She'd leave us both, leave you to me....*

Grace knew that her mother probably wouldn't leave her. But she didn't believe anyone could love her after finding out something like that. And her father had left, hadn't he? He'd *said* he cared about them, but not enough to stick around. He'd left and never come back, and although Irene had tried to locate him, it was as if he'd just disappeared.

Putting a hand to the wall to steady herself, Grace lowered her head and took several deep breaths so she wouldn't pass out.

"Why don't you sit down?" Clay said at her elbow. "You could watch as I pack everything."

"No, that's not enough," she said. Somehow she had

to summon the strength to dismantle this place herself. Maybe it was because she thought she should've put up more of a fight against the reverend. She'd always wondered...if she'd been less obedient and more assertive, like her sisters, would she have escaped as they did? What was it about her that tempted Barker to do what he did?

There's my pretty baby. Hold still and it'll feel good this time, I promise.

"Grace?"

It was as if it had happened yesterday. She could even smell her stepfather's breath....

Clay repeated her name, finally dispelling the reverend's soft, grating voice. Wiping her upper lip with her forearm, she turned to her brother. "What?"

"Where do you want to start?"

"Here," she said but felt as though someone had given her a tranquilizer when she tried to open the filing cabinet. Her arm was heavy, uncooperative.

Eventually, she managed the button that released the catch and gazed into the top drawer. She knew it wouldn't be locked. Clay and her mother had thrown away the key the night they buried the reverend—right after they'd destroyed the pictures.

Grace knew there'd been a lot more than the ones they'd found. The photos were Barker's way of reliving his fun. But he must've destroyed the rest for fear of being caught with them, because even the police, when they went through his things, hadn't discovered any. They'd bagged several items as evidence—a terse note from Irene threatening to leave Barker if he didn't start treating her better; a picture Grace had drawn of a man who looked suspiciously like Barker hanging from a tree; a bank statement that showed Irene had bounced several checks on her account while Barker had plenty of money in his; and the life insurance policy that named Irene beneficiary of a $10,000 policy she never even tried to collect. Except for the insurance policy and bank statements, they were things Irene and Clay had missed in their hurry to get rid of the body, clean up the blood and drive the reverend's car into the rock quarry.

The evidence gathered by the police had been enough to raise suspicions but, fortunately, not enough to make a case.

Now, the small wooden box in which Barker had kept the pictures held only the silver dollars he'd collected, a tie clasp in the shape of a cross and a driving award he'd received as a young man. Grace's hand shook as she poked through the contents, marveling that, except for Madeline, the sum total of the reverend's existence had come down to twenty bucks in silver dollars, a few worthless trinkets and an intense hatred from the only people who really knew him.

"Fraud!" she cried and threw the box against the wall. It left a dent before splintering on the floor.

Clay looked up at her sudden outburst. But he didn't stop her when she ripped out every file, overturned the reverend's neatly arranged desk, smashed the pictures he'd hung on the wall, destroyed the small air-conditioning unit that used to rattle and hum over her head while she was pinned to the floor, and threw his radio at the window.

After cracking one of the panes it squawked on the floor, like a wounded chicken, as the fight drained out of her. Then she stood, panting, in the middle of the room.

"You had enough?" Clay asked, his voice low, his eyes watchful.

She stared down at the nicks and gouges on her hands. "He used to play Big Band music to cover any noise I might make. He was such a cautious man. So mindful of appearances."

"He got his due, Grace."

"No, he didn't," she whispered. "I can only hope you're right about hell."

Moving closer, Clay took hold of her shoulders. "Don't let him ruin the rest of your life. Please."

That was the idea. Whether or not she'd succeed remained to be seen.

Nodding, she straightened and took a deep breath. She'd go to her garden. She'd rake and hoe and weed until the pain receded.

But then she saw the room through her stepsister's eyes and realized what she'd done. "What are we going to say happened here?" she asked.

Clay pushed her gently into a chair. "That someone broke in searching for clues and trashed the place."

"Will Madeline believe it?"

He wiped the blood oozing from a cut on her hand. "The way this town feels toward us? I'm sure she will."

Dropping her head, Grace covered her face. "Poor Maddy. He was her father. I shouldn't have done it. Maybe, if not for me, the reverend would've been a different man."

"That's not true. Don't even think it," Clay said.

But the reverend had certainly told her that, time and time again. At thirty-one, her mind rejected it. Her heart, however, was more easily convinced.

When she didn't answer him, Clay tilted her chin so that she had to meet his eyes. "Don't worry," he said. "You had every right."

She held his hand to her cheek. Clay tried to carry the burden for all of them. But even his shoulders weren't broad enough for what the reverend had set in motion.

That night, Kennedy went to the pool hall as usual. He wasn't particularly interested in playing this week. But there was no better place to catch up on town gossip, and he wanted to know who stood with him and who had, at the Vincellis' urging, defected to the Nibley camp.

Joe, Buzz, Tim and a friend he hadn't seen for a while, Russ Welton, were there by the time Kennedy arrived. They hollered a greeting as soon as he walked through the door and called him over to their favorite corner. Kennedy had spoken to Joe on the telephone a couple of times since he'd seen the Nibley flyer. Joe claimed he was staying out of the fight, but Kennedy suspected something or someone was fueling the rift between the Archers and Elaine, Marcus and Roger Vincelli. The news that Kennedy had taken Grace camping might've made them angry. It might've made them phone him and ask what the hell he thought he was doing. But they'd taken immediate action, without so much as contacting him.

Joe had to be the instigator. Maybe he was pretending to be an innocent bystander because he didn't want Kennedy to tell his parents about the gambling debts. Kennedy wasn't sure of his motivation. But he became even more convinced that Joe wasn't acting like himself when Kennedy beat him at pool and he didn't complain. Casual acceptance of defeat wasn't his style.

"You were *on* tonight," Joe praised, taking a swig of his beer.

Kennedy put his cue stick in the rack and shrugged. He didn't really care whether he beat Joe or not, so he saw no point in provoking him. "I got lucky this week."

"In more ways than one?" Joe asked with a grin.

Kennedy felt the other men's attention settle on him. "What do you mean by that?"

"You're still seeing Grace, aren't you?"

"We're friends," he replied.

"She's turned out to be a real beauty," Buzz said, obviously trying to keep the peace.

Joe toyed with the eight ball. "Only friends?"

Kennedy picked up his own beer. "Why are you asking? You preparing a report for your family?"

The eight ball clacked against several other balls as Joe sent it rolling across the table. "I already told you. I'm staying out of the problems between you and my folks. But I will say that you can't blame them for being unhappy that you'd choose Grace over us. Our families have been friends for a long time. The Vincellis have always supported the Archers."

"Your parents can vote for whomever they like," Kennedy said. "I don't have a problem with that."

"You might have a problem with it if you lose the election."

"I'm not going to lose the election."

Joe smiled slyly. "I'm just saying that it'd be a shame if you did. Especially when you had all the support you needed—until you got involved with Grace."

"I'll see whoever I want," Kennedy said with a scowl.

"Of course. I'm not trying to tell you any different."

Kennedy didn't believe it. But before he could say anything else, someone touched his arm. When he turned, he saw Janice Michaelson, a woman about four years older who was currently living with a female friend she'd met on the Internet. Because she'd never married—or apparently even dated—rumor had it that she and her friend were lovers. With her boyish haircut, lack of makeup and choice of wardrobe, Janice certainly fit the stereotype, but if she was a lesbian, she'd never admitted it. Kennedy didn't blame her for keeping quiet. Being gay wasn't easy in a town like Stillwater.

"Wanna dance?" she said.

Joe made some wisecrack about which of them would lead, and Tim and Randy started to laugh. Buzz pretended he hadn't heard.

"Sure." Kennedy put his hand on the small of Janice's back, hoping to steer her away before Joe could insult her again. But she stood her ground and leveled Joe with a look.

"At least the women I know like me," she said. "That's more than I can say for you."

Joe flushed as Tim said, "Oh, she burned you, baby. She burned you bad." Even Buzz laughed.

"You think that's funny, you fat ugly dyke?" Joe said. "At least I'm not suffering from penis envy."

Her gaze fell pointedly to his crotch. "With the size of your dick, you *should* be."

The muscles bunched in Joe's arms as he shoved off the edge of the table. He opened his mouth to make a retort, but Kennedy recognized the gleam in his eyes and yanked Janice onto the dance floor.

"Joe's an idiot," he said as he led her through the crush of bodies into the very middle.

"If you're just figuring that out, you're a little slow on the uptake," she murmured.

"He saved my life."

"He probably pushed you in to begin with."

Kennedy had never danced with Janice before. Typically, she and her friend—or partner, if the rumors were true—hung out at the bar or played pool. Sometimes they sat in back, watching football on the big screen and eating chips and salsa.

"Where's Constance tonight?" he asked.

"She went to visit her father in Nashville."

"Is that where she's from?"

"That's where her father's from. She was raised in Michigan by her mother."

He was already running out of small talk. "So you're on your own tonight?"

"I'm not staying long. Actually, I was on my way home until I saw you come in."

"Me?" he responded in surprise.

"Yes. This is probably really stupid of me, but—" she glanced to either side and lowered her voice "—I need to tell you something."

Now he was really befuddled. What could Janice have to say to him? "About what?"

"I've heard you're seeing Grace Montgomery."

"Don't tell me I've lost your vote, too," he said with a grimace.

"Whether or not you date Grace won't affect my support. But there's a lot more at stake here than an election. That's why I feel I need to say something."

"If you're waiting for my full attention, you've got it."

She bit her lip, looking uncertain.

"Well?"

"I hope I don't live to regret this," she said with a small groan, and gestured him closer.

Kennedy could see Joe straining to get a peek at them and turned Janice the other way. "What is it?"

"I saw Clay driving Reverend Barker's car the night he disappeared."

"What time was that?"

"Late. Very late."

Kennedy missed a step and nearly crashed into her. Instead of trying to continue dancing, he pulled her off to the far side, well away from Joe and the others. "Want to repeat that?"

"You heard me," she said.

"But that can't be. All the Montgomerys say they never saw Barker or his car after he left for the church at six o'clock."

"The only member of their household who might tell you the truth was staying at a friend's house, re-member?" she said.

It was his turn to look around, to be certain no one was listening. "You're *sure* it was him, Janice?"

"Positive."

Kennedy hated the confidence in her voice. "How?" he asked, feeling sick.

"Because I *saw* him. I was coming the other way."

His mind raced as he tried to absorb the significance of Janice's words and what they meant to Grace, his family, the Vincellis, the rest of the Montgomerys, the whole town. "Where were you?"

"Gossett Road. I was coming back to town. He was heading out. His mother was following him in that old Fairlane she used to drive."

Kennedy pressed his fingers to his temples. After all these years, why was Janice divulging this *now?* "Why didn't you tell anyone at the time?"

"I was only seventeen."

"So?"

When she answered, she mumbled so badly, he couldn't understand her. "What?" he prompted.

"I said I would've had to reveal what I was doing out that night!" she snapped.

Lou Bertrum turned to stare at them, and Kennedy motioned Janice even farther into the corner. "What *were* you doing?"

"I don't want to say."

"It's too late for that now."

She put a fist on her hip, shifted her weight, sighed. Finally, she said, "I was coming back from Lori Hendersen's house, okay?"

Lori Hendersen? Although it had been years since he'd seen her, Kennedy immediately remembered his sophomore history teacher. Along with several of her friends from Jackson, she'd organized a Gay Rights parade that marched through the center of town his senior year—and had her house burnt to the ground for her trouble. "Oh," he said as he realized exactly why Janice had maintained her silence for so long.

"Yes," she said. "I *couldn't* say anything. It was after midnight. My parents didn't even know I was out of the house. Lori would've lost her job. I don't have to tell you that this town isn't very forgiving of—" she lowered her voice yet again "—alternative lifestyles, to say nothing of a teacher-student relationship. It's been thirteen years, but nothing's changed there."

"So why are you telling *me?*" At this point, Kennedy would rather not have known. He already cared about Grace, didn't want to see this destroy her life. He'd hidden the Bible and decided to keep his own mouth shut.

"Why do you think?" she whispered harshly. "I'm

trying to warn you that the Vincellis are probably right about Barker. What else could've happened that night? Clay was on his way out of town. The reverend's car hasn't been seen since. *You* put it together."

Hank Pew bumped against Kennedy, nearly throwing him into Janice. Catching himself, Kennedy waited until Hank had muttered an apology and gone to the bar for another drink.

"Who else have you told?" he asked.

"No one. No one else *can* know. Lori might've moved away, but my parents still live in this town, and they're begging me to get married and have a family. I have no desire to hurt them in their old age—or have my own place get torched. I'm sort of partial to my flower farm, you know?"

"So this is only for my benefit?"

"It's for Raelynn and your boys, too. You're good people. I don't want to see you get mixed up with the Montgomerys. Even if Grace didn't have anything to do with the actual murder, she's kept silent all these years—working as a district attorney, no less. They'll lynch her for that alone, if they ever find out. Think about your kids. If they become attached to her, what would seeing her go through a trial and possibly wind up in jail do to *them?*"

Kennedy couldn't imagine. He'd never had to worry about anything like that before.

"Joe's coming," Janice said. "I gotta go."

Kennedy caught her arm. "Wait—"

"No, I've done my part. I don't ever want to talk about this again. Whether you take my advice or not is up to you," she said and slipped into the crowd.

Kennedy watched her pass through the front door just as Joe reached him. "What was going on over here?" he asked. "That bitch looked like she had something serious to say to you."

"She's worried about the road near her house," Kennedy replied. "If I get elected, she wants me to see about making some improvements."

Joe wore a skeptical expression. "That's it?"

"That's it," he said and went through the motions of playing another two games of pool, just to keep up appearances. But his mind was on Grace the whole time—and the fact that he could no longer ignore the past and simply hope for the best.

He had to know what happened that night.

Clay didn't answer his door right away. Kennedy thought maybe Grace's brother wasn't there. He was about to give up and head home to relieve Kari Monson, his Thursday-night babysitter, when the porch light snapped on. Then a curtain moved in the window, and he felt rather than saw someone looking out at him.

Finally, the lock clicked and the door opened.

"Kennedy," Clay said, his expression curious yet guarded. "What can I do for you?"

Kennedy had hoped Clay would invite him in, but judging by the way he was dressed—in a pair of jeans with no shirt or shoes—this wasn't a good time. "I'm sorry to bother you so late. But could you spare me a couple of minutes?"

Clay glanced back over his shoulder, leading Kennedy to believe he wasn't alone. If it had been a Friday night, Kennedy might've expected him to have company. But not during the week. Clay worked too hard. Occasionally he showed up at the Let the Good Times Roll tavern, but more often he went to bed early.

"Clay? Who is it?" A woman's voice. Kennedy thought it might be Alexandra Martin, who owned the breakfast café in town, but he knew it could be any one of a number of women. Eligible members of the opposite sex didn't seem to care that Clay might've been involved in a murder. Some of them were making a career out of trying to win him over. They cooked him dinner, baked him cakes, occasionally accompanied him to the tavern and far more often kept his bed warm. But much to the disappointment of his many admirers—and the relief of their relatives—Clay remained as aloof as ever. Kennedy was willing to bet Grace's brother would never marry.

"Should I come back tomorrow?" he asked, even though he felt like he needed to talk to Clay *now,* before he could spend one more second thinking about what Janice had said.

"That depends," Clay said softly. "Does this have anything to do with my sister?"

It had everything to do with Grace. But Kennedy didn't want to put it that way. "It has more to do with the past."

Clay stepped outside and closed the door. "What do you have to say?"

Kennedy considered telling him that Janice had come forward. He knew it would increase his chances of reaching the truth if he could name a witness. But she'd put herself at risk to protect Heath and Teddy. Maybe Clay would guess, if he'd seen her that night eighteen years ago, but Kennedy wouldn't reveal her identity.

"Someone saw you driving the reverend's car the night he went missing," he said.

Kennedy wasn't sure if he'd expected a visible reaction to this news. If so, he should've known better. Clay was too good at poker to give himself away—and he'd been playing this game for far too long. "And five other people saw five other things," he said.

"This is someone I trust."

"Well, I don't know who told you that, but they're mistaken. The reverend never let me drive his car."

"His lack of permission is part of the problem," Kennedy said.

A muscle flexed in Clay's cheek, but Kennedy wasn't about to back off. "I caught Grace with the Bible the reverend carried around everywhere. I *know* you or someone else in your family was involved that night."

There was a slight narrowing of Clay's eyes, but nothing more. "So why don't you go to the police?" he asked.

Kennedy scowled. "You know why."

"You like Grace."

Like was a pretty mild word for absolute infatuation. "I care about her," he admitted.

Clay seemed to measure him in some way. "Then leave the past alone." He started to go back into the house, but Kennedy grasped his arm.

"I have my own family to protect, Clay. That's why I'm here."

Clay looked at Kennedy's hand, but Kennedy didn't let go. "What do you want me to tell you? That you have nothing to worry about? That you can have Grace right along with everything else?"

"I want the truth."

"Whose version?"

"I'll take yours, for starters."

Chuckling mirthlessly, Clay shook his head as though Kennedy was crazy for even asking.

"If this person stepped forward, there could be others," Kennedy said, hoping to convince him. "Who knows when something new might come out?"

"'What if' is a tough thing to live with," Clay agreed. "That's why, if I were you, I'd keep my life simple and start seeing someone else. Grace isn't meant for anyone around here. She—" his eyebrows clashed as he struggled for words "—she's too good for this place."

Kennedy had never had anyone suggest a woman was too good for him before. But, considering how he'd behaved toward Clay's sister in high school, he accepted it. "She's been through a lot. I know that."

"I'll take care of her," Clay said, almost fiercely. "Don't think she needs you."

The door opened and Alexandra stood there, wearing only a sheet. "Oh. Hi, Kennedy," she said with a giggle.

Kennedy barely had a chance to wave before Clay told her to wait for him inside.

She pouted at the impatience in his response but obeyed him. Kennedy got the impression that Clay would simply send her home if she didn't. He made no secret of the fact that he didn't care deeply for her or any of the other women he entertained. His indifference was probably the very thing that kept them coming back.

"You're right," Kennedy said with a sigh. He was making this harder than it needed to be. He had to stay away from Grace, just as she'd tried to tell him. That would solve everything. Then, if the truth emerged, it wouldn't affect him, his kids or his parents. Life would continue as it always had.

"Good night." Turning, he walked to his truck. But

once he was on his way home, he found that Grace had left a message on his cell phone.

"Hi, Kennedy. Give me a call when you can, okay?"

He told himself he wouldn't respond. He'd just made the decision to steer clear of the whole Montgomery mystery. How many people did it take to warn him that he was traveling hell-bent for trouble?

But he didn't get more than a block from Clay's farm before he made a U-turn and headed back to town. He wasn't going to call Grace. He was going to *see* her. Because part of him stubbornly believed they still had a chance—if she cared about him. If she cared enough to tell him the truth.

17

Anxiety surged through Grace the moment she saw Kennedy's SUV pull into her drive. She'd been trying to come up with a good reason for contacting him. But it'd been two hours since she'd called his cell phone, and she still hadn't thought of anything beyond the truth—that she wanted to hear his voice.

"Grace? It's me," he said and knocked again when she didn't immediately answer.

She considered pretending she was asleep or gone. But since his mother had come by, and she and Clay had boxed up all the reverend's things, she felt…renewed. As though she was on the verge of something really fantastic. She was sure Kennedy had some part in that. Everything seemed to center, in one way or another, on him.

"Grace?" he called a second time.

Smoothing her tank top and shorts, she quit stalling and opened the door.

His eyes ran over her as if he wanted to pull her into his arms. But he kept his distance. "Hi."

The butterflies in her stomach made it difficult to breathe. "Hi."

"You called earlier?"

She thought of offering him some of the excuses

she'd already devised. *Heath left his swimsuit here, and I wondered if you'd like to pick it up…. I made some cinnamon rolls I bet the boys would enjoy for breakfast.* But she didn't see the point.

"Yes."

He waited expectantly for her to continue, then finally asked, "What did you want?"

She took in the green of his eyes, admired the squareness of his jaw. "To see you," she admitted.

His eyebrows rose in obvious surprise. "Tonight?"

"Why not?"

"Why not?" he repeated to himself as though it was a loaded question.

She moved back so he could come inside, but hesitated before closing the door behind him. "You might want to move your truck."

"For the Vincellis?" he said. "Forget it. I'm not moving anything."

Evidently, he was more like his mother than she'd thought. "I'm afraid you and your family are too proud for your own good."

"People can think what they want of my being here."

"You're running for office."

"And if I'm elected, I'll do the best job I can. That's all I owe the voters of this town."

"I can't believe you don't care more about winning."

"I care about it," he said. "But I'm not willing to let other people use it to dictate what I can and can't do."

She shook her head at his stubbornness. "Fine. I guess that's up to you."

He said nothing.

"So…can I get you a glass of wine?"

"Sure."

She led him into the kitchen, where she took a bottle of merlot from the cupboard. She was just starting to uncork it when he took hold of her hands.

"What happened?" he asked, examining the nicks and gouges she'd sustained while destroying the reverend's office.

She shrugged. "I got a little too aggressive with my gardening." She let her gaze fall to his thumbs, which gently brushed the insides of her wrists. She wanted to touch him, she realized with a sharp pang of desire. Intimately. She imagined sitting astride him, watching his face as she took him inside her.

Finally, at thirty-one years of age, she craved physical intimacy—and it was creating an unexpected and incredible high.

He entwined his fingers with hers. "Grace…"

The tone of his voice made her nervous. "What?"

"I know you're not going to want to talk about this, but…"

Tensing, she waited for the rest.

"…I need to know what happened the night the reverend died. Before whatever's going on between us goes any further."

She pulled her hands away. "Nothing happened. I've already told you and everyone else. He just…disappeared."

He looked torn. "I'd like to believe you. I really would. But we both know that's not the truth. Finding you with his Bible told me that much."

She didn't know how to respond. She wanted to level with him—but she couldn't. Tomorrow, next year, he might not feel the same way toward her as he did right now. "It's the only truth I can give you."

"I have to protect Teddy and Heath, my parents," he explained. "I can't see you if I don't know what I'm getting myself into."

Grace froze inside. What had she been thinking? Just because his mother had asked her to stay, just because she entertained his boys so often, didn't mean anything had changed between them. He was right. There were still too many risks. For both of them.

"I understand," she said, folding her arms defensively. Every time she dared to hope, the shadow of her past stretched toward her like the reverend's arm from his grave. She was stupid to think she could get beyond it, especially here in Stillwater. "I—" she pushed the wine aside "—I made cinnamon rolls for the boys. Why don't you take some home with you for breakfast?"

"Stop it," he said.

"Stop what?" she snapped, anger filling the sudden void in her chest, replacing the happiness, the optimism, of a moment earlier.

"Don't withdraw from me, damn it. You were… *there*. I could feel it."

"What do you want me to do?"

Taking her by the elbows, he pulled her up against him. "Trust me," he whispered. Then his mouth covered hers.

She'd been starved for the taste of him—and suddenly he was there, giving her what she needed. Wrapping her arms around his neck, she returned his kiss more passionately than she'd kissed any man.

"Can you trust me?" he said against her mouth. "Please?"

She wasn't sure. She was feeling too many sensations. He was yanking off her shirt, and she was try-

ing to help him. She kept waiting for the moment she'd
go cold inside, when she'd want him to stop. But as
long as he was kissing her, touching her, murmuring
in her ear, she felt nothing but warmth. This was
Kennedy. It seemed as if she *belonged* in his arms.

"Tell me what happened to the reverend, Grace," he
said, cupping her breasts and kissing the swell of them.

Think, she told herself. But she didn't want to do
anything that might end the arousal coursing through
her. The desire for more of Kennedy, his touch, his
taste, his smell nearly consumed her. She wanted to
cast all care and caution aside, to escape them for
once.

"Grace?" he prompted breathlessly.

"I…can't," she said.

He drew back, stared at her long and hard. Then he
lowered his head and took her nipple in his mouth.
"Don't make me choose," he said, his tongue moving
against her.

Every nerve began to tighten and tingle. She closed
her eyes at the pleasure he gave and let her head fall
back. This was what other women experienced. This
was healthy.

"Tell me it's not going to hurt the people I love if I
love you, too," Kennedy said, the hoarseness of his
voice telling her he was every bit as affected as she
was.

It was the Bible that was making him so dogged,
she thought. She had to give him some explanation or
he'd keep pressing her. Fighting to control her career-
ing emotions, she began to make up whatever she
could think of—anything to obfuscate the reality of
eighteen years ago. "I don't…know what you mean.
I—I found the…reverend's Bible in the barn when I

got back to town and…and I was going to plant it in Jed's shop so—"

He took a step back. The expression on his face was one she'd never seen there before, one full of desire *and* deep regret. "You're saying you were going to frame Jed? I can't believe that."

"No, of course not. Not really. I—"

"Forget it," he said. The hard edge in his voice indicated that he was struggling with his own conflicts. "I have to go. I can't keep pretending you're telling me the truth. Teddy and Heath mean too much to me."

Closing her eyes, Grace listened to his footsteps recede. He was right; he was better off without her. But when the house fell silent before he could have reached the front door, she looked up to find him watching her from across the room.

"I'm falling in love with you, Grace," he said softly. "Do you know that?"

She shook her head. It was a lie. It had to be.

At her adamant rejection, he swore and started through the living room.

Grace stood at the kitchen counter, her nails curving into her palms. *Don't go, please.* She knew, if he walked out, that would be the end of what they had. He'd just bared his soul —and she'd given him nothing in return.

But she couldn't speak, couldn't overcome the fear.

I'm falling in love with you…. His words seemed to swirl through her head, growing larger and then smaller. She wanted to grab hold of them, believe in them, let them anchor her to something better than she'd known. But how? Eighteen years of silence clogged her throat, choking off all sound.

When the front door opened, she told herself to let

him leave. But she couldn't. Not yet. He was the only one who could make her forget.

Grabbing her shirt and clutching it to her chest, she ran after him. "Kennedy?" she managed to call.

He turned in the doorway, his gaze hopeful.

Her mouth was too dry to speak. Swallowing hard, she pushed past the fear. "Stay with me tonight."

His eyes filled with emotion. "Grace…"

"You can walk away in the morning," she said. "One night won't change anything."

Kennedy wished he could refuse. But it was impossible. He'd been telling the truth when he said he was falling in love. And he knew it was the greatest of ironies, after the arrogant way he'd treated Grace when they were younger, that he should want her so badly now.

Dimly, he thought of Heath and Teddy. He'd never knowingly allow them to be hurt. His folks mattered a great deal, too. But spending just one night in Grace's arms suddenly didn't seem that threatening. Maybe if he fulfilled his terrible craving for her, he'd be able to forget her.

Shutting out the voices in his head, he stepped back inside and closed the door. He wanted Grace too badly to listen to reason. Even his own.

The moment he reached for her, Grace dropped the shirt she'd been holding against her chest and went into his arms. She couldn't believe it. Kennedy hadn't left. He was still here with her.

They had tonight.

One hand came up to fondle her, and he sighed as if she felt better than anything he'd ever touched.

Euphoria filled Grace as she brought her lips to his. This was unlike anything she'd experienced before; this was heaven. Strange that she'd find it in Still-water. Or maybe it wasn't so strange. It was here that she seemed to experience every extreme.

"Grace?" he murmured, his mouth hot and wet as he kissed her deeply, hungrily.

She could hardly speak above the pounding of her heart. "What?"

"The only birth control I have is an old condom Joe stuck in my wallet a year ago."

"You're that sexually active, huh?" she teased, her skin hypersensitive, her knees weak.

"I haven't been with anyone since Raelynn," he said.

"That condom won't do the job?"

"Don't you have anything else?"

"No." George had insisted she go on the pill, but she'd stopped taking it when he ended their engage-ment over a month ago.

"It'll get us by," he responded.

She laughed at his sudden conviction, because she wasn't concerned. She certainly wouldn't get pregnant on purpose, not without Kennedy wanting the same thing. But neither would she cry over an accident. She'd craved a baby for the past several years. She could sup-port one, would absolutely adore it. Wanting a child was partly why she'd planned to marry George. Consid-ering the way she felt about Kennedy—as if she'd sim-ply die if he walked away from her now—she couldn't imagine anything more wonderful than having his child. That would make her return to Stillwater well worth any cost.

"It'll be okay," she agreed and, taking his hand, led him upstairs.

* * *

Kennedy paused in their lovemaking to lean back on one elbow and admire Grace. He wanted her beneath him so he could finally bury himself inside her, take her with long, powerful thrusts that would end the torturous wait. But after the disregard and abuse she'd suffered as a child and then as a teenager, he wanted to be extra-gentle, to let her know that this meant something to him. He wanted it to mean something to her, too. If these few hours were all they'd have together, he was determined to make the most of them.

"What?" she murmured, staring curiously up at him.

Her skin seemed to glow in the moonlight streaming through the window. With her dark hair a halo on the pillow next to him, her expression one of trust and expectation, he knew he'd never seen a more beautiful sight. "You're gorgeous."

A sexy smile curved her lips as her fingers combed through his hair. "You're nothing like I expected."

"Knowing what you thought of me, I'm sort of glad to hear that."

She chuckled. "I'm sorry. I was wrong."

He kissed the tip of her nose. "I'm the one who should be sorry, Grace. I was so…young and stupid. Tonight I just want to make you forget."

Her hand slid over his chest, down to his navel and lower. "Now's probably a good time for that," she said and pulled him down on top of her.

Kennedy's arms shook with anticipation as he supported the bulk of his weight while pressing inside her. The feel of her body accepting his was almost enough to send him over the edge. Especially when she groaned and arched into him, pulling him deeper.

"That's it," she said. "That's what I want. For the first time in my life, that's what I want."

He knew there was something significant in those words, but he couldn't focus on it. He was too overwhelmed by what he was feeling. "Incredible," he whispered as he began to move.

She threw an arm over her face as though savoring each sensation, but he stopped until she lowered her hand and blinked up at him. He wanted to see the dreamy look in her eyes that had held him spellbound since he'd first touched her, wanted to witness every reaction. Then he rolled her nipple in his mouth before sliding into her again, and again, and again.

Soon the rhythm grew frantic and sweat slicked their bodies, but it was a perfect meshing of needs, of touching, tasting, seeking. A complete abandonment of individuality to become one.

"That's...nice," she whispered between breaths, her arms tightening around him. "So nice."

He wanted it to be better than nice. He wanted it to be perfect for her. So he forced himself to slow down, to draw the pleasure out as long as possible. But it was only a few seconds later that she gasped out his name and shuddered in his arms. And then he couldn't have held back for anything.

Grace listened to Kennedy's deep, even breathing as he slept with his body tight against hers. Contentment flowed through her veins. She was warm and comfortable, complete in a way she'd never experienced, but she refused to succumb to sleep. She already felt as if she was dreaming. Staying in Evonne's house, making love with Kennedy Archer. Was it even real?

She moved slightly, adjusting her pillow. His hand closed possessively over her breast, making him feel real enough. But she didn't roll over as she wanted to. She knew if she gave him the opportunity, he'd want to make love again. They'd already tried several alternatives. Nothing else could compare to that first time, but they'd used their only condom, and she doubted he'd see anything positive in giving her the baby he didn't even know she wanted.

"Grace?" he murmured after a moment.

"What?"

"I still think we should go to the fireworks tomorrow night."

Grace wished she could agree, but she knew it wouldn't be wise for them to go together. Like her, he just didn't want their brief affair to end. "No."

"What about Teddy and Heath? They'll be disappointed."

She hated the thought of hurting Kennedy's children. But she couldn't allow them to grow any more attached to her. "I'll see you all there, I guess. I need to start weaning them from me."

He didn't seem pleased with her response. "Why not tell me what we're fighting here?"

She couldn't burden him with her secrets, or he'd face the same torment she did. "*You're* not going to be fighting anything."

"If you really want to protect me, tell me."

It didn't work that way, and he knew that as well as she did. But when she didn't respond, he climbed out of bed. "Fine. It's late. I'd better go."

"Do you think your babysitter will be watching the clock?" she asked to temper the sudden estrangement between them.

"I'm sure she's asleep. Thursdays are my usual night out, so she typically stays over. I doubt she'll even notice when I come in." Completely unconcerned with his nudity, he bent to gather his clothes, which were strewn on the floor.

Grace couldn't help enjoying the sight of his muscular physique. She couldn't believe how easily she'd been able to make love with him. It had come naturally, without the crippling memories and distaste she'd experienced so often with George. At times she'd felt *close* to normal when she was with her old boyfriend. Last night, she'd felt *completely* normal. Whole. In love. Nothing else could compare.

She knew it was a sign of how much she wanted to be with Kennedy. But acknowledging that didn't make their situation any easier. He'd always been out of reach.

"Good night," he said and started from the room.

Grace winced at the sting of his withdrawal. He was angry with her. He was like Clay; he expected her to hand everything over to him and let him be in charge.

"There's something I should tell you," he said, turning back as he reached the door.

Grace sat up, drawing the sheet with her. "What's that?"

"If there's anything more you can do to protect yourself from whatever happened in the past, do it."

"What do you mean?" she asked, the old tension returning.

"Someone saw Clay driving Barker's car the night the reverend disappeared. It was late, around midnight, and he was heading out of town. Your mother was following him."

She could tell that Kennedy was watching her closely, so she absorbed what he said without letting the shock of it register on her face.

"Grace?"

She was trying to say he shouldn't worry, that it wasn't true—or make up some other lie—but she couldn't. What had passed between them was too fresh, too honest. So she said nothing.

His eyes swept over her as if he'd come back and make love to her again right now, if only she'd tell him the truth.

It was certainly a temptation. She already felt she'd trade just about anything for one more kiss.

"God, Grace, are you really going to let me go so easily?" he asked.

"There's nothing I can do," she said helplessly.

"I know you care about me. A woman doesn't make love like that unless she cares."

She blinked against the tears that threatened. She couldn't endanger her family because of her own selfish desires. "You should be glad," she said softly.

"Glad that you won't even give us a chance?"

"Glad that I won't tell you anything else. Go home, Kennedy," she said. "We both knew it could only last until morning."

Kennedy cursed as he hurried to his truck. Grace had said that one night wouldn't change anything. But that was bullshit. He'd known it then, too. He just hadn't been able to resist her offer. And now he was going to pay the price. He could smell her on his clothes, his skin, still craved her. He knew he'd never be able to look at her again without wanting to feel her beneath him, just the way it had been a few hours ago.

She'd given herself without reserve—given everything except the one thing keeping them apart.

As he got to his truck, something moved in his peripheral vision and he whipped around to find Joe standing in the shadows.

"Have a good night?" Joe asked, his face contorted in the light thrown off by his lighter as he lit a cigar.

Joe rarely smoked, unless he was drunk. "Don't start," Kennedy said. "I'm not in the mood."

His friend motioned toward the house. "She's quite a change after Raelynn, isn't she? Or maybe that's the attraction, what I'm missing in all of this. You clean-cut, successful guys occasionally like to go slumming. You want to take a walk on the wild side, Kennedy? See what you can get from a whore like Grace?"

Kennedy clenched his jaw. "I don't know what you're doing here, but you need to leave—now."

The end of Joe's cigar glowed in the dark as he lifted it to his mouth. "Why?" he said, laughing. "It's my turn, isn't it? That was how it worked in high school. We passed her around. With a woman like her, there's no need to be selfish. Maybe when I'm finished with her, I'll give Buzz a call."

Kennedy didn't know he was going to do it until it was too late, until he'd already launched himself at Joe and taken him down. In one part of his brain, he knew Joe was purposely provoking him and told himself to ignore it. But then he slugged Joe right in the face.

Joe had obviously been expecting a reaction, but not one as explosive as he got. "What the hell are you—" He didn't finish. Blood was pouring from his nose, filling his mouth. He tried to get out from under Kennedy, take a few swings. But his attempt to fight back only gave Kennedy an excuse to really let go. He hit Joe again and again, as if Joe was his worst enemy and not the man who'd once saved his life.

"You son of a bitch," Joe cried, throwing his own punches. But Kennedy was in too close for Joe to do any harm.

The flash of shock and anger that caused Joe to fight back quickly dissipated. Soon he simply covered his face and hollered for Kennedy to stop.

Kennedy finally allowed Joe to get up, but the moment he stood, Joe took another swing.

Dodging the blow, Kennedy tackled him again, this time slamming his head into the cement of the driveway.

Joe immediately capitulated. "I give. Kennedy, stop! I'm sorry, okay? I'm sorry. Let me up."

Kennedy was breathing hard when he released Joe. Slowly he backed off, ready to defend himself if necessary. But Joe didn't try anything else. He wiped at the blood on his mouth and chin as they stood there, glaring at each other.

"This isn't over," Joe said, spitting blood on the ground. "You wait. Even the Archer name won't be able to save you now."

"Why don't we finish it here?" Kennedy asked.

Grace's door opened before Joe could respond, and she came hurrying out in a bathrobe. "What's happening?" she cried. "What's going on?"

Joe gave her a murderous look. "*You* are," he said. Then he slung the blood dripping from his chin at her with his fingers and stomped off.

Kennedy cursed silently as he watched Joe leave. He'd just thrown a match on fresh kindling, and he knew it.

Shaking the pain from his hands, he climbed into his truck.

Grace grabbed the door before he could shut it, but he couldn't look at her just then.

"Are you okay?" she asked, sounding worried.

"Stay inside and keep the house locked," he said. Then he pulled his door out of her grasp, backed up and burned rubber as he drove away.

18

The next morning, Kennedy peeked into Teddy's room to discover that he was already awake and counting the money he'd been keeping in a large plastic ice cream tub.

"How much do you have now?" he asked, leaning a shoulder against the doorjamb.

Teddy glanced up. "Almost a hundred and fifty dollars."

"That's a lot of money. What are you going to do with it?"

Kennedy knew his youngest child had been saving up, but Teddy wouldn't say what for.

"There's something I want to buy."

"How much does it cost?"

"A lot."

"Is it a toy?"

Teddy shook his head.

"How much more money do you need?"

"I'm not sure." Teddy pursed his lips. "Maybe two hundred dollars?"

"Wow, that *is* a lot." What could an eight-year-old desire for three hundred and fifty dollars? "If you won't tell me what you want, how are you going to go and buy it?" he asked.

Teddy contemplated the neat stacks of quarters and piles of dollar bills. "Maybe I'll ask Grandma to take me."

"I guess you could do that." He sauntered into the room. "You've certainly been saving for a long time."

"Ever since Mom died," he said.

Kennedy sat on the bed. He was self-conscious about his hand, which he'd injured fighting with Joe last night. But Teddy would see it when they had breakfast if he didn't see it now.

"What happened?" his son asked, spotting his swollen knuckles almost immediately.

Kennedy tried to make a fist, but the pain was too great. He'd iced his hand all night, hoping to alleviate the swelling, but it wasn't gone down yet. He doubted he'd broken anything. He could move all his fingers. But it hurt like hell and would probably take a few days to heal.

"Dad?" Teddy prompted.

Heath stuck his head in the room, his hair mussed from sleep. "You guys are up already? Wow, look at that," he said, also zeroing in on Kennedy's hand. "How'd you get hurt?"

Kennedy wanted to tell them he'd had an accident of some sort, but the way word spread in Stillwater, he knew they'd learn the truth at some point and he didn't want to be caught in a lie. "I hit Joe."

"You got in a *fight?*" they cried.

Kennedy could hear the echo of every lecture he'd given them on solving problems without violence and wondered how far he'd set himself back on that issue. *Do as I say, not as I do....* That wasn't the kind of parent he wanted to be. And it wasn't the kind he'd been in the past. He still wasn't sure why he'd attacked Joe last night. It was as if he'd been trying to force a change physically, since he couldn't affect circumstances in any other way. When he'd made love to Grace, he'd been fighting to erase the past and create a more hopeful future. When he'd hit Joe, he'd been fighting to force him to back off and leave Grace alone.

Unfortunately, he'd only made the situation worse—for everyone.

"Joe was drunk," he explained. "He said some stupid things, and I lost my temper." He stretched out his hand so they could get a better look at the results. "I wouldn't recommend ever doing this. I'm sure I hurt him. And I certainly didn't do myself any favors, as you can see."

"Did he hit you first?" Teddy asked.

Kennedy cringed inside. "No."

Teddy's eyebrows went up. "Did he hit you back?"

"He tried."

"But you beat him up, right, Dad?" Heath said proudly, and began to hop around, shadowboxing.

"Fighting doesn't solve anything," Kennedy replied. "I'm sure there'll be more problems resulting from this than would've occurred otherwise, and I've got only myself to blame."

Heath stopped his Rocky imitation. "What kind of problems?"

The phone rang, saving Kennedy from venturing a guess.

"I'll get it," Heath said and ran down the hall.

Kennedy figured the problems he'd just mentioned were already starting when Heath brought him the cordless phone. "It's Grandma."

Wonderful. If Camille was calling him this early, she'd probably heard the news.

Using his good hand, Kennedy held the phone to his ear. "Hello?"

"Is it true?" Camille said without preamble. "Did you really break Joe Vincelli's nose?"

"I hit him a few times. I don't know if I broke his nose."

Silence.

"Mom, you there?" he said.

"According to his mother, you broke his nose *and* you gave him a black eye."

"Oh, well—" he studied his swollen hand "—that's good, I suppose. I wouldn't want it to have been for nothing."

"You think this is funny?"

"Does it matter? I can't change it now." He would've added that the expression on Joe's face *had* been kind of funny, but he didn't want the boys to hear him acknowledge it.

"So, why did it happen?" she asked.

Kennedy let go of a long breath and walked over to the window. "We got in a fight. That's all."

"That sounds like an explanation I might get from Teddy."

"Why elaborate? I'm not particularly proud of myself. How'd you hear about it so fast?"

"Elaine called me less than five minutes ago. She's nearly hysterical, saying they're going to sue you, file charges for assault and work tirelessly to see that you never hold public office in this town. She even said they're going to start a petition demanding your resignation at the bank."

"Is that all?" Kennedy said dryly.

"Kennedy," his mother replied. "What's going on? You've never been in a fight before."

He had no answer for her. He was hiding evidence, sleeping with Grace, punching Joe. He'd be better off without any of it, but one thing seemed to lead to the next. And he couldn't say he regretted sleeping with Grace. He knew he'd do it again if she ever gave him the chance. Last night had been satisfying in a very primitive way. He felt his body stir just thinking about it.

"Is it your father?" she asked, lowering her voice. "Is this some sort of reaction to his illness? I know it's affecting you. It's affecting all of us."

"I gave Joe what he deserved," he said. "What happened doesn't have anything to do with Dad." The fact that life could be fleeting, that he didn't want to waste a moment of it, might've played a role. But that was only a small part of everything going on. Mostly it came down to wanting something he couldn't have. He knew what it was like to love as deeply as he'd loved Raelynn. And he knew what it was like to lose the woman who'd meant so much to him. He wanted to fill the hole that had been left in his family when she died. Not just for himself, but for his children.

Unfortunately, they seemed to have chosen a woman whose past made that impossible.

"Elaine claims the fight was over Grace. That you were at her house at three in the morning."

This was where it all grew worse…. "That's true."

"I can guess what you were doing there. What I can't figure out is why Joe was with you."

"He wasn't with me. He was lurking outside."

"Lurking?" She hesitated as though tempted to give up her antagonistic approach. He could hear her sigh. "You were still stupid to do what you did."

"Thanks," he said with a grimace. "It helps to have you spell out the things I already know."

She ignored him. "We have to do something to stem the tide of public opinion."

"What can we do, except tell the truth? He was trespassing, he called Grace some unflattering names and I hit him. What more is there?"

"We have to prove that Grace isn't what everyone's always thought, that she was abused, like you said. Then you'll come off like a white knight for seeing the truth when no one else could. She'll finally get the respect she deserves, and—"

"She deserves?" he interrupted. "Don't tell me you're having a change of heart, Mother dear."

"Stop, will you? I'm working on damage control here. We have to make Joe look like the bad guy."

"Joe *is* the bad guy. He's a complete—" Kennedy turned to see Heath and Teddy, listening to every word, and quickly amended his remarks "—moron. But we can't do what you're suggesting."

"Why not? You told me you have proof."

"Forget it. I won't drag Grace's most tragic moments out for everyone to see. If she wanted that, she would've done it herself."

"We'd be doing her a favor. What happened to her makes her very sympathetic."

"*No.*"

"I'm willing to befriend Grace, Kennedy, but not at the cost of what it could do to you."

The automatic sprinklers came on, sending a spray of water against the window. Kennedy watched the droplets roll down the pane. "We have bigger things to worry about."

"Bigger than your future?"

He shoved a hand through his hair. "My future will be what it is. How's Dad feeling?"

There was a long pause. "He's going to be fine."

"Just take care of him, okay, Mom?" Kennedy said, imbuing his voice with some of the urgency he felt. He didn't want the decisions he'd made to affect his parents at such a critical time. "I can take care of myself."

He expected her to respond with something like, "You haven't been doing a very good job of it lately," but she didn't.

"I know it was hard to lose Raelynn," she told him. "But your father's going to make it."

"I'd better go," he said. "I've got to get to the bank." He could predict the kind of day he'd face as the story of the fight spread through town, but he figured he might as well get it over with. It beat talking about death with his mother. All the talk in the world wouldn't stop the Grim Reaper if he was on his way.

"Are you bringing the boys over here, or to Grace's house?" she asked.

He turned to watch Teddy gather up his money. "I won't be seeing Grace anymore."

"What about the fireworks tonight?" Teddy cried, overhearing.

Kennedy covered the phone. "She's going with her sister. She'll see you there."

"No," the boys cried, almost in unison.

Kennedy gestured for silence. "You'll see her, I promise."

"Isn't it a little late to give Grace up now?" Camille asked.

He thought of what Janice had told him and wondered where Clay had hidden Barker's car. "The stakes only go up from here," he replied.

* * *

Camille Archer perched on the couch in her living room, facing her husband, who sat across the coffee table from her, drinking the green tea she'd made for him. "So what do you think?" she asked.

Otis ran a hand over his jaw. He hadn't shaved yet, but he'd decided to edge the lawn before the sun grew too hot. The scent of fresh-cut grass lingered on his clothes. Camille had tried to talk him out of exerting himself. She didn't know what she'd do if they couldn't get his cancer into remission. She didn't want to live without him and constantly pleaded with him to take it easy. Kennedy had promised to edge the grass tonight, since the boys weren't old enough to do that part of the yardwork. But Otis wasn't the type to sit around. As long as there was half a breath left in him, he'd work at something. She supposed he had to, for his own peace of mind. He probably enjoyed the menial tasks he insisted on doing now that he wasn't feeling well enough to spend many hours at the office. At least he took what he did slowly, at his own pace, and often came in to rest.

"Sounds to me like he cares about her," he said simply.

"He and Raelynn had a good relationship. He could be on the rebound."

"I think it goes deeper than that. He's fighting it, but no other woman's even turned his head since Raelynn." Otis stared off into space before focusing on her again. "And if I don't make it—"

She stiffened. "Don't talk like that."

"Listen to me," he said gently. "If I'm not going to make it, I want to die knowing my son is happy."

"But would you trade happiness now for sorrow later?"

"She was only thirteen when Barker disappeared. I suspect she's as innocent as he claims she is."

"What about her family?"

"It's time this town forgot the past and moved on."

"That's easy for us to say. It's not our loved one who's missing."

"I want to support Kennedy in the relationship. It might be the last thing I'm able to do for him."

Camille had talked to Grace several times since the boys had started going over there so often and had begun to like her in spite of her earlier prejudice. Heath and Teddy worshipped her. And Kennedy was, at the very least, infatuated with her.

"If only he'd give us the proof he told me about," she said. "The fact that he attacked Joe, who nearly drowned saving his life, tells me he'd sacrifice anything to protect her. But I think it might be best for both of them if the truth finally came out. It might be the only way they can be together."

Otis winced as he shifted his position, and worry burned like hot acid in Camille's stomach.

"Are you okay?"

He grinned slightly. "Stop worrying, woman. I'm fine."

"Maybe you should lie down—"

He put up a hand to stop her fussing over him and went back to their conversation. "Can't you talk Kennedy into telling you what this proof is?"

"I don't think so. I've tried."

"Do you want me to speak to him?"

Camille thought Otis could get the information out of him—if anyone could. But she didn't want to force Kennedy to choose between the woman he desired and the father he loved. If only she could figure out what he had, she'd know whether it could help them in some way. Then, if it turned out not to be worth the pain it might cause Grace, she'd forget about it. "Maybe later," she said. "I'm going to talk to Buzz."

"You think Buzz might know something about it?" Otis asked in obvious surprise.

"He and Kennedy have been close for years. If anyone knows anything, it'll be Buzz."

"Have you seen Joe's face?" Grace asked as she, Madeline and Irene carried a blanket, a picnic basket and a bag of fireworks through the gate of the Stillwater High football field. The fact that one of the town's mayoral candidates had left her house in the middle of the night and beaten up the guy who'd once saved his life had started a big scandal. Grace didn't want to be here tonight, giving all the gossips a focal point. But Madeline and her mother wouldn't hear of her skipping out. Besides, Teddy had called to make sure she was coming. She didn't want to disappoint him and Heath.

"Not yet," Madeline said. "But I've heard plenty about how bad he looks. I've even heard that Joe filed assault charges."

"Those won't stick," Grace said. "Joe was trespassing. Besides, Judge Reynolds knows both of them."

"And in this town, a fight is still just a fight," Madeline added. "They happen occasionally at the tavern. As long as it's one-on-one between two grown men and no one's permanently injured, the police pretty much ignore it. Especially when one of those men might be their future mayor."

"He'll be fine," her mother responded. "Joe got the

worst of it." She smiled triumphantly. "His nose is crooked and swollen, he has a cut on his cheek, and both eyes are puffy."

"Sounds like Kennedy made his point," Madeline said.

Irene raised her chin. "Couldn't have happened to a nicer guy."

Grace agreed, but she also felt horrible about it. Kennedy had tried to go home earlier in the evening, but she'd asked him to stay.

Madeline moved the picnic basket to her other arm. "That kind of violence is so unlike Kennedy."

"He's always been calm and rational," Irene said.

He wasn't very rational last night, Grace thought. They'd both lost all inhibitions, thrown everything they had into their lovemaking. Knowing their affair couldn't last had made it that much more frenetic.

"What set him off?" Madeline asked.

"I don't know for sure," Grace admitted. "I heard some hollering and came rushing outside to find Joe bleeding."

"Kennedy wasn't hurt?" Irene asked.

Grace lowered her voice because they were entering a more crowded area. "He seemed fine last night, but Teddy told me his hand was swollen this morning."

"I hope he didn't break it," Irene said.

Madeline found them a nice spot on the grass and began to spread out the blanket. "No, from what I heard, Dr. Phipps X-rayed it this afternoon. It's just a bad sprain."

"Then we can still be happy about Joe getting what he deserved!" Irene said.

Grace would've been happier if she hadn't seen the

glint in Joe's eyes last night. He'd retaliate in some way. She knew it.

Cindy was with her sister on a blanket nearby. Sensing her attention, Grace was tempted to move to a new location. Cindy had tried to warn her to stay away from Kennedy, and instead of taking her advice Grace had created more problems for him.

She was embarrassed about that. But there was nowhere else to go, at least nowhere that would be any more private. *Everyone* seemed to be whispering and watching her.

"I hate this," she muttered.

"Really?" Her mother fluffed her hair. "I love it. So, are you meeting Kennedy after the show?" she asked far too loudly as she arranged their picnic.

"Stop it," Grace muttered under the breath. "I'm not going to see him at all." But then she spotted the object of their conversation only three blankets to their left. His T-shirt and baggy shorts revealed his lean, muscular build, but it was the memory of what lay beneath those clothes that made her cheeks burn.

He met her gaze and held it for several seconds. She told herself to look away, but couldn't. Finally, he bent to answer Teddy, who was tapping his arm.

"Let's go," Grace said, turning back to her mother and sister.

Irene and Madeline hadn't seen Kennedy yet, which made her think she might have a chance of convincing them. Clay was supposed to be coming tonight, with Alexandra, whom he'd been seeing off and on lately. They could find him if they were lucky. But it was no good. Irene and Madeline were far too pleased with the reversal in their situation to want to be discreet about their presence.

"Are you kidding? This is perfect," Madeline said.

"Just about everyone can see us," her mother added.

That was the problem. Grace didn't want to be so close to Kennedy. And she knew that if Teddy and Heath saw her, they'd make a big deal about coming over, which meant she'd be even more visible.

Sitting down, she did her best to hide behind the people between them, and once again felt Cindy watching her from the other direction. She turned, prepared to stare her down. But Cindy didn't appear to be angry. As soon as their eyes met, she nodded to her right and Grace followed the direction of her nod to see Joe. He was talking to his parents about thirty feet beyond Cindy, but even from that distance, Grace could tell that his face was as beat-up as Irene had said.

Grace glanced back at Cindy to find her smiling broadly—and couldn't help smiling back.

Joe watched the crowds visiting the restrooms and the concession stand located to one side of the football field, searching for Buzz. He hadn't wanted to come tonight. But, as his mother had pointed out, it was important that he let as many people as possible see what Kennedy had done. He also needed to work fast to insure that all his friends, who were also Kennedy's friends, didn't immediately side with Kennedy. If he could reach Buzz before Kennedy did and give his side, Buzz would probably stay out of it, and Ronnie and Tim and the others would likely follow his lead.

That was all Joe hoped to accomplish. He didn't want to feel isolated. He wouldn't allow Grace—or even Kennedy—to do that to him.

Walking restlessly back and forth, he glared sullenly at anyone who dared get too close. Unless it was someone he felt he should acknowledge. Then he'd grunt and wave as though he was in too much pain to do more.

And he was. But that wasn't the worst of it. He looked terrible. People were treating him like Frankenstein's monster....

Where the hell was Buzz? He had to be here somewhere. The fireworks wouldn't start until twilight deepened into darkness. They had at least fifteen minutes, and if he knew Sarah Harte, she'd have Buzz at the concession stand, getting her something calorie-laden. If she'd been *his* wife, Joe would've put a stop to the weight gain right away. But when she acknowledged her widening hips, Buzz simply laughed and called it "happy fat."

Joe just called it *fat*. And he didn't find it appealing.

A laugh came from somewhere behind him—a laugh he immediately recognized—and he pivoted to see Grace standing next to Madeline at the cotton candy machine not ten feet away. "I haven't had this stuff since I was ten years old," she said.

Joe's stomach knotted with a mixture of resentment and admiration. Maybe Grace was white trash and liked to pretend she wasn't. And maybe she'd cost him his best friend—he'd never forgive her for that. But she sure was beautiful, and getting prettier every day. Since she'd come to Stillwater, her skin had tanned to a deep golden color and looked soft as satin, and her eyes had begun to sparkle with a liveliness he'd never seen there before. In that sundress, she was the epitome of feminine. She always exuded sensuality, but tonight more than ever. Knowing that Kennedy had

been in her bed last night drove Joe crazy. His muscles bunched as he imagined Kennedy pumping into
her....

"Remember mixing butter and sugar together and
eating it when Mom wasn't home?" he heard Madeline
ask.

Her voice carried to him as easily as Grace's had.
They were in a good mood, enjoying themselves.

Joe resented that, too. He was miserable because of
Grace. Why should *she* be having fun?

"Yes!" Grace licked a piece of cotton candy from
her lips and laughed again. "Wow, that brings back
memories."

Circling wide, Joe came up behind them. "What about
those bleachers?" he said, speaking into Grace's ear.

Her spine practically snapped as she whirled around
to face him. "What about them?" she challenged, the
levity gone from her wide, thick-lashed eyes.

"Do they bring back memories, too? That was our
spot, remember?" He licked his fingers and rubbed
them in front of his bandaged nose. "I can still smell
you, Grace."

Blanching, she threw the cotton candy she'd just
purchased into the trash can. "With what's left of your
nose, it's funny you can smell anything," she said and
grabbed Madeline's arm. "Let's go."

Joe had meant to intimidate her, upset her. But like
every encounter with Grace these days, this exchange
hadn't given him the satisfaction he craved. Somehow, he wanted to make her need him again. Like she
used to, back when she wasn't fit to lick his boots.

He reached out to stop her from going, but dropped
his arm when the crowd parted and he spotted Buzz
talking to Camille Archer.

"What's that bitch want with Buzz?" he muttered to himself and slipped through the people between them. He hoped to get close enough to hear. But Kennedy's mother nodded, touched Buzz's arm affectionately in parting and headed to the field before he could catch even a wisp of their conversation.

"Hey," Joe called, striding up.

Buzz had been wearing a puzzled expression as he watched Camille disappear into the crowd, but it turned to surprise when he saw Joe. "Damn, you look even worse than I expected. What the hell did you do to make Kennedy tear you apart like that?"

"I could've stopped him," Joe said. "But I was trying not to hurt him. We've been friends all our lives, you know. I still don't understand what made him come at me like that. I was just joking around."

Buzz didn't seem completely convinced, but he didn't argue. "Come on, Sarah and the kids are hungry," he said and got in line at the snack bar.

"What'd Camille want?" Joe asked conversationally. "To tell you how I've mistreated her boy? First, I save Kennedy's fool life. Then he dates the woman who probably murdered my uncle and busts up my face for not liking it. I don't know how anybody could feel too sorry for him."

"Camille didn't say anything about the fight," Buzz said, glancing over his shoulder as though he knew his wife would be getting impatient for her food.

"What, then?"

Buzz shook his head.

"You don't want to tell me?"

"It's not that. It's just that I'm sure it wouldn't mean any more to you than it did to me."

"Try me. What'd she say?"

Buzz's eyebrows rose as he shrugged. "Maybe you *should* know," he said. "Maybe it would get you to back off the Montgomerys."

"What?" Joe pressed.

"She says Kennedy has something that'll prove Grace's family is innocent."

Joe shoved his hands in his pockets to hide the clenching of his fists. He wanted the Montgomerys to be guilty. He *needed* them to be guilty. Or Kennedy would come out of this looking like a hero, and he'd be dog shit. "What kind of proof?"

"I have no idea. Kennedy hasn't mentioned a thing to me. Did you hear him say anything unusual at the pool hall last night?"

"Nothing."

Buzz jingled the change in his pocket. "Whatever it is, she thinks he buried it somewhere. She kept pressing me, as if some detail might jog my memory. But it doesn't make any sense to me. If he has proof that Grace is innocent, why would he hide it?"

Kennedy *wouldn't* hide anything that proved Grace's innocence, Joe thought. There'd be no reason for that. He *wanted* her to be innocent.

He'd only hide something that proved her guilt....

Joe's heart suddenly slammed against his ribs as the meaning of Buzz's words became clear to him. Kennedy had something, something Joe needed.

Joe blinked several times, his mind racing. Where would Kennedy hide it? At his house? In his car?

No, Buzz had said he'd buried it. But where?

The line moved forward, and Joe moved with it. Then he froze in place. *Buried* it? That was it! That was what Kennedy and Grace had been doing in the woods up at the lake!

Remembering the small mound of earth he'd noticed not far from the restrooms made Joe feel giddy with relief and hope. He knew where it was. Just when he was beginning to panic, just when he feared Grace would get the best of him, Kennedy's own mother handed him everything he needed to destroy the Montgomerys for good—and maybe Kennedy, too.

"Joe?" Buzz said, sounding perplexed.

Joe told himself to breathe deeply, to calm down. "What?"

"You okay?"

"Yeah. Listen, my head is hurting like hell. I'm going home to take a couple of aspirin, okay?"

"The fireworks haven't even started yet. Are you sure you don't want to tough it out a little longer?"

"No, I'm out of here." Joe wasn't worried about missing the show. If he found anything at the lake, the real fireworks wouldn't start until he got back.

19

Teddy and Heath located Grace just before the fireworks began. Kennedy let them sit with her because he knew they'd beg him until he relented, even if he tried to say no. She reminded them too much of their mother. In most ways, Grace and Raelynn were very different people, but they both had a gentle way with children. Like Raelynn, Grace didn't talk down to Teddy or Heath, or act as though they were a bother. She was genuinely interested in what they had to say. And they thrived on the attention.

After the fight with Joe, Kennedy would've preferred to let the gossip die down before allowing Teddy and Heath to associate with Grace again. Lord knew he'd given the Vincellis sufficient fodder for their campaign against him. But Grace would be gone after the summer ended. How could he deny his boys the chance to enjoy her company while she was here?

Heck, he wanted to be with her, too. He'd tried to convince himself that a few hours in her arms would be enough. But what they'd shared last night only made the situation that much more difficult. Now he had a slew of erotic images to contend with, images that burst upon his mind when he least expected it. Grace eagerly meeting his thrusts as they made love.

Grace's satiated smile as he ran his fingers along the curves of her body. Grace's eyelashes resting against her cheeks as she lay peacefully in his arms. He might have broken down and gone over to the Montgomery blanket himself, except his parents had joined him, with some of their close friends and neighbors.

"So are we going to have the funds to build that new wing at the elementary school this year?" Tom Greenwood asked Kennedy's father. They'd been talking about town business for a few minutes. Usually this interested Kennedy. He had strong opinions on what should happen with the school, plenty to say. But tonight he could think only of Grace and how or when he might be able to get his hands on her again.

Glancing toward her for probably the millionth time, he saw her smooth Teddy's hair off his forehead and wished he could move closer. But then he caught his mother watching him and quickly looked away.

"It's a possibility," Otis was saying. "But I'm still not convinced we shouldn't start over. That building is getting too old."

"You're talking about more money, money we don't have."

"In the long run, it'll be cheaper than sinking a hundred and fifty thousand into that old school."

"So where would you build? On the Corte property?"

"No, that's too far out of town." Otis started naming possible sites, enumerating the pros and cons of each, but Kennedy just pretended to listen. He wasn't interested in any issues right now. He was only interested in Grace.

A boom signaled the beginning of the show. Conscious of his mother's attention, Kennedy stretched out on the blanket and watched several fireworks explode in the sky. The kids around him gasped at the shimmering display of red and blue. But as soon as his mother entered his father's conversation with Tom, Kennedy's eyes drifted back to Grace.

She was lying between Teddy and Heath, gazing skyward.

Kennedy remembered the smell of her, the smooth texture of her skin, and knew he'd been more than crazy to believe last night would solve anything. He still wanted her, more than ever.

Go home, Kennedy. We both knew it could only last until morning....

Had she meant it?

"What about the middle school?" he heard his mother say to Tom and Otis. "That needs repairs, too. I hear the roof's leaking in several places...."

The little boy on the next blanket moved, blocking Kennedy's view of Grace. He shifted to compensate, and found her looking right at him. And then he knew. Whatever was happening between them wasn't over yet. The longing in her face told him she felt the same driving need to be close, to kiss deeply, to touch.

"How do you like the show, Kennedy?" his mother asked.

Kennedy pulled his gaze away. "It's great," he said. But he wasn't thinking about the Fourth of July. He was thinking about buying more condoms. Several boxes. He and Grace had most of the summer. They'd be foolish to waste it.

Camille leaned forward. "Are you okay?" she asked.

"I'm fine," he said. But he wasn't so sure. He was

imagining how he'd feel when it was time for Grace to leave. Would he be able to give her up?

Of course he would, he told himself. He'd have to.

Grace breathed in the scent of baby shampoo that lingered in Teddy's hair. He and Heath felt so perfect in her arms. Teddy's face was sticky from the cotton candy he'd eaten earlier. And they wiggled a lot, which made Madeline complain. But Grace couldn't think of anywhere she'd rather be than sandwiched between them.

Unless it was with Kennedy. She wanted him there, too. But she was trying hard not to show it. By downplaying their relationship, she hoped to take away Joe's power. If they didn't appear too interested in each other, it probably wouldn't matter so much that they'd been together once or twice. Kennedy was a widower. He had to get lonely. A brief affair to assuage that loneliness was completely forgivable—especially, in a community as misogynistic as Stillwater—for a man.

As long as this town didn't perceive her as a threat to Kennedy's heart, she figured he might still be able to win the election. Provided everything calmed down. But in order for that to happen, she and Kennedy needed to keep their distance.

"Kennedy's watching you again," her mother murmured gleefully.

Grace kissed Heath's head, then smiled at the fireworks bursting across the sky. She didn't think she'd ever been so happy, at least not since before her mother had married the reverend. Only Molly was missing. If Molly were here, she'd want the show to last forever.

"He doesn't make any secret about what he wants, does he?" Madeline's girlish giggle was infectious. "He acts like he can't take his eyes off you."

"He's just checking on the boys," Grace said.

Irene shook her head. "No, he's not."

"If Kirk ever looked at me that way, I think I *would* marry him," Madeline said dreamily.

"Who's looking at you?" Teddy asked, finally tuning in.

"No one," Grace replied. But Heath answered at the same time.

"Dad."

Obviously Kennedy's oldest had picked up more than Grace had realized. She made a surprised face at Madeline over his head.

"He thinks she's pretty," he said.

"Maybe he'll marry you!" Teddy chimed in.

"No, we're just friends," she said. She knew that could never happen. But she had this moment. For now it was enough. Or so she believed until the fireworks were over. Then she felt strangely bereft as she kissed Teddy and Heath goodbye.

As they ran to their father, she forced herself to turn away. But Kennedy bumped into her as everyone jostled to get out of the stadium, and thrust part of a napkin into her hand.

She shoved it in the pocket of her skirt without response. The Vincellis were on her left, glaring at her. But the moment Madeline dropped her off, she hurried into her house, pulled the napkin out and opened it.

Come over, it said.

It was after midnight. Grace held a glass of wine in one hand and Kennedy's brief summons in the other. She'd been telling herself for hours that she wouldn't go. They had an understanding. Last night was supposed to be their only concession to how they felt. She knew she'd be doing Kennedy and his boys a favor by refusing to continue the relationship. She also knew she probably didn't have enough willpower. Last night didn't feel like the end. It felt like the beginning.

The clock chimed twelve-thirty, jerking her out of her thoughts. She was going, and she knew it. No use prolonging the wait. But she'd have to be careful. Joe seemed to be keeping a close eye on her place. If he was out there somewhere, waiting as he'd been waiting last night, she certainly didn't want him to know where she was going.

Gathering her purse and keys, she walked outside and circled the house. No one skulked about in the garden or the garage. No one lurked in the drive. She even sat in her car for a few minutes to see if his truck went by.

Firecrackers popped a few streets over, a little late celebrating. But there was no sign of Joe.

He couldn't spy on her twenty-four seven; he had to sleep sometime. With his face so badly injured, he was no doubt home in bed.

Chastising herself for being paranoid, she started her car and pulled into the street. She wouldn't park at Kennedy's, she decided. She'd leave her car a few blocks away and walk.

Kennedy's house was rather intimidating. Perfectly restored, it had three stories with a turret and a gabled roof. It was by far the best in Stillwater—the town's only historic building, besides the old post office.

Grace felt as though she had no right to venture inside. She almost turned back three times as she advanced toward the wide verandah. Maybe Raelynn had passed on, but this was still her house, her man, her children.

The voices of Kennedy's friends echoed in Grace's mind. *Hey, babe, come and give me a little sugar... You know what I like.*

Biting her lip, she lowered the hand she'd just raised to knock. What had she been thinking? She had no business here.

She hurried down the steps. But a click behind her indicated someone had opened the door.

"You weren't going to knock?" Kennedy asked.

Silently cursing the weak will that had brought her here in the first place, she pivoted on the flagstone path leading through the tulips and irises of Kennedy's parklike yard. "I didn't want to wake you."

"I wasn't asleep."

A car passed on the road. Grace held her breath until she could be sure it wasn't Joe.

"What's wrong?" Kennedy asked.

"This place...changes things," she replied.

The deep shadows made it difficult to read his expression. "How?"

"I don't feel comfortable here."

He studied her. "Why not? I don't think you've been over before, have you?"

"I went by this place a lot. I can still remember seeing you and your friends celebrating Lacy Baumgarter's sixteenth birthday party right there." She motioned to the side yard. "I was on my way to the pizza parlor. You were pushing the girls on the tree swing."

He said nothing.

She cleared her throat. "Anyway, it reminds me of all the reasons we don't belong together."

"I would've come over to Evonne's, but I can't leave the boys alone," he said.

"I know."

"Does that mean you're not coming in?"

"I can't."

Stepping outside, he closed the door quietly behind him. "Grace…"

"What?"

He strode down the path. He was wearing nothing but a pair of blue jeans, and she tried not to let her eyes linger on his bare torso.

"I'd really like you to come in," he said softly.

She shook her head, gazing beyond him, at the house.

He lifted her hands and kissed her fingertips. "I think you'd like the place, once you got used to it."

"You hurt your hand last night," she said as she noticed the swelling.

"Not too bad. The doctor said it'll be fine in a week or so."

"That's good."

He tried to tug her toward the door, but she resisted. "Come on, Grace. What's wrong?"

"I don't want to make love to you with you wishing I was Raelynn," she admitted.

Dropping her hands, he scowled at her. "I don't want you to be anyone other than who you are."

When she didn't respond, he put his arms around her and pressed his lips to her temple. "That party wasn't as much fun as it looked," he whispered. "None of them were."

She nodded. "We're just so different, Kennedy."

"Who says?"

Everyone knew it. She'd *lived* it.

"Come on," he said and led her onto the lawn.

"Where are you taking me?" she asked in surprise.

He pointed to the old tree swing. "It's your turn."

Still bent on leaving, Grace hesitated. But the envy she'd felt all those years ago kept her where she was, and the expectant look on Kennedy's face convinced her. Sitting in the swing, she held on to the ropes as he started to push.

The chair creaked as he sent her flying higher and higher. With each lift of her stomach, Grace's heart raced with exhilaration.

Closing her eyes, she smiled at the heady sensation of Kennedy's firm hands helping her sail through space. Difficult though it was to believe, the girl who'd been the laughingstock of the whole town had finally been invited to the party.

By none other than the prince himself.

The inside of Kennedy's house was as elegant as the outside. Expensive furniture and paintings filled room after room. Persian rugs covered richly polished hardwood floors. Crown molding lined the ceiling. And there were plenty of built-in cabinets and shelves.

Grace began to feel out of place again as he walked her through the parlor, the living room, the sitting room and the kitchen. Especially when she saw the family portrait hanging in the dining room. But Kennedy held on to her the whole time, as if he sensed that she might bolt.

Fortunately, she saw numerous little reminders that Teddy and Heath lived here, too. That helped.

"Can I see the boys?" she asked.

He took her upstairs to the second story. Heath's room was on the right. Teddy's was just past it. Grace smiled as she stood at each boy's bedside and stared down at his sleeping face. "They're wonderful, aren't they?" she whispered, rubbing her knuckles against Teddy's soft cheek.

"They think you're pretty special, too." Kennedy kissed her neck. "They'd be mad if they knew you were here and they didn't get to see you."

"It'll be hard to leave them when I go back to Jackson."

"Don't talk about leaving."

The grandfather clock chimed in the entryway below.

"I don't know anyone else who has a grandfather clock," she said with a smile.

He nipped at her ear. "If you don't like it, I'll get rid of it."

"Right now?" she teased.

"First thing in the morning. It can wait that long, can't it?"

"I don't know," she said more seriously. "I don't like being reminded of the passing time."

"Neither do I," he admitted. "Not when you're here."

He drew her away from Teddy's bedside, but she stepped on something that made her pause. "What's this?" she asked, picking up the page of a magazine, folded into a tiny triangle.

"I don't know." Taking it from her, he stood in the light spilling from the hallway to see what it was. Then he looked back at his son. "Oh, my gosh, this is it."

"What?"

He turned the paper so she could see. It showed a marble statue of an angel and two different birdbaths, along with ordering information for each. "What he's been saving up for," Kennedy murmured.

Remembering Teddy at her door the day she'd first met him, Grace took a closer look. He'd told her he was saving up for something special. "He wants a birdbath?"

"He wants the angel."

"How do you know?"

"Because Raelynn clipped this out herself. She was considering buying it for the garden. When she died, Teddy wanted me to get it for her headstone."

"You didn't want an angel?"

"I preferred something rectangular, something that could be more easily inscribed." He frowned as though disappointed in himself. "I guess I was so caught up in my own sorrow that I didn't realize how important the angel was to him."

"It's been two years. How sweet of him not to give up."

"He's quite a child." Refolding the clipping, he placed it on the dresser. "I'll have to talk to him when I get an opportunity, see if I can help him somehow."

"I think he wants to do it himself," Grace said. "Otherwise, he would've come to you."

Kennedy rubbed a thumb over her cheek and bottom lip. "You're probably right. But now that I know, maybe I can hire him to do some extra work around the house."

The desire Kennedy inspired as he touched her coiled in the pit of Grace's stomach. "That's a better idea."

He pulled away long enough to adjust his son's covers, then guided her out of Teddy's room and through a set of double doors that led to a large master suite with a tall four-poster bed. A small retreat branched off to the left, containing a secretary and a couch with lots of pillows. Two large walk-in closets and a giant bathroom were located to the right.

"This is nice," she said, but the tender moment they'd shared in Teddy's room was gone and she was feeling nervous again, supremely aware that she was in another woman's domain.

She must have communicated her anxiety in some way because Kennedy told her to relax as he walked into the bathroom and turned on the Jacuzzi tub.

"I'm not nervous," she lied.

Coming back to her, he slipped his hands around her waist. "Maybe it's me. I'm afraid you're going to walk out of here while I'm dying to make love to you."

She glanced once more at the bed—Raelynn's bed. "I'm considering it."

"Last night, you asked me to stay. Now I'm asking the same of you."

"But I don't belong here, Kennedy."

"I want you with me." He tugged her bottom lip into his mouth. "Tell me you want that, too."

"What I want doesn't change anything."

Slipping his good hand under her shirt, he unfastened her bra, and she caught her breath as his palm covered her breast. "There's nothing to worry about. I've got plenty of birth control this time."

"If I had my way, we wouldn't even use it," she said.

He jerked back as though she'd given him an electric shock. "What?"

"I want a baby more than anything," she told him. "I want *your* baby."

An emotion Grace couldn't quite interpret appeared in his eyes. "But—"

"It's impossible," she interrupted, shaking her head. "I know."

He kissed her again, more tentatively at first. But as she put her arms around his neck and began to respond to the teasing of his lips, his kisses began to deepen.

"The tub's going to overflow," he said and pulled her into the bathroom, where he tested the water and stripped off their clothes.

When he stood before her completely naked, she smiled. They were nearly surrounded by mirrors that showed her at least ten reflections. "Wow," she said.

He grinned, then urged her into the water with him, where he lathered her entire body with soap. "Grace?"

The sensation of his wet skin sliding against hers made her feel as if she were floating on air. "What?"

"If I give you a baby, will you stay?" he murmured.

"The night?"

"Forever. Will you marry me?"

Grace felt as though he'd opened the drain and she was spinning down with the water. *"What?"*

He threaded his fingers through hers. "You heard me."

"We're crazy to even consider it. You know that."

"Just tell me you're innocent," he said. "Tell me you had nothing to do with Barker's disappearance and I'll give you a baby, marry you, let you share Teddy and Heath."

Grace's heart was beating so hard she thought it might leap out of her chest. "Kennedy, no…."

"Yes," he insisted, letting go so he could search out her most sensitive parts.

Grace gasped at his bold exploration. What he was doing made her weak, shaky…and eager for more. "I…can't."

"I know what I want, Grace. To be together. To

know you'll be here with me at the end of each day. Don't you want the same thing?"

"More than I ever thought possible," she whispered.

"Then you have to trust me. We can make a future together, but only if we trust each other."

She remembered Clay telling her she deserved a chance at happiness. Did she really? Could it happen? Kennedy seemed to be offering her everything she'd ever dreamed about. But the price was absolute honesty.

"Grace?" Kennedy pleaded, kissing her temples, her eyelids, her cheeks. "Come on. I'll never hurt you. We could be a family."

Every muscle tensed—with hope, expectation, desire. And fear.

"We could have a little girl, a sister for Heath and Teddy."

There were voices in her head, screaming that she was never supposed to tell. The world would come to an end if she opened her mouth. But her heart was begging her to believe, just this once.

"It was my fault," she whispered.

He froze but didn't remove the hand that cupped her in a very private way. "How?"

"He—he wouldn't leave me alone." Her chest suddenly grew so tight she had to fight for every breath. "He—he had Molly locked out of the r-room. And then my m-mother came home and knew something was wrong. H-he wasn't even supposed to be home. He'd sent her away on purpose." Kennedy didn't move, but he was watching her intently. "She started accusing him, screaming that she was going to the police, that she'd reveal him for the filthy scum he was, and he…he couldn't take it. Appearances were everything to him. He denied it, again and again, but my mother knew. She knew at last." The words started coming quicker, like a torrent of water breaking through a dam. "The screaming escalated and things got violent. He started to hit her. I didn't know what to do. I tried to stop him, but he threw me off and kept going after her. Then Clay came home and—" she gulped for more air "—and he got into it, to save her, to protect me."

"And the reverend turned on him?"

She nodded. "My m-mother had to stop it, had to get him off my brother."

"How'd she do it?" Kennedy asked softly.

"She hit him on the head with the butcher block that held our knives."

"And?" he prompted.

"He fell," she said simply. "He collapsed right there on the kitchen floor. We—we never dreamed he was dead. But there was so much blood and…" She blinked rapidly, trying to hold back tears. "He wasn't moving, wasn't breathing. We didn't know what to do. We couldn't call the police. No one here liked us, no one would believe that it was merely an accident. My mother knew she'd go to jail and the rest of us would be split up."

"The Barkers and Vincellis wouldn't have tolerated the humiliation. They would've fought you," Kennedy agreed. "They would've demanded revenge."

"He was the town preacher, above reproach. *Everyone* would want revenge! It was an accident, Kennedy. But it wouldn't have happened if it weren't for me. They were fighting about me."

The end of her confession met with dead silence. Kennedy stared at her. He seemed to be shocked that she'd finally admitted the truth she'd hidden for eighteen years.

The tears Grace could no longer hold back rolled down her cheeks, and she gazed up at him, terrified by what she'd just revealed. But he didn't let the fear last.

"You were only thirteen."

"I'll never forget it. Molly huddled in the corner, crying. My mother screaming hysterically. And Clay taking calm and deliberate control of everything. 'We'll bury him behind the barn,' he said."

Grace wondered if Kennedy would ever look at her the same way again. But he ran a finger tenderly over the curve of her jaw. "I won't let any of that stand between us. I'll do whatever I can to protect you," he promised, kissing away her tears. Then he tossed the condoms on the ledge of the tub into the garbage, settled his hips between her thighs and sealed his promise with his own risk.

After breaking a small window at the back of Evonne's house, Joe removed his T-shirt, wrapped it around his forearm and reached inside to unlock the door. He expected the noise to bring Grace stumbling sleepily down the stairs—and eagerly anticipated the panic in her voice when she called out to see if someone was there.

But he heard nothing.

Carrying his uncle's Bible with him, he shut the door quietly and felt his way through the dark. It would be even better to surprise her in bed, he decided, and smiled as he imagined how she might plead with him. He'd tell her what she could do to stop him from going to the police, let her think she could avoid the vengeance this Bible would launch. Then, after he'd used her all he wanted, he'd call the police anyway.

She shouldn't have messed with him. He'd get his

revenge on her and—he gingerly touched his injured nose—Kennedy, too.

His footsteps creaked on the old boards as he climbed the stairs, but he heard no response from above.

"Gra-ace," he murmured, a singsong quality to his voice. "Oh, Gra-acie. Have I got a surprise for you."

Still nothing.

He poked his head inside the first bedroom. A spare. The next one was empty, too. The last room on the right obviously belonged to Grace, but she wasn't there. Her perfume and hairbrush lay on the dresser. Her bed was neatly made. There was a skirt tossed on the rocking chair and a pair of panties lying on the floor near the hamper.

Crossing the room, he held the panties to his nose and breathed deeply, looking forward to the pleasure to come. Then he shoved them inside his pocket and headed back downstairs. Maybe he'd passed her without realizing it. She could've fallen asleep on the wicker couch in the screened-in porch, the hammock in the yard, or the sofa in the living room.

"Grace?" he called, turning on the lights. Finding an empty wineglass on the coffee table, he licked the rim. She'd taste as good as she smelled.

"Where are you?" The house was empty. So was the screened-in-porch and the hammock. Jogging to the alley where he'd parked his truck, he retrieved the flashlight he'd used at the campground and looked through the windows in the door of her garage. When he first arrived, he'd taken a quick walk around the place, just to make sure she was alone. Because he didn't see her car in the drive, he'd assumed it was in the garage, where she usually parked.

Unfortunately, the garage was as empty as the driveway.

"Gone," he muttered, feeling deprived. What now? He hadn't expected it, but she could be staying with Madeline, her mother, Clay or even Kennedy.

After last night, he was betting on Kennedy. But he didn't want to go there; he wanted to confront her when she was alone. He'd deal with Kennedy later, when he could tell him how many times she'd brought him to a mind-blowing orgasm.

Using his flashlight to check his watch, he saw that it was nearly two in the morning. If she was with Kennedy, she'd probably be home soon. Kennedy wouldn't have a woman in his bed when the boys woke up.

So he'd wait for her, he thought, heading back into the house. He'd have to delay his gratification a little longer, which certainly didn't make him happy. But there were some positives to waiting. He could make himself at home, look through her stuff, drink a glass of wine—and let the anticipation build.

20

Kennedy kissed Grace's shoulder and pulled her a little closer to him. If they hadn't made a baby in the past few hours, it wasn't for lack of trying. Grace was now his to love and protect, just as he'd loved Raelynn, just as he loved his boys. He knew there'd be sacrifices. He might even have to pull out of the mayoral race. But somehow that didn't upset him. Not when he thought of waking up with Grace in his arms for the rest of his life.

Rolling onto his back, he let go of her and stared up at the ceiling, searching his heart and mind to see if loving Grace changed how he felt about his first wife.

No. Raelynn was still there, as much a part of him as ever. It wasn't a matter of loving one or the other, he concluded. It was a matter of loving both, which was what made his relationship with Grace feel so right. He could bring her into his home, let her enjoy Teddy and Heath, even make love to her without any guilt— because Raelynn would've wanted him to be happy. He was certain of that; he'd want the same for her.

"It's late. I'd better go," Grace murmured.

Kennedy hadn't realized she was awake. "How do you feel?"

She smiled sleepily. "Good."

"No regrets?" he asked, wanting to calm her if she was having second thoughts. He knew she might be a little overwhelmed by what they'd promised each other, by what they'd done.

She leaned up on one elbow and gazed down at him, her hair puddling like silk against his chest. "No regrets." She touched the side of his face. "What about you?"

"None," he said and meant it. He was a little apprehensive about the future, but only because he was afraid he couldn't completely protect her from the reaction of their small community.

"You might feel differently in a couple of months."

He could tell she was referring to the possibility that she might be pregnant. "No," he said. "Seeing you carry my baby will make me proud."

"If you lost the election, would you ever consider moving away from this town?" she asked.

He skimmed his hand over the curve of her hip. "If you couldn't be happy here. But…I wouldn't be able to go for a while."

"Because of the bank?"

He brought her hand to his mouth and kissed her slim fingers. The future was far brighter now that good things were occurring along with the bad. Kennedy had thought his days of being as content and fulfilled as he'd been with Raelynn were over.

And now there was Grace.

He smiled as the more critical events in his life suddenly seemed more like change than loss.

He still didn't want to say goodbye to his father, though. "My dad has melanoma, Grace," he said, sobering. "I couldn't go anywhere until…until we see what happens with that."

"I had no idea."

"No one else knows, except my father's family in Iuka."

"I'm so sorry," she whispered.

The fan whirled slowly overhead, around and around. "My mom believes he's going to beat it."

She kissed the side of his mouth. "Your mom? What do *you* believe?"

"I don't know. I hope she's right."

"So do I. For you. And for Teddy and Heath."

Kennedy thought about the next few months. "It means we might be here for a while. Are you okay with that?"

She nodded, but she didn't say anything to make that nod more convincing before settling her head on his shoulder.

"Grace?"

"Hmm?"

"What about your job?"

"I'll have to quit."

He could smell her perfume, feel her soft flesh against him. "Will you mind?"

"No. I can always go back to work when the kids are older. Even if we don't have a baby right away, I want to be home with Heath and Teddy. They're more important to me than any job."

She was the missing piece, the piece that made his family complete. He couldn't believe how fortunate he was to have found her.

His body stirred, and he rolled over to make love to her again. Kissing her deeply, he buried his hands in her long hair. "The next few months won't be easy," he murmured against her mouth. "But you'll hang in there with me, won't you? You won't give up on us—no matter what?"

"I won't give up," she promised. "I'll do whatever it takes."

On the surface, her answer was the one he'd been looking for. Only there was a ferocity to "I'll do whatever it takes" that gave him pause. He would've questioned Grace about it. Except he lost that thought almost the second it entered his mind. He couldn't concentrate on anything else when Grace closed her eyes and surrendered to his touch.

She was committed to him—that was all that mattered.

He hoped.

Once Grace reached her car, she sat there, staring out at the dark farmland that stretched on either side of her. So much had changed in the last few hours. *Everything* had changed. And yet nothing had changed at all. She'd agreed to marry Kennedy Archer. They planned to raise a family together. But loving him still put him and his children at risk. Joe, the other Vincellis and Madeline still sought the truth. The reverend was still dead at her family's hand—and buried in too shallow a grave.

What if the reverend's car turned up one day. A find like that would, no doubt, lead to another search of the farm. If the police ever came back, Grace knew it would be the beginning of the end. They'd leave no stone unturned. McCormick would be running the show this time, and he wasn't inept, like Jenkins had been before him.

She had to do something, she decided. Something to insure that the worst never happened.

Starting her car, she pulled onto the highway and headed home. Whether Clay liked it or not, it was time to give the Reverend Barker a new resting place. Getting rid of his remains was the only way to protect them all.

Joe saw Grace's headlights swing into the drive and quickly stepped to the side of her front window, out of sight. She'd learn what was waiting for her soon enough. In the privacy of her own home. Where no one could hear if she made a fuss.

He smiled, eager to see her cowed. He couldn't wait to make her try just about anything he could imagine.

But she didn't come in. When the garage door rolled up, she pulled only partially inside.

He moved to another window so he could see better, but all that was visible from the house was the back end of her Beemer. He assumed she'd gotten out and left the engine running because the taillights stayed on long after the brake lights went off.

What the hell was she doing out there?

He parted the drapes and changed positions yet again, but he could no longer see her. Not until she emerged from the garage carrying something long and dark. Something that looked like—he dropped the glass he'd been holding, which shattered on the hardwood floor—a shovel!

Despite the alcohol he'd consumed, Joe's heart began to race as she put it in her trunk. What was she doing? Considering what he'd just turned up at the lake, he could think of only one possibility. What else would motivate her to go digging in the middle of the night?

He watched her close the trunk and hurry into the

garage. Her brake lights flashed, then she backed up and the door rolled down.

She was on her way.

Joe stayed at the window long enough to make sure she turned left toward the farm. Then he ran to the alley, jumped in his truck and headed out in the same direction. With any luck, he'd catch sight of her tail-lights within minutes, he thought. And he was right. Four minutes down the road, where Main Street merged with the highway, he saw her driving about a mile ahead of him.

He slowed down. No need to give his presence away. If he had his guess, he'd soon be able to tell the whole town exactly where they could find his uncle's body.

Grace parked in the thicket of trees that lined the back side of Clay's property, along the canal, and gathered up the shovel, gloves and flashlight she'd brought. She knew if Clay realized what she was up to, he'd stop her immediately. He expected her to leave everything as it was. But there was too much at stake. She had to do whatever she could to make sure her past wouldn't eventually ruin her future—and Kennedy's.

Clay, her mother, Molly—they deserved the chance to forget and move on. This was something she could do for all of them.

The deep croak of a toad broke the silence as she crossed the cotton fields toward the farm. The pond wasn't far. She could hear the trickle of water as she drew closer and struggled to concentrate on that instead of the creak of the weather vane atop the barn, which shifted at unexpected moments. That creak set her teeth on edge. She could remember lying in bed the summer the reverend died, her windows open wide to catch any hint of a breeze, and hearing that sound. No matter how hard she tried not to, she'd think it was the barn door sliding open and imagine the reverend leaving his office for the night—and coming for her. Pulling the sheet up to her chin even though she was already damp with sweat, she'd stare at the darkness beyond her window until her eyes burned, or the sun finally came up.

Those memories threatened to rob her of the strength she needed to use her shovel. Stopping, she bent over to catch her breath, but then marched on. She'd made her decision. She couldn't live in Stillwater another day knowing that proof of what had happened was right on the farm, exactly where so many people suspected it to be.

To get through this, she had to break what she was doing into very small steps. Perform one action at a time and think no further. Soon it would be over. And afterward, without the constant fear of discovery, she'd be fine. There were too many other, happier things to dwell on now.

When she reached the clearing on the other side of a copse of trees about twenty yards from the barn, she set the shovel against the trunk of a weeping willow and pulled on her gloves. This was the spot. She felt as though she could've found it with her eyes shut. It was far enough from the barn that Jed hadn't been able to hear them above the radio he had blaring, but close enough that Clay didn't have to push the wheelbarrow over too much rough terrain. Time had been an issue that night. They'd had far too little of it....

Don't remember. Act. For Kennedy. For Teddy and Heath. For everyone I love.

Her flashlight swept over a cotton baler, a wagon, a tractor and some tractor wheels piled next to a relatively new shed. There was also a '57 Chevy truck parked beside a plough. Because Clay wasn't a horse lover—his only experience with horses had been with the reverend's stallion, which had bitten him at every opportunity—he'd ripped out the stalls and used the space to restore old cars. He was working on a Thunderbird and a Mustang. She'd seen them when she and Clay had dismantled the reverend's office, and figured this truck was either a future project or a rejected one. In any case, Grace was pretty sure it was parked right on top of the reverend's grave. Which made sense—but also made her task more difficult.

How would she accomplish this? And how gruesome would it get? Her professional background assured her that after eighteen years, the reverend would be reduced to bones and bits of fabric. But Grace wasn't sure she could stomach even that much. Not when she was pulling it from the ground.

Pretend you're somewhere else. At the office in Jackson. Pretend this is no one you know, simply Exhibit A from one of the many cases you've worked on. One step at a time, remember? One step at a time...

Circling the vehicle, she forced open the old door, which complained loudly, and wiped away the cobwebs that suggested this truck had been sitting there for years. The keys dangled from the ignition, but the truck wouldn't start. It was in pretty bad shape. She doubted it even had an engine.

She'd have to excavate the dirt from the side, she decided as she climbed out. But how long would that take? The sun would be up in three hours—and Clay with it.

Leaving the door of the truck ajar, because she couldn't stand the noise of closing it, she got on her hands and knees and shined her flashlight beneath the truck. They'd buried Barker in a tattered quilt her mother had bought at a garage sale when Grace was just a baby.

She looked for any hint of that blanket, or anything else that would indicate Barker's remains might be as easy to uncover as she'd always feared. If she found it, she'd dig tonight. A foot of soft dirt couldn't take too long to move. If she found nothing, she'd get an earlier start tomorrow night.

A sound brought Grace's head up. Holding her breath, she listened.

The weather vane creaked, but she couldn't hear anything else. Only the cicadas and the frogs.

It's the wind. That's all.

Flipping her hair over her shoulder to relieve the heat of it on her neck, she crouched closer to the ground and angled her light toward the back tires. She thought she saw something pink in a narrow rut. Was it part of the blanket?

Grabbing her shovel, she swung it under the truck, trying to scrape what she'd found toward her. But the snap of a twig made her freeze in midmotion. As much as she wanted to attribute that sound to an animal or the wind, she knew she wasn't as alone as she'd assumed.

Was it Clay? She wanted to call out to him, in case he had his gun. He might well shoot first and ask questions later. But she wasn't willing to give herself away just yet. What if he'd seen a glimmer of light and was only coming to investigate? She could still hide. If he caught her out here tonight, she'd have a much more difficult time slipping onto the property tomorrow.

Snapping off her flashlight, she shoved it beneath the truck and rolled under with it. The smell of damp leaves filled her nostrils as she lay flat on her stomach and waited. She tried not to think about the reverend in the ground directly beneath her. That invited images of a bony skeleton reaching through the dirt to pull her into his grave....

Another twig snapped as whoever it was drew closer. Grace told herself to breathe lightly and evenly. She wasn't afraid of Clay, only of the risk that he'd catch her and make it impossible for her to do what had to be done. She couldn't rest until she'd hidden the reverend's remains in a place where they'd never be found.

She'd scatter his bones deep in the forests of Tennessee. Then, even if some part of him was eventually found, no one would be able to connect it to a person who'd gone missing two decades earlier in another state.

Lee Barker would finally be gone. For good. She'd be free to marry Kennedy.

But the boots that slowly approached didn't look like Clay's boots. They were some kind of fancy cowboy boots. Even in the dark she could tell that much, just as she knew that this person didn't walk the way her brother walked.

Who was it?

"Gra-ace, oh, Gra-ace. Where are you, huh? I know you're here somewhere."

Her heart jumped into her throat. It was Joe!

"Quit playing games with me," he said. "I have the Bible."

She curled her fingers into fists. He couldn't have the Bible. Kennedy had destroyed it. Kennedy had told her so himself.

"I spent the past hour or so reading some of the nice things he wrote about you. He really liked you, you know that? He doesn't even mention Madeline, his daughter by *birth*."

Grace had no idea what he could be talking about, didn't want to think of the possibilities. Kennedy wouldn't have given Joe the Bible. So how did he get it? And what could the reverend have written about her?

Her stomach churned.

"And look what you and your family did to him," he went on. "You did do it, right? I saw you get the shovel from your garage. I know what you're up to out here."

Since leaving Kennedy's, she'd checked her rearview mirror at least a thousand times. She would've taken a circuitous route, too, except there was only one way to get to the farm from town. Still, she'd seen no headlights behind her. She'd passed one small compact car at an intersection, but the driver was a woman. How had he followed her?

She wondered about all of that, but now that he was here, it didn't matter. Even if he didn't have the Bible, he knew about it. And she'd led him right to Barker's remains.

She'd risked everything for one chance at happiness. A chance she was about to lose.

The phone brought Kennedy out of a deep sleep. He was exhausted and wanted to ignore it, but he feared it might be his mother calling about his father.

Burrowing through the mess he and Grace had made of his bedding, he grabbed for the phone on the opposite nightstand. "'Lo?"

"Kennedy?"

It was a woman, but not his mother. He couldn't place the voice.

"Yes?" He tried to get his bearings.

"It's Sarah."

Buzz's wife. Raising his head, he frowned at the alarm clock. It was three-thirty in the morning. Why was Sarah calling him at this hour?

"Is everything okay with Buzz and the kids?"

"They're fine. It's Grace I'm worried about."

A ball of nervous energy formed in the pit of Kennedy's stomach. "Why are you worried about Grace?"

"Maybe it's nothing but…"

Sarah wouldn't have called him in the middle of the night if she really believed it was nothing. "But what?"

"I just saw her heading toward the farm."

"The farm?" he repeated because her words didn't make any sense. Grace hadn't left his house that long ago. She should've been on her way home.

"And Joe was following her."

Kennedy sat up and kicked the rest of the covers away. "Where were you when you saw them?"

"On the north edge of town."

"What were you doing there?"

She sounded dejected when she answered. "Buzz and I had an argument. I left to spend the night at my mother's."

"I'm sorry to hear that."

"We're going through a rough patch, that's all."

"Are you sure it was Grace you saw, Sarah?"

"Pretty sure," she replied. "I didn't get a good look at her face, but she's the only one in town with that kind of BMW."

"And Joe?"

"He was in his truck."

"Alone?"

"From what I could tell."

"What made you think he was following her?"

"He came barreling out of that side street by her house with his lights off. It was kinda weird."

Kennedy's mind raced as he tried to imagine what this was about.

"After your fight with Joe last night, I thought you might want to know. I like Joe, but lately…I don't know, he seems a little too obsessed with Grace, if you ask me."

Kennedy began looking for some clothes to put on. "Thanks, Sarah. Hang in there with Buzz, okay? He's a good man."

"I know he is," she said. "We'll work it out."

Kennedy certainly hoped so. But he was more concerned with what Sarah had told him about Grace. Where was she going? And why was Joe hot on her trail?

He said his goodbyes, hung up and paused in his dressing to dial Grace's cell.

"Hello, this is Grace Montgomery. I'm unavailable at the moment, but if you leave your name and number, I'll get back to you as soon as possible."

At the beep, he said, "Call me immediately." Then he sent her a text with the same message and called Joe's cell.

"You're up awful late tonight," Joe said, sounding as happy as though he'd just hit the lottery.

"What's going on?" Kennedy asked.

"What makes you think anything's going on?"

Joe's tone made him even more leery. "Why are you following Grace?"

"Oh...that. Boy, you do keep an eye on her, don't you?"

"Just answer the question."

"To be honest, I was curious to see what she was planning to do with the shovel she put in her trunk."

Shovel? The word filled Kennedy with dread. "Stay away from her, Joe," he warned.

"I'm not sure I like the way you're talking to me, Kennedy," he said. "It's taken me a long time to realize it, but you're an ungrateful son of a bitch, you know that?"

"Because I have a little compassion for people who've already been through enough?" Kennedy said.

"Because you chose a woman like Grace over me. You know what I'm talking about. You stabbed me in the back, Kennedy."

"That's not true, Joe."

"Well, you're not the friend I thought you were. And now it's time for the truth to come out."

"What truth?"

"I have my uncle's Bible. I know you're the one who buried it."

Kennedy's hand tightened on the phone. "Joe, listen to me. Don't do this."

"Why not?"

"Because I know you can be a better man."

"Like you?" he scoffed. "Tell me, does a *better* man help cover up a murder?"

"There was no murder!"

"We'll soon see, won't we?"

Kennedy jerked a T-shirt over his head. "How do you plan to do that?"

"It's easy. Thanks to Grace, I know where my uncle's buried."

The farm. Grace had talked about the farm. And the shovel Joe had mentioned made Kennedy even more nervous. Had Grace really put a shovel in her trunk? If so, what was she going to do with it? And what would it mean to the future they'd talked about? The baby she could be carrying?

"Joe, please. Give Grace a break."

"Hell, no. This is just the beginning, Kennedy. The police are on their way, and this time I can almost guarantee they'll come up with the evidence they need to press charges."

Kennedy couldn't fasten his pants using only one hand so he left his fly open and went for his shoes. "If you're looking for blood, go after me. But leave Grace alone."

Joe laughed softly. "Why, when I can hurt you a lot worse the other way?" he said and hung up.

Kennedy stared down at the phone. After eighteen years of dodging and denying the accusations launched at her and her family, Grace had taken a wrong turn and the wolves were circling.

This was exactly what Kennedy had feared—that he wouldn't be able to protect her. If the police found a body, he wouldn't be able to do a damn thing.

After waiting for a dial tone, he called his mother and asked her to come out right away to sit with the boys. Then he called Clay.

The phone at the farm rang and rang and rang. When there was no answer, he tried McCormick on his cell.

"Chief McCormick here."

"Dale, this is Kennedy."

"What's up, Kennedy?"

Kennedy began to pace. "Can you come over? I need to talk to you."

"I can't right now. I'm on my way to the Montgomery farm."

"Joe doesn't know what the hell he's talking about," Kennedy said.

There was an awkward silence. "Kennedy, he says he has proof. He also says you've been keeping a few secrets you should definitely have passed along."

"Grace and her family aren't guilty of murder, Dale."

"Are you sleeping with her, Kennedy? Is that much true?"

"Whether I'm sleeping with her has nothing to do with her guilt or innocence."

"It makes a difference to what you're willing to believe about her, my friend. I sympathize with you. But I have to do my job. If Joe's got proof, I have to act on it."

Shit! Kennedy's growing fear and agitation spurred him to move faster. "Act how?"

"I've got Hendricks over at the judge's house, trying to get a search warrant."

"But you already searched the farm! You found nothing."

"We found plenty, but nothing conclusive enough to build a solid case. A body would change that. And Joe's convinced he knows where to look."

Kennedy stopped in the middle of the floor. "Dale, listen to me, Joe's doing this out of spite. He's a vengeful son of a bitch, that's all."

"If we don't find anything, I'll shut him down,

Kennedy. I promise. I know what Joe's like. But first I have to determine if there's any validity to what he's telling me."

Kennedy descended the stairs two at a time, dashing to the kitchen for his keys. "Grace was just a girl when the reverend went missing."

"I've heard of stranger things. Anyway, someone's responsible for his disappearance. And it's my job to figure out what happened, who did it. I'll do my best to be fair. You know that."

His words offered Kennedy little comfort. He kept hearing Grace say, *It was my fault…but I didn't mean for it to happen. It was an accident.*

An accident… Would the proof support that? Probably not. If so, the Montgomerys would've contacted the police when it happened, right? In any case, after eighteen years it would be difficult to establish the details, and the details were everything. It would be far easier for McCormick to let public opinion—and the Vincellis—pressure him into charging Grace or someone else in her family with murder.

"The facts aren't always what they seem," he said.

"The facts are still the facts, Kennedy, and I have to be true to them. I'll be in touch."

Kennedy cursed as McCormick hung up. Now what? He tried Judge Reynolds, only to receive a similar answer. If there was new evidence, they had to act on it.

By the time Kennedy's mother arrived, he was down to contacting Irene Montgomery, anything to bring Grace some support. He had to call information for the number, but Irene was listed.

"Hello?" she said, answering on the second ring and sounding as groggy as he'd expected.

"Irene, this is Kennedy Archer."

"Kennedy?" she repeated as though she'd never heard the name.

He dared not take the time to explain. "Meet me at the farm as soon as possible. Grace is there, along with Joe Vincelli. The police are on their way."

"What's going on?"

"They're getting another warrant," he said and slammed the phone down on the counter.

Camille grabbed his arm as he hurried past her toward the garage. "Do you want me to have your father place a few calls?"

"I've already called everyone I can think of. Just stay with the boys. I'll let you know what's going on as soon as I can," he said and ran out the door.

21

"That was your boyfriend. He's a little worried about you," Joe said. He still hadn't found her, but he was so close Grace was afraid to breathe. He'd turned on a flashlight and searched the work shed and the trees. Now he was looking inside the cab of the truck.

"I betcha he's coming over here," he went on. "Which is fine. He might as well be around when the police arrive. Seeing his face when you're arrested for murder will be almost as good as what I had planned. Almost, but not quite," he said with a laugh.

Grace stared at the glimmers of light that seeped through the spots where rust had eaten away the floor of the truck. Joe's feet were only a few inches from her. She had to come up with some way to stop the inevitable. And she had to do it fast. It was a matter of seconds before he found her. There weren't that many places to hide.

Searching the ground, she found a small rock as he closed the door of the truck. She imagined he was about to bend, to look underneath. And that left her with only one chance.

Hoping to make Joe believe she was dashing off in the opposite direction, she tossed the rock toward the other side of the work shed. It skittered, then hit something with a solid *clunk*. But Joe wasn't fooled. Dropping to the ground, he pointed the flashlight right in her face.

"My, my, look what we have here."

Grace screamed and tried to scoot out the other side. But it was no use. He simply ran around the truck and dragged her the rest of the way by her hair.

"Where's the shovel, Grace?" he said as he slammed her up against the wheel-well. "What were you going to do with it?"

"I don't know what you're talking about."

"Sure you do." He held her in place with his lower body, grinding his hips into hers. "The police'll be looking. You know that, don't you? You're going to prison."

"And you're going to hell," she said.

"Hey, be nice and I might give you one for the road." He licked her neck, laughing when she flinched. "You can't tell me you're looking forward to being locked up with a bunch of women." He rubbed against her again. "You've had a lot of men. Won't you miss the ride?"

"I wouldn't miss it a bit if all men were like you."

Even in the dark she could see the malicious glint in his eyes. "If the police weren't already on their way, I might be tempted to show you how much I've changed."

"Are you trying to make me sick?"

Clenching one hand in her hair, he jerked her head back and bit her breast where it swelled above her shirt. But Grace barely felt the pain. She'd been waiting for an opportunity to break away from him. If she could reach her car, she could leave Stillwater behind forever, as she should've done in the first place. Then she wouldn't have to face Madeline when they unearthed her father's bones, wouldn't have to drag Kennedy and his boys through everything to come.

She jerked her knee up, trying to hit Joe in the groin.

He sensed it coming and moved at the last second, but it changed his focus just enough that she managed to wrench away from him. She started to run, and thought she was actually going to escape, when he caught her and smacked her across the face.

The force of the blow threw Grace's head back and left her cheek stinging and numb. But she wasn't about to give up. She hit Joe on the bandage that covered his nose, which elicited a violent curse—and another blow to her face.

Lights flashed behind Grace's eyes, but she still gave the fight everything she had, biting, kicking and slugging for all she was worth. She broke away once more and was at the edge of the clearing before Joe hauled her back by yanking on her hair.

He looked like he'd hit her again, and take great pleasure in doing so—but a deafening shot exploded through the air.

Clay! With a mixture of guilt and relief, Grace realized her brother had joined them.

"You have about three seconds to let go of my sister and get off my land."

Grace's ears rang. But she heard the hardness in her brother's tone, knew he meant business.

Joe hesitated—but ultimately decided to gamble. "No way. Put down the gun, Clay. You can't help her. You're in over your head already."

Grace stared at her brother, trying to make out the expression on his face. It was too dark to pick up on nuances, especially from ten feet away. But the absolute conviction in Clay's stance was hard to miss.

Would he really shoot? Would they have another body to bury beside the last one?

Grace couldn't stomach the thought of it. "Clay, don't. Please. He's not worth it."

Clay ignored her. "You're assaulting my sister. I'd shoot a man for less."

"Clay—"

He didn't let her finish. "I said let go of her—now!"

Joe jerked Grace in front of him, using her to shield what he could of his body. "You're wasting your time threatening me. The police are on their way. It's all over."

Clay raised the gun a fraction of an inch higher, clearly aiming for Joe's head. "Nothing's over."

"It will be when they find my uncle's body," Joe said, but his voice rose while he was speaking, revealing his fear.

"This is your last warning," Clay said quietly. "If you don't let go of her right now, the only body they'll find will be yours."

"Let go." Grace believed it was the panic in her voice that finally convinced Joe. He shoved her away from him with such force that she nearly landed face-first in the dirt.

Clay didn't move to help her. He was still staring down the barrel of his rifle. "I should shoot you anyway. You're not worth a damn. Just like your uncle."

"I *knew* you hated him," Joe whispered vehemently. "Finally, you've admitted it, after all the lies…."

"I could tell you a thing or two about pretenses," Clay said. "About men like you who care for no one but themselves and the dark impulses that drive them. You're a waste of space, you know that, Joe?"

Joe lifted his hands in a defensive posture while

backing away. "You—you're the one who's going to jail."

"Then I have nothing to lose, right?" Clay raised his gun another inch or two.

Grace could sense her brother's rage mounting, knew the past eighteen years had scarred him, too. The frustration, fear, turmoil and anger he'd endured seemed to be coming to a head. He'd been caught up in a situation he was too young to handle, one he'd never asked for or sought. He'd been through so much that now he cared more about vengeance than self-preservation.

Grace felt helpless to stop what was happening, but knew she had to try. She couldn't let the police arrive to find Joe dead and Clay holding the gun that killed him. It was bad enough that they were going to find Barker.

"Clay!" she said.

"Stay out of it, Grace."

Grace thought she saw his trigger finger tighten and hurried toward him. She paused as she reached him, dared not touch him for fear he'd pull the trigger. "Clay, put the gun down," she said, lowering her voice to a soft plea. "For me. You're not the kind of man to do this."

"I think most people in Stillwater would disagree with you," he said.

"They don't know you like I do," she said. "Don't become what they've made us out to be. Don't prove them right."

His eyes flicked her way, but he seemed determined not to let her change his mind. He repositioned the rifle as if he'd fire anyway. But something she'd said must have gotten through to him. After several long seconds, he pointed the barrel at the ground.

Grace shut her eyes in relief. She would've put her arms around him, but the sirens that had begun to wail in the distance came closer and several police cars tore down the drive.

Chief McCormick rushed out of the lead vehicle. He had someone with him, someone Grace couldn't see because of the glare of flashlights. "Put the gun on the ground and step away from it, Clay," he said.

Clay looked at Grace. She got the impression he was considering opening fire and going down in a hail of bullets.

She put out a hand to stop him, just in case. But then his lips curved into a mysterious grin and he stepped away from the rifle, exactly as McCormick had directed.

They were going to dig. After so many years of fearing this moment, Grace could hardly believe she was now facing the very thing she'd dreaded for so long. She stood watching as Chief McCormick and Officers Hendricks and Dormer had Clay use the tractor to pull the Chevy out of the way. Stood without moving when they set up perimeter lights. Stood, a numb observer, as they found the shovel and flashlight she'd left lying on the ground and cast her a knowing glance. She didn't even blink as they brought a few of their own shovels from their cars and started to scoop up the dirt.

Joe followed them around as they worked, begging for a backhoe and nagging them to be as thorough as possible. McCormick agreed to the backhoe, provided they didn't find anything in the next couple of hours— but Grace knew they wouldn't need to go to the trouble. The reverend was buried right where they were digging. It wouldn't take more than a few minutes to find him.

Kennedy had shown up soon after the police. He held Grace's hand, his shoulder brushing Clay's as the others swarmed around them. Grace had tried to push Kennedy away from her, to convince him to leave her alone and go back home to his boys. She didn't want him to be associated with her now that the end was in sight, didn't want him to witness what the police were about to unearth. She preferred to remember their time together as it was—perfect, beautiful, priceless…and unspoiled by all this.

But he wouldn't listen. His expression grim, he held his injured hand close to his body as the police began to pile dirt at the edge of the clearing. He didn't have much to say, but he seemed as resolute in his support of her as Clay was. Menace filled his eyes every time he looked at Joe.

"What're *you* staring at?" Joe finally asked. "You should be gettin' ready to kiss Gracie goodbye because she won't be putting out for you anymore, buddy."

A muscle flexed in Kennedy's jaw, which inspired Grace to cling to him even more tightly. She was afraid he might start another fight. For a mayoral candidate, he'd surprised her more than once. But he didn't make any threatening moves. "I was wrong to believe you were my friend," he said.

"What would you call me, if not a friend?" Joe snapped. "I saved your freakin' life. Or have you forgotten about that?"

"You have a few redeeming qualities. Too bad you don't have more," he responded.

"You're the one who turned on me, Kennedy. You're

the one." He motioned to get the attention of the others. "Look at him! He supports her even though her shovel's right here. And he thinks he should be mayor!"

McCormick shot Joe a look that said the vendetta between him and Kennedy wasn't helping. "We haven't found anything yet," he said.

"You will," Joe told him.

The police chief went back to supervising the digging as Irene came up the drive.

When Grace saw her mother, she felt even worse about what she'd caused. As angry as she'd been, as much as she'd blamed Clay and Irene simply because she had no better target for her disappointment and disillusionment, she knew what her mother and Clay had faced and, in a way, admired their strength. The situation eighteen years ago had spiraled so quickly out of control. After the reverend had fallen and they'd realized he was dead, they'd done what they had to do to keep the family together.

If only McCormick would accept the truth for what it was!

But she sincerely doubted he could. Even now. The community wouldn't allow it. Not when everyone believed so completely in Barker's goodness. They'd championed their preacher; learning what he really was would make those who thought they knew him feel like fools. And, as Kennedy had said, it would humiliate and embarrass the Vincellis.

"Grace," her mother said, walking toward her.

Irene's ashen face revealed the extent of her fear and concern. Grace didn't think she'd ever seen her mother looking so old or so fragile.

"I'm sorry, Momma," she said, but as she gave her

mother a hug she saw Jed Fowler near the barn. She was about to ask why he was there, who'd called him, but when he reached them, he looked at Irene in such a way that Grace's mouth dropped open. She'd never seen him so unguarded, so openly sympathetic. Was he the man her mother had been seeing?

It *couldn't* be. Not Jed. Her mother was at least ten years younger and far more attractive.

"Hello," Grace said to him.

He nodded in acknowledgement but remained silent, his eyes on the work being performed by the police.

Grace edged closer to her mother and lowered her voice. "You could've told us you were seeing Jed. There's nothing wrong with that. Why make it such a secret?"

"What?" Irene followed Grace's gaze and seemed startled to see him standing there. "I'm not seeing Jed," she whispered a moment later.

"Then how'd he know—"

"I called him," Kennedy said. "I figured he might be able to persuade Chief McCormick that you couldn't have buried the reverend out here, at least not while he was in the barn."

"That was a nice thought, Kennedy," Irene said. "And it's kind of you to be here."

"I'll do whatever I can," he promised.

The polite smile she offered him wilted as Officer Hendricks dragged up a piece of the quilt Grace had been looking for earlier. "I think I've found something, Chief."

Seeing that scrap of fabric nearly buckled Grace's knees. She might have crumbled to the ground if not for Kennedy. Sensing her panic, he moved behind her and slipped his arms around her waist.

McCormick shot Irene a subtle glance before responding. "What is it?" he asked, striding over.

"Beats me," Hendricks said. "Fabric of some kind."

"*Fabric?*" Joe echoed. "That's not what we're looking for. Keep digging. You have to keep digging."

McCormick ignored him. "Set it aside."

"Be careful with it," Joe said. "It could be evidence."

Slipping the strip of pink cotton into a paper sack, Hendricks went back to work. Grace expected him or one of the others to find the reverend with the very next shovelful. But just as they brought up something that showed bone through the dirt, Jed Fowler stepped forward.

"It was me," he said. "I did it."

Every shovel stilled as the men turned to stare.

McCormick's bushy eyebrows met above his piercing brown eyes. In the east, the sun was just showing the first hint of daybreak, making it easier to see. "You're saying you killed the reverend?"

Grace tightened her grip on Kennedy's hand as Jed nodded.

The police chief sent Irene another glance, then spat on the ground. His slow response gave the impression that he was mulling this information over in his mind, seeing how well it fit his instincts. The look on Irene's face was…strange, too; almost as if they shared some secret. But as far as Grace was aware, her mother barely knew Chief McCormick.

"How'd you do it?" he asked Jed.

Irene stepped between them. "It's not true. You know it's not true," she said.

"With a piece of wood," he said.

"You hit him with it?"

"Yes, sir. On the back of the head."

McCormick rubbed his chin. "Okay. *Why'd* you do it?"

"Chief McCormick…" The hand Irene laid on the police chief's arm could simply have been a beseeching gesture. But Grace thought she noticed something just a little too familiar about it. "He didn't do it."

"Of course he didn't," Clay added.

Joe Vincelli had come over the moment Jed spoke. Now he crowded closer. "They should know," he said.

McCormick raised a hand, signalling them all to stay out of it. "Jed?"

"He didn't want to pay me for my work," Jed muttered.

"Come on, I know you," McCormick said, lowering his voice. "I've seen the stray animals you adopt, the unassuming life you lead. Hell, you've fixed my cars since I can remember. You expect me to believe you killed the Reverend Barker over a repair bill? And you've kept silent all these years while suspicion swirled around the Montgomerys?"

Jed looked at Grace's mother, and Grace thought she could imagine why he'd hidden the Bible. Was he in love with her? In any event, he knew what had happened that night. At least he knew part of it. He'd hidden that Bible for Irene's sake.

"I should've come forward earlier," he said.

"I won't let you do this," Irene murmured. "I won't let him," she said to Chief McCormick.

The quick glances between the police chief and Irene had ceased. Suddenly he seemed reluctant to even look at her. "I've never seen you get angry in the forty-some years I've known you," he said, staring intently at Jed.

"I was angry that night."

Grace believed he *had* been angry, angry on behalf of Irene. Had he heard the shouting? Seen the fighting? Watched them drag the body from the house? She guessed he had. She also guessed he'd helped clean up after they'd left with the car. That was how he'd come by the Bible.

"So his skull should be smashed in," McCormick said.

"Should be," Jed responded.

"And what did you do with the body?"

"That's it right there." He pointed to the bone showing through the dirt in Officer Hendrick's shovel.

"He's lying," Joe said. "He's trying to protect the Montgomerys."

"Shut up." McCormick motioned for Hendricks to pick up whatever he had in his shovel.

Tension made Grace's muscles ache. She held her breath as Hendricks carefully dusted off what was clearly a skull. But—instinctively she stepped closer—it was too elongated to be human. And it certainly wasn't smashed.

Clay folded his arms. "Wonderful, McCormick. You've exhumed our family dog. He died of natural causes when I was only fifteen, but feel free to cart him off to a forensic anthropologist if that'll reassure you."

Joe glared at him. But McCormick seemed to breathe more easily as Hendricks placed the skull next to the fabric.

"Keep digging," Joe said. "I know my uncle's here somewhere."

McCormick cocked an eyebrow at Joe as though tempted to refuse. Grace could feel the weight of her mother's will, pressing him to do just that. And she could tell that it had an effect on him. There was a tangible intimacy between them that surprised her.

And then it all made sense. Her mother wasn't seeing Jed. She was seeing Chief McCormick.

Grace covered her mouth as she studied her mother. Irene returned her gaze, but wouldn't hold it, which told Grace almost as clearly as an admission that she was right. Her mother was having an affair with a married man—as they'd feared. But not just any married man. She was sleeping with Stillwater's Chief of Police!

Turning in Kennedy's arms, she tried to make out his expression. Was what she saw apparent to everyone? But he didn't seem to notice anything amiss.

"What is it?" he murmured.

"Nothing," she said and turned back.

McCormick rested a hand on top of his shovel. "I think we've done enough here."

Because they'd really done enough? Or because he wanted to let Irene off the hook?

Grace watched Irene close her eyes, probably saying a silent prayer of thanks. But Joe wasn't about to let things go. "Wait a second," he said. "You've got a warrant. You can't waste the opportunity. You have to dig."

"I don't have to do anything," McCormick said. But when Joe glanced from him to Irene, Grace could tell it pricked the chief's conscience. No doubt he felt as though he was wearing a scarlet letter. In any case, he quickly backed off. "What the hell," he said, once again avoiding Irene's gaze. "We've come this far. We might as well make damn sure."

They dug for another four hours, until dust and sweat ran down their faces in rivulets. By midmorning, the rest of the Barkers appeared. Even Vicki Nibley placed a call to Chief McCormick, throwing her weight behind getting the backhoe Joe wanted. That came at noon. But they found nothing. By the time Grace heard Madeline running down the drive, the police were packing up.

"Word's all over town that the police have found a body here," she gasped. "What's going on?"

Grace was too tired and numb to answer.

"You can't find something that isn't here," Clay said.

Hendricks wiped the sweat from his forehead. "The only thing we've got is your father's Bible," he said to Madeline. "Joe claims it was out by Pickwick Lake."

"Where Grace and Kennedy buried it when they went camping recently," Joe inserted.

Madeline's eyes filled with tears as Joe handed her the Bible. She gently touched the inscription, then turned to Grace for an explanation. But it was Kennedy who answered—by speaking to Joe. "You were there, too, Joe."

"What are you saying?"

"I'm saying *you* must have buried it."

"What?"

"I don't know how else it could've gotten there," Kennedy said. "If we'd found it, we would've given it to Madeline immediately, right, Grace?"

"Right," Grace murmured. She knew she should probably make more of an effort to convince her stepsister. Poor Maddy looked thunderstruck. But Grace couldn't get beyond her own shock. Where were Barker's remains? The police should've discovered them. Unless...

She glanced up to find Clay watching her, and that

was when she realized. He'd moved them. She didn't know how or when—and she certainly didn't know where—but they were gone because of him.

Forever the Guardian...

"Your cousin found Grace out here with a flashlight and a shovel," McCormick told Madeline. "He thought she might be trying to move whatever's left of your father."

"A flashlight and a shovel?" Once again, Madeline's gaze moved expectantly to Grace.

Grace glanced guiltily at Clay—silently sending him an apology, as well—and gave the only excuse that might be believed. "I—I just wanted to make sure that what I've heard for so long isn't true."

"That mom or Clay might have killed Dad?" Madeline asked, her jaw sagging.

Grace stared at the ground. "I know. I feel silly. But everyone in this town seems so positive, and...it finally got the better of me. I want to know what happened. I can't take the questions anymore."

"Grace..." Madeline reached for her hand. "I understand completely. It's so hard. But you can't lose faith. I know Clay and Mom would never hurt anyone."

"Then you don't know them as well as you think," Joe snorted.

Madeline turned on him. "You found *nothing*. Doesn't that send any kind of signal to your pea-sized brain?"

"Yeah, that we're looking in the wrong place!"

"I'd know if these people were capable of what you suspect, Joe. I lived with them. I grew up with them."

"*Somebody* had to have done *something*," he retorted.

"Regardless, we had to check," McCormick said,

almost apologetically, and Grace wondered if he was trying to explain his position to her mother.

"Don't waste your time here," Madeline replied. "Get out and look for the real culprit instead of harassing the people I love. Look what you've done to Grace. You have her doubting her own family. But you're not going to do the same to me. I've already lost my father. I won't lose anyone else!"

The tears that were streaming down Madeline's cheeks made Grace feel terrible. As she started to comfort her stepsister, Kennedy whispered, "Some lies are blessings," and she understood what he meant. Guilty though she felt, telling the truth wouldn't solve anything. It would only destroy the most important relationships Madeline had left.

"It's going to be okay," Grace said, hugging her stepsister. "I made a mistake. But they're all done digging. It's over."

"You satisfied?" McCormick asked Joe.

"No, we need to look elsewhere," he said. "We're missing something. I know it."

McCormick picked up a shovel and slung it over one shoulder. "We've torn this place apart. Your uncle isn't here."

Joe cut him off before he could take two steps. "He *is* here. He's probably right under our noses!"

"If you know where his grave is, then by all means show us," McCormick challenged. He waved a hand at the disturbed dirt. But when Joe couldn't pinpoint a spot, he walked away.

Joe's eyes darted to the cotton fields, the barn, the house. "What about the Bible? Kennedy knows more than he's saying about this whole thing or he wouldn't have gone to such lengths to hide it."

McCormick whirled on him. "Now you think Kennedy Archer's involved?"

"He is!" Joe insisted.

"Do I have to remind you that his father is the mayor of this town? Otis has called me twice this morning to tell me I'd better watch my step. He won't stand by while I slander his son."

"No one's slandering anyone," Joe argued.

"You can't go around accusing innocent people of covering up a murder, Joe," McCormick shouted. "Not unless you have proof."

In the ensuing silence, everyone looked at everyone else. Joe flushed red, but the stubborn set of his jaw said he wasn't about to give up yet. "The Bible is evidence."

McCormick's hands curled into fists and he stepped right up to Joe. "Of *what,* exactly? Finding that Bible off in the woods somewhere tells us nothing—except that maybe we're digging in the wrong place."

Joe pointed at Kennedy. "Ask *him* where it came from, okay? Just ask him."

The police chief rubbed his neck as if trying to ease the tension there. He seemed to consider Joe's request, reject it, then entertain the idea again. "Kennedy, any chance you want to answer that?" he asked at last.

Kennedy shrugged. "I don't know what he's talking about."

"That's what I thought." McCormick motioned to his men. "Put everything back as close to the way it was as possible. Let's get out of here while we still have our jobs."

Joe grabbed the chief's arm. "What about Jed's confession?"

"What about it?"

"He knows something, too."

"If he knew where your uncle was, he wouldn't have tried to confess he'd killed what turned out to be a dog."

Jed was watching Irene closely, as if he, too, suspected what Grace already knew. She wanted to go to him, put a hand on his arm and thank him, but Joe was still causing problems. "Clay must've moved the body," he said. "We should search the root cellar, the basement of the house, the—"

"A search warrant isn't a blanket document that includes everything you want it to, Joe."

"You could go back to Judge Reynolds—" Joe started.

"No," McCormick interrupted. "We're out of here. And if you know what's good for you, you'll go, too—before Clay leaves you worse off than Kennedy did. He's got the right, you know. The way I see it, you're trespassing."

Clay arched an eyebrow at Joe, and Joe took a quick step back. "Let's go, son," Mrs. Vincelli said. Obviously, even she'd had enough.

"I never dreamed you, of all people, would take her side," he said to Kennedy.

For the first time, Grace felt a twinge of sympathy for Joe. He'd always admired Kennedy, had nearly worshipped him, in fact.

Kennedy linked his fingers with Grace's. "I'm sorry, Joe. Regardless of our past, Grace's past, the upcoming election or anything else, from now on, she and I stand together."

The color had drained from Joe's face. "Who would've thought you'd end up with Grace Montgomery?"

"Soon to be Grace *Archer,*" Kennedy said.

Madeline gasped. "You're getting *married?*"

"To *Kennedy?*" Irene said, her tone implying that all her dreams had just come true.

Joe obviously had the opposite reaction. He looked as though he'd been struck through the heart. But Grace felt a smile bloom on her face. The sun was now shining brightly, bathing everything in uncompromising warmth. The night had stolen nothing. She was going to be with the man she loved. "Yes."

Madeline grinned and, with another glance at McCormick, who had his back to her, Irene hugged both her daughters.

"When?" Clay asked.

Kennedy brushed his lips over Grace's knuckles. "As soon as possible."

"You'll be sorry," Joe called back. "She's no Rae-lynn."

"I don't want her to be Raelynn," Kennedy said. "I love her just the way she is."

There was nothing more Joe could say. He'd never be Grace's friend. But he couldn't hurt her anymore, either.

His family dragged him off as Grace looked at the farm, waiting for her memories of the reverend to steal the light from her soul, to dim her happiness, the way they always did. But as her eyes roved over the uneven ground, she realized he was gone. Gone for good. Like the files and mementos that had cluttered his office. Like the threat of the police, who were already packing up and pulling out. Like the darkness.

Kennedy gave her arm a gentle tug. "Let's go tell the boys about the wedding."

Grace could hardly wait. "I'm going to love being

their mother," she said and silently promised Raelynn that no matter what happened, she'd do right by the whole family. But before she left, she had a question for her brother.

"Why didn't you tell me?" she asked, pulling him aside.

He folded his arms and gazed out over the land. "I knew it had to come to this," he said.

"You knew they'd search? You wanted them to?"

"It was the only way to set you free."

"Why didn't you let them search before?"

"An invitation would've seemed staged. This way…it was real, you know? They did what they wanted to, even though they thought I was against it. That should keep them happy."

She double-checked to make sure no one was close enough to hear their conversation. "So, where did you put…*it?*" she whispered.

He smiled and shook his head. "That's one question I'll never answer. He's not your problem anymore. That's all you need to know."

"Grace?"

Grace looked up to see Madeline standing off by herself. She'd been reading through her father's Bible, turning each page as though it was more precious than gold.

"What is it?" she said gently when she noticed the tears in Madeline's eyes.

Madeline pointed to a page at the beginning of the Bible that was usually blank. Only this one was covered with small, neat handwriting that included dates, scriptural references and passages, notes. "You should read all the beautiful things Dad wrote about you. You were so special to him."

Special? More than Madeline would ever know.

Grace's eyes locked with Kennedy's. Then she smiled at her stepsister. "You're the one who's special, Maddy."

Epilogue

Grace lay on her back beneath the Baumgarters' giant oak, the one that now belonged to her and Kennedy, staring up at the dappled sunshine. The winter had been especially mild, and it was a glorious day, one of those days that felt like spring. Kennedy had dropped out of the mayoral race so he could spend more time with the family. But he didn't seem to regret it. Especially since his father's chemotherapy had gone so well.

"How old is Grandpa today?" Teddy asked.

"Sixty," Kennedy said. He was pruning back some of the wisteria vines that grew onto their porch, while Teddy and Heath lay on the grass beside Grace, still dizzy from their spinning contest.

"Wow, that's old."

They were having Kennedy's parents over later to celebrate Otis's birthday. She needed to start cooking—and cleaning, too. Molly was coming for a visit after Valentine's. But she was having a difficult time pulling away from her kids. "Thank God it looks like he's going to be around for a while longer."

"Is he all better?" Heath asked.

A vine snapped as Kennedy's pruning shears cut through the stem. "The doctors say he's in remission, which means he's good for now."

"Can I feel the baby?" Teddy asked, crawling closer to Grace.

Grace chuckled at his eagerness. He asked almost every day. "The baby's not moving right now."

"How big is it getting?"

"She's probably about four pounds," Kennedy told him.

Heath gave his father a funny look. "How do you know it's a she?"

"Just guessing," Kennedy said without pausing in his work. "Wouldn't you like a little sister?"

"If she'll play ball with us," Heath said.

"Yeah, if she plays sports, I guess that would be okay," Teddy agreed.

Grace put a hand on her stomach, just as excited as the rest of the family about the child growing inside her.

"It's taking forever," Teddy complained, as though the thought of having to wait overwhelmed him.

Kennedy dragged a severed vine to the pile he was creating on the lawn. "You started out that little."

"And look at you now," Grace said.

Teddy snuggled closer to her. "I was that little when I was in my other mommy's tummy?"

"Mmm-hmm." Lazily, she slipped her fingers through his fine hair, wondering how any woman could be happier than she was at this moment.

"I was eight pounds when I was born," Heath said, scooting closer.

Grace smiled at her older son, wishing she could capture this lazy moment and hold it inside forever. Teddy and Heath had accepted her so readily, so easily. Half the time, they treated her as though they were afraid to let her out of their sight for fear she might not come back. After what had happened to their mother, she could understand why.

"What about you?" she asked Teddy. "How much did you weigh when you were born?"

He shrugged. "Beats me."

Kennedy dragged another severed vine to his pile. "Six and a half pounds."

"There're some pictures in your baby book," Grace said. "Shall we ask Daddy to take a break so we can go in and look?"

Teddy immediately sat up. "Sure!"

"I'm almost finished," Kennedy said.

"I want to see something first," Heath told her.

Grace watched as her oldest boy leaned up on one arm and studied the sky above them. "What is it?" she asked.

"Do you really think our mom's looking down on us?"

Closing her eyes, Grace felt the gentle wind on her cheeks. "I do," she said. "I can't see her, but if I try real hard I can feel her. Can you?"

"Sometimes," Heath said.

"Do you think she has wings like that angel I bought?" Teddy asked.

The statue Teddy had wanted now sat in the cemetery in a prominent place near Raelynn's headstone. "Maybe," she said. "In any case, I'm sure she's safe and happy and very pleased with your gift."

"You really like that statue," Teddy said. "Don't you?"

Grace smiled. She liked it, all right. It was elegant. But she valued it more for the fact that it had been a young son's gift of love to his mother. "It's one of my favorite things."

Teddy grinned at her words, and exchanged a glance with Heath.

"What are you up to?" Grace asked.

Teddy smiled shyly. "It's supposed to be a surprise, but—"

"Don't give it away—" Kennedy started to say. But it was already too late.

"Me and Teddy are saving up to buy one for you." Heath's words came in a rush. "Dad said you could put it in the garden."

A lump rose in Grace's throat as they waited for her reaction. Trying to hide the tears welling in her eyes, she pressed a kiss to each boy's forehead. "What a wonderful gift. Thank you."

"Are you *crying?*" Heath asked.

"Happy tears," she said with a watery smile.

Kennedy stopped working and came over to help her up. "I knew you'd like it. But it was their idea."

A police car pulled up at the curb, and a small, dark-haired woman got out. "Grace?" she said. "Grace Archer?"

Grace dashed a hand across her wet cheeks. "Yes?"

She met Grace halfway up the walk and pulled her sunglasses low enough that Grace could see a pair of brown eyes fringed with long black lashes. "You used to be Grace Montgomery?"

"Yes."

She offered her hand. "I'm Allie McCormick."

Grace felt slightly uncomfortable at the woman's last name. She'd tried to convince her mother to stop seeing the chief of police—before someone figured out what was going on between them. Irene had promised she would, but Grace was willing to bet they were still sneaking around. Grace knew her mother was hoping Chief McCormick would leave his wife and marry her; Grace hoped just the opposite. As much as she wanted her mother to be happy, she didn't agree with stealing someone else's husband. And she knew what might happen if Joe and his family ever got wind of the affair. They'd claim McCormick purposely turned a blind eye to any possible evidence when he searched the farm, which would put them right back under the microscope.

"Are you any relation to Chief McCormick?" she asked, trying not to reveal her sudden unease.

"His daughter. I was a junior when you were a freshman, but I remember you."

Grace couldn't place her, but she'd blocked out much about those years. "Nice to meet you."

Allie looked around at the home Grace had never dreamed she'd own. "The Baumgarter place was always beautiful, but you've done a lovely job with it."

"Thank you." Grace eyed her badge. "You work with your father, I see."

Allie smiled. "Fighting crime runs in the family. Until he retired, my grandfather was a detective in Nashville. My uncle's still a highway patrolman in California. My brother's a sheriff in Florida."

Why was Allie McCormick telling her this? Grace felt Kennedy take her hand, knew he was wondering the same thing. "What can we do for you, Officer McCormick?" he asked politely.

She pushed her sunglasses back up to the bridge of her nose. "Seeing that I'm back in town, I thought I'd drop off my card, is all. I've been living in the big city, working cold cases for the Chicago Police Department, so—"

"Cold cases?" Grace hoped her voice didn't sound as tremulous as it felt.

"Yeah, it was a tough job, but I enjoyed it," she confided. "There's nothing more satisfying than solving something that's ten, twenty, even thirty years old."

"I bet."

She patted the top of Teddy's head, who, together with his brother, kept crowding closer to her, obviously fascinated by the gun on her hip "Someone told me you were a prosecutor," Allie said.

"That's true."

"Then I'm guessing it must drive you especially mad not to know what happened to your stepfather."

"It's been…difficult," Kennedy said, trying to help out.

"That's really why I'm here. I wanted to let you know that I'm going to do what I can to answer that question for you."

"How nice," Grace said numbly.

She tucked the dark hair falling from her ponytail behind her ears. "Madeline stopped by the station, asked if I would."

"So you're opening the case again?" Kennedy asked. Grace cringed inwardly.

"Not officially, no. I'm just going to tinker with it a bit, in my off hours."

"I'm afraid you might be wasting your time, Officer McCormick," Grace said.

"That's okay. I'd like to use my skills, you know? And sometimes even small, seemingly unrelated things can help." She reached into her pocket. "Here's my number, in case you remember anything new about the night Reverend Barker disappeared."

Grace accepted the card Allie thrust toward her. "It's been eighteen years. What makes you think I might remember something now?"

"You never know." Her smile was still friendly enough to make Grace believe she didn't know about her father and Irene. "Anyway, I can't resist a good mystery. Can you?"

* * * * *

Can Grace and Clay keep their secret forever?
What happens when an inquisitive cop takes
an interest in the case?
Read DEAD GIVEAWAY to find out!
Coming from MIRA Books.
Turn the page for an excerpt from the
second book in this exciting series.

They hadn't meant to kill him. That should've mattered. It probably would have—in a different time, a different place. But this was Stillwater, Mississippi, and the only thing smaller than the town itself was the minds of the people living in it. They never forgot and they never forgave. Nineteen years had passed since Reverend Barker disappeared, but they wanted someone to pay for the loss of their beloved preacher.

And they'd had their eye on Clay Montgomery almost from the beginning.

The only bit of luck was the fact that, without a body, the police couldn't prove Clay had done anything. But that didn't stop them—and others—from constantly poking around his farm, asking questions, suggesting scenarios, attempting to piece together the past in hopes of solving the biggest mystery Stillwater had ever known.

"Do you think someday he'll come back? Your stepdaddy, I mean?" Beth Ann Cole plumped her pillow and arranged one arm above her head.

Annoyance ripped through Clay despite the beautiful eyes that regarded him from beneath thick golden lashes. Beth Ann typically didn't press him about his missing stepfather. She knew he'd show her the door.

But he'd let her come over too much lately and she was beginning to overrate her value to him.

Without answering, he kicked off the blankets and began to get out of bed, only to have her grab hold of his arm. "Wait, that's it? Wham, bam, thank you, ma'am? You're not usually so selfish."

"You didn't have any complaints a minute ago," he drawled, glancing pointedly over his shoulder at the claw marks she'd left on his back.

Her bottom lip jutted out. "I want more."

"You always want more. Of everything. More than I'm willing to give." He stared at the delicate white fingers clinging to his darker forearm. Normally, she would've recognized the warning in his expression and let him go. Tonight, however, she went straight into her "how can you use me like this" mode, an act she put on whenever her impatience overcame her good sense.

But the cloying sound of Beth Ann's voice bothered Clay more than usual. Probably because he'd recently had bad news. The police chief's daughter, a police officer herself, had returned to town. And she was asking questions.

Clay had seen her. A small woman, Allie McCormick didn't look like much of a threat. But Clay's sister had called to tell him she'd been a cold case detective in Chicago—a damn good one.

And Allie wasn't his only problem....

Swallowing a curse, he rubbed his temples, trying to alleviate the beginnings of a headache. But the pounding only grew worse when Beth Ann's voice rose dramatically.

"Clay, are we ever gonna move beyond a physical relationship? Is sex all you want from me?"

Beth Ann had a gorgeous body and occasionally used it to get what she wanted—and he knew what she wanted right now was him. She often wheedled or pouted, trying to coax him into a marriage proposal. But he didn't love her, and she understood that, even if she liked to pretend otherwise. He rarely called her, hardly ever asked her out, never made any promises. He paid her way if they went anywhere, but that was a matter of courtesy, not a declaration of undying devotion. She initiated most of their contact.

He remembered the first time she'd come to his door. From the moment she'd moved to town nearly two years ago, she'd flirted with him whenever possible. She worked in the bakery of the local supermarket and did her damnedest to corner him the moment he crossed the threshold. But when he didn't immediately fall and worship at her feet, like all the other single men in Stillwater, she'd decided he was a challenge worthy of her best efforts. One night, after a brief encounter at the store where she'd made some innuendo he'd purposely ignored, she'd appeared on his doorstep wearing a trench coat—and not a stitch of clothing underneath.

She knew he couldn't ignore that. And he hadn't. But at least he didn't feel guilty about his involvement in her life. Of course, if it suited her purposes—usually when she was hinting that he should buy her some necklace or other gift—she liked to act as though he was the sex-fiend and she the benevolent provider. But after experiencing her voracious appetite over the past several months, he definitely had his own opinions about who'd become the provider.

"Let go of my arm," he said.

She blinked at the edge in his voice, looking uncer-

tain, and then released him. "I thought you were starting to care about me."

Presenting his back to her, he pulled on his jeans.
Normally, sex relaxed him, helped him sleep. Which
was why he'd let his relationship with Beth Ann continue for so long. But they'd just made love twice, and
he felt more wound up than ever. He couldn't quit
thinking about Office Allie McCormick and her exten-
sive background in forensics. Would she finally bring
an end to it all?

"Clay?"

Beth Ann was getting on his last nerve. "I think
maybe it's time we quit seeing each other," he said as
he yanked on a clean T-shirt.

When she didn't answer, he turned to see her gaping at him.

"How can you *say* that?" she cried. "I asked one
question. One!" She laughed as though he'd completely overreacted. "You're so jumpy."

"My stepfather is not a subject I'm prepared to discuss."

She opened her mouth, then seemed to reconsider
what she was about to say. "Okay, I get it. I was tired and
didn't realize how much it would upset you. I'm sorry."

He scowled. She hadn't told him to go to hell and
walked out, as she would've done a week ago, which
indicated that their relationship was changing. Although he'd tried to make clear to her that he was the
most emotionally unavailable man she'd probably ever
meet, she was becoming attached. He didn't understand how, but there it was, written all over her face.

He couldn't allow her to come back. He wasn't
even willing to admit he had a heart, let alone open it
to anyone. "Get dressed, okay?" he said.

"Clay, you don't really want me to leave, do you?"

He used to send her home as soon as they were finished, so there could be no confusion about the nature of their relationship. But the past few times he and Beth Ann had been together, she'd faked sleep and he'd let her spend the night.

Now he knew that softening his stance had been a mistake, although he had to admit they probably would've ended up at this point sooner or later. Eventually, whoever he was seeing got tired of guessing at his thoughts and feelings and gave up on him. Only occasionally did he have to prod someone out the door.

To his chagrin, Beth Ann seemed to be falling into the "needs prodding" category. "I've got work to do, Beth Ann."

"At one in the morning?"

"Always."

"Come on, Clay. Stop being a grump. Get back in bed, and I'll give you a massage. I owe you for that dress you bought me."

She grinned enticingly but with enough desperation to make his neck prickle. He hated what he had to do, wished he could avoid it. But it was long past due. He should've said goodbye a month ago. "You don't owe me anything. Forget me and be happy."

Her eyebrows shot up. "If you want me to be happy, that means I matter to you, right?"

Determined to be completely honest—or at least stay in keeping with his hard-ass image—he shook his head. "No one matters to me."

Tears slipped down her cheeks, and he silently cursed himself for not seeing this coming. Perhaps he'd relied too heavily on the fact that Beth Ann wasn't a particularly deep person. Anyway, she'd get over him as soon as some other man strolled through the Piggly Wiggly.

"What about your sisters? You love them," she said. "You'd take a bullet for Grace or Molly, even Madeline."

What he'd done for his sisters was a case of too little, too late. But Beth Ann wouldn't understand that. She didn't know what had happened that night long ago. No one did, besides him, his mother and his two natural sisters. Even his stepsister, Madeline, Reverend Barker's only natural child, had no clue. She'd been living with them at the time, but she'd spent the night at a girlfriend's.

"That's different," he said.

Silence. Hurt. Then, "You're an asshole, you know that?"

"Probably better than you do."

When he wouldn't give her a target, she drew herself up onto her knees. "You've been using me all along, haven't you!"

"No more than you've been using me," he replied calmly, and pulled on his boots.

"I haven't been using you. I want to marry you!"

"You only want what you can't have."

"That's not true!"

"You knew what you were getting into from the start. I warned you before you ever peeled off that trench coat."

She glanced wildly around the room, as though stunned to realize he was really through with her. "But I thought…I thought I could change you. That…that for me you might—"

"Stop it," he said.

"No. Clay." Climbing out of bed, she came toward him as if she'd wrap her arms around his neck and cling for dear life.

He put up a hand to stop her before she could reach him. Not even the sight of her full breasts, swinging above her flat stomach and toned legs, could change his mind. Part of him wanted to live and love like any other man. To have a family. But he felt empty inside. Dead. As dead as the man in his cellar. "I'm sorry," he said. "But you can't say I didn't warn you."

When she recognized how little her pleading affected him, her top lip curled and her eyes hardened into shiny emeralds. "You son of a bitch! You—you're not going to get away with this. I...I'm going to..." She gave a desperate sob and lunged toward the nightstand, grabbing for the phone.

Because Beth Ann was so prone to histrionics, Clay guessed she was playing some kind of dramatic game, possibly hoping to get one of her many male admirers to pick her up, even though she had a car parked outside. He watched dispassionately. He didn't care if she used the phone, as long as she left right afterward. This was a blow to her pride; not her heart, and it couldn't have come as a surprise.

But she pressed only three buttons and, in the next second, screamed into the receiver, "Help! Police! Clay Montgomery is trying to k-kill me! He knows I know what he did to the rev—"

Crossing the room in three long strides, Clay wrenched the phone from her and slammed down the receiver. "Have you lost your mind?" he growled.

She was breathing hard. With her gleaming, frantic eyes and curly blond hair falling in tangles about her shoulders, she looked like an evil witch. No longer pretty.

"I hope they put you in prison," she breathed, her voice a low, hateful murmur. "I hope they put you away for life!"

Scooping her clothing off the floor, she hurried into the hall, leaving Clay shaking his head. Evidently she didn't realize that she already had her wish. Maybe he wasn't in a physical prison, but he was paying the price for what had happened nineteen years ago—and would be for the rest of his life.

Officer Allie McCormick couldn't believe what came through her police radio. Pulling onto the shoulder of the empty country road she'd been patrolling since midnight, she put her cruiser in Park. "What did you say?"

The county dispatcher finally swallowed whatever she had in her mouth. "I said I just got a call from 10682 Old Barn Road."

Allie recognized the address. It was written all over the case files she'd been studying since she'd moved back to Stillwater six weeks ago. "That's the Montgomery farm."

"There's a possible 10-31C in progress."

"A homicide?" Allie thought there might have been one murder committed on that property, long ago. But she had a hard time believing there was about to be another. For starters, if Reverend Barker was dead and not missing, as some claimed, Stillwater had already exceeded its fifty-year quota for violent crimes. Secondly, Clay lived on the farm alone and, judging from what she knew of him, he led a pretty solitary life.

"That's what the caller said," the dispatcher responded.

Who would he kill? And why? Certainly not any

member of his family. He was the poster child for absolute loyalty. It was the Montgomerys against the world, not against each other.

It was probably some kind of prank.

"Was it a man or woman you spoke to?"

"A woman. And she seemed damn convincing. She was so panicked I could barely understand her. Then the call was disconnected."

Shit. That didn't sound good. "I'm not far. I can be there in less than five minutes." Peeling out, Allie shot down the road.

"You want me to rouse Hendricks for backup?" the dispatcher asked, still on the line.

The other officer who worked graveyard wasn't the best Allie had ever worked with, but if there was trouble, he'd be better than nothing. "Might as well try. I'll bet he's sleeping at the station again, though. I caught him with his chin on his chest over an hour ago, and once he's out an earthquake won't raise him."

"I could call your dad at home."

"No. Don't bother him. If you can't get Hendricks, I'll handle this on my own." Hanging up, she flipped on her strobe lights to warn any vehicles she might encounter that she was in a hurry, but didn't bother with the siren. When she approached the farmhouse, she'd turn it on to let the panicking victim know that help had arrived. But until then, the noise would only rattle her nerves. She wasn't completely comfortable being a street cop again. She was too rusty at the job. She'd spent the past five years working mostly in an office as a cold case detective in Chicago. But her divorce, and coming home so that she and her daughter would be closer to family, meant she'd had to make some sacrifices. Hitting the streets was one of them.

Rain began to plink against her windshield as she raced down Pine Road and hung a skidding left at the highway. It had been a wet spring, but she preferred it to the terrible humidity they were facing as June approached. Staring intently at the shiny pavement ahead of her, she ignored the rapid *swish, swish, swish* of her windshield wipers, which were on high but beating only half as fast as her heart. "You wouldn't kill again," she muttered. "You're not that stupid." Heck, she didn't even know Clay had killed the first time. She only knew that Reverend Barker's disappearance—an incident she still clearly remembered—was highly suspicious. She didn't believe such a well-respected man, the community's spiritual leader, would drive off without saying a word to anyone and without packing a stitch of clothing or withdrawing any money from his bank account. No one would do that without good reason. And what reason, good or otherwise, could Barker have had to leave his farm, which was the only property he owned? If he was alive, someone would've heard from him by now. He still had plenty of family in town: a wife, a daughter, two stepdaughters, a stepson, a sister, a brother-in-law and two nephews.

His daughter Madeline was certain he'd met with foul play. She refused to accept that he might have abandoned her.

Allie had seen fathers walk away from their children before, knew it was a distinct possibility. But in this situation, she tended to agree with everyone else. Something violent had happened to Reverend Barker.

She was determined to find out what. For Madeline. For Barker's nephew, Joe, who was also pressing her to solve the case. For the whole town.

Gravel spun as she reached the farm and whipped into the long driveway. Briefly, she realized that the property looked far better than when Reverend Barker had lived there. The junk he'd stacked all around—the rusty old appliances, flat tires, bits of scrap metal and other odds and ends—were gone. The house and buildings appeared to be in good repair. But she didn't have time to look the place over very carefully. She was too busy coming to a screeching halt and turning off her lights and siren.

Jumping out of the car as soon as she rammed the transmission into Park, she hurried toward the front door, only to be intercepted by a woman wearing a pair of slacks unbuttoned at the waist and holding a shirt and purse to her bare chest. "There you are," she cried, stumbling toward Allie from the direction of the carport.

The woman appeared to be alone, so Allie relaxed the hand she'd put on her gun and reached out to steady her. It was Beth Ann Cole, the woman who worked in the bakery at the Piggly Wiggly. Allie had seen her several times. Beth Ann wasn't someone she—or anyone else—was likely to forget. Mostly because she had the kind of face and body people admired. Tall, elegant and model-pretty, she had porcelain skin, long blond hair and slanted, cat-green eyes.

Allie had most recently spotted her with Clay at church. Like a lot of others, Allie hadn't been able to stop staring at them. With their impressive height and exceptional looks, they made the most stunning couple imaginable. Yet Allie couldn't really claim she'd thought they were an item, even after seeing them together. Clay's body language hadn't indicated that he felt the slightest bit *connected* to Beth Ann. Mrs.

Peabody, sitting in the pew next to Allie, had whispered that he showed up with someone new almost every time he attended—which wasn't often enough to save his soul, the old lady had added with a judgmental sniff.

Of course, Allie had watched Clay and Beth Ann through only one service, which wasn't efficient to draw any conclusions about someone like Clay Montgomery. She'd never met a more difficult man to read. She'd gone to high school with him—he'd been a senior when she was a junior—and had certainly noticed his swarthy good looks. But she'd never gotten close to him. No one had. Even back then he'd made it abundantly clear that he wasn't interested in making friends.

"Tell me what's going on," she said to Beth Ann.

Suddenly, the woman was crying so hard she couldn't speak.

"Try to get hold of yourself, okay?" Allie used her "cop" voice, hoping to cut through Beth Ann's near-hysteria, and it seemed to work.

"I—I'm cold," she managed to say, glancing toward the house as if she was afraid Clay Montgomery might come charging out after her. "C-can we get in your car?"

She helped Beth Ann into the passenger side. Then, checking again to make sure Clay wasn't about to spring out of the bushes near the house, she circled the car and slid behind the wheel. After locking the doors, she twisted in her seat and studied the other woman as well as she could in the dark. A flood light attached to the barn had come on when she pulled in, revealing Beth Ann's smudged mascara. But it had been activated by a motion sensor and chose that moment to go off, and Allie didn't want to turn on the car's interior light until Beth Ann was fully dressed.

"Take a deep breath," she said, and tried starting with a simple question to relax the crying woman. "How'd you get out here?"

"I drove." She pointed to a green Toyota Avalon not far from where Allie had parked. "That's my car right there."

"Do you have the keys?"

She nodded, sniffling. "In my purse."

"What time was it when you arrived?"

"About ten."

"Are you the one who called in the complaint?"

"Yes, he's an animal," Beth Ann responded, crying some more. "He—he killed that reverend guy everyone's always talking about. The man who's been missing for so long."

The hair rose on the back of Allie's arms. Beth Ann had stated it so matter-of-factly, as though she had no doubt. And her words definitely supported the majority opinion. "How do you know?"

She rocked back and forth, still covering herself with her shirt but making no attempt to put it on. "He told me. He said if I didn't shut up, he'd beat me to a bloody pulp, like he did his stepfather."

Clay was physically capable of beating just about anyone. Nearly six-four, he had a well-defined body with shoulders broader than any Allie had ever seen. The long, physically gruelling hours he worked maintaining a farm that should easily have taken two or more people to run, kept him in shape.

But he hadn't been very big at sixteen. From the pictures, and Allie's own memory, he'd been a tall, lanky kid with a shock of shiny black hair and cobalt-blue eyes. When he wasn't aware he was being watched, he occasionally looked lost, even weary, yet he consistently resisted any and all kindness. He hadn't filled out until sometime after she'd left for college—presumably in his early twenties.

"Did he explain how he killed his stepfather?" she asked.

"I told you. He—he beat him." Much to Allie's relief, Beth Ann finally pulled on her shirt. Allie had seen a lot in her days working for the law—more dead bodies than she cared to count—but having the very busty Beth Ann sitting next to her bare-chested, and knowing she'd probably just left Clay's bed, was a little too up-close-and-personal. There was no cushion of anonymity in Stillwater.

"You're telling me he killed Reverend Barker with his bare hands? At sixteen?" Now that Beth Ann was dressed, Allie snapped on the interior light so she could read the nuances of the other woman's expressions. But storm clouds covered the pale, waning moon outside, and the light was too dim to banish all the shadows.

"He's strong. You have no idea how strong he is."

Allie knew Clay's reputation. He'd broken all kinds of weight-lifting records in high school. But that was mostly as a senior, when he'd had a little more meat on him, not as a skinny sophomore. "He probably weighed 160 pounds at the time," she pointed out.

Silence met the skepticism in her voice, then Beth Ann said, "Oh, I think he used a bat. Yeah, he used a bat."

Something about this interview wasn't right, but Allie tried to go with it, just in case. If Beth Ann was telling the truth, what could Reverend Barker have done to make Clay take a bat to him? Had he grown too strict? Was his discipline too severe?

It was possible. Allie remembered Barker as a particularly zealous preacher, and Clay had never been puritanical. He'd always liked women—there'd never been a shortage of females eager and willing to do whatever he wanted—and he'd been involved in a few fights. But he was kind to his mother and sisters. And, as far as she knew, he had no problems with drugs or alcohol.

"The police never found a murder weapon," she said, hoping to draw more information out of Beth Ann.

"He must've gotten rid of it somehow."

"Did he *tell* you he used a bat?"

She glanced out at the house. "No, but he must have."

He must have... Allie bit back a sigh. "When did Clay make this confession to you?"

"A—a few weeks ago."

"Did you tell anyone?"

"No."

"What about your mother or father? A friend?"

"I didn't talk about it. I—I was too afraid of him."

"I see," Allie said. But she didn't see at all. Beth Ann had shown no fear of Clay on Sunday. She'd touched him at every opportunity, clung to him like lint when she could, even though he continually brushed her off. "And you came out here tonight, although you're afraid of him, because..." She let the sentence dangle.

"I'm in love with him."

"But—"

"He attacked me!"

"What precipitated the attack?"

"We…had an argument."

Allie said nothing, merely waited for Beth Ann to continue. Generally, people kept talking when the silence in a conversation stretched out, often revealing more than they intended to. Sometimes it was the best way to reach the truth.

"I—I told him I was pregnant." She wiped at a falling tear. "He…insisted I get an abortion. When I refused, he started slapping me around."

It was difficult to tell in the eerie glow of the interior light, but Allie couldn't see anything more than smeared makeup on Beth Ann's face. There was certainly no blood. "Where?"

"In the house."

The rain began to fall harder, drumming against the hood of the car and making the air smell of wet vegetation. "No, where did he hit you?"

Beth Ann made a general motion with her hands. "Everywhere. He wanted to kill me!"

Allie cleared her throat. She wasn't sure how she felt about Clay Montgomery, but he'd been pretty tight-lipped over the past two decades. She doubted he'd suddenly divulge his culpability in a capital crime to someone like Beth Ann, and then let her run straight to the police. Besides, if he'd really wanted to hurt her, she wouldn't be sitting here safe and sound—in his driveway, no less. By her own admission, Beth Ann had her car and her keys. Yet she'd chosen to wait for Allie instead of speeding away from danger. "How did you manage to escape him?"

"I—I don't know," she said. "It's all a blur."

Allie pursed her lips. Apparently only Clay's confession was crystal clear.

Grabbing the notepad she kept in her car, she scribbled down Beth Ann's exact words, then peered thoughtfully at the house. "Stay here. I'd like to ask Mr. Montgomery what he has to say. Afterward, you can follow me downtown and give me a sworn statement. Unless you feel you need to go to the hospital first," she added, her hand on the door latch.

Beth Ann didn't even respond to the hospital suggestion. "A sworn statement?" she echoed.

"Attempted murder is no small crime, Ms. Cole. You want the D.A. to press charges, don't you?"

Beth Ann tucked her hair behind her ears. "I—I think so."

"You told me he assaulted you. That he tried to kill you."

"He did. See this?" Beth Ann shoved her arm out.

Allie saw a rather superficial wound that resembled claw marks. Hardly the type of damage she would've expected Clay to inflict. In a fight, a man typically aimed for the face or midsection. But it was her job to document the injury, just in case. "We'll get pictures of that. Do you have any other scrapes, cuts or bruises?"

"No."

"And yet he hit you how many times?"

"I guess he didn't hit me that hard," she replied, suddenly retracting what she'd said earlier. "He grazed me with his nails when I was trying to get away. It frightened me more than it hurt me."

An accidental scratch was a far cry from attempted murder. "What about his confession? Is that how you remembered it?"

"Yes. Of course."

Allie had her doubts about that, too. "You'll swear to it?"

Beth Ann stared at the house. "Will he go to jail if I do?"

"Would it make you happy if he did?"

"Me and almost everyone else in this town."

Allie hesitated before answering. "If what you say is true, prison is a possibility. But your story would require corroboration. Can you offer any supporting evidence?"

"Like what?"

"The location of Reverend Barker's body? The location of Reverend Barker's car? The murder weapon? A taped or signed confession?"

"No, but Clay *told* me he killed him. I heard it with my own ears."

Allie didn't believe a word of it. She didn't even believe Beth Ann had been attacked. But she radioed dispatch to see if her backup was en route.

"I couldn't reach Hendricks," the dispatcher told her. "Are you sure you don't want to wake your father?"

Allie flipped off the interior light and considered the quiet farm. Getting wet seemed to be the only threat within fifty yards of them. So she decided to check it out alone. "No, I'll take care of it. If you don't hear from me in fifteen minutes or so, go ahead and rouse him."

"You got it."

Adjusting the gun on her belt to keep it from biting into her waist, Allie stepped out of the car. "Sit tight and lock the doors."

"What will you say to Clay?" Beth Ann asked.

"I'm going to tell him what you've told me and see how he reacts to it."

Beth Ann stopped her from closing the door. "Why? You can't trust someone with his reputation."

Allie didn't respond. She knew there'd be plenty of people willing and eager to put him away based on such flimsy testimony. But she wasn't one of them. She wanted the truth. And she was going to use everything she'd ever learned about solving cold cases to find it.